THE SLAUGHTER
PEN

THE SLAUGHTER
PEN

A Story about the Horrific Marine
BATTLE FOR TARAWA

DAY TWO

BY JAMES F. DWYER

ISBN: 1536995894
ISBN 13: 9781536995893
Library of Congress Control Number: 2016913138
CreateSpace Independent Publishing Platform
North Charleston, South Carolina

DEDICATION

This is probably the most enjoyable part of the book writing process...because this is where you get to say thank you to all the people who helped make this possible. My list is not a very long one...but it's an important one...because without them...this book would never have been written. So here goes...

I would like to acknowledge my Father in Heaven...and His Son...Jesus Christ...who is my Lord and Savior...and His Holy Spirit...for all the wonderful blessings They have bestowed on me. Without my faith, I would have nothing...and I am truly blessed beyond words.

The genesis of this book began when I was a little boy...when my younger brother...Bobby...was sick with leukemia. A young marine...whose name I do not know...learned about Bobby's illness and sent my brother a stuffed marine bulldog and a typed message addressed to M/Sgt (Honorary) Bobbie Dwyer. The message read as follows: *It has been brought to the attention of this command that you are a brave and obedient young marine. Bravery and obedience are taken as a matter of fact in the case of every marine. However, due to the degree that you have exhibited these qualities, we are privileged to award you the Good Conduct medal.* The message was signed by *John C. Smith, Maj. General, U.S. Marine*

Corps, Commanding. Bobby died a few months later...in May of 1968...and I never forgot that kind act. It was my first contact with the Marine Corps...and one that left a lasting impression on me. I would like to thank that marine...whoever you are...for making my nine-year old brother an honorary marine...and for sparking my first interest in the Marine Corps. Without you...I may never have written this book.

I would like to thank my father...a former FBI agent...and the most generous and kind-hearted man alive. My dad tried to enlist in the Marine Corps in 1944...but he was turned down due to his having asthma as a boy...so he became a Navy radar man and he served aboard the U.S. Navy cruiser *Portsmouth* in WWII. This man gave me a love for all things military...since he took me to my first war movie...and many others...and he paid for my subscription to the Military Book Club...and he took me to the Army-Navy game in 1973. It is because of my dad...who I love and respect...that this book was written.

The next group of men I would like to thank all served in the 2nd Division, U.S. Marine Corps and all were at Tarawa...and I feel a special connection to each of them...

Second Lieutenant* Joseph Sexton...who grew up down the block from my dad in Brooklyn, New York...and who fought with the 1st Battalion, 2nd Regiment and lost has life in the battle. I first thought of writing a story about Tarawa as a way of honoring Joe... who never returned...and the little girl...his daughter...that he never got to meet. Joe's sacrifice was the inspiration for this book.

Corporal Robert George...who fought in the battle and experienced more acts of valor than he could count. Bob graciously took my calls and he spent several hours on the phone telling me what the battle was like and he described everything he saw with such emotion and detail that I will never forget him. My only regret is that he did not get to read these books...as he passed away in Sacramento, California before they were finished.

Colonel Paul Millichap...was at Tarawa and I am the proud owner of his Springfield rifle...which was given to me by his daughter...Denise. Major Millichap was the Second Division's Ordinance Officer at the time of the battle and he was paid the highest compliment possible...when retired Colonel Ed Bale...who led his tanks ashore as a first lieutenant on the western end of Betio Island on Day One of the battle...told me over the phone that he was a great officer. Denise's kindness and love for her father helped motivate me to start writing my story again.

Without the inspiration of these four men above...a Navy man and three Marines...all members of the greatest generation...and their families to motivate me...I might never have written this story.

I would like to thank my mother...who never complained when her boys came back to the house coated in dirt and sweat...after spending an afternoon playing war...and for letting me hang those World War II models from the ceiling in our bedroom...a simple act...but one that let my imagination run wild and encouraged my love for the military. Without my mother's love, guidance, and willingness to sacrifice for her children...I would never have made it to West Point...which gave me the foundation I needed to write this book. My mother is one of a kind...and her love for our Country... which she received from my Irish grandmother...who was born in County Tipperary...motivated me to write this book.

I will always be indebted to Sergeant Colin Jackson of the Atlanta Fire Rescue Department...who told me that I needed to finish what I had started fourteen years ago...*Just get something done,* he told me... Well I listened to his advice...and now Book One...and Book Two... are done.

And last but not least...I wish to thank my wonderful, patient wife who has kept the house operating while I was working on my two stories...especially the second one...which was finished while

I was incapacitated with a torn Achilles tendon. My wife has done everything I have asked of her...without complaint...and there is no better person to be with when the chips are down. She was gracious in letting me read long passages from my story to her...even though she had things to do...to see how they sounded and to show her that I was a good writer. She gave me confidence to keep going... and I love her for spoiling me. She is my treasure and without her love, compassion, and encouragement...I may never have been able to finish either book. And as Jesus told us...those who should be first must be last...and a servant to all...and you fulfill those words to the letter...which is why I put you last in the order! Thank you, Darling...I love you!

Semper Fi!

---

*Second Lieutenant Sexton's rank was incorrectly identified as First Lieutenant in early editions of *Annihilation Beach*

ACKNOWLEDGEMENTS

The formulation of this book began many years ago...when I first discovered military books...while I was suffering through seventh grade detention in our junior high school library...in 1970. Over the last forty plus years or so, I have read hundreds of war books...both fiction and non-fiction alike...and I have watched every war movie that came across the airwaves or was shown in a movie theatre near where I lived at the time. Many of the battles and the men I read about and watched on television or in the movies were very interesting...but nothing captured my attention the way the battle of Tarawa and the men who fought in it did. Tarawa stoked my imagination the very first time I read about it...which must have happened when I was in junior high school...because I can remember spending time later on in our local town library investigating Tarawa in a Marine Journal that listed details about marine battles of World War II. All these years later, I can still remember the feeling I had when I saw the name of Second Lieutenant Joseph Sexton with a KIA listed next to his name in the index for the battle. This young officer had grown up right down the street from my father in Brooklyn, N.Y. and seeing his name brought the battle to life for me…since my father remembered seeing him walking down the street in his dazzling marine uniform when he was home on leave during the war. Then…without realizing it…my father mentioned something that changed my life. In talking about Joe…my dad said how sad it was to see his wife…a girl who had grown up directly behind my dad's own brownstone…pushing a baby carriage up the street with a little girl inside. That little girl was Second Lieutenant Joe Sexton's daughter…and he never got to see her…nor she him… since he was killed fighting for his Country in the battle for Tarawa. Even at that young age, I swore that I would do something…someday…to honor that man and the little girl who would spend the rest of her life without her father. That goal never really left me…and I remember the first time I tried to do something about it. I was in my late 20's and I began writing a movie script about the fight for Tarawa in a small apartment in New Milford, New Jersey. I didn't get very far…but I had made my first attempt at fulfilling my dream… and that's what counted at the time. That spark would reignite almost ten years later…when I decided to write a book about a military figure that I thought a younger audience would find interesting. I was going to call it, "A Marine Lieutenant at Tarawa," and I wanted to model my book after the Hardy Boys series by Franklin W. Dixon. These were the very first books that I had ever read as a kid…and I loved them. If I was successful in this first endeavor…I planned on producing a series of books like it…using different characters in different branches of service to describe the battles that were fought in World War Two. I was hoping that they would generate the same level of excitement in the young boys of today that I had experienced when a new Hardy Boys book hit the shelf in our local department store. With that in mind, I began writing the story about my lieutenant…and I found the exercise very exciting. Without realizing it, I had stumbled back into my real calling…the one that had been lying dormant for so many years. So I continued to write…giving life to my marine lieutenant…and before long I realized that my simple story had morphed into something far more sophisticated than a simple child's story and I was now writing for a far more mature audience. And in the whole process, I found out...most importantly... that I really enjoyed writing. I spent the next sixteen years working on this story...writing when the urge hit me...putting it off when it didn't. Had I not become a firefighter after 9-11, my story might have been finished earlier...but life has a funny way of interrupting our pursuits at times...so my endeavor has taken a little longer than I anticipated...but Book Two is now finished. The story you are about to read is the second of a series of three books about the battle for Tarawa....and it deals with the actions that took place on the second day of the battle. As you will see...I have tried to arrange the books in chronological order...but some scenes...out of necessity... will take the reader back to the actions of the day before...and to other places than the island of Betio. I have attempted to capture the battle through the eyes of the marines who fought there...and to some degree...through the eyes of the brave Japanese soldiers who fought there as well. To this end, I have created my own cast of characters who will experience as much of the battle as possible... while rubbing elbows with the actual marines who fought the battle. I have tried to stay as true to the real story of Tarawa as possible... and I relied on the superb books below to assist me in this regard:

Utmost Savagery
The Three Days of Tarawa
By Colonel Joseph H. Alexander USMC (RET.)

ONE SQUARE MILE OF HELL
THE BATTLE FOR TARAWA
By John Wukovits

Tarawa
a legend is born
By Henry I. Shaw, Jr.

Mantle of Heroism
Tarawa and the Struggle for the Gilberts, November 1943
By Michael B. Graham

Bloody Tarawa
A Narrative History with 250 Photographs
By Eric Hammel and John E. Lane

Tarawa
Too young to Vote
By Robert L. George

Tarawa
20-23 November 1943
A Hell of a Way to Die
By Derrick Wright

tarawa 1943
the turning of the tide
Praeger Illustrated Military History Series
By Derrick Wright

"The bravest are surely those who have the clearest vision of what is before them, glory and danger alike, and yet notwithstanding, go out to meet it."

Thucydides…Athenian historian and general…460 - 395 BC

If you faint in the day of adversity,
Your strength *is* small.

Deliver *those who* are drawn toward death,
And hold back *those* stumbling to the slaughter.

Proverbs 24:10-11

Conversation between Colonel David Shoup and Father Francis Kelly on the night before the invasion of 20 November 1943:

Colonel Shoup: *Padre, I want you to pray for me.*
Father Kelly: *What sort of prayer, Colonel?*
Colone Shoup: *I want you to pray that I don't make any mistakes out on that beach; no wrong decisions that will cost any of those boys an arm or a leg, much less a life. I want you to pray for that, Padre.*

ABOUT THE AUTHOR

 James F. Dwyer is a 1980 graduate of the U.S. Military Academy at West Point. While a cadet, he attended the U.S. Army Paratrooper School at Fort Benning, Georgia and earned his wings in the summer of 1978. He also served in the U.S. Army as an armored cavalry officer in the 2nd Squadron of the 9th Cavalry Regiment at Fort Stewart, Georgia from 1981 until 1984. After leaving the Army, he worked as a trader on Wall Street for nine years before leaving for Sandy Springs, Georgia where he worked as a stock broker for another nine years with A.G. Edwards & Sons. He left the financial world after 9-11 and became a firefighter with the City of Atlanta Fire Rescue Department at the age of forty-six. He has been with this department for thirteen years and worked as a part-time firefighter for seven and a half years with the Sandy Springs Fire Rescue Department from 2007 until 2015. He has been married to his wife, Meryl, for nine years and they have three dogs and two cats

at home in Acworth, Georgia. He and Meryl belong to Freedom Church, a non-denominational Christian church in Acworth and on Sundays he participates in a bible study program for inmates at the local jail. This is his second literary work and he is currently working on the third book of his three part series about the battle of Tarawa.

ORDER OF BATTLE

(The names of the men below…or the units they served in…appear in the story. Their fictitious counterparts are listed as well. This is only a partial list of the entire force involved in the invasion of the Tarawa Atoll.)

U.S. Forces

V Marine Amphibious Corps (VMAC)

Commanding Officer

Major General Holland Smith

2nd Marine Division
(approximately 20,000 men)

Commanding Officer

Major General Julian Smith

Assistant Division Commander

Brigadier General Leo Hermle

Division Chief of Staff

Colonel Merritt Edson

Division Supply Officer

Lieutenant Colonel Jesse Cook, Jr.

Assistant Division Supply Officer

Captain Ben Weatherwax

Division Ordinance Officer

Major Paul Millichap

Observers

Lieutenant Colonel Evans Carlson
Lieutenant Colonel Walter Jordan

2nd Amphibious Tractor Battalion
(approximately 480 men)

Commanding Officer

Major Henry Drewes KIA

<u>2nd Tank Battalion</u>
(approximately 700 men)

<u>Commanding Officer</u>

Lieutenant Colonel Alexander Swenceski WIA

<u>C Company, I Marine Amphibious Corps (IMAC) Tank Battalion</u>
(approximately 700 men)

<u>Commanding Officer</u>
First Lieutenant Edward Bale, Jr.

<u>1st Platoon Sergeant</u>
Platoon Sergeant Charlie Sooter

<u>3rd Platoon Commander</u>
First Lieutenant Lou Largey

2nd Marine Regiment
(approximately 3,250 men)

<u>Commanding Officer</u>

Colonel David Shoup WIA

<u>Regimental Operations Officer</u>

Major Thomas Cullhane, Jr.

<u>Regimental Surgeon</u>

Lieutenant Herman Brukhardt USN

Regimental Chaplains

Lieutenant Francis Kelly USN
Lieutenant Norman Darling USN
(portrayed by Lieutenant Aaron Johnson)

Regimental Scout-Sniper Platoon

Platoon Commander
First Lieutenant William Deane Hawkins KIA
Platoon Sergeant
Gunnery Sergeant Jared Hooper

1ˢᵗ Battalion, 2ⁿᵈ Marine Regiment

Commanding Officer

Major Wood Kyle

A Company CO
Captain William Bray WIA

B Company CO
Captain Maxie Williams WIA

B Company XO
First Lieutenant Edward Maher
(portrayed by First Lieutenant Kevin Kelly)

C Company CO
Captain James Clanahan

C Company XO
First Lieutenant Justin Mills KIA

C Company Platoon Commanders
First Lieutenant William Seeley WIA
Second Lieutenant William Howell
Second Lieutenant Joseph Sexton KIA

2nd Battalion, 2nd Marine Regiment

Commanding Officer

Lieutenant Colonel Herbert Amey, Jr KIA

E Company CO
Captain Edward Walker, Jr. KIA
(portrayed by Captain John Ring)

E Company XO
First Lieutenant Maurice Reichel KIA

E Company Platoon Commanders
Second Lieutenant Lewis Beck KIA
Second Lieutenant William Culp KIA
Second Lieutenant Donald Dahlgren KIA
Second Lieutenant Carl Mesmer
(portrayed by First Lieutenant Daniel Hackett)
1st Platoon Sergeant
(Name of actual combatant is not known but he is
portrayed by Platoon Sergeant Thomas J. Roy)

F Company CO
Captain Warren "Lefty" Morris WIA

F Company XO
First Lieutenant Wayne Sanford WIA
(portrayed by First Lieutenant Kenneth Konstanzer)

F Company Platoon Commanders
Second Lieutenant Joseph Barr WIA
Second Lieutenant George Cooper WIA
Second Lieutenant Laurence Ferguson, Jr. WIA
Second Lieutenant Raymond Marion WIA
Second Platoon Sergeant
Platoon Sergeant Arthur Maher

G Company Commander
Captain Alan Cason

G Company Platoon Commander
Second Lieutenant Fred Martin WIA
(portrayed by Second Lieutenant Conner Orr)

K Company Commander
Major Harold "K" Throneson WIA

3rd Battalion, 2nd Marine Regiment

Commanding Officer

Major John Schoettel

I Company CO
Captain William Tatom KIA

I Company XO
First Lieutenant Sam Turner

K Company CO
Captain James Crain

K Company XO
First Lieutenant Clint Dunahoe KIA

K Company Platoon Commanders
First Lieutenant Joseph "Ott" Schulte WIA
Second Lieutenant Thomas Becker KIA
Second Lieutenant James Fawcett
Second Lieutenant Wilbur Hofmann KIA

L Company CO
Major Michael Ryan

L Company XO
Captain Robert O'Brien

M Company CO
Major Stoddard Courtelyou

M Company XO
Captain George Wentzel KIA

6th Marine Regiment
(approximately 3,250 men)

Commanding Officer

Colonel Maurice Holmes

1st Battalion, 6th Marine Regiment

<u>Commanding Officer</u>

Major William Jones

<u>2nd Battalion, 6th Marine Regiment</u>

<u>Commanding Officer</u>

Major Raymond Murray

<u>3rd Battalion, 6th Marine Regiment</u>

<u>Commanding Officer</u>

Lieutenant Colonel Kenneth McLeod

<u>8th Marine Regiment</u>
(approximately 3,250 men)

<u>Commanding Officer</u>

Colonel Elmer Hall

<u>1st Battalion, 8th Marine Regiment</u>

<u>Commanding Officer</u>

Major Lawrence Hays, Jr. WIA

<u>2nd Battalion, 8th Marine Regiment</u>

Commanding Officer

Major Henry "Jim" Crowe

2nd Battalion Executive Officer

Major William Chamberlin WIA

E Company XO
First Lieutenant Aubrey Edmonds WIA

F Company Platoon Commander
Second Lieutenant George Bussa KIA

3rd Battalion, 8th Marine Regiment

Commanding Officer

Major Robert Rudd

10th Marine Regiment
(approximately 3200 men)

1st Battalion, 10th Marine Regiment

Commanding Officer

Lieutenant Colonel Presley Rixey

<u>C Battery Forward Observer</u>
Second Lieutenant Thomas Greene

18ᵗʰ Marine Regiment
(approximately 2500 men)

<u>A Company, 1ˢᵗ Battalion Assault Engineer Platoon</u>
Staff Sergeant William Bordelon KIA

<u>C Company, 1ˢᵗ Battalion Assault Engineer Platoon</u>
First Lieutenant Sandy Bonnyman KIA

<u>Japanese Forces</u>

<u>Gilbert Islands Garrison Force</u>

<u>Commanding Officer</u>

Rear Admiral Keiji Shibasaki

3ʳᵈ Special Base Force
(formerly known as the 6ᵗʰ Yokosuka Special Naval Landing
Force…approximately 1100 men)

<u>Commanding Officer</u>

Commander Keisuki Matsuo

7ᵗʰ Sasebo Special Naval Landing Force
(approximately 1500 men)

<u>Commanding Officer</u>

Commander Takeo Sugai

111th Pioneers Construction Battalion
(approximately 1,250 men)

Commanding Officer

Lieutenant Isao Murakami

4th Construction Unit
(approximately 1000 men)

Fictitious composition of the 1st Platoon, E Company
2nd Marine Regiment

Platoon Commander

First Lieutenant Daniel Hackett

Platoon Sergeant

Platoon Sergeant Thomas Roy

Right Guide Sergeant

Sergeant Gene Flockerzi

Demolitions Corporal

Corporal Oscar Robertson KIA*

Messengers/Runners

Private First Class Gene Petraglia
Private First Class Lerman Mudd
Private First Class Larry Rickard

Platoon Corpsman

Pharmacist Second Class Thomas Fumai

1st Squad

Squad Leader

Sergeant Tom Endres

Assistant Squad Leader

Corporal Tim Staggs

BAR-men (2)

Private First Class Chip Newell KIA
Private First Class Marty Vandrisse KIA

Assistant BAR-men (2)

Private Joe Agresta
Private Bruce Elliot KIA*

Grenadier

Corporal Dwyane Edge KIA*

Riflemen (5)

Private Pete Delaney KIA
Private John Scott

Private Jeff DeGeralamo KIA
Private Ted Rosenau KIA
Private Steve "Whitey" Thompson WIA

2nd Squad

Squad Leader

Corporal Phil Oliver

Assistant Squad Leader

Corporal Markus Wilson KIA**

BAR-men (2)

Private Rick Friedman KIA
Private First Class Kevin Lewis

Assistant BAR-men (2)

Private Sean Feeney
Private Terry McGowan

Grenadier

Private First Class Bart Moore KIA

Riflemen (5)

Private First Class Doug Tuchmann
Private Dave Low KIA

Private Lorin Fetzer KIA
Private Ragnar Svansson KIA
Private Cam Johnston KIA

3rd Squad

Squad Leader

Sergeant Jeff Varner

Assistant Squad Leader

Corporal Derek Hullender*

BAR-men (2)

Private First Class Michael Reisman
Private First Class Paul Rampley

Assistant BAR-men (2)

Private Tyler Smith
Private Dave Osby KIA*

Grenadier

Corporal Robert Minkewicz KIA

Riflemen (5)

Private Chris Nelson
Private Billy Jefferson KIA*

Private Vinny Grasso WIA
Private Brian Hennessey
Private Doug Schonkwiler KIA

*referred to by rank or position in story

**Corporal Wilson is incorrectly identified as the Assistant
Squad Leader of the 1st Squad in the List of
Fictional Characters Section in *Annihilation Beach*

**Members of 1st Platoon, E Company who rode in
the amtrac nicknamed, "Widow Maker"**

1LT Hackett
PFC Petraglia
PhM2 Fumai
SGT Endres
CPL Staggs
CPL Edge
PFC Newell
PFC Vandrisse
PVT Agresta
PVT Thompson
PVT Devaney
PVT Scott
PVT Elliot
PVT DeGeralamo
PVT Rosenau
CPL Wilson
PFC Moore
PVT Friedman
PVT Feeney

PVT Low
PVT Fetzer

Members of 1ˢᵗ Platoon, E Company who rode in the amtrac nicknamed, "Rum Runner"

PLT SGT Roy
SGT Flockerzi
PFC Mudd
PFC Rickard
CPL Robertson
CPL Oliver
PFC Lewis
PVT McGowan
PVT Svansson
PVT Tuchmann
PVT Johnston
SGT Varner
CPL Hullander
CPL Minkewicz
PFC Reisman
PVT Osby
PVT Grasso
PVT Hennessey
PFC Rampley

PVT Smith
PVT Schonkwiler
PVT Jefferson
PVT Nelson

(ranks in the section above are listed in their abbreviated form)

CHAPTER 1

For many people around the world, November 21, 1943 would be just another day...much like day before it...and the day before that even. However...for those in the Armed Forces of the United States...this day could have deadly consequences...depending on what branch of service you were in...and where you were located at the time. If you were a pilot or an air crewman in the U.S. Army Air Force stationed in England for instance...you could be shot down while flying on a fighter or bomber mission over Europe that day... since the air war was in full swing by this point in time. In fact, on battlefields all across the globe...on the ground...on the water and under the water...and in the air...men in the Army and Navy were losing their lives daily while fighting an enemy who considered their cause to be just as noble and worthwhile as the American men they were fighting did. It was happening in places like the Atlantic Ocean...where the battle against the German U-boat menace that had ravaged the British and American Merchant Marine convoys for three years was finally turning...and in Southern Italy...where U.S. Army infantrymen were slogging their way up the muddy slopes of the Italian countryside trying to dislodge the German Army that was fighting tenaciously under the brilliant leadership of Luftwaffe General Albert Kesselring.

It was just as deadly in the Southwest Pacific near Australia. There U.S. Army troops under the mercurial Five-Star General Douglas MacArthur were battling their way up the eastern coastline of jungle-invested New Guinea using a new strategy called, "island-hopping." Conceived and implemented by MacArthur, the strategy involved ignoring large concentrations of Japanese troops who were entrenched and waiting for battle. Instead...in a brilliant move not seen before...MacArthur simply bypassed these areas and had his men land in the areas that were lightly defended further up the coast. This left the Japanese Army surrounded by the American Army on both their northern and southern flanks and by the menacing, headhunting New Guinea tribesmen...who hated the brutal Japanese more than the Americans did...to their west. And with the shipping lanes of the shark-infested Bismark Sea to their east blocked by the U.S. Navy and Army Air Force, the Japanese were cut off from their lines of supply and they began to whither on the vine... just like the Japanese Army on Guadalcanal had. In essence, the bypassed Jap bases became nothing more than large POW camps and before long thousands of Japanese soldiers...with nowhere to go... began dying of starvation and malnutrition as the war dragged on.

To the southeast, the campaign for the South Pacific was progressing at a rapid pace as well...as the forces of the U.S. Navy and Marine Corps under Admiral William "Bull" Halsey advanced up the island chain of the Solomon Islands. Halsey's latest target was the island of Bougainville near the northern end of the Solomon's... and while the Japanese fought tenaciously to defend it...the jungle and weather conditions on the island proved to be far more formidable...even worse, some said, than Guadalcanal. Incredibly, several marines were listed as KIA - killed in action - after large trees toppled over on them during the incessant rain storms that blanketed the island.

In addition to the grueling land battles fought in the Solomon's, Halsey's men would also fight several surface actions and wage numerous air battles with the Japanese forces stationed at Rabaul. And Halsey's forces won them all...thus continuing the American dominance in the area following the American victory at Guadalcanal. And these victories would have a tremendous impact on the action taking place on a small island that lay several hundred miles to the northeast in the Central Pacific Ocean.

• • •

The campaign for the Central Pacific was the brainchild of Admiral Ernest J. King, the Commander-in-Chief of the U.S. Fleet in Washington, D.C. He believed it was necessary to launch a simultaneous drive across the Central Pacific Ocean in conjunction with the combined drives in the Southwest and South Pacific theatres of operations. The man he tasked with completing this job was Admiral Chester W. Nimitz...the Commander-in-Chief of the Pacific Fleet in Pearl Harbor...and he was no rookie. Nimitz had already planned the retaliatory and successful raid by sixteen B-25 bombers on the Japanese home islands from the carrier *Hornet* in April of 1942 and experienced the Battle of the Coral Sea in May of 1942...the first carrier battle of the war...and the very first sea battle in history where ships fought without ever seeing one another. Then came the monumental Battle of Midway Island in first week of June in 1942. There the Japanese were solidly defeated...having lost all four of their carriers to American dive-bombers while the American force lost only one of the three carriers that made up their ambush team... the valiant *Yorktown*...which finally succumbed after taking numerous bomb and torpedo hits.

Nimitz's last conquest had been the Solomon Islands campaign which involved the retaking of Guadalcanal and then a series of other island invasions as he moved up the chain towards the Japanese naval bastion at Rabaul. With all these scalps hanging from his belt, Nimitz then set his sights on the various island chains that the

Japanese had taken in Central Pacific in the first months of the war. After careful consideration, Nimitz decided that his first target for the U.S. Navy's march across the Pacific would be the Tarawa Atoll that was part of the Gilbert Islands.

Within the Tarawa Atoll was a small island named Betio Island. And since this obscure island had an airfield on it, Nimitz made the occupation of the island the main priority in his plans. The assignment for taking this little island had fallen to the 2nd Marine Division...since the legendary 1st Marine Division was already scheduled for the Bougainville operation to the southwest. And this is how it came to be that the marines from five battalions of the 2nd Division found themselves fighting for their very lives in one of the most deadly places on the face of the Earth. And so begins November 21st...the second day of one of the most legendary battles ever fought in the history of Marine Corps.

CHAPTER 2

As dawn broke over Betio Island on Monday morning, approximately thirty-five hundred battle-weary marines were staring over the desolate landscape that had once been a thriving Japanese airbase. Hidden somewhere among the shattered ruins was what remained of Admiral Keiji Shibasaki's defense force. The Japanese Commander had started the battle with a force of nearly four thousand eight hundred men...twenty-six hundred being crack infantry troops from the 6th and 7th Special Naval Landing Forces. Another one thousand two hundred and fifty men were combat engineers from the 111th Pioneers...the men who had poured their hearts and souls into preparing the island's defenses to resist an enemy attack. The remaining nine hundred and fifty men were in the 4th Fleet Construction Battalion...half of whom were conscripted Korean laborers. These men did the heavy lifting...working alongside the Pioneers where and when they were needed. Just how many of Shibasaki's defenders had survived the hellacious fighting on the first day of battle was anyone's guess, but the marines figured that they had to have killed a bunch even though they had seen very few bodies to confirm it. Still, no one could have imagined that the ones left would be able to put up as nasty a fight as they had the day before.

• • •

This second day certainly couldn't be any worse than the day before had been for the tired, seasick men of Major Lawrence Hays's 1st Battalion, 8th Marines. Held in reserve, they were still aboard their Higgins boats when the sun began to appear along the eastern horizon. They had been out there for nearly twenty hours now... rocking back and forth the entire time...all the while waiting for orders to land. This mishap, like so many others, was the result of the communications failures that had plagued the whole landing operation from the very beginning. And this problem was about to rear its ugly head yet again...another bad omen for the men of Hays's battalion.

Their long nightmare had begun around mid-day of Day One... when Colonel Shoup tried to get a message to the 2nd Division Staff aboard the battleship *Maryland*. Shoup was adamant in his desires: he wanted the 1st of the 8th to land on a *specific* part of the Red 2 beachhead. Having seen Kyle's and Rudd's battalions being slaughtered as they came in across a broad front on Red 2 and Red 3, the Colonel wanted Major Hays to concentrate his force on the Red 2 beachhead by coming in along the right side of the pier instead. The pier would provide Hays's men the cover and protection that Rudd's and Kyle's men had not had and thus they would have a much better chance of getting ashore intact. Once they landed, Shoup wanted Hays' men to attack westward towards Red 1 in order to link up with Major Ryan's orphans who would be attacking eastward from the Bird's Beak on the northwestern corner of the island. This dual-pronged assault would eliminate the deadly *Pocket* in the Red 1 Beachhead that had caused so much trouble to the landing teams the day before. Once the *Pocket* was eliminated, additional reinforcements could land unhindered along Red 1 and Red 2...and then a concentrated attack towards the tail of the island could be initiated.

Unfortunately, most of the radio messages that Colonel Shoup sent from the island never reached Major General Julian Smith... the fifty-eight-year-old Division Commanding General...CG for short...or his staff on the *Maryland*. And the few that did make it through were so confusing that Major General Smith had no idea what Colonel Shoup actually wanted. Based on the fragmentary information he had received from the beaches, Smith issued orders for the 1st Battalion to land to the left of Red Beach 3 along the tail end of the island instead. The Japanese on the eastern end of the island could then be destroyed in a pincers movement as Hays's men attacked westward while Major Crowe's men attacked eastward out of their perimeter...a maneuver which mimicked what Colonel Shoup had planned for the western end of the island. When a Navy Kingfisher observation plane later reported that the 1st Battalion had begun landing, it was assumed that General Smith's orders were being carried out and that things were finally going according to plan. Unfortunately, the pilot and observer in the Kingfisher were mistaken...the fog of war now rearing its ugly head to bedevil the operation. What they saw were the artillery batteries still trying to land on Red 2...and they confused their attempts with the 1st of the 8th. Ironically, the order to land never reached Major Hays at all! Instead, he and his battalion remained on station at the line of departure... milling about in their cramped LCVP's for the rest of the afternoon and night.

It was well past midnight when the Division Staff realized the error over the disposition of the 1st Battalion and their frustration over the faulty communications reached new heights. The staff... though dog-tired and crammed for time...scrapped the old plan and began working on yet another one that would land Hays' men along the tail at first light. This plan was torpedoed in midstream as well... when word finally came in via messenger that Colonel Shoup wanted the battalion to land on Red 2. Sadly, the staff officers had no way of knowing that these instructions had passed through several layers of command along the way and that the most important component of the message - that Shoup wanted the 1ˢᵗ Battalion to come in along the pier instead of landing in the middle of Red 2 - had been filtered out! Unaware of what Shoup wanted and why...the staff directed Hays' battalion to land along the western side of Red 2...and right into the teeth of the bristling defenses of the *Pocket*.

• • •

First light of Day Two on the island found the men in Lieutenant Dan Hackett's CP up and alert. Most of all, they were gratified that they had survived the night. They were in good spirits and astonished that the Japanese hadn't launched an attack against their lonely outpost during the night. "Why didn't they come?" The question was on everyone's mind and it was asked over and over again by the men in the crater as they passed two cans of rations between them. It was a meager breakfast...but it was better than nothing... and someone had been gracious enough to share them...so they ate without complaint.

The men came up with various rationales to explain why the Japanese had left them alone throughout the night. Some were sound...while others were crazy. One man proposed that the Japs might have been evacuated off the tail of the island by a fleet of submarines under the cover of darkness. The lieutenant was listening as well and laughed when he heard that one and said, "It wouldn't be the first time something like that was done."

"Oh, here we go...yet another history lesson," Private First Class Gene Petraglia, the lieutenant's runner, moaned.

"Since you asked...you shall receive. What I was referring to was one of the early battles that took place during our Revolutionary War. It took place right near where I grew up in fact...and it was called the Battle of Long Island...even though it was fought in Brooklyn," the lieutenant explained to the men. Everyone except Petraglia seemed to be genuinely interested in the lieutenant's story. The runner rolled his eyes in mock boredom and said, "Lemme guess who won...the Germans?"

Private First Class Saul Cohen looked at the lieutenant's runner askance and said, "You can't be that dumb. You look dumb...I'll give ya that...but no one is that stupid. Although you might be."

"Don't worry...he's just acting stupid. He likes to do it to aggravate me. He knows it was us versus the British Army...and the British won...sort of," Hackett said lightheartedly.

Petraglia just glared back at Cohen...not sure he liked the man's tone. The much-taller Cohen caught his look and glared right back at him...defying him to do something. The stare off lasted a few seconds and then Petraglia just smiled which caught the barrel-chested Cohen off guard. Startled, Cohen said, "Just let the LT finish the story...it's interesting...at least I think it is."

"You still have the floor, sir," Petraglia said, holding his hands up in mock surrender.

"Thank you. As I was saying...the Brits won the battle but the interesting thing about it was that General George Washington...the guy that cut down the cherry tree when he was a kid...well, he saved the day for us Americans."

"How'd he do that, sir?" Cohen asked while glancing over at Petraglia...who just shrugged his shoulders in response.

Lieutenant Hackett watched the exchange between the two men and when he saw that the situation was defused...he continued. "Well, after the Americans lost the battle, they were forced to retreat. They could only go so far though and eventually they got hemmed in against the East River...which separates Manhattan...which is an island... from Brooklyn. The British had them surrounded on three sides and it looked like it would be a massacre when the British Army...who had a lot more guys...attacked the Americans in the morning."

At this point, Private Kevin McCaffrey interrupted and warned, "Sounds a whole lot like what we got right here...no, lieutenant?"

"You make a real good point...we are surrounded...like they were...but this time we have reinforcements in those ships behind us to back us up…whereas Washington and his men were on their own. And those men will be landing soon enough…so while the two situations are sort of the same…there are important differences between the two. See my point?" Hackett asked.

"I do," McCaffrey answered, and then added, "So how'd the battle end up…how'd our guys keep from getting massacred?"

The lieutenant's face lit up as he explained the final stage of the battle to the men. They could tell by his enthusiasm that the lieutenant obviously liked and admired George Washington and his excitement drew them in as well. Hackett told them how an eerie fog had descended…almost miraculously…over the battlefield…which shrouded the movements of the Americans from the British sentries. Washington then ordered his men to keep fires burning along his entire line to give the impression that all his men were still there. Next, he called up a special group of men who were part of his army…the fishermen from Marblehead, Massachusetts. These men were skilled sailors and he had them round up every boat they could lay there hands on. In complete darkness, the Marbleheaders began shuttling Washington's entire army across the river to Manhattan…and safety. The evacuation went on all night…and the last man to leave the Brooklyn encampment in the early morning was General Washington himself. When the sun finally burned the fog off several hours later, the British were shocked to find that the American ragamuffins had escaped their grasp…yet again…and Washington and his army were thus free to carry on the dream of the American Revolution.

"That's an incredible story, sir," Cohen said, mesmerized.

"Yeah…I didn't know it happened that way. I must've been asleep in that part of the history class," McCaffrey agreed.

"So it's possible that the Japs could've been taken off the island," Hackett said, nodding to the man from the machine gun squad who had made the remark that started the whole conversation, "but I don't think this Jap general…Shibasaki…is in the same league as our General Washington…so they're probably still here."

Most of the younger marines seemed to champion another explanation for why the Japanese had failed to attack during the night. They were hoping that the Japanese were contemplating giving up. They were debating the merits of this possibility when a gruff voice broke in.

"Don't count on it. Nips don't surrender. Ever. They fought almost to the last man on the *Canal*. It'll be the same way here. Trust me," Sergeant Ricardo Upshaw offered…the tone of voice immediately dashing any hopes the men had for an easy day ahead.

"Runner comin' in, sir."

The lieutenant looked up at the marine who made the announcement. He was pointing forward…indicating that the runner was coming from Sergeant McGovern's position…not along the beach from the direction of Regimental headquarters. Hackett crawled up the slope of the shell hole in time to see a marine scampering towards them. He was zigzagging from side to side and he stopped occasionally when he was able to find adequate cover. The man finally scrambled over the lip of the crater and slid down to the bottom. He was breathing heavily, exhausted from his run. He took his helmet off and scratched at his scalp, causing his matted hair to stick up at odd angles. He looked around, spotted the lieutenant, and smiled.

"Morning, sir."

"How are things, Feeney?" the lieutenant responded good-naturedly, glad to see the private first class. Hackett reached across and handed him his canteen. Sean Feeney took it, unscrewed the top, took a swig, recapped it, and handed it back with an appreciative nod.

"Oh, not so bad really. Could be worse I guess."

"Well if you came lookin' for some breakfast, you came to the wrong place. Sorry we can't offer you anything."

"That's alright, sir. Some of the boys up front had some chow on them and we passed it around. It wasn't much, but it was enough."

"That's good. Did you lose anyone last night?"

"No, sir. Sergeant McGovern's pretty shocked that we didn't get hit last night. We had some light probing out to our front, but nothing like we were expecting. No one fired a shot so I don't think the Nips know we're here yet…or if they do, then they're not worried about us." Feeney looked around and noticed that none of the other men - except the corporal from the machine gun crew - were paying any attention to what he was saying. They were acting like he wasn't even there…each attending to his own private task instead. One man was sharpening his knife with meticulous attention…while another was blowing into the chamber of his rifle to remove any sand that had gotten into it during the night. They all had one thing in common though…they looked haggard…and as a result they seemed numb to what was going on around them. "Most of us were up all night…just waitin' for them to hit our line. From the look of it, you guys didn't get much sleep either," he stated flatly.

"I can't figure it out. I thought for sure they would've tried a banzai attack last night. They always have in the past. Maybe the Japs are getting smarter."

"Sure as hell hope not, sir. These damn Japs have been hard enough to kill already. The last thing we need is for them to get better at stayin' alive."

"Anything else?"

"Sergeant McGovern said to let you know that everything is status quo along our line. There hasn't been any activity to our direct front to speak of. We can see a little movement around that large bunker complex that's covering the cove about four hundred yards ahead of us on the right though. He thinks the Japs will try to hang on to that place 'til the very end."

"Yeah, they probably have some heavy stuff in there. There's bound to be some smaller bunkers around it. It'll be hard to get at if we have to go after it head on. I wish to hell we had some of those damn flame throwers to use against it." Lieutenant Hackett turned his gaze from the bunker complex back to the beach and the lagoon.

Feeney thought about the dilemma for a moment and then said, "I didn't see any on the beach where we came in at, sir, but there might be some engineers further down the beach. Or maybe some demo guys with some satchel charges."

"Good idea. I'll send someone back to find some. In the meantime, tell Sergeant McGovern that we'll sit tight for now. We should be getting some word from Regiment shortly. They know we're here. And from the looks of it…we might be getting some help over here sooner than we thought."

"You got it, sir."

Feeney didn't fully understand what the lieutenant meant by "help" until he got up to leave and looked out over the lip of the crater. It was lighter now than when he had started out for the CP. Scanning the lagoon, Feeney could now make out a long line of Higgins boats churning towards the reef some five hundred yards away. It looked like these marines were going to be making their landing right on top of them.

"Okay, then. Go ahead and head back. Be careful. Snipers are gonna be looking for runners now that the sun's up."

"No problem there, sir," Feeney replied confidently as he inched up to the lip of the crater. Looking over, he checked the ground quickly and then glanced back at the lieutenant. "I sure hope those boys have it easier coming in than we did," he said before dashing off towards the trench line in the distance.

CHAPTER 3

From his Regimental CP, Colonel Shoup could see the same thing and was furious. Knowing that Major Hays' battalion was coming in, he had ordered his commanders on shore…Majors Crowe and Rudd on the left…Lieutenant Colonel Jordan and Major Kyle in the center…and Major Ryan on the far right…to conduct a general advance at first light. Shoup hoped the lull in firing would continue until these attacks started and then he figured the hornet's nest would be stirred up once again. What he wanted most though was for the three-pronged attack to divert the attention of the Jap gunners away from the three rifle companies that were trying to land. Now…to his unending frustration…he could tell that his wishes…yet again…had been ignored. The LCVP's carrying the 1st of the 8th were not orienting on the pier like he had wanted but were heading too far west. The colonel knew that this approach would put the 1st Battalion's landing in jeopardy since it would be riding right into the devastating guns of the *Pocket*. "If we can't get those damn boats to shift closer to the pier, those men will catch hell over there!" he roared out to his staff. Colonel Shoup then turned to Lieutenant Colonel Rixey and told him to reposition some of his

75mm pack howitzers so they could fire on the Jap bunker complex in the *Pocket*.

"Already working on it, sir," Rixey quickly responded. "I've got two guns moving now. We got lucky somehow and got a bulldozer in last night. They built us two berms on the beach. These guns will be able to blast anything over there on Red Two as soon as they're set up."

"Good. That's good," Colonel Shoup replied. "Your guns may be about the only help we can give those boys. I've ordered everyone to attack but if that fails…you're it. Ryan is pinned down on the Beak with his own problems. Jordan's doing the best he can with what he's got right here. Down the beach to the right is still unsecured for all intents and purposes. We've got some scattered units in there but not enough to make a difference. Hell, they're still complaining that the machine gun fire is so heavy that they can't get off the damned beach. Hawkins and his scout-snipers are headed down there to clear out the Jap strong points behind the seawall. If anyone can do it, he can. You know what he told me before he left?"

"No, sir," Rixey answered.

"He told me that it was a perfect mission for them since his one platoon could still lick any two-hundred-man company in the world."

"Didn't he lose some men attacking the pier yesterday?" Rixey asked.

"Yeah, a few…then some others around here after they landed. He lost another last night when the Japs charged the pier. That crazy man started out with thirty-four men and now he's got about twenty left. He was wounded yesterday morning too when a mortar round exploded near him on the beach. He seems to be okay though. I wish I had more like him."

"He reminds me of that Greek philosopher…Heraclitus. He said something very profound about warriors…how out of a company of one hundred men…ten were completely worthless…and had no business being there."

"I don't think this Heraclitus ever encountered a company of marines, Rix. I've seen one or two deadbeats in a company in my time...but ten...that seems way too high...even for an Army unit," Shoup countered, smirking.

"I gotta agree with you, sir, but maybe the Greeks had more slackers then. Anyway, this Heraclitus went on to say that eighty out of the one hundred were basically cannon fodder...pardon the pun."

"None taken...of course...but again...I think this Heraclitus had an axe to grind against the Greeks. He obviously wasn't talking about the Spartans...even though they were from Greece too. They were more like us. And that number eighty is way too high...even for a run-of-the-mill Greek outfit. You see I studied military history too," the colonel replied evenly, "and I'll be damned if there were any shirkers in that group of three hundred that fought at Thermopylae."

"Touché," Lieutenant Colonel Rixey said in agreement, then continued, "but now we come to the good part...the part where he was talking about men who are more like our marines here. He said that only nine out of the hundred are real fighters...and that they were lucky to have them...since it was those guys who made the battle--"

"We just got a runner in from Jordan," Major Culhane, Shoup's executive officer shouted over, cutting Rixey off abruptly. Rixey knew Tom Culhane well and thus wasn't waiting for an apology. "He says it's as bad as yesterday...that his men are trying hard to advance...but they're meeting heavy resistance," Culhane continued, shaking his head. The dark frown on his face left no one wondering how he felt about the set back.

"Got it, Tom," Shoup acknowledged as the deep sound of gunfire could be heard out to their front...where Jordan's men were waging their attack.

"Tell Jordan to keep pushing. Once we get Hays in we'll get him some help."

"Yes, sir," Culhane replied as he turned on his heel to relay the message to Jordan's runner.

"I got my fingers crossed that today is going to be better than yesterday…but it won't be if I keep gettin' messages like that," Shoup said, turning his attention back to Rixey. "Now what were you saying?"

"Oh…I was quoting Heraclitus…and how he felt that there were only nine real fighters out of a hundred men. Too low an estimate in my opinion…but he was around back then and I wasn't…so maybe he knew something about those men that I don't. But then he went on to say that out of that one hundred…there was one guy… the ultimate warrior of them all…and upon whom the whole unit depended. 'He would end up bringing them all back,' was how he put it. Well, I think our Greek philosopher was referring to your scout-sniper platoon leader…Lieutenant Hawkins," Rixey said, finally finishing his point.

"If I had a hundred like him this battle would've been already over," Shoup replied affirmatively as the sound of the battle continued to swell around them.

"Well, sir, we'll do our best to keep those Jap gunners' heads down. Those seventy-five 's of mine can be pretty deadly firing at these short ranges."

"Thanks, Rix. I know your men will do a great job. That's about all I can do for Hays now I guess. I just hope it's enough."

• • •

The 1st Battalion, 8th Marine Regiment was packed into some twenty-five Higgins boats that were organized into five landing waves. The men had boarded the boats in the early morning hours of D-Day and they had been rocking back and forth in them ever since. They were fatigued, soaking wet, seasick, and miserable. Most of them couldn't wait to get out of the landing craft and put their feet on dry ground to end their torment.

When the order to commence the landing was finally communicated to the boats, a rousing cheer went up among the men. Their spirits rose even more when the men were told to unload their weapons to prevent any friendly-fire incidents from happening. It was a necessary precaution since they would landing along a sector of the beach that had been - as far as they knew - already secured by the 2nd Battalion, 2nd Marines. The last thing anyone wanted was for one marine to shoot another accidentally as they charged through friendly lines to take up their forward positions on Red 2.

The chilling realization that the landing wasn't going to be quite as easy as they envisioned hit as soon as the boats of the first wave left the line of departure at 0615 hours. These landing craft began taking fire from the direction of the *Niminoa* almost immediately. During the night, the Japanese had sent more men out to reinforce the infantrymen still hidden aboard the derelict and now their machine gun fire swept down the length of each oncoming wave... raking the LCVP's and causing the first casualties. The well-dressed lines that the landing craft had maintained began to unravel as the coxswains were forced to take evasive action to avoid this vicious fire.

As disruptive as this initial fire was, all hell broke loose when the Japanese shore batteries and heavy machine guns opened up. Enemy gunners in bunkers in the *Pocket* and along the eastern tail of the island began zeroing in on the Higgins boats out in the lagoon. Of all the weapons the Japanese were using to repel the marine landing, the most deadly were the twin-mounted 13.2-mm heavy machine guns, the 70-mm howitzers, and the dual purpose Type 88 75-mm and Type 89 twin-mount 127-mm DP guns. They were labeled DP for dual-purpose...since they were exceptionally good at both bringing down aircraft in an anti-aircraft role and sinking landing craft in an anti-boat role. The devastation these guns wrought on the oncoming marines was horrific. Several LCVP's suffered direct hits and were literally blown out of the water before they even reached the reef. Marines in adjacent boats...who only seconds ago had been waving to their friends across the way...were now staring blankly at clouds of smoke where their friends' boats had just been.

Sadly, the situation continued to deteriorate...and the day had only just begun. Like the day before, the water depth covering the reef was still too shallow to permit the Higgins boats to cross it. The coxswains did their best to get the marines as close to shore as possible, but the reef forced them to drop their bow ramps some five hundred yards away from the beach. Most of the marines leapt into chest or waist deep water, caught their balance on the coral apron, and then scrambled over the reef. Others jumped into water over their heads or fell into shell holes and plunged to the bottom. Some of these men...especially the ones who were really loaded down with equipment...drowned when they couldn't shed their combat loads... which could weigh as much as ninety pounds...quick enough. The same fate befell the marines aboard the boats that were hit beyond the reef and sank in deeper water. As a matter of survival, scores of men were forced to abandon their weapons and gear as they struggled to reach the shallow water near the reef. Most of battalion's heavy weapons - the machine guns, the mortars, and the flame throwers that were sorely needed ashore - were lost in this manner.

And as the marines waded in and got closer to the beach, individual Jap gunners punished them with an unrelenting torrent of rifle and machine gun fire. It seemed even worse than the day before because all the Jap fire was directed solely against this one lone battalion. Marines who were pinned down behind the seawall turned around and watched the horrific scene unfold behind them. Like an audience at a play, they watched helplessly as the 1st Battalion was cut to pieces on the theatre's main stage.

CHAPTER 4

"I need a corpsman."

No one inside the cramped bunker paid any attention to the marine at the entrance. The silence was broken by a ripping sound as one of the men inside tore open the utility shirt of the man lying on a makeshift table in the center of the darkened room.

"Hold that light up. I can't see…"

A young corpsman, obviously tired, obeyed the order and stretched his hand higher. The signal lamp he was holding illuminated the gruesome chest wound on the marine before him.

A third man…the doctor…opened one of the man's eyelids, checked the pupil, and then placed his ear to the man's chest. "This one's not dead…not yet anyway. Get him on one of the boats that are going out. He'll make it if we can get him back to the transports." The doctor said this as he was packing the wound with gauze and bandaging it tightly. He finished the procedure, patted the unconscious man on the arm, and said, "Good luck, marine." The man was quickly carried out of the bunker on a stretcher and was taken to an amtrac that was parked near the pier only ten yards away for the dangerous trip back to the support ships.

Lieutenant Brukardt straightened up, stretched out his arms, and yawned loudly. He was twenty-nine years old and an accomplished surgeon and he had not slept in twenty-four hours. He and three corpsmen had made it to the island the day before with Major Rudd's battalion and they had been working on the wounded ever since. They had set up their aid station in this abandoned Jap bunker and it was now fully occupied with wounded marines. Without missing a beat, he turned to the marine who had just shown up and asked softly, "So who needs a corpsman?"

"Well, sir, I'm sorta here on my own. I'm with Hawkins," the marine stated expectantly.

The doctor squinted at the marine, the bright glare of the doorway obscuring the marine somewhat and replied, "Uh huh," apparently unimpressed with his introduction.

The marine looked at the doctor quizzically and then it dawned on him that the doctor did not realize who Hawkins was. "Sir, I'm a scout-sniper in Lieutenant Hawkins' platoon. We just got orders to take out some Jap bunkers down the beach some and, well, we're probably gonna need some medical help on this one. Lieutenant Hawkins is kinda crazy...well, not kinda crazy...just plain crazy. You see he's already been wounded, and if he gets hit again, well, we want a corpsman to be there just in case."

"I have heard about this Hawkins now that you mention it. Never met the man, but I have heard of him," Lieutenant Brukardt said, thinking the request over in his mind. "Didn't he lead the attack against the pier yesterday morning?"

"Yes, sir, he sure did. He ran down the pier like a wild man too, shooting Japs left and right as he went by. He knocked out some Jap pillboxes right over there once we landed. That's when he got hit by the mortar."

"Well, as you can see here, I don't have any men I can spare. I wish I could help you but--"

"I'll go, sir," a voice said, interrupting the doctor. Pharmacist Mate Fumai emerged out of the darkness from the rear of the bunker where he had been taking a much needed nap.

"You sure you want to go?" the lieutenant asked, adding, "You've been up all night."

"I'm fine, sir. I just got some rest and I feel fine. It's getting kinda crowded in here anyway. I could use some sunshine," he replied cheerfully, obviously faking it.

"Okay, I won't hold you here. Thanks for your help last night. Several marines who wouldn't have made it are going to get home alive because you were here to lend a hand."

"Don't worry, sir, I'll be back. The Japs seem to be having a hard time getting rid of me!" Fumai said as he slung an aid bag over his shoulder. He gave a wave to Lieutenant Brukardt and then turned to the scout-sniper said, "Ready when you are."

"Follow me...and oh, make sure to keep your damn head down if ya wanna live long," the marine warned as the two men left the bunker and headed for the cover of the seawall.

CHAPTER 5

At the other end of Red 2, PFC Feeney had just begun briefing Sergeant McGovern. Feeney - who had landed as a private but was given a battlefield promotion by Lieutenant Hackett for his bravery in conducting a recon mission soon after they had landed - had just made it back to the trench line and was telling Sergeant McGovern what Lieutenant Hackett wanted done when Japanese fire exploded above them. The noise sent shock waves through their bodies and they looked at each other in disbelief. McGovern wondered immediately: *If there are enough Japs left to put up this kind of firepower...why didn't they attack us in strength last night?* And he shrugged his shoulders as if to say *beats me* to Feeney...who was wondering the same exact thing. He then glanced cautiously over the sandbags that lined the trench and he could see flashes coming from the large sand-covered bombproof that sat in middle of the curve of the parrot's neck. This position was about seventy yards behind the seawall and it dominated the entire cove area and could fire accurately at targets that were well beyond the reef. McGovern also saw gunfire flashes coming from smaller bunkers that were to the left and right of the bigger one. He knew that the Japs had designed the position so that each bunker had interlocking fields of fire with the one next to it...which made the complex virtually impregnable to head-on attacks. Closer in, not more than a hundred yards away, he could make out two more machine gun emplacements that were protected by coconut logs...just like the ones they had taken out yesterday. McGovern turned to Feeney and shouted, "Get the men on the left firing on those two bunkers right there." He kept pointing at them until Feeney saw them...since they blended in with the rubble around them.

"I see 'em," he said confidently.

"We'll have to knock out those guns before we do anything else. At least we'll take some of the heat off the men coming in. It's not much but it beats doing nothin'."

"You got it, sarge," Feeney said. He then turned and made his way down the line, alerting the men to the new targets in front of them.

Sergeant McGovern watched Feeney go and then he started down the trench to the right to do the same thing. He had gone about ten feet and was looking at Sergeant Endres when his body suddenly pitched forward and thumped the ground with a sound like a stuffed duffel bag being thrown from the bed of a truck. He landed face down, let out a muffled grown that the sand absorbed, and then died. He had been shot in the side of his head...just above the brim of his helmet...which had a jagged hole in it now. The helmet had not stopped the bullet...since it was not really designed to. Instead, the helmet was worn to deflect small pieces of shrapnel and other debris that might land on a person's head if an explosion occurred nearby. And the shot that had gotten him was one of sheer luck...or so it seemed.

The enemy gunner had swung his weapon over to engage the sneaky Americans who had just started firing at his bunker from a trench line not far away. He had been raking the boats near the reef line unhindered but bullets were now pinging off the logs of the pillbox he had so painstaking helped to build many months ago. Annoyed by the distraction, he was about to fire a controlled burst at the trench line when he was hit squarely in the chest by an M-1 rifle slug. Stung by the impact of the bullet, the Japanese private took his eye off the sight to see where he was hit. In doing so he traversed the gun slightly to his right and squeezed off three rounds before slumping over the gun. Although one of his rounds would find its mark, the young Japanese soldier would never know it. His body was roughly pulled off the gun by the assistant gunner and he fell to the dusty floor of the bunker. Bullets were smacking against the bunker's walls and no one had time to help him….since they needed that gun back in action immediately.

Weak from the loss of blood and wracked with pain, the gunner dragged himself slowly into the corner and sat against the coconut log wall. With no expectations of medical help, he knew he would eventually bleed to death. The thought of it didn't depress him though; luckily, over the course of his twenty years, he had found very little that did. He had lived a good life and had always been told he was funny. He had found enjoyment in making others laugh and he knew that was one of his gifts. In the hour before he died, he thought fondly of the good times he had shared with his friends in the squad…who he would miss dearly…and of his family back home…who he would miss more.

CHAPTER 6

"How far down we goin'?"
"Not much farther. The lieutenant said he'd meet us at that disabled amtrac up there."

The scout-sniper and the corpsman were crouched over and making their way slowly down the beach along the seawall. Japanese fire was still pouring over the top of the barrier in an effort to stop the marine reinforcements from getting ashore. Up ahead they could see an amtrac that was leaning against the seawall. It looked like it had almost made it over the log wall when it had either been hit, stalled out, or just gotten hung up. Pharmacist Mate Fumai could see a group of marines huddled by it…looking in their direction.

"That's gotta be the one," Fumai said.

"It is. I can see some of our guys from here," the scout-sniper acknowledged.

As they got closer, several men began waving at them to stay low and one shouted a warning, "Stay down! The Japs are right behind the seawall!"

Once they made it to the amtrac, the men welcomed their buddy with silent nods.

"Where's the lieutenant?" a grizzled marine asked the scout-sniper.

"I don't know. I thought he'd be here already. I stopped to get a corpsman. I figured we could use him for this one."

The tough-looking men gave a casual glance at the corpsman but said nothing to him.

"We'll wait another five minutes for him. If he's not here by then, we'll go ahead and attack the bunkers ourselves," another man said, obviously in control of the group in the lieutenant's absence.

"Okay. But don't count the LT out yet. He wants to handle this one himself. He told me that back at the CP," the scout-sniper advised.

A young marine who was sitting off to the side...by himself... heard this and asked, "You mean your lieutenant goes with you when you take the bunkers out?"

The others turned to face this marine and one answered, "He doesn't go with us. He goes alone. We provide cover fire for him."

"Let me get this straight. Your lieutenant does the attacking and you guys sit back here? I've never seen an officer do that," the outsider replied incredulously.

"Well, there ain't too many officers like Lieutenant Hawkins... that's for damn sure," another man shot back.

Fumai watched this exchange and realized that the young marine was not part of the scout-sniper platoon. *He's another nomad, just like me*, Fumai thought, so he decided to join him. He crawled past the other men and slid in next to him against the seawall. The corpsman held out his hand and introduced himself to the small marine. The marine stuck his hand out and grabbed the corpsman's hand in his own...and the two hit it off instantly.

"I'm Private First Class Bob George. I guess you're like me...an orphan out here."

Fumai agreed and explained the circumstances that led up to why he was there. When he had finished the story of his travails, he looked at George quizzically and asked, "You mind if I ask you a personal question?"

The private knew what was coming. "Let me guess? How old am I, right?"

"I didn't mean to hurt your feelings or nothin'. Heck, I just met you," Fumai countered, trying to apologize.

"I don't take nothin' by it. I get it all the time. I've always looked pretty young for my age I guess. I joined the *Corps* the day before my seventeenth birthday. Recruiting sergeant cut me a break. I thought all the hard marine training and Guadalcanal might've aged me a bit. Looks like it hasn't, huh," he said good-naturedly and then he went on and told his story.

"I'm a machine gunner from A Company…First of the Tenth. Our job is to protect the seventy-fives from getting overrun. I got to the beach sometime around four this morning. We spent all day yesterday looking for an opening through the reef. We had been in that darn Higgins boat since before daylight. The lieutenant in charge finally lost his patience and ordered the boat driver to drop us off at the end of the pier. That was around seventeen hundred. So the guy pulled up to the seaplane ramp and let the bow down…and wouldn't you just know it…the ramp just missed the wood planking and it sank underwater. Next thing you know, sea water is pourin' in and the darn thing sank right there. We only got one of our fifty cals out. We lost the other three. The thirty caliber section lost all their guns. What a waste."

Confused, Fumai asked, "But you said you only got ashore a couple of hours ago? It took you that long to make it in from the pier?"

"Yup. That pier was under fire all night. We lost one guy right away to a Jap machine gun. We knew right then and there that this wasn't gonna be no picnic. I crawled in the whole way. Our whole section got split up somehow when it got dark. I haven't seen anyone else since I got to the seawall. I was so tired I crapped out right there. When it started getting light out this morning, I woke up and got a shock. The two marines I had crawled in between were both dead. One had half his face blown off. I thought I had a lotta company by the seawall and that it was fairly safe. There were marines laying all over down there. It didn't take too long to figure out that nearly half of them were dead. There must've been a hundred or more that were killed on that beach alone. A lot of good marines that are laying back there aren't ever gonna see home again."

"You're right about that," the corpsman agreed somberly. "I never could've dreamt it was goin' be this bad."

Neither man said anything for a while after that. They were both lost in their own thoughts until Fumai finally broke the silence. He felt foolish asking the question, but he went ahead and asked it anyway. "Bob, have you noticed anything strange on the beach around here?"

"Strange? No… nothing at all. Other than the fact that it looks like we might get wiped out here…nothing strikes me as particularly strange," the private replied sarcastically.

"What about the chickens?" Fumai asked inquisitively.

"Oh…them. Whatta about 'em?"

On the way to the amtrac, Fumai had noticed that there were dead chickens lying on the beach and inland of the seawall. There must have been at least two hundred carcasses scattered about by his count. It seemed like there were feathers and chicken parts strewn all over the place.

"Whatta about 'em? What the hell are they doing here? That's what I wanna know," Fumai replied.

"The Japs eat the eggs…and probably the officers get to eat a chicken every so often. What else ya think they have 'em for. You must be a real city boy if you couldn't figure that one out for yourself," George answered, laughing as he said it. "Heck, I grew up in the Ozark Mountains…in eastern Oklahoma…and my daddy had a farm. Chickens aren't a strange sight to me. Their pens must've been hit during the naval bombardment. Some of them must have got away, but they didn't make it very far. Nothin' stays alive very long out here…not even the chickens." George's voice softened suddenly as he continued, "I actually caught one earlier…before I got here. This small bird came staggering down the beach. It was bleeding pretty badly…it had been hit in the neck by some shrapnel. I guess it was dazed cause it walked right up to me as I was lying against the seawall. The poor thing didn't ask to be here. I gave it some water from my canteen but it just poured out of its neck wound after it drank it. I just let the bird go after that. There was nothing else I could do for it."

A few minutes passed and then someone shouted expectantly, "Here he comes!"

Both George and Fumai looked down the beach to see what all the excitement was about.

"Who the hell is that?" Fumai asked one of the scout-snipers.

"That right there is the finest officer in this here Marine Corps. That crazy son-of-a-bitch is our Lieutenant Hawkins," the man responded proudly.

Striding confidently towards them was one lone marine. Incredibly, he was not crouching behind the seawall for cover. Instead, this man was walking fully upright down the beach. He was wearing a cloth sniper's cap instead of a protective metal helmet and had a .45 caliber pistol holstered on his hip. He was carrying an M-1 carbine in his hand. He had a defiant look on his face that was a cross between a scowl and a penetrating glare and his demeanor conveyed the sheer contempt and hatred he had for the enemy.

Fumai turned to George and said incredulously, "I just came down that seawall. There are bullets flying all over the place over it. A damn bug wouldn't stand a chance out there. How is he not getting hit?"

George…continuing to stare at the lieutenant…looked mystified and said, "Beats the heck outta me."

"Is it luck or divine providence?" Fumai wondered.

"Nobody's that lucky. Somebody upstairs is obviously watching over him," the private responded.

"Well, if that's the case, I wouldn't want to be one of those un-fortunate Japs on the other side of the seawall?"

"Why's that?"

"Because I have a feeling the wrath of God is about to descend on them in the form of one mean-assed marine lieutenant...that's way," Fumai answered back matter-of-factly.

"Amen to that," George replied coldly.

• • •

Lieutenant Hawkins strode in among his men and looked the group over. Both Fumai and George noticed the intensity in the man's dark eyes when he glanced in their direction. "Who are you?" he asked, pointing at George.

"George, sir. Private First Class. I'm a machine gunner with Alpha...First of the Tenth. I--"

Lieutenant Hawkins cut him off before he had a chance to fin-ish. "Well, we're the Scout-Sniper platoon. Are you any good with a rifle?"

"Good enough hunter to put a meal on the table, sir. I grew up in the Ozarks. Money wasn't too easy to come by at times. I shot rabbits and small deer mostly."

"I'm from El Paso, Texas," Hawkins said, and added, "You're hired. Welcome aboard."

Hawkins then turned to Pharmacist Mate Fumai and said, "And what about you?"

Fumai began to speak but the scout-sniper that had recruited him jumped in and interrupted the corpsman. Fumai was content to let the other man do the talking for him. When he was done with the explanation, the lieutenant seemed satisfied. "If any of my men get hit...do the best you can for them. Understood?"

"Yes, sir. I will. I won't let you down. Do you want me to take a look at that shoulder wound you got?"

Hawkins glanced down and touched the bloody spot on his shirt where the mortar fragments had cut into him. "No. Don't worry about me. I'm okay. Just take care of my men. These Japs can't hit me. They couldn't hit me with a shotgun at point-blank range."

Without being told to do so, the lieutenant's men began handing him their hand grenades that they had unclipped from their web belts. He hooked them on to his belt, nodded to the men, and then boosted himself up onto the top of the seawall. Then he ran at the bunkers out ahead and several scout-snipers rose up and began firing at the apertures to pin the Jap gunners down. Hawkins was like a wild man…dashing from one pillbox to the next…firing his carbine and throwing grenades into them. He destroyed the first two positions this way.

In route to a third bunker, Hawkins came across a small machine gun nest. This position was protected by coconut logs instead of concrete and it was covered in sand…just like the others were. The two Japanese *rikusentai* inside had been firing their rifles at the crazed marine who had charged the bunkers to their right. Although neither man had said so, they had both determined that this man was a Samurai of some sort. No other type of warrior would attack with such ferocity and courage. They might have been able to bring him down with their Type 99 7.7mm light machine gun…but…unfortunately…they had run out of ammunition only minutes before. The crew commander and another man had left to retrieve more ammunition for their gun but they were spotted as they headed to the larger bunker next to them. They only made it about ten feet before being shot down by the marines hidden behind the seawall.

Now this devil-possessed American was headed for their position and the two remaining men became frightened. The man seemed to have an aura of evil surrounding him…since his face was contorted with rage and he was yelling words they could not understand. They continued to fire at him with their *Arisaka* rifles…but…try as they might…none of their shots hit him. Too late, the men realized that they should have spent more time at the firing range perfecting their rifle marksmanship instead of concentrating solely on their machine gun accuracy. And it was a mistake they would not recover from… since the enemy soldier was getting closer by the second.

The man that was hunting them was obviously under some kind of *divine force* that protected samurai warriors as well…and this made them even more anxious. As the range narrowed, they realized they would never be able to kill this maniac…so they both bolted out the rear of the bunker. They scrambled down the trench and jumped over the dead bodies of their two friends. They were almost to the main bunker when a grenade landed next to them. It exploded in their midst…killing one and wounding the other. The wounded man was knocked down and began crawling…his legs now useless. He could hear and feel rifle bullets smacking into the sides of the trench above him, and he cringed from the pain coming from his shattered legs. Finally, he rolled over onto his back in time to see a pair of blazing black eyes staring down at him over the sight of an M-1 carbine. The man raised his arms in protection but it did no good…as two bullets slammed into his upper chest.

"That's for the boys out in the water," the lieutenant hissed.

The words meant nothing to the Japanese gunner…but he could feel the anger in them. And somehow he knew this warrior standing over him would kill many more of his countrymen before the battle was over. The thought saddened him…for many of the men were his friends…and his only wish…before he lost consciousness… was that they could all survive and return to their families back home. He never felt the third bullet striking home…insuring that he never would.

• • •

Private First Class George dropped down below the seawall and started reloading his weapon. "I've never seen anything like that before. That's one hell of an officer," he said to Fumai and the corpsman nodded in silent admiration.

George rose up again and watched as the lieutenant now attacked the third…and largest…bunker. Using the same technique that he had perfected on the other two, Hawkins blasted away at the gun slits with his rifle as he ran towards it. When he got closer, he threw hand grenades in the openings and dove for cover. This time the outcome was different however. The men along the seawall heard the muffled *currrummph* of the explosions inside the bunker and they stood up to survey the damage. To everyone's surprise, a single grenade came sailing back out and Hawkins dove for cover yet again. The grenade exploded harmlessly…but it seemed to enrage the lieutenant none the less. He raced back to the seawall and vaulted over it…landing squarely on the sandy beach below.

"I'm outta grenades…anybody…got any?" he asked, short-of-breath.

His men began handing him more grenades and he put them in his shirt pockets. He then mounted the disabled amtrac and began firing one of the side-mounted .50 caliber machine guns at the bunker. His aim was accurate and sand and concrete dust began flying up as the bullets hit all around the bunker's gun ports. Then he eased off the trigger of the heavy machine gun….reached into his pocket…and quickly threw a grenade at the aperture. The grenade was a perfect strike and it went right into the bunker. Incredibly, it came flying back out in the direction it had been thrown. Hawkins saw it coming and jumped over the gunwale of the amtrac to avoid it. The grenade burst while he was in mid-air and the explosion knocked him forcefully to the ground.

When he stood back up, George could see that the lieutenant had been hit by some of the shrapnel and he was a little shaken. His shirt was torn in more places and soaked with blood. The fragments had cut a swathe across his upper chest and the new wounds were bleeding profusely now. Fumai and his men scrambled over to him but he pushed them back.

"I'm okay. I'm fine," he said brusquely.

"But, sir, you're hit bad. Let me take a look at you," Fumai pleaded.

He grabbed the corpsman by his shirt, looked him directly in the eyes, and said calmly, "I didn't come here to get evacuated. I came here to kill Japs."

Fumai realized there was nothing he could do. The lieutenant's dark eyes told him all he needed to know. This man was going to keep on fighting until there was no fight left in him.

"Just watch over my boys, okay."

Before Fumai could answer, the officer was climbing the seawall and charging the bunker again. He reached it safely and standing on its roof, he threw more grenades into the front and side gun ports. Fumai could hear him yelling and screaming all sorts of epithets and curses at the Japanese inside.

"Come out and fight like men, you dirty bastards!" the lieutenant raged, challenging them. As if hearing him, the back door of the bunker suddenly swung open and three Japanese came tumbling out...scrambling for their lives. But Hawkins had anticipated this move...and that was as far as they got. He sprayed the group with his rifle and they crumpled down dead in front of the doorway.

The lieutenant stepped over the pile of Japs and examined the interior of the bunker. There were four dead bodies inside. He approached the bunker's gun ports cautiously - the last thing he wanted was to be shot by one of his own men - and looked outside. He had a clear view out to the reef and he could see men still being fired on as they were trying to come ashore. *At least these Japs won't do any more damage*, he thought with satisfaction...and then he headed back to his men...exhausted.

CHAPTER 7

O nly a few hundred yards down the beach from where Lieutenant Hawkins was waging his one-man war, Lieutenant Hackett and his men were engaged in their own desperate struggle with two bunkers to their front as well. And their fight had just cost them their first casualty: Sergeant McGovern.

Sergeant Endres saw McGovern get hit and knew immediately that he was dead. He had seen guys get hit before and could tell by the way the sergeant fell…like a sack of potatoes…that he wouldn't be needing first aid. But Endres didn't let his death paralyze him the way the loss of some of his squad members had the day before. This time he reacted immediately and took command of the marines in the trench line. Looking around quickly, Endres saw that the men on the left were still firing at the bunkers to their front so he ignored them for the time being. Since Sergeant McGovern had not made it very far, none of the men on the right were engaged however…they were still waiting for orders. Endres shouted as loud as he could and got their attention. With hand signals and yelling he was able to get them firing at the bunker as well. He then looked back to his left and he saw PFC Feeney coming back from giving Corporal Ingunza and Private First Class Mornston their orders. Feeney saw Sergeant McGovern laying there and he crawled up to his body and rolled it over. Once he saw that he was dead, he released his hold on the body and quickly crawled over to Sergeant Endres.

"You up for another trip to the CP?" Endres asked him.

"Do I have a choice in the matter?" he answered him right back.

"Nope. Tell the lieutenant that we need that machine gun crew up here. They're not doing any good back there. It doesn't look like the Japs are gonna try to overrun us. Not yet anyways. But if the Japs do decide to charge, that gun could do a hell of a lot more good up here than back there. Tell him we got two bunkers pinning us down. We could use the machine gun to keep their heads down while we try to outflank them. See what the lieutenant thinks."

"Right," Feeney answered flatly and he rolled out of the trench and started low crawling towards the CP.

Low crawling is a slow and tedious method of maneuver...and when Feeney finally reached the CP...he was completely exhausted. He had gotten up and ran when he could but the enemy fire was so heavy that his instincts told him to stay low most of the time. His elbows were bruised from supporting his body as he pulled himself along and the back of his neck was aching from trying to hold his head up to see where he was going. It took him several seconds to catch his breath...and when he was finally able to speak...he saw that the lieutenant was already getting the CP group ready to move out.

The lieutenant spoke first. "Is that fire on us coming from the bunkers by the cove?"

"No, sir, it isn't. We got at least two pillboxes out to our direct front that are firing at us. We didn't even know they were there until they started firing. We're firing back, but it's our rifles against their machine guns. Sergeant Endres thinks that the machine gun team should come forward."

"Sergeant Endres? What happened to Sergeant McGovern?"

"He's dead, sir. Machine gun fire got him. He never knew what hit him," Feeney answered matter-of-factly.

The lieutenant was quiet for a few seconds...the pain of the news etched on his face as he digested the grim news. "Okay," he stated firmly...back to normal. "Tell Endres we're coming. I'm bringing everybody up."

"Aye aye, sir. I'll tell him. And tell the guys to stay low out there. The Japs on these machine guns got good eyesight. None of them are wearing those thick, coke-bottled glasses like ya see in the movies...trust me."

• • •

The journey across the open ground from the CP to the trench line was fraught with danger. Machine gun and rifle fire laced the air around Lieutenant Hackett and the seven enlisted men as they made their way over. The group suffered one casualty when one of the men in the machine gun crew was hit and killed. This man had lagged behind the others for some reason and when they reached the trench ahead of him...he panicked. Instead of crawling forward through the gauntlet of fire as the others had done, the marine stood up and started running frantically for the trench. A Jap machine gunner saw him and cut lose a burst of fire that brought the man down in a spray of blood and guts. He got hit in the lower body and his insides seemed to explode out of him, soaking the sand around him. The man screamed in agony for a few moments and then began to moan for help but no one moved to help him. Even though they wanted to, they could tell the man was too severely wounded to do anything for him. The man was a goner...it was plain and simple... and no one wanted to get killed in the wasted effort of trying to save a man who was beyond help anyway. It was a cold calculation...one without much mercy...but war alters your motivations in a hurry. And the horrors of Betio had quickly converted any do-gooders into battle-hardened men who knew when and where to risk a life to save another. A minute or so later the man's pleading ceased...but it seemed like an eternity while it lasted. Thankfully…the man died quietly…much to the relief of the marines in the trench that he had failed to reach.

Lieutenant Hackett watched the life slowly ebb out of the man and remembered him from the night before. The lieutenant had thought it odd that the man had hardly spoken to anyone the entire time they were in the shell hole together. His behavior indicated that he was sort of a loner and Hackett had asked Corporal Upshaw about it. Upshaw explained that the man had been assigned to his platoon just before they shipped out. No one had really had a chance to get to know him all that well. He was good at his job, but he didn't make any effort to meld with the other men in the weapons platoon. Over time, Upshaw had learned that the man had served on Guadalcanal and that he was one of a few survivors from his last platoon. "You tend to isolate yourself from others once you lose a lot of your good buddies," Upshaw explained. The lieutenant agreed since he had seen traces of the same behavior in some of his own men after Guadalcanal. Neither man needed to address why the man had broken and run…since it was an insane act and it had cost him his life. They both knew that every man had a breaking point…and this man had obviously reached his…so they left it at that.

• • •

Despite the loss of one of his men, Sergeant Upshaw and the other man got the .30 caliber machine gun set up and into action moments after they reached the trench…and its fire had a marked effect on the balance of the fight. Now the Jap pillboxes were receiving just as much fire as they were giving out and after a while a back-and-forth duel developed…with each side firing at the other and then ducking for cover. It wasn't long before both sides grew tired of the game however and each decided to up the ante to finish the other side off.

• • •

Having been trained to seize the initiative and keep moving, Hackett concluded it was time to act yet again…instead of waiting for those orders that might never come. *We can't sit around here forever...waiting for a runner from Regiment...that may never reach us. For all I know he may have been killed already...just trying to get over here. Hell, we're only one damn platoon anyway and the Colonel's got at least five battalions to direct. He's got bigger fish to fry than worrying about us,* he reasoned. *And knowing the Colonel, he wouldn't want us just sitting around on our damn asses waiting anyway. The Colonel would want us to attack.....so that's exactly what we're going to do...* and he quickly formulated a plan to take out the two Jap bunkers. He signaled the three squad leaders to meet him in the middle and Ingunza, Mornston, and Endres scrambled quickly down the trench and knelt beside him.

"Here's what we're gonna do," the lieutenant said, pointing at Sergeant Endres and PFC Mornston. "I want your squads to lay down a base of fire against the far bunker. Alternate it so that we'll have continuous fire on it. Sergeant Upshaw will concentrate his thirty cal on the bunker closest to us. We'll take that one out first with a flank attack around the left side. Corporal Ingunza's squad has that job. Once we've knocked out the first one...I want the machine gun to shift over to the pillbox on the right. You've got ten minutes to get everybody ready. Then we go." When he finished speaking, the lieutenant looked each man in the eye and they gave him an affirmative nod to indicate that they knew exactly what he wanted done. Then he reached over and grabbed Ingunza by the arm and said, "Make sure your men have enough grenades to do the job. Get some from the other squads if you're short."

• • •

Across the way, the Japanese in the pillboxes decided it was time to get rid of the annoying marines in the trench line out in front of them so they could concentrate on the bigger fish out in the lagoon. In a stroke of luck, their position possessed one of the rarest of commodities on Betio: the two pillboxes still had wire communications with each other and with the large bunker complex behind them and with the positions around the cove. Putting this advantage to use, Petty

Officer Okagi…an experienced combat veteran…called back and requested help from one of the batteries of the two Type 92 70mm guns that they knew were dug in along the cove. These two-wheeled, short-barreled howitzers were already registered on the reef and were firing at the Higgins boats as they came up to it…causing tremendous damage. The battery commander told them that it would be difficult since the trench line was so close but that he would change the setting on one of his guns to max elevation and give them three rounds. That was all he could spare for now since his gun had been firing all morning long and their ammunition was running low. He told the men in the pillboxes up ahead to give his gun crew a few minutes to make the adjustments and then they would start firing.

• • •

The ten minutes ticked off quickly and Lieutenant Hackett could see that everyone was ready. As he signaled the start of the attack with a wave of his hand, a tremendous explosion shook the ground on the right…directly in front of Sergeant Endres' men. He pulled his hand down instinctively, but not before a piece of white-hot shrapnel had sliced into it. He winced in pain and noticed that the wound was bleeding but he didn't have much time to worry about it because two more thundering explosions then hit off to his left. He hugged the side of the trench to protect himself as flying shards of red-hot metal from the exploding rounds went whizzing over him. When the dust settled, Hackett looked around and yelled, "Everyone alright?" PFC Mornston…nearest to the lieutenant…took a quick headcount, nodded, and replied, "All okay here." Looking to his right, Hackett saw that the first explosion had rattled most of the men, but no one looked like they had been hit. Hackett could even hear Sergeant Endres yelling for his men to get up in case the Japs charged.

The scene on the left was much worse however. The second round had hit near the section of the trench where the machine gun team had set up. Smoke and dust still hung above the ground and the sides of the trench had collapsed around the area where the shell had gone off. Corporal Upshaw and his assistant gunner were both down...their bodies sprawled out...and Hackett knew they were dead.

The third and final round had seemed to possess eyes as well: it landed near the end of the trench line where Corporal Ingunza and his squad were beginning their flank attack against the enemy pillbox. Ingunza, the consummate fighter, and three others had just left the trench and were weaving their way through a thicket of scrub and broken coconut trees that covered their approach to the enemy bunker. The other four men left behind in the trench would then join them as soon as the corporal signaled them forward. Before they had left, Ingunza had pointed out several hide positions that they could use while circumventing the pillboxes in the distance and he intended to leapfrog their way from one hideout to the next without drawing enemy fire along the way. Ingunza took the lead to show the way over and he was several yards ahead of the others when he apparently stumbled over something on the ground. He lost his balance and then he flopped down in the sand...at the exact same time the enemy round exploded behind him. The force of the explosion knocked Ingunza senseless...and his inert body lay where it had fallen.

The rest of the men in the trench behind him were dazed as well...but only one man appeared to be hurt...since there was blood running down his face. But the real horror of what had happened sank in when the dust cleared and the survivors saw what was left of the three men out in front of them. They had caught the brunt of the explosion and their bodies were mutilated beyond recognition. The injured marine in the trench slumped down and shook his head in stunned disbelief...while two other marines pressed themselves tightly against the front side of the trench to protect themselves from any other rounds that might be dropping in. The fourth marine came to his senses quicker than the others and he was able to yank the two who weren't wounded back into firing positions. Then he jumped up and ran over to Corporal Ingunza. He didn't bother to check to see if he was alive though. Instead, the man just grabbed one of the corporal's shirt sleeves and hurriedly dragged him back to the trench as fast as he could. Only then did he check to see if Ingunza had a carotid pulse.

"That's the way to do it. Now pour it into them!" Hackett screamed as loud as he could. The marine heard him, pointed at Ingunza, and flashed the thumbs-up sign to show that the corporal was alive and that he had no intention of giving up. The lieutenant returned the gesture with his good hand and beamed with pride. Hackett had seen men rally when the chips were down on Guadalcanal and he knew that a display of courage like this...especially coming from a young private...could become infectious and energize the other men. Without thinking...acting purely on impulse...the lieutenant stood up and looked to his left and then to the right. Then he started to scramble out of the trench. *This might not be the smartest maneuver... but what the hell...they're paying me to be a leader!*

CHAPTER 8

The Japanese *rikusentai* manning the pillboxes saw the shells exploding along the trench line and let out a cheer.

"Excellent shooting. All three rounds hit the target!" Saburo Okagi, the petty officer in charge of the pillboxes, yelled into the handset.

"I wish we could give you more rounds, but we must save them for the boats that are still coming in. We blew up several yesterday... and we've already sunk two so far this morning. You will have to hold off the filthy American infantry yourselves from this point on," the voice on the other end to the line said excitedly.

"Don't worry about us. That should hold them back for a while," Okagi replied confidently.

"Long live the Emperor," the man replied and then the line went dead.

A fierce explosion followed by a huge fireball suddenly thundered behind the pillbox and the petty officer flinched instinctively as he felt himself being knocked forward by the force of the shockwave that came through the opening at the back. As he fell to his knees Okagi thought, *it's surprising that the American planes took so long to find us...*

since he believed that his positions had finally been identified by the American planes that were flying overhead. He did not realize…at this point…that the explosion had actually taken place behind the bunker complex near the cove…and not beside the two bunkers that he and his men were manning. He had no way of knowing that the American pilots - who were flying by at over three hundred miles per hour - had yet to identify them as targets…since his bunkers were much smaller and so well camouflaged that they were almost invisible from the air.

The large defensive position along the cove was not so lucky however. It was easy to spot and it was being bombed and strafed without let up by the American bombers and fighters that were so plentiful above them.

The veteran petty officer was no novice when it came to this kind of warfare. He had experienced his share of air attacks on Guadalcanal…thus he knew what to expect…so he had prepared for them accordingly in the months before the attack. Okagi re-membered how his men had complained bitterly throughout the summer as he pushed them to work harder. In their eyes, he was a tyrannical slave driver and he didn't care one wit about them. They were convinced that Okagi's sole goal in life was to work them to death under the hot equatorial sun…while their friends in other squads got to take swimming breaks in the cove during the day. "Is it really necessary to drive us like animals, Sabo?" they often wailed as the sweat soaked their tan-colored uniforms a dark brown color. Unmoved by their pleas, the petty officer would point to the sandy ground and say simply, "Keep digging. It's still not deep enough."

"Just how deep and how thick do we have to make these things? If I have to cut another coconut log or lift one more bucket of sand… my arms will fall off," a bold private groaned one day after working several hours without letup. "What's the point anyway? You know as well as we do that the Americans aren't going to come here," he added, trying a new tact that he felt made perfect sense.

"The Americans are coming here. Trust me," Okagi stated emphatically.

"How do you know for sure? What do you know that we don't?" another one countered, not willing to concede the argument.

"The Americans will come here for one thing and one thing only," he said, the tone of his voice even more serious now.

"Let me guess, Sabo. They're coming here to see if we have any island beauties that we can share with them. When they see there's nothing but ugly soldiers here...they'll turn right around and go to the next island without firing a shot!" another one shouted out. This one fancied himself a comedian...since he always seemed to make the men laugh when he made a point...right or wrong.

"I wish it were that simple, my friend. What the Americans want is right behind us. They will come for that airfield....just like they did at Guadalcanal."

"Even if they do come...won't our planes be able to hold them off?" a third man asked innocently. "Why just the other day I counted twelve Zeros out there. Those twelve plus the six Betty bombers will be able to hold them off...won't they?"

"Not very long I'm afraid," Okagi answered. "When the Americans come...and they are coming...they will have more than enough planes to handle ours."

"Even so, Sabo, we're building these bunkers like fortresses. Are you telling us that the Americans are good enough flyers that they can get through our anti-aircraft fire and still hit us? I sat next to one of the gunners the other day in the mess hall...and he said his crew was so good that they could knock down a sea gull flying over the island if they wanted to," the comedian stated proudly. He looked at his friends for support, and they all shook their heads in agreement.

"Wait until a bomb goes off near you and then you'll thank me," he chided them. "Better yet," he added, "wait until you see one of their fighter planes coming down at you with their wings twinkling. I want to see your faces then. When the ground erupts around you and the bullets zing by like humming birds and you realize that death is knocking on your door. And if you somehow survive that...you know what?"

"No...what," they all responded in unison, riveted to their leader's words.

He eyed each one in turn and said menacingly, "Know that I'll be inspecting the backs of your pants to see how many of you have crapped in your drawers!"

That had been back in the summer...a period the men were now referring to fondly as *the peaceful time*...long before the deadly air raid of mid-September and the ones that had been occurring daily since the thirteenth of November. During *the peaceful time*, Betio had been bombed occasionally by high-flying B-24 Liberator bombers...but the Japanese garrison had written them off as nuisance raids since very few bombs had found their mark and very little of value had been hit. But that all changed on the eighteenth of September when the men first heard...and then saw...aircraft of a different sort approaching the island. This time the raid was conducted by Navy carrier pilots flying aircraft that were far better suited for the job than the Army bombers had been. Before they could gather their wits about them...the enemy F6F Hellcat fighters...the SBD Dauntless dive bombers...and the TBF Avenger bombers had roared in low and pounded the island for what seemed like an eternity. When the American planes finally left...Betio was nothing but a smoky ruin. The men had tried to put the blazing fires out using buckets of seawater...but their efforts were in vain and several storage facilities eventually burned to the ground. Worse yet...many...if not all...of the planes that had been based on the island had been riddled by machine gun fire and shrapnel while they were parked in their protective revetments. The very planes that the Japanese leaders were relying on to identify and help destroy the American Fleet if it approached had been rendered useless...never to fly again.

In the days following that raid, each of Okagi's men had taken the time to personally thank him for staying on them and pushing

them during those hot summer months. Were it not for his determination and fortitude, any one of them could've ended up like
their friend from another company who had apparently gone crazy.
This man had endured repeated bombings and strafing in a large
bunker that had been identified as a key target in photos taken by
American reconnaissance aircraft that had come over the island
weeks ago. Their pillboxes...on the other hand...had survived unscathed since they were nearly invisible from the air and thus were
never targeted by the Navy pilots. Afterwards, the man had seemed
to be okay...but a few days later he had simply broken down when
he heard the engine noise of a friendly Betty bomber that was turning around on the large airfield apron near his position. The story
of what had happened to their friend began making the rounds so
one of the men went over to verify his condition. "All he does is
sit around and mumble to himself now," the man who had seen
him personally said. "I wouldn't have believed it if I hadn't seen it
with my own two eyes. It is very sad to see my friends. One of the
men stationed in the bunker with him told me that he is so scared
of planes now that they found him digging the ground up with his
bare hands...thinking he could tunnel his way to safety. He said he
was so frantic that he even tore the nails off his fingers and he kept
right on digging."

Seeing the fear in their eyes, Okagi stressed, "And that is after only
a few bombing raids." To drill home the point, he added, "Wait until
you have to go through this for days on end...maybe even months!"

"Months?" one of the men said incredulously.

"Yes...months...think you can handle it?" Okagi replied dryly.

The man thought about it...picturing what it would be like...and
said sourly, "Just in case...I'm going to shave down my fingernails...
so I don't tear them off when I try to dig my way off this island!"

Another man...the comedian...said, "Let me know when you're
going so I can get in behind you and save my nails the trouble!" The

rest of the men burst out laughing…all the while hoping that day would never come.

• • •

Petty Officer Okagi knew firsthand what it was like to endure bombing raids that seemed to go on without end. He had already experienced the strain of unrelenting air attacks and knew that even the best soldiers could be turned into piles of weeping jelly if they allowed themselves to break under the strain. That was why he had made his men work so hard on preparing their positions. And Okagi was now confident that the camouflage work they had done on the bunkers would protect them from the air attacks that would come during the initial stages of the battle. What worried him though was what would happen once the enemy invaded the island and their bunkers were discovered. Like everyone else, Okagi wanted to believe that the island was so well prepared that the garrison could hold out indefinitely. *Maybe Admiral Shibasaki knows more than I do and we can hold out forever…*but then Okagi's memories of Guadalcanal had reared up and he knew they wouldn't be able to. *Betio is just too small and there is no jungle for us to hide in once the Americans overwhelm us.* He wasn't foolhardy enough…or cruel enough…to tell his men that of course. Instead, he wanted them thinking and believing that they were truly invincible. *Their confidence in their positions and fighting ability will be all they'll have to rely on once the real fighting starts. It will give them the courage to fight on and it will have to sustain them for as long as it takes…*just as it had sustained him back on the *Island of Death* not so long ago.

CHAPTER 9

When Petty Officer Okagi arrived on Guadalcanal in late August of 1942, the Japanese Air Arm was considered one of the most formidable air forces in the world. And it certainly appeared that way in the beginning. During his first three months on the island, Okagi always saw planes with the red circles on their wings and the emblem of the Rising Sun on their sides flying in the skies over the island. The sight of these brave Japanese flyers tangling with the enemy planes high above the island had filled him with awe and pride…and the Japanese pilots had always seemed to dominate the action in both numbers and outcome as far as he could tell.

And in the early stages of the air war over Guadalcanal, the Japanese pilots were decidedly better than their American counterparts in air-to-air combat. They had more experience and there were more of them. The American pilots were quick learners however… and as the battle dragged on, they gained invaluable experience as they fought against the Jap fighters and bombers. All of a sudden, the Japanese Air Command noticed a disturbing trend taking shape: fewer and fewer pilots were making it back to Rabaul after fighting in the air battles over the dangerous skies of Guadalcanal. And as their fighter force was slowly thinned out of experienced pilots, the Japanese Air Command had only one option to meet the crisis: they were forced to replace the veterans who had been shot down with younger, less-skilled pilots. The results were disastrous...and the large, evenly-fought battles that had defined the early stages of the air campaign became rare events indeed. Instead, the battles became one-sided events...and marine aces like Major John Smith and Captain Joe Foss...who both flew out of Henderson Field...were soon dominating every engagement and racking up kill after kill.

• • •

Petty Officer Okagi noticed this shift in control of the air war over Guadalcanal as well. By November, the vaunted Japanese Betty bombers and Zero fighters were not as prevalent or ubiquitous as they had always seemed to be. And as control of the air shifted to the Americans...the Japanese ground units began attracting far more attention from an American squadron that didn't have to tangle with the enemy fighters that it had been forced to dogfight in the early months of the battle.

Okagi had no way of knowing that this shift in power had triggered a similar shift in tactics for the Army pilots that were part of the 67th Fighter Squadron that was based on Henderson Field. These pilots were now given free rein to concentrate on the enemy units in the jungle...since the planes they were flying...the slower and less nimble Bell P-400's and P-39's...were far better suited for ground attack missions than dog fighting. And to that end, the 67th Squadron was now flying sorties up and down the northern coastline of Guadalcanal looking for signs of Japanese activity. After a while, these sweeps became so effective that it was nearly impossible for a Japanese unit to maneuver in the open without being detected and engaged. One of Okagi's commanders was so leery of these *long-nosed* planes...as they were fearfully called...that he forbade his soldiers from marching on the roads, paths, and trails before sunset to prevent air attacks against them. "Moving in daylight increases the odds of being seen by those damn air patrols," this officer had warned, "and once you're spotted...you're guaranteed a trip to an early grave."

Okagi remembered one particularly horrible scene that had played itself out right in front of him. His platoon had drawn beach defense duty and they had waited until dark before moving up to their assigned positions...in accordance with the major's order. The men they were replacing looked like veterans...and as they filed out... the rude comments and pleasantries that were typically exchanged between the outgoing and incoming units took place here as well. The position was located in a grove of coconut trees that ran along the beach...and it consisted of a series of foxholes that the men had constructed the day before. As Okagi was approaching it, one of the men - he was wearing the stripes of a petty officer - pulled Okagi over and pointed to the position he had just left and said, "Take that one...I spent a lot of time on it. It'll give you good luck too...since I prayed to the gods in it last night."

"Thanks," Okagi replied, "I will." As the man moved on, Okagi heard one of the other men who was leaving say to the man behind him, "Hey...you can take mine...and if it smells like piss...don't worry about it...since that's all I did in mine." The petty officer just shook his head at the exchange and said to his own man, "Don't worry about that rat...you can join me in mine...since it looks like there'll be plenty of room."

"Thank you, Sabo. I appreciate that," the man said gratefully... and the two of them walked over to the foxhole that the petty officer had identified. It had been dug along the front edge of the grove about seventy-five yards from the water. It was a perfect position because it was concealed from the air by palm fronds and he could see far down the beach in both directions. Both men jumped in and began some housekeeping to make their new home as comfortable as possible. Before long, the other man was snoring gently...

and Okagi let him sleep…since the night was quiet. Then he looked up at the star-filled sky…and admiring the Creator's work…he knelt down and silently prayed to his God as well.

• • •

As the sun broke out to start a brand new day, Petty Officer Okagi noticed a thick, gray haze hanging over the water off shore…but it burned off quickly as the day worn on…revealing a clear view of the Sound out in front of him. He estimated that he could see about a mile out from the beach. *It's probably closer to two, but how can I really tell*, he wondered. *Whatever it is, I'll have plenty of time to react to an American attack if one comes.*

The petty officer warned himself to stay vigilant even though this section of the beach was several miles away from the forward lines. All the men in the platoon were aware that the Americans had already tried a landing in this direction back in early August. That time an American raiding party of twenty-five men had come ashore near the Matanikau River…an area slightly east of where they were currently dug in. It came about because a marine intelligence officer…Lieutenant Colonel George Goettge…had been tricked into believing that the Japanese in the area wanted to surrender. His naiveté and lack of respect for the Japanese fighting spirit had cost him his life however. Except for three men who managed to escape by swimming out to sea, the entire patrol had been wiped out when they were trapped against the shoreline. To celebrate their glorious victory, the Japanese officers had rushed up, drawn their ceremonial samurai swords, and hacked the bodies of the dead marines apart.

It was not lost on Okagi that every man in his platoon was secretly hoping that the marines would try another landing in their area… so they could duplicate this early Japanese victory. In doing so, they would bring honor and prestige to their unit…and it would be a wonderful gift to present to their Emperor and citizens back home. But Okagi was a fairly realistic person, so he realized the odds of this happening were very slim. As much as he wished for it, he felt the

marines were just not brave enough to risk another attack like that…
at least not anymore. *Now they sit in their foxholes behind their barbed wire
and wait for us to charge. And once we oblige them…and we always do…they
rip us to shreds with their machine guns and artillery. No, these Americans are
not stupid enough to launch an attack like that anymore. Those days are over…
unless we can somehow trick them into one….but we'll never get a chance like
that…*. and he dismissed the idea entirely from his mind.

As the hours slid by and nothing happened, Okagi began to think
that the day might actually end on a quiet note. *Nothing wrong with that,*
he thought, and a quick glance at his watch told him it was nearly
seventeen hundred hours. He had always felt that the late afternoon
was the most beautiful part of the day and the setting sun always
reminded him of his village back home on the China Sea. Since he
was a little boy he had loved to sit on the hillside with his friends and
watch the fishing boats returning with their catches. Even at that
distance, he could always pick out his father's boat from all the others…and as it got close to the quay…he would race down and meet
the boat at the dock. The memory of that much gentler and happier
time brought a smile to Okagi's face and the petty officer could feel
his body starting to relax at the very thought of it. Surrendering to
the impulse, he eased up against the back of the foxhole and closed
his eyes for the first time all day. No sooner had he done so then a
commotion over to his left made him sit up and take notice. As inconceivable as it seemed, a platoon had emerged out of the coconut
grove and was marching down the beach towards them. An officer
wearing an impeccable uniform was leading the formation and a
sergeant was calling cadence to keep them in step in the soft sand.
The men in the platoon were all wearing fresh uniforms and they
were well groomed so this unit must have just arrived on the island.
The reinforcements had probably been dropped off by a Japanese
destroyer at a point just up the beach during the dead of night almost
fifteen hours ago. Okagi figured that the officer had rested the men
in the tree line during the day and then had received orders to move

the platoon to a new location. Maybe the officer didn't know any better. Or maybe they were just behind schedule and the officer was trying to make up the lost time. Whatever the reason, the officer had chosen to take the most direct route...right down the beach...to get to wherever they had to go. Several men in Okagi's platoon began yelling at the green soldiers as they marched by. Some shouted dire warnings of what could happen to them while others jeered at them in mocking tones. Okagi remembered one taunt a man had yelled out in particular: "You're not on the parade ground in Yokohama, you idiots. You're on the *Island of Death* now!"

The words had barely made it out of the man's mouth when a more ominous sound could be heard in the distance. From experience, Okagi's men knew immediately what it was and they began warning the men on the beach to head for the jungle. Most of the men in the platoon...including the officer...assumed the men were still heckling them and thus ignored their shouts and warnings. The tight formation marched on blissfully...the noise above them drowned out by the rattling of their equipment and the crunching sand under their boots. Okagi's men quickly stopped their taunting and began ducking down in their foxholes...pulling whatever cover they could find over them. He was about to do the same, but first he shielded his eyes and looked upward. They were hard to see at first...but then he spotted the *long-nosed planes* as the sound of their engines grew louder. It was a flight of two P-400's Caribous and two P-39 Airacobras from the vaunted 67th *Jagdstaffel* Squadron under the command of Captain John Thompson and they had seen the juicy infantry target on the beach. The pilots flying the two P-400's... affectionately referred to as *klunkers*...immediately nosed over from an altitude of seven thousand feet and began descending at four hundred miles per hour. The other two fighters...the P-39's...which were more maneuverable than the P-400's...maintained their height at eleven thousand feet to provide top cover in case any Jap fighters showed up to interrupt the party.

Intent on their mission, the officer and sergeant were oblivious to the danger coming their way and they continued on. Some of the men in the ranks sensed what was happening however and they began looking skyward. At the last moment, the officer looked up as well and immediately realized the dire predicament the platoon was in. He began to issue a command but his voice was drowned out by the bark of the 20mm nose cannon and six .303 inch machine guns mounted in the wings of the lead P-400. Sand erupted from the beach in geysers and fell like a shower on the men as the rounds slammed into the formation. Pieces of bodies and equipment flew in the air as the formation disintegrated under the first plane's raking fire and then from the second P-400 flying several hundred yards behind it. When the first two planes had finished their runs and regained altitude, the two P-39's winged over and headed for the beach. They began firing at a range of five hundred yards and the cumulative effect of their weapons was devastating. The explosive shells from each plane's 37mm cannon and the bullets from its two .50 caliber machine guns which were mounted in the nose and the four wing-mounted .303 inch machine guns tore into the men still lying on the beach. Incredibly, none of them made an effort to run for the cover of the tree line. Instead, they had remained where they were...dutiful to their leader's last command.

The four planes made several more firing passes over the platoon...and when their ammunition was exhausted, they joined back up and headed for home. Flying in one of the P-39's behind and several thousand feet above the P-400's, Captain Thompson glanced over at the plane beside his and realized he needed to radio his wingman.

"You planning on landing with that five-hundred-pounder slung to your belly?" he asked.

First Lieutenant Michael "Roddy" Rodriquez didn't understand him at first, but it dawned on him soon enough. His ground crew had loaded his plane with a big bomb since their original mission had been to attack some Jap shipping that had been spotted by a coast watcher up the Slot.

The Australian coast watcher's radio message stated that several Japanese merchantmen and a destroyer were hiding in a cove of one of the nearby islands...a new tactic the Jap Navy had begun using to offset the American air superiority in the waters around Guadalcanal. The ships would sail down the Slot and when they reached the outer range of the American planes, they would find a good anchorage... one that was hopefully hidden from the prying eyes of the American scout planes. Then...under the cover of darkness...they would sail for Guadalcanal and offload their cargo as soon as they got there. Once their mission was completed, they would head back up the Slot before daylight hit. And while this strategy was working tactically... since less shipping was being intercepted and sunk...it was failing strategically...since the amount of supplies reaching the island had been drastically reduced.

Looking for such a lucrative target had excited the four pilots initially...since Jap ships in hiding rarely had air cover over them... lest their hiding spot be given away. Without Zero fighters to worry about, the pilots could attack the ships with impunity...an Airacobra pilot's dream...since the American plane was not as maneuverable as the Jap Zero fighter was and thus it suffered when it tried to dogfight with its enemy counterpart.

But their search had found nothing and they were heading back empty-handed when they spied the activity on the beach. In a matter of seconds, the pilots' mission went from ship interdiction to ground attack...and they were just as well-equipped to accomplish this second mission as they were the first...if not more so.

• • •

"No, I think I'll let the Japs keep it as a present," Lieutenant Rodriquez radioed back, referring to the five-hundred-pound bomb attached to the belly of his plane. "I didn't have time to wrap it real nice...but I'm sure they'll appreciate it all the same," he joked, his spirits much improved now that they had accomplished a meaningful mission in attacking the Japanese infantry. "That is…with your permission, sir. I'll deliver it to them right now in fact…if you let me," Rodriquez added, holding up his crossed his fingers to the captain flying beside him.

"Seein' that I'm in a good mood and all…I'm gonna grant you permission. But don't get too cocky…since my decision is based on mere survival…not on your competence as a pilot. Everyone knows you're probably the worst pilot in the squadron. If I let you try to land with that bomb, you'll end up blowing up the rest of the pilots and the ground crew back at Henderson when you crack up. So I hereby grant you full permission to deliver your present to those bastards down below!"

"Yes, sir! Thank you, sir! Now if you boys don't mind waiting… this shouldn't take but a few seconds," Rodriquez said as he turned his plane around and dipped its nose to begin his bomb run.

• • •

Having seen the planes head off, Okagi and the men in his platoon figured the air attack was finished. Some of them, mostly the ones closest to the beach, stood up and began brushing themselves off. Their uniforms were covered in sand…by bits of foliage that had blown off the trees around them…and…worst of all…with body fragments from the mangled soldiers…twenty-nine in all…who were laying on the sand in front of them.

Turning to the man in the hole beside him, Okagi shook his head mournfully and said, "Another waste. Will it ever end?"

"Not as long as we have men for them to kill…and dumb officers to lead us to the slaughter pen I guess," he replied, just as exasperated.

"Those brave boys came all this way to die for nothing. It is not right. And there is nothing we can do for them. Their bodies will end up decaying here…on this island…just like all the rest. Who has the time to see that their ashes are sent home to their loved ones? It is a disgrace."

"I don't know who they are...and neither do you, Sabo. And it's a good bet that no one else on this island does either. Don't trouble yourself with problems you can't solve," the soldier offered in return.

"Yes, in the end, I guess you are right my friend. I only--" Okagi was about to finish his thought when he heard the dreaded sound again. It came out of nowhere and caught his men by complete surprise. "Get down!" he screamed as loud as he could...but it was a second too late.

• • •

With his P-39 gathering speed in its dive, Lieutenant Rodriquez looked through the windscreen and saw nothing moving on the beach below. As he got closer, he shifted his eyesight to the sight reticule and began lining up the crosshairs on the intended target below him. And what he saw nearly sickened him: the beach was littered with shattered bodies and equipment and blood had stained the sand a deep reddish brown color. *Nothing could be alive in that group*, he thought, and with a deft adjustment he angled his plane inward, so he could drop the bomb in the jungle behind the beach. *If anyone survived our attacks, they're gonna be hiding in there...*and he toggled the bomb loose.

The plane got so close that Okagi swore he could see the expression on the pilot's face. And had he been able to speak English and read lips, Okagi would have been able to tell that the pilot from Clearwater, Florida had said, "Enjoy the gift...I hope it's somebody's birthday!"

CHAPTER 10

Petty Officer Okagi was trying to get up but he just couldn't seem to get his body to respond to the orders he was giving it. His coordination seemed to be off…and he realized he may have banged his head on the gun sight as he was blown forward by the force of the explosion behind him. He was leaning on his knees and he had steadied himself by placing one hand on the floor. He was trying to grab onto the pedestal mount of the machine gun with the other hand but he kept missing it as he reached for it. Seeing this, the machine gunner left his weapon and grabbed Okagi under the arms and lifted him up. Okagi felt along his scalp and checked his face to see if there was any blood on it…but his hand came back clean. *Lucky*, he thought, trying to steady himself. The petty officer shook his head and regained his senses quickly and the first thing he did was peer out of the aperture at the marines in the trench. Strangely, one of the enemy was holding his arm up and shaking his fist at them. "Get back on that gun!" Okagi shouted and the man let go of him and jumped right back on the *Nambu* Type 99 Light machine gun. Just then an F6F Hellcat fighter zoomed by…its six .50 caliber wing guns flashing. Okagi figured it was the same plane that had just dropped its bomb…and now it was hanging around to strafe anyone that had survived. *That felt like a five-hundred-pounder,* he reasoned… *given the force of its explosion.* He was slightly off on its weight though… since the bomb weighed in at only one hundred pounds…but it had hit the ammunition dump for the 70mm howitzers. It was a perfect strike and it ignited the rounds that were stored for the guns to use and the massive explosion had taken everything nearby with it. One howitzer crew was completely wiped out and several *rikusentai* in the big bunker next to them were killed by the concussion alone. Okagi glanced out the back door of the bunker and saw a large plume of black smoke hanging over the cove near where the howitzer battery had used to be…and Okagi knew instantly that their artillery support was over.

Okagi had experienced this kind of slaughter before…and he immediately thought back to the horrible image of the beach at Guadalcanal…and he shivered yet again at the memory of it. He could still remember thinking how lucky they had been to be hidden by the jungle…and thus out of the gun sights of the four fighters. But then…out of nowhere…he saw a lone fighter plane coming in at them again and it was so close he could even see the pilot. Then he glimpsed a large bomb tumbling end-over-end. He had screamed a warning and he and the man with him had instinctively dropped down inside their foxhole while most of his men stood around… oblivious to the danger hurtling down at them. The bomb sailed past Okagi's foxhole and exploded amidst the men further down the line with such force that eight of them were obliterated by the blast… and nine were wounded so badly that they would never survive their injuries. He had waited several minutes to let the ringing in his ears go away and then he finally stood up. The sight that met his eyes was one that he would never forget. The man in the hole next to his had been killed by a flying piece of shrapnel and it had taken the top of his head clean off just below his nose. He must have raised his head up just high enough to look over the lip of the foxhole when the bomb went off. The man's body was still in the same position it had been when he was killed...like nothing had happened. He was lying on his stomach and he had propped himself up on his elbows. The only thing different was that he was missing the top of his skull and his cloth hat...of course. His bottom row of teeth and the white neck bone were all that was left behind and it was as gruesome a sight as Okagi had ever seen.

Incredibly, Okagi and the man with him didn't have a scratch on them. And that's when he realized how lucky he had been to have chosen such a well-built foxhole when they occupied this position the night before. *That guy that dug this thing was no liar...and the extra effort he put into it saved my life.* It had also taught him a good lesson for the future: if you're going to take the time to construct a position... make it a good one. The hole had been deep enough to provide full protection for both men and its sides had been reinforced with pieces of drift wood that had been taken from the beach. These two attributes had mitigated the force of the bomb's explosion...which had been so powerful that its shrapnel had even sheared several co-conut trees right in half. It had also left some of his dear comrades so disfigured that he was having a hard time figuring out who was who. Two men actually looked like they had been put through a meat grinder. They were both just piles of red meat lying on the jungle floor with bits of uniform mixed in.

The wounded were no better. Some had arms blown off...while others were missing a leg or two. He wanted to help them, but there was nothing he could do for them. Medical supplies, like everything else, were hard to come by and so they had made do with what little they had left. Okagi offered encouragement and compassion to the wounded but he could tell by the looks in their eyes that they under-stood their predicament. Most of the injured...especially the severely wounded...would never make it off the island alive and they knew it. It was depressing to see them this way, but rendering a kind word to them was not too much to ask since they were his men and they had done everything he had ever asked them to do. As they lay on the ground awaiting death, he was all they had left and he vowed that he would make their passage to the hereafter as comfortable as possible. *If I ever find myself in this position, torn apart and near death, I hope someone will offer me some comfort and a moment of solace before I go.*

CHAPTER 11

The men had those desperate looks on their faces again...*just like they had had when they were aboard the amtrac yesterday morning*...and Lieutenant Hackett could almost sense them pleading for someone to do something. *Somebody's gotta lead this charge...and since I'm the officer...it's gotta be me.* So, with blood dripping from his wounded right hand, Lieutenant Hackett stood up and yelled, "Who's comin' with me?" He had just begun to jump out of the trench when he felt a hand on his shoulder forcibly restrain him.

"You stay put, lieutenant! I'll get 'em over there. Just get the rest of the men to cover us!" It was Sergeant Endres...and he slid behind the lieutenant and made his way down the trench...with Private Scott following closely on his heels.

• • •

Sergeant Endres had seen what had happened on the left...just like the lieutenant had. And he figured that with Ingunza down...their planned attack would falter...if not fail completely. So someone had to do something fast...and he sprang into action. After corralling the lieutenant, he had scrambled down the trench to get a status on PFC Mornston's men. He found them to be okay...but two of them were still acting groggy from the effects of the deafening explosion that had hit nearby. He yelled, "Keep firing! Keep it up! Pour it on them!" The urgency and sharpness of his commands seemed to be what the doctor ordered, and within seconds Mornston's entire squad was engaging the enemy inside the two bunkers. Satisfied, Endres turned to Private Scott and said, "Things might get dicey from here on out. Just stay with me and you'll be fine. Let's go!"

Since he had climbed down the landing nets the day before, Private Scott had followed his platoon sergeant's instructions to the letter. He had stayed as close to his squad leader...Sergeant Endres... as he possibly could and he had managed to survive when a lot other guys hadn't. Then Endres had ordered him to spend the night at the CP. Scott wasn't thrilled with the idea...being away from Sergeant Endres and all...but orders were orders so he gone back without a gripe. But now he was back with him and he felt as confident as ever. During the night, the private had thought often about the advice Platoon Sergeant Roy had given him...and...so far...Sergeant Roy had been right...since he was one of the few that were still left alive from the old squad. *And I did it by staying right on Endres' tail and that's where I'm gonna be the rest of this fight.* So when Endres told him to follow him...that's exactly what Private Scott did...no questions asked.

Now the two men were dashing down the trench towards Corporal Ingunza's squad...or what was left of it. They left the trench for only a brief moment as they skirted around the destroyed machine gun section, and then they hit the deck when a Jap machine gun zeroed in on them. Bullets began smacking off the back of the trench right above them so they ended up crawling the last few yards until they reached Ingunza's men.

"I didn't think you two were gonna make it. That Jap fire is comin' over as thick as flees on a junkyard dog right now," Private First Class Saul Cohen said nonchalantly as he squeezed off three quick rounds from his M-1 Garand at the pillbox in the distance. A high-pitched pinging sound came from his rifle and a metal clip flew up and away indicating that his rifle was out of ammunition. Without removing his eye from the rear sight, Cohen reached down and took a new eight-round clip out of an ammo pouch and deftly reloaded the rifle in one smooth motion. He fired three more rounds and then glanced over the stock of his M-1 and winked mischievously at them.

"Just lucky I guess," Scott responded happily.

"Really….we'll maybe you can bring us some good luck too. Are you Irish?" Cohen asked casually and resumed firing until the clip was expended.

"I might be, but I think I'm more English…a little German too."

Sergeant Endres cut him off. "I hate to break up this tea party but we've got two pill boxes to knock out. Interested in joinin' us?"

"Sure…why not?" the tall, dark-countenanced marine replied confidently.

Sergeant Endres glanced over at Ingunza and the other wounded marine and realized that neither was in any condition to help at this point. Ingunza had been stunned from the blast and was still very woozy while the unfortunate private had taken a chunk of shrapnel in the face…and he was now missing an eye. Ingunza would certainly survive but it was impossible to tell how long the wounded marine would last. Endres told the other private who didn't seem to be hurt at all to bandage the wounded man up and then to fire on the bunker to the left. "Cohen here is gonna come with Scott and me. Watch for us. We're gonna move up the side over there by those palm trees. Now don't get trigger-happy and fire on us when we come out, okay."

The private nodded and Endres said to Scott and Cohen, "Okay, let's go. And don't do anything stupid. Use whatever cover's out there. If one of us gets hit, don't stop…just keep going. We've got to knock out those bunkers."

• • •

Darting in and out of shell holes and hiding behind piles of rubble and debris that lined their path, Sergeant Endres, PFC Cohen, and

Private Scott made their way stealthily forward…all the while evading the prying eyes of the Japs inside the two bunkers. Finally, they crawled up behind a huge tree trunk that was laying on the ground and stopped. The position was perfect since it was located about twenty yards off the flank of the two bunkers.

Endres let the two privates catch their breath, and then he pulled two hand grenades out of his pocket and handed them to Cohen. "I want you to use one grenade on each bunker. Get as close as you can to the gun port on the first one and lob it in. Scott will cover you. I'll take the back side and get anyone that tries to come out that way. We'll go after the second one the same way. Got the picture."

Scott and Cohen turned their heads in unison and looked at each other confidently. Then they shook their heads at the sergeant, indicating they were ready to go.

"Okay then….let's go kill some Japs," Endres said matter-of-factly…and he dashed off.

• • •

None of the Japanese in the bunkers were aware of the danger that was closing in on them. Up until then, things had been going pretty much their way, so they had no reason to think that their defenses had been penetrated. From what they could see, it appeared that most of the marine landing forces had been repelled…slaughtered even…if the number of landing craft burning along the reef meant anything. Granted, some of the enemy were making it ashore, but in numbers too few to have any meaningful impact on the outcome of the battle thus far. And when they had been confronted by some marines directly, Petty Officer Okagi had called for…and gotten… impressive artillery support and it had decimated the marines in the trench line to their front. Up to this point, they had only suffered one casualty in the engagement so far: the machine gunner who had been shot in the chest had died a little over an hour ago. He had been the comedian of the squad…and…as usual…he had made light of his condition and had even left them laughing as he died. Sitting against the rear wall of the bunker - he felt it too undignified to be laying on a dusty floor during the last moments of his life so he had forced himself to sit up - he had managed to croak out, "Tell Sabo… we should've made…that gun port smaller."

Then an American fighter had flown over and dropped a big bomb on the cove complex behind them…and while the explosion had been huge…no one had been killed. Okagi…their intrepid leader…had been knocked down by it…but he was back up in seconds… so their luck seemed to be holding.

Given these circumstances, it was easy to understand why Okagi's men in the bunkers were still confident about their prospects of survival at this stage of the battle. And the positive outlook they had didn't change when the pesky marines in the trench line began firing at them yet again.

• • •

"Watch your front! They're not done yet!" Okagi yelled out suddenly as bullets began hitting all around the firing aperture.

The machine gunner stopped firing and he lifted his head off the stock and asked the man next to him what Okagi had said. The man told him brusquely, "Don't worry about it. Just keep firing you dummy." The gunner gave him a quizzical look and lowered his head back down on the gun and tucked the stock firmly into his shoulder. Every time he saw a marine pop his head up, he fired a short, three-round burst at him. He knew he was a pretty good shot - he had trained all summer long on the Type 99 7.7mm light machine gun with its telescopic sight - and he was fairly certain he had killed a few of them already. He was just about to squeeze the trigger when something flew past him and thudded off the wall behind him. Having never seen anything like it before, he just kept on firing until he heard the terrified voice of the man next to him yell, "Grenade!" Okagi spotted it too and screamed, "Look out!" Reaching down, the assistant gunner picked up the deadly device and tried to throw it out, but his aim was off and it hit right above the narrow firing slit. The grenade bounced off the front wall and exploded in the air…killing both him and the machine gunner instantly…and Okagi was thrown against the back wall. The two other men…a rifleman and an ammo bearer…were stunned from the force of the explosion…which was magnified by the tight confines of the pillbox… and they were bleeding after being hit by the metal shards that had flown everywhere. The ammo bearer recovered more quickly from his wounds than the other two did and he stumbled groggily out the rear exit of the bunker…and right into the business end of a Thompson submachine gun.

• • •

Sergeant Endres raced over to the first bunker and knelt down to reduce his silhouette. *No sense letting a sniper nail me now that I made it this far,* he reasoned. He watched Scott and Cohen run over and then he crept down the side until he reached the back corner and peered around it. The rear of the bunker had an open doorway with a log stairway leading down to it since the lower half the bunker was built four feet below ground level. This made spotting the upper half of the bunker from the outside very difficult since very little of it appeared above ground. The rear entrance didn't seem to be guarded so Endres just low crawled over to it and waited.

Dust suddenly blew out the exit and Endres gripped his Thompson tighter. He waited two seconds and then sprang up to a kneeling position so he could see the entire doorway. In no time at all, a Jap soldier emerged out of the haze like a ghost. His tan uniform was blood-streaked and he was staggering…as if in a daze. Endres placed him squarely in the sights of his machine gun and squeezed the trigger. The Jap soldier had no time to react and his body absorbed the full impact of the .45 caliber slugs that Endres had fired into him. Just as quickly as he had come out, the Jap was knocked right back inside the bunker.

Out front, Cohen waited two seconds after the grenade went off and then stood up. He was about to stick his M-1 into the slot when

69

JAMES F. DWYER

Scott grabbed it and said, "Use this instead." Scott handed Cohen a BAR...a Browning automatic rifle...which was considerably heavier than the standard M-1 Garand. Scott had found it laying on beach next to a marine who had been killed when he tried to land the morning before. No stranger to weights, Scott immediately traded his M-1 for the heavier BAR and the large ammo belt that went with it...and he had been firing it all morning long.

Cohen...a big guy himself...hefted the BAR with its twenty round magazine easily and he jammed the barrel inside the firing slit and pulled the trigger. He swept the automatic rifle back and forth...the big .30 caliber bullets ricocheting inside...and two rounds hit the rifleman cleanly...and finished what the grenade had already started. Cohen released the pressure on the trigger and heard someone moaning inside the bunker so he fired off another burst and then the moaning stopped.

Out back, Sergeant Endres jumped down and landed beside the stairway...his weapon raised and ready. Endres took a couple of steps, braced himself against the thick log that was buttressing one of the sides of the entrance, and looked through the dusty haze. The man he had just shot was lying on his back and Endres kicked his boot to make sure he was dead. He could see five other bodies sprawled out...and they appeared dead too...so he yelled out, "Scott...Cohen...you guys alright?"

"Okay here," Scott said as they both scurried around to the back.

Scott looked at Cohen and said, "That BAR sure does some nice work, huh."

Cohen...who was cradling the BAR like a new-born baby... handed it back to him sheepishly and replied, "Yeah...I thought it would be harder to handle...but it felt awfully good in my hands. I might even volunteer to carry it on our next operation if I can make it through this one alive."

Scott gave the M-1 back to Cohen and ejected the empty magazine from the BAR. He reached down and took out a fresh clip from the large ammo belt he had taken off the dead marine on the beach...

70

and with the deftness of a veteran…he loaded it easily. Then he took a deep breath and tried to steady his nerves for the next charge.

Endres waited until the two men had caught their breath and when he saw they were ready, he said, "Good job, you two. One down. Now let's go get that next one!"

• • •

The three *rikusentai* manning the other bunker knew the one on their flank was under attack…but there was nothing they could do to stop it. The fire coming at them from the trench line was so strong that they risked getting hit if they stood up to fire back so they stayed low until the marines were forced to reload. When they sensed a lull in their fire, they would pop back up and fire their machine gun at whatever targets they could see…and then drop back down when the marines started firing back at them. They were doing the best they could…at least they thought they were…since this was the first time they had been in combat…and they had managed to hold off the marines so far. That changed when they saw dust and debris flying out the front and rear openings of their sister bunker off to the side and they figured that the marines they had just seen running up to it had managed to blow it up. They had gotten a few shots off at them as they approached the bunker but not enough to do any good obviously. Now the three marines were on the far side of it…so they still couldn't fire at them. The assistant machine gunner picked up an *Arisaka* rifle and took up a position outside the rear entrance of their bunker. "You two watch our front…I'll take care of the rear," he yelled back at them. Then he saw a marine firing his weapon at the back of the other bunker, but before he could get a shot off, the man had ducked inside. Then he came back out and he saw the two others join him. They looked like they were discussing something…and then they began running in his direction. He stood up and lowered his rifle at the marine in the lead. He pulled the trigger and was surprised at the buck of the weapon against his body. He never remembered it kicking that hard when he had fired it at the rifle range. He knew his shot had found its mark though. He watched it strike a marine and he saw him drop. He had never killed anyone before and he felt a strange sense of satisfaction at seeing the marine fall. He wanted to fire at the other two who were still coming, but he found that his body wouldn't respond to the commands his mind was giving it. He tried to slide the bolt back to eject the spent cartridge but nothing seemed to be happening. He glanced down at his chest and noticed that his uniform top was torn and dark patches were starting to appear all over it. He didn't remember them being there before and wondered just where the holes and the splotches had come from. *I was always meticulous about my uniform, I must be more careful in the future*, he thought to himself. Things began to get cloudy in his mind all of a sudden and he slumped down against the entranceway of the bunker. He felt his body relaxing and a gentle serenity descending over him. It was a feeling that he had never really experienced before. All the awful sounds of the battle were going away too. Then it became very quiet outside and he found it extremely calming. He looked up into the sun, the *Rising Sun*, and he felt its warmth and thought, *what a beautiful day it has turned out to be.*

• • •

Sergeant Endres was running as fast as he could to the next pillbox when a Jap rifleman stood up, aimed his rifle, and pulled the trigger. PFC Cohen, running behind the sergeant, saw him first and yelled, "Look out!" Endres made a slight dodge to his left and the bullet went right by him. It then made a sickening sound as it smacked right into Cohen with a meaty thud.

Cohen was hit in the upper body and he yelled, "Damn it!" as he fell down. He immediately tried to see where he was shot... hoping all the while that it wasn't in a fatal spot...when Scott caught up and knelt beside him. "The grenade...give me your grenade!" Scott yelled, poking and patting his pockets, trying to feel for it. Cohen stopped moving and dug into his shirt pocket and gave it to him. "Make it...count," he eked out...gritting his teeth...the pain kicking in.

Scott took a quick glance at the wound, said, "You took one in the shoulder. You'll be okay...it doesn't look real bad," and he jumped to his feet and ran ahead.

Endres was running hard so he fired his submachine gun from the hip at the Jap rifleman. His aim was good and the burst hit the man in his chest and stomach. A spray of blood flew off the man as the bullets hit him and Endres saw a strange look of shock etched on the Jap's face as he fell back...apparently dead. Endres stopped several feet away from the rear exit to see if anyone else was going to come out...but no one did.

Private Scott caught up to Sergeant Endres and the two of them approached the back of the bunker and knelt down. They could hear the machine gun firing and a Jap chattering away inside...probably a loader identifying targets out in the cove for the man operating the machine gun. Instead of going around to the front, Scott just lobbed the grenade through the opening in the back.

The two *rikusentai* manning the *Nambu* never saw the grenade rolling up behind them. They were so focused on the marines out in front of them that they weren't even aware that their friend was now lying dead at the exit...leaving them open to an attack from the rear. The grenade struck one of the loader's boots and before he could look down to see what it was, it exploded, killing both men instantly.

Sergeant Endres got up and said, "See if anything's still alive in there."

Scott disappeared into the haze that enveloped the doorway, made a fast sweep of the interior, and came back out. "Only two inside...both dead. Plus this one," he said, pointing the barrel of his BAR at the body of the Jap soldier sitting up. Scott stepped around the man but suddenly stopped and looked at the man more closely. "Hey, sarge," he called out, "Did you get a good look at this guy?"

Sergeant Endres replied, "No, why?" and wondered if the man he had shot was a high-ranking officer and Scott had found something useful. "What's he got? A map...codebook...what?"

Scott glanced at the man one more time and he yelled over, "No...nothing like that. I've just seen a lotta dead men lately, but this guy...this guy looks like he actually enjoyed the trip home. Look at him...he looks like he should be sittin' in a recliner down at the Cape."

The sergeant looked at Scott quizzically and said, "Here I'm thinking you got somethin' the intel boys would want." He shook his head at the absurdity of it...that Scott was trying to analyze the last thoughts of the guy he had just killed...and he replied, "Just get your dumb ass over here, Private Scott."

Private Scott left the smiling Jap behind and scrambled over to his squad leader. Endres was scanning out ahead for more targets but turned to Scott and said, "Here's some good advice for you: worry less about the dead Japs and more about the live ones. They're the ones that are gonna kill ya."

Private Scott looked at the sergeant and said right back, "No problem there, Sergeant Endres. Your wish is my command."

"Well that's just great to hear," Endres replied, knowing that the mild scolding had gotten the attention of the young marine. Then he added, "I'm real happy you agree with me. Now go tell the lieutenant to come up. I'll see to Cohen."

Sergeant Endres watched Scott trot off in the direction they had come from. He was crouched over at the waist and held his BAR out in front of his body in case he needed to fire quickly...a movement technique that was all but mandatory on the island if one wanted to stay alive. The sergeant was about to yell at him to be careful when he saw him duck behind some cover, wait a second, and then move out again. Even though they had just knocked out these two bunkers...moving through this area was still fraught with danger. There were still several buildings...or what was left of them...off to the left that probably housed Japanese snipers or machine gun teams and the enemy stronghold on the cove to their right was still pouring fire at the marines in the water and the landing craft by the reef. Besides that, Endres heard machine gun fire in the distance...and although he couldn't see it just yet...he knew the large nexus of the main runway had to be close by...maybe a hundred yards or so past those trees up ahead of them. *The Japs must have multiple gun emplacements set up to defend that piece of real estate,* he thought grimly. *It's gonna take us a lot longer to take this place than those generals planned...a hell of a lot longer.* And though he had no way of knowing it at the time, his premonition was spot on...since their next challenge...that of crossing the airfield... was looming right ahead of them. And this one would be just as daunting and just as challenging as surviving the landing the day before had been.

• • •

Not far away, Private Cohen struggled to get up. The pain in his shoulder was increasing by the moment and he instinctively knew he had to get out of no man's land. He rolled onto his right side and pushed himself up with his good arm. The movement made it feel like a knife was being plunged into his shoulder, but he ignored it and ran back to the rear of the first bunker they had attacked...his left arm dangling uselessly by his side. He took a seat and pulled a dressing out of a pouch on his web belt. Then he pressed it against the hole in his shoulder to stop the bleeding...just like he had been trained to do.

It wasn't long before Sergeant Endres trotted up and said, "Here, let me help you with that."

"Thanks. I can't get it to stay up on its own."

Endres knelt down, pulled the bloody gauze away, and examined the entrance wound. Then he slid the utility shirt off Cohen's damaged shoulder and had him lean forward. An ugly, jagged hole about the size of a quarter marked the spot where the bullet had exited the private's upper back. "You're lucky. The bullet went clean through. You feel okay?"

Grimacing, the private replied, "It's pretty damn sore, but I guess I'll make it. If it had hit anything important I'd probably be dead by now...right?"

"Yeah...it's the ones that bounce around inside that do the most damage," Endres said, trying to reassure him.

"Yeah...good thing mine went right through then," Cohen agreed, having heard the same thing in training.

"You know," Endres went on, "I once saw a guy get hit where you did and the bullet came out near his hip on the opposite side. It must have hit a bone or something and deflected downward...it tore him up inside and he was dead in seconds. You, on the other hand, have hit the jackpot so to speak. Once we get you back to the beach and back to the ships...you should be headed home. This type of wound takes a while to heal up. I should know since we used to talk about it a lot back on the *Canal*. We had endless bull sessions on which kinda wounds were the best to get. Things were sorta rough...we'd been there for way too long you see...and some of the boys startin' thinking it would be better to shoot themselves in the foot or somewhere else on the body to get evacuated out rather than stay there. One guy figured out that the shoulder was the best place to get hit. Imagine that. We told him he was crazy, but he seemed to think he was right. He ended up getting killed not long after that so he never did get a chance to test his theory out. Oh well."

"Can you imagine that," Cohen said incredulously.

Endres pulled out a field dressing and placed it against the wound on his back. "Now lean back," he said, using the back of the bunker to hold the dressing in place. Then he put the original bandage back over the front wound and applied pressure to it with one hand while taking another dressing and a sulfa packet out from his own medical pouch with his other hand.

"Hold that for a second," he said to the private, and Endres placed Cohen's right hand over the dressing. Endres then tore open the sulfa packet, put Cohen's hand back down, pulled the bandage away, and applied some of the white powder to the wound. He then put the new dressing over the old one and wound it tightly around Cohen's shoulder, armpit, and neck so that the bandage held both the front and back dressings in place. He tied it off and it held fairly well. "That'll have to do for the time being," he said, patting Cohen's good shoulder, comforting him.

Cohen relaxed and let his head fall back against the log wall of the pillbox. Then he looked up slowly and thanked the sergeant.

"Don't worry about it. You'd do the same for me. Now just take it easy for the time being. The lieutenant's almost here. Once we got this place secure, we'll get you headed back to the beach and home. You got anyone special waitin' on you back in...?"

"Novato....little town...just north of San Francisco. I've got a wife and a four-year-old son back there. It'll be nice to see him again. I'm gonna take him fishing when I get back. He was too young...to teach him how to do it...last time I was home in the States."

Sergeant Endres noticed that PFC Cohen seemed to be weakening somewhat. He studied him for a second and noticed that his breathing had slowed down, but other than that he seemed to be okay.

"You sure will. Now take it easy. We'll get you outta here as soon as possible. They got some good medical teams back on those ships. They'll patch you right up. And by the way...thanks for saving my life. I'd be lying here if you hadn't called out. I don't know why I didn't see the bastard myself," Endres said guiltily.

CHAPTER 12

After the grenade bounced off the wall in front of him, Petty Officer Okagi turned to his left and ducked down in a vain attempt to shield himself from the coming explosion. The grenade detonated when it reached waist-level and the blast blew Okagi's body against the back wall, splattering blood against it. The blast shattered his left thigh so badly that it looked like it had been chopped up with a meat clever and his left calf was blown completely off, exposing the tibia and fibula bones between his knee and ankle. He had also lost his pinky and ring fingers on his left hand...which he had put out to shield himself... and the top of his thumb had been sliced off and was a pulpy mess. Yet despite the severity of his wounds...Okagi was still alive...somehow.

At first, Okagi thought he might be dreaming...as thoughts of home danced through his mind. He pictured his lovely mother padding around their little home on the hillside, preparing dinner for her family, and seeing her face light up with joy as he and his father arrived at the door after trudging up the trail from the village below. Then he experienced an overwhelming sense of contentment...and he was convinced that he had died. *If this is what it feels like...then dying isn't so bad*, he thought blissfully...and he slowly drifted off to sleep.

He awoke with a start however...a distant explosion jogging him back to reality. As he regained consciousness and the fog that had settled over his mind seemed to lift, Okagi knew he was not in Heaven as he had hoped - Okagi was in fact a Christian...but he had kept it a secret from his Emperor-worshiping brethren - but was still laying on this back inside the bunker. *How'd this happen*, he wondered...but all he could remember was one of his men yelling out a warning...and then a brilliant flash of light. *The marines must have gotten a grenade into our bunker...that explains everything*, he reasoned. *And I must have gotten hit...but I don't feel any real pain like I did when I was wounded back on Guadalcanal.* But something else...a gut feeling... told him that he was seriously hurt...so he tried to find out what was wrong. After several attempts Okagi found that he could only move his right arm...and his left leg seemed to be twisted up underneath him. *I must have fallen on it somehow*, and he tried to shift his body so he could move the leg out from under him. *Once I get it straightened out it'll feel alright. Other than that I feel okay...only tired...I feel so very, very tired* and when the leg wouldn't move...he gave up the effort. Laying his head back down on the sandy floor, Okagi began to consider every-thing that had happened and thought, *we should've been able to hold out longer. We didn't even last two days against them this time. And the Admiral had been so sure that we could destroy them as they came in. I admired his con-fidence at first...but deep down I knew. The Admiral had never fought these Americans before...like I had...so how could he know? He should have been on Guadalcanal. Then he would've known that it was useless. These Americans never stop coming.* And then he passed out again.

He had no way of knowing how long he was out, but when he came to he sensed that someone else was standing next to the bunker doorway. He glanced up and saw a marine looking in to see if there was anyone left alive. Hidden in the shadows, the petty officer had laid still...feigning death to fool him...and his ploy must have worked since the marine left without discovering his presence. As Okagi con-tinued to lay there, he remembered another time when he had found himself in a similar situation and just smiled. *They had missed me then too, but this time, unlike the last, there is nowhere to go. This time I'm on Betio, and there's no place to hide. Not like the last time…back when I was on Guadalcanal.*

• • •

After losing most of his men to the fighter plane attack in the coconut grove, Petty Officer Okagi and the other lucky survivors were merged with an Army company that had suffered heavy casualties as well. Unfortunately, the only thing that seemed to change was the food situation…which went from bad to worse…if that were even possible. The same American planes continued to hound the Japanese Army units up and down the coast and the commanders on the ground seemed incapable of organizing a massed resistance against the ruthless marine invaders who seemed to be growing in numbers and boldness. And as their supplies dwindled and the losses mounted, it became harder and harder for the Japanese soldiers to envision the defining victory that they had been promised by their officers. The fact that they were no closer to dealing the American forces a death blow after all these months of fighting was the ultimate betrayal…and the fact that their valiant efforts and sacrifices had amounted to so very little was beyond frustrating. The reality of it brought tears to Saburo Okagi's eyes.

The only saving grace was the Army major who now led Okagi and his men. Major Heizo Takizawa was a smart, brave, and noble officer who did his best to look after the men who served under him. Since most of his original command had never made it to the island - many having drowned in Iron Bottom Sound when their landing barge had been sunk a half-mile from the beach by an American dive bomber in mid-October - the officer had begun organizing a patchwork unit filled with survivors from other decimated units. And when he found that Okagi and his men fell into this category, he quickly added them to his new company.

When the petty officer and his men reported to the major, they found him instructing his soldiers on the fine art of downing an enemy fighter plane by using deflection shooting. And when the major explained that it was no more difficult than shooting a bird in flight, Okagi chimed in with, "And if any of you can, please do so, since none of us have eaten much lately and a seagull would make a wonderful meal for all of us!"

Major Takizawa stopped the lecture, turned around, and looked at Okagi sternly and said, "Do you make it a habit of interrupting an officer in front of his men?"

"No, sir! I was merely--"

"Merely what," the major demanded harshly, interrupting Okagi.

"Sir," Okagi stammered, "I was...merely...trying to--"

"Trying to what?" Takizawa said condescendingly, cutting him off again. As he waited for the petty officer's answer, the major struck an imperious pose by folding his arms across his chest. At the same time he glanced over Okagi's shoulder and considered his men. He noted their rigid position of attention and thought, *these men are disciplined, always a good sign.*

"I'm waiting," Takizawa pressed, since Okagi had still not replied to the major's last question. Then the major stepped around Okagi and carefully inspected the men's uniforms and equipment, and he saw that they were in better physical shape than most of the men currently under his command.

"Sir," Okagi finally blurted out, "I have brought shame--"

"Petty Officer Okagi," Major Takizawa interrupted once more, "You have done no such thing. In fact, after inspecting your men, it is I who would be honored if you and your men would like to serve under my command. And if you agree to do so...I promise you and your men will get a decent meal tonight...at least...as good as we can manage!"

"Sir," Okagi piped up, "I don't know what to say!"

"Say yes," Takizawa replied, "so I'll be happy!"

"Yes...of course we will!" Okagi answered right back, a broad smile etched across his beaming face. And then he raised his right arm, slowly, almost ceremonially, and saluted his new commanding officer to seal the deal.

• • •

Major Takizawa recognized Petty Officer Okagi's value as a small unit leader immediately and before long Okagi was tasked with assignments that would have been ordinarily handled by an officer. But good officers were in short supply and since Okagi had so much ability and talent...the enlisted man often got the job instead. The major justified his unorthodox, problem-solving approach by saying that *Guadalcanal was a strange place and, as such, required even stranger methods to get important things done.*

Petty Officer Okagi, for his part, respected the major tremendously and found it very easy to serve under him. He knew what it was like to serve under officers who cared only for themselves and nothing for the men beneath them...yet Major Takizawa did not fit that mold. On the contrary, the major cared deeply about his men and treated them all with dignity and fairness. Of course, some men had misinterpreted his kindness for weakness and a few wily ones had even tried to take advantage of him. But the major was no pushover and those who violated his rules or regulations quickly found out that getting admonished by Takizawa was akin to standing in front of a blow torch. It was...to say the least...a terrifying experience and...as a result...there were very few disciplinary problems in a unit comprised of castaways and refugees...which made the petty officer's job that much easier.

Major Takizawa also trusted his men implicitly...a rare quality among Japanese officers. As a result, he always took the time to explain the details and key aspects of the operations they were undertaking and answered any questions they might have. Okagi found this fascinating...since officers had never consulted with the underlings in any of the units he had served in thus far. This approach was also extremely useful to Okagi and his men...since it addressed a glaring battlefield weakness that surfaced every time they were engaged with the marines. Okagi knew from experience that once the company officers were killed in a battle, the rest of the men sort of muddled around since no one knew what to do or what the plan called for. And since the men had never been trained or taught to exercise initiative, the unit was…in most cases…slaughtered in place. Knowing the parameters of the mission and what the major was trying to accomplish gave Okagi and the others a latitude of action they had never experienced before…and for once they felt they actually had a hand in sculpting their own success. Okagi and the rest of the enlisted leaders found it incredibly empowering and they cherished the trust that the major had placed in them. Now they could act on their own within the framework of the overall plan and not have to worry about having their heads removed for doing so.

The men also knew that the major would never ask any of them… no matter what his rank…to do anything that he wasn't willing to do himself. This selflessness was so infectious that it bound the men together and while other front line units were suffering from desertions - some men simply reached their limits and snuck into the jungle…never to be seen again…or they attached themselves to the support units in the rear areas - Major Takizawa's command grew in numbers as word of his superior leadership skills made the rounds among the men on the north coast of the island.

Okagi's opinion of his commanding officer soared to new heights after the petty officer heard the tale about how the major had volunteered to come to Guadalcanal on his own. It was almost too incredible to believe, but the man who had told him the story was pretty reliable - he was in the intelligence section of the *Sendai* Division and Okagi had run into him by luck - so Okagi figured it must be true. According to the man's sources, the major was the youngest and favorite son of a senior member of the Imperial General Staff back in Tokyo. His father, a major general who knew General Tojo personally, used his connections to secure a soft staff job for the major back home. When he learned of the posting, Takizawa had politely - some said emphatically - declined the offer...like any good samurai warrior would have. His next move was to request a transfer to Guadalcanal instead...where he could lead Japan's elite soldiers in the war against the Americans. But when Okagi retold the story word-for-word to his own men...many of them...as much as they loved and respected the major...refused to believe it. "Are you out of your mind," one of the dissenters said incredulously, "No one would come to this hellhole on his own. If the major did volunteer to come here...then he was insane...and Major Takizawa is not insane!" Then, pointing a bony finger at all of them, he said, "No, we're the crazy ones...for believing everything those officers told us when we were back at Rabaul. How we would come here and have an easy time of it. Now look at the fix we're in. As far as I'm concerned...the only officer I'll ever trust again is our major!"

• • •

The Japanese forces on Guadalcanal had been fighting the Americans for nearly four months and had nothing to show for it. If anything, the situation on the island had grown progressively worse. Now nothing...save withdrawal...which the generals and admirals at Rabaul had yet to consider...or surrender...which was simply unheard of... could stop or prevent the Japanese losses from mounting. The island was like a wild animal with a voracious appetite...and it was devouring everything the Japanese High Command fed it. Conditions became deplorable...and Takizawa's men...through no fault of his own...were suffering...just like all the rest. By early December, battle deaths, disease, and, worst of all, hunger had reduced his company by nearly seventy percent...and the thirty or so survivors were wondering if they'd ever get off the cursed island alive.

Major Takizawa was doing everything he possibly could to improve their morale, but one incident made him realize how bad things had gotten when Okagi had come to him abruptly. "Sir, you need to come with me," he said, concerned. Okagi then led him silently into the jungle and stopped. Pointing, he said, "They're ours. I heard rumors that this was happening, but I didn't want to believe it."

Takizawa saw two bodies lying together in the distance and knew immediately what they had done. It was a pitiful sight, and unfortunately, one that was becoming more common as time went on. The two emaciated soldiers, their uniforms in tatters, were linked together in a death embrace. One of them had placed a hand grenade between their stomachs and the other had pulled the pin. The major knew there was nothing honorable in this blatant act of suicide... but he excused it nonetheless...since he knew it was born of desperation. If nothing else, these brave men had chosen a foolproof method to end their pain and suffering as quick as possible. "I have heard these very same rumors, Okagi," the major said, nodding in agreement. Then he added somberly, "But, like you, I didn't think it was possible. I know now that I was wrong to think that way. This is my fault. I need to find something for these men to do...something that will give these men a reason to live. If not...we will find more and more of them this way...and I...as their commander...cannot let that happen."

• • •

The plan Takizawa devised suited his needs to the letter. His company - in reality, he had no more men than an under-strength platoon did in numbers...but they were still calling it a company - was dug in behind the Mantanikau River...a large river that meandered out of the mountains to the south and eventually emptied into Iron Bottom Sound. The river was the key terrain feature in the area...as most rivers tend to be...and the major's men were responsible for guarding a sandbar that ran between the eastern and western banks of the swampy, brackish river. Both the Japanese and the Americans alike had been using the sandbar as a main crossing point for their forays into each other's territory and, lately, Takizawa's men had been getting harassed by the American unit that was operating in their vicinity. The major's experience led him to believe that a company of marines was probably responsible for it, but Takizawa knew that attacking an entire company with the men he had left was out of the question. The major had never accepted the insane illusion that most of the other officers did...that Japanese bravado alone could offset their lack of numbers and firepower in a fight with the enemy. Thinking that way was courting death...and he had lived too long to simply toss his life away on a pipe dream. But he did not sell the fighting ability of his men short either...and he was certain that they could destroy a small, isolated group of marines if his men could catch them on their own terms. So all the major had to do was figure out a way to lure one of the marine platoons...or even a patrol...away from the rest of the company and then engage it. Hopefully, the scheme he devised would do just that.

"This plan is audacious to say the least," the major said as he explained his idea to his trusted confidant, Petty Officer Okagi. "I wonder myself if we can really pull it off," he continued as Okagi remained silent...thinking it over. "But I believe it is my duty...our duty...to do something. I will not sit by while my men are dying of hunger or by their own hand. If we must die...we will die honorably...and we will take as many of the enemy with us as we can."

"I think it can work," Okagi said adamantly.

"You think so," the major replied, and he felt a surge of confidence creeping into his psyche...something that had been missing for quite a while.

"Yes. It is certainly worth a try. I will go get the men so you can explain the details to them yourself. I guarantee they'll go for it once they hear it." While walking away, he shouted over his shoulder, "And if it doesn't work out, then so be it. At this point, I would rather go down fighting than starve to death or die of sickness in a month or so."

• • •

When Okagi returned with the men, the major motioned for them to sit down and relax. Once the men were seated comfortably, he began to explain his two-part plan. "My plan is based on deception and timing. First off, I will need five volunteers to act as decoys," the major said, and when five arms shot up...he smiled approvingly. "Good," he said, "I knew I could count on you," and he continued on. "My five decoys are going to stand out there in the river by the sandbar and splash around until you are spotted by one of those American fighter planes that seem to be everywhere lately."

"So you want us to act like we're just taking a bath out there, sir? Do we really smell that bad, sir?" one of the volunteers asked sheepishly.

"Well, I'd never mistake you for a bunch of *geishas*, that's for sure," the major said jokingly, and the men laughed as well. "But the real reason," he said, motioning them to quiet down, "is that you will be the bait that draws the marines to us. This whole plan hinges on one of their planes seeing you...so make sure you put on a good show." Takizawa then explained what he thought would happen once the men in the river were identified as Japanese soldiers and not some friendly natives trying to catch their morning breakfast. "I believe the pilot will radio your position in," he said, "and then a marine patrol will be sent to check it out. This is what I am counting on...but he may also try to take you out on his own. I realize this is a deadly gamble, but I do not think these American flyers are so trigger-happy that they would waste their ammunition on such a small group of soldiers who are simply trying to wash up."

"He might if he thinks we are surrendering," one man offered.

"The Americans do not look at surrender the same way we do," the major countered. "In fact," he continued, "they think there is nothing wrong with it. We are taught that is cowardly and dishonorable to surrender, but the Americans, and the British too, for that matter, are not. In the Philippines, thousands of American soldiers surrendered to General Homma and an entire British Army laid down their arms in Malaysia. We consider it our duty to fight to the death...but the Americans do not...so I do not think the

American pilot will fire on you if he thinks you are simply surrendering. However, if the plane does attack for some reason, I do not expect you to act like targets in a shooting gallery. I want you to do everything possible to survive, but as the plane passes by, I want the ones who have not been hit to act like you have been too." The men laughed nervously when they heard that part of the plan, but stopped when they realized that the major was deadly serious. "If any of you are having second thoughts," Major Takizawa said, looking directly at his five gallant volunteers, "and want to back out...I will not hold it against you." None of the men indicated that they did, so the major nodded and continued, "Very good...and don't worry...I'm going to be right beside you." There was an audible gasp from the men and some of them began to protest but the major cut them off. "Did you actually think I was going to let you take that risk all alone?" he asked

"But, sir," one of the volunteers pleaded, "what will we do if you get killed?"

"You will carry on...as brave and obedient soldiers always do," he replied matter-of-factly. Then the major changed his tone and reassured the man, saying, "But do not worry...I have no intention of getting killed. I am certainly too crafty and savvy for that to happen."

"Well, sir," the man replied slyly, "I hope you won't mind if I stand right beside you when that plane comes over then..." and everyone roared in laughter.

Okagi allowed the men to enjoy the moment but then he signaled them to quiet down. The major waited a second, relishing the excitement that seemed to be spreading throughout his men. "Of course I would be honored for you to stand next to me," Takizawa said, and the soldier's face beamed in appreciation as the men beside him clapped him on the shoulder in celebration and in an expression of camaraderie that develops amidst men who share danger together. Then the major reiterated that the main goal of this part of the plan...which seemed suicidal at best...was to get the pilot to report their location so a marine patrol would be dispatched to check it out. He explained that if the pilot did fire on them, then the marines would be sent out to confirm the pilot's handiwork…to verify that he had gotten them all. And if he didn't fire on them…as was hoped…and just reported their location…then the marines would probably send out a patrol to try to capture them for intelligence purposes. Naturally, Takizawa's intrepid volunteers were praying that the pilot would just radio the report in and move on to bigger game…or…better yet…return to Henderson Field and take the rest of the day off.

Timing was the critical aspect of the second part of his plan and Major Takizawa told them that it would begin when the American plane was out of sight. "I will count off ten minutes to make sure the plane does not double back on us," he told them. Then, after the ten minutes were up, Okagi and the rest of the men who had been hiding on the western side of the river would merge with the men in the water and together they would all cross over to the American side and set up an ambush position along the main trail leading to the river. Finishing up, the major placed his hands on his hips, struck a martial pose, and said defiantly, "Now, if the Americans react like I think they will…and I know they will…then we can anticipate a marine patrol to come marching down that trail…and when it does… we'll be waiting for it!"

The men reacted immediately to the major's stirring words and jumped to their feet yet again with new-found energy suddenly coursing through their tired bodies. Petty Officer Okagi walked out in front of them and faced the major. Then, coming to a rigid position of attention, the petty officer proclaimed, "Sir…if you will lead us…we will follow you wherever you go!"

Major Takizawa was filled with pride as he eyed his band of dirty, disheveled soldiers and he knew they had a lot of fight left in them…despite their ragged appearance. *They just need someone to lead them*, he thought, and then a scene from home - he had been raised in the Tochigi Prefecture…the mountainous region north of Tokyo - flashed through his mind. It was an image of the family cat stalking and trapping a field mouse in the beautiful garden outside his house. *We'll stalk our prey just like that cat did…silently and stealthily,* he thought, *and the marines will have no more luck than that poor mouse did.* Then, mirroring Okagi, the major came to a position of attention and shouted, "It will be an honor to lead you, my brave comrades!" And as the men beamed, he yelled, "Banzai…Banzai…Banzai!"

Flushed with pride, the men raised their rifles in the air and shouted *Banzai* three times to the delight of their glowing commander.

• • •

Later on that afternoon Major Takizawa approached Petty Officer Okagi and said, "Make sure the men get a decent meal tonight…and a good night's rest. I know it's an impossible task…but try anyway. Use all your connections and see if you can scrounge up some fresh fish and rice…not the spoiled stuff. I want the men ready in the morning…since I intend to kick off our plan at first light."

"We're going tomorrow morning, sir?" Okagi asked, and then added, "So soon?"

"No time like the present, Okagi. You've been around me long enough to know that I don't like to waste time," the major replied.

"That's certainly true," Okagi said right back, and then asked, "But don't you think the men need a little more time to prepare?"

"No, my good friend, the men are as ready as they're ever going to be," the major countered. "In fact," he said, "they get weaker with each passing day so I see no need to delay it."

Okagi thought for a second and said, "You are right, sir. I'll do the best I can with our dinner. Someone's bound to have some food hidden somewhere. If they do, I'll find it."

"That's the spirit!" Takizawa exclaimed. "With that kind of attitude we can conquer the whole world!"

• • •

As confident as he was, Takizawa could never have imagined that the first phase of his plan would unfold exactly the way he had designed it. He and the men had only been in the water an hour or so when one of those terrifying, *long-nosed* planes - it had a gaping, saw-toothed shark's mouth painted on the cowling under its nose...just like the ones that had attacked the ill-fated platoon on the beach - appeared in the sky overhead. The plane seemed to be on a westerly path but it began a gentle turn to the left and reversed course. The men watched it tensely, tracking it path, and then shouted, "Here it comes!" as the plane stood on its right wing and swooped down. It made several passes over the men as the pilot marked their position, and then the fighter turned on its wing and flew away.

"Did you see? Did you see!" one of the men yelled excitedly.

"The pilot was talking on his radio!" another one answered, "Just like the major said he would. He came in so low that last time I could even see his face. He looked right at me!"

A third man held his head in his hands, and, in amazement, turned to the major and said, "I can't believe he didn't fire a shot at us! Sir, how did you know?"

"I can't believe I'm actually still alive!" a fourth man chimed in.

The fifth man just stood there, frozen in place, as if in shock, his jaw gaped open. One of the others tapped him on the shoulder and asked him if he was okay, but he said nothing.

"The answer is simple, men," the major said, jubilant that his daring plan was working out so far, "either the gods heard your prayers last night...or we are just lucky and we got a pilot who fights with honor and chivalry." To commemorate the moment, Major Takizawa lifted his arm and waved *sayonara* to the departing fighter pilot...a simple gesture of respect from one warrior to another. As if on cue, the plane began rocking its wings up and down, the pilot answering the major's wave with one of his own...in an obvious display of comradeship. Smiling, he watched the plane disappear in the distance and thought, *we could be good friends...that pilot and I... were we not trying to kill each other. It is good to know that the insanity of this war has not corrupted everything it has touched.* Then he looked at his watch and noted the time. With that simple act, the second phase of his daunting plan kicked into action.

• • •

Petty Officer Okagi watched the plane fly off and realized, thankfully, that his misery was almost over. He had been laying in a nasty foxhole since daybreak…and he couldn't wait to get out of it. Staring at his watch, he thought *If I have to spend one more hour in this dung hole, I might just kill myself and save the Americans the trouble…*and he willed the minute hand to move faster.

It had been very dark when the company arrived at the tree line beside the river and the men had begun to dig in. The position suited their purposes in three ways: hidden among the trees, the holes they had scraped out could not be seen from the air or from the opposite side of the river…where the Americans were. In addition, they were close enough to the sandbar that Okagi and the others could provide excellent covering fire for the men in the river if they needed it. The only problem was that the ground was so swampy and the soil so porous that water…stagnant and putrid…had filled the holes almost as fast as they could dig them and the edges had caved in at even the slightest touch. Okagi had been laying in a muddy soup for over three hours as a result…which was an eternity as far as he was concerned since he liked to keep his body and uniform as clean as possible. Now, with the plane almost out of sight, he thought ruefully, *I'd pay that pilot a small fortune if he'd stay away for just a few more minutes so we can leave these holes behind us and get across that sandbar undetected.*

The minutes dragged by slowly, but the major stuck to the timetable and yelled for the rest of platoon to stay under cover. If they left too early, and were discovered crossing the sandbar, the plan would be foiled…since the next stage hinged on stealth and surprise. So Takizawa scanned the sky continually, looking for the plane, wondering if he had underestimated the American pilot, thought, *a shrewd*

pilot would double back just to make sure nothing had changed, but, thankfully, he was nowhere to be seen. He looked at his watch again…and at
the ten minute mark…with the skies still clear…he finally signaled
the others across.

Petty Officer Okagi…who hadn't taken his eyes off the major…
said, "Let's go!" as soon as the officer began waving his arm back
and forth. This was the prearranged signal that everything was okay
and for Okagi to bring the covering force over to the far bank of the
river. Hearing the order, the others scrambled out of their foxholes
and followed Okagi across the sandbar…mud and water dripping
from their uniforms…staining the sand brown in their wake. When
he reached the far bank, Okagi knelt beside the major and took a
headcount to insure that no one had been left behind. With everyone
accounted for, Okagi pushed his way into the jungle and headed left,
away from the trail that led directly to the sandbar.

After moving twenty-five yards or so, Okagi turned the column -
the men were following Okagi in a single file - to the right so they
were now traveling parallel to the trail off to their right. As they
moved deeper into the jungle, Okagi slowed the column down and
the men crept along silently…their senses razor sharp…looking and
listening for any sign that would indicate that a marine patrol was
coming down the trail beside them. They saw and heard nothing
to alert them…so they continued on…and before long Okagi was
within sight of the spot where the major wanted to establish his ambush site. At that point Okagi held up, and as they walked past, the
petty officer pointed out the spot where he wanted them to set up
for the coming ambush. He was almost done with the assignments
when the Major's well-crafted plan suddenly fell apart.

• • •

Major Takizawa's experience had served him well when it came to
designing his plan since he had been right when he estimated that
a marine company was located on the opposite side of the river
from their position. However, he had no way of knowing that the

enemy company he was targeting - Echo Company of the Second Regiment - was in the process of readjusting its lines westward. In an uncanny coincidence, the company was moving one of its platoons closer to the river...at the very same time he was formulating his plan. The major might have learned of his target's intentions if active scouting of the American positions had been taking place, but he had put a stop to it only days before. Sadly, four of his best men had never returned after they had left on this type of mission and he couldn't risk losing any more men without getting something of value in return for their efforts. What made it worse was that they never learned the fate of these men...their brothers in arms...their friends. They had gone out in teams of two on separate mornings and never returned. If they were lucky, then they had been killed by the marines in a fight...but if not...then the possibilities were endless...and all bad. They may have been captured...by either the marines or the local natives...and no one wanted that to happen to them...since it was considered a disgrace to be taken prisoner. It was also common knowledge that both the marines and the islanders tortured their captives horribly before killing them. Worse still, the men could have become disoriented within the featureless terrain of the jungle and they were still out there...alive but wandering around hopelessly lost. If that had happened, then they would be slowly starving to death...and probably losing their minds as well in the green hell that now owned them. One man even hinted that they may have been eaten by crocodiles...and no one thought he was crazy for suggesting it.

Sadly, the major had gained nothing for his men's sacrifices. He knew no more about the Americans or their positions than he did before and if he continued to lose men at this rate...there would be nothing left for him to command in a few weeks or so. Faced with these grim circumstances, Takizawa had been forced to cancel the very thing that could have supplied him with the information he needed most to develop his plan properly.

With no one keeping an eye on the American positions, Takizawa was blind to the fact that a platoon had been moved up…and was now based less than a half a mile from the river. Ironically, this slight adjustment in positioning threw the timing of his ambush plan off by just a few minutes…but they were minutes that were critical to the implementation and success of his overall plan.

In designing it, Takizawa had allotted his platoon thirty minutes to reach the ambush site and then another three minutes for setting the ambush up. With the marines further back, he figured their patrol would reach the sandbar in an hour or so…which gave his men plenty of time to prepare their ambush site and wait for the Americans to arrive. However, since the Americans had moved closer to the river, the marine patrol was able to reach the ambush site much quicker than Takizawa had calculated. As a result, the major's troops didn't get the ambush set up properly and they were forced to spring their trap prematurely. Too late, with fire erupting around him, the major realized that his meticulous attention to detail had cost him dearly. If he had been more aggressive and left the sandbar five minutes ahead of schedule…instead of worrying about the American plane returning…the marines would have stumbled into a perfect trap.

• • •

Petty Officer Okagi knew something had gone wrong the second he heard the *Nambu* open up and he screamed for the men to get down. Dropping to one knee, he screamed the order again but no one seemed to hear him. Instead, they kept standing…firing their weapons feverishly in the direction of the path. Since he couldn't see what they were shooting at and it didn't seem like anyone was shooting back at them, he yelled at them again…but this time he told them to cease firing. The men around him paid no attention to his order. Okagi cursed… and then stood up to see what they were firing at….but his view of the trail ahead was blocked by the leafy jungle that hung on either side of it. *This is crazy… why are they doing this?* Then a hand grenade came arcing in from the direction of the trail. Okagi saw it and dove out of the way, but the man standing next to him didn't and the grenade landed in the soft ground beside him. He was lifted into the air by the force of the explosion and metal fragments peppered both his legs and abdomen and nearly blew off one of his hands. Another chunk of shrapnel hit him in the face and sliced his cheek open and knocked out a few teeth. Okagi had been hit too, but his wounds were minor compared to the man who had taken the brunt of the explosion. Okagi heard more explosions in the jungle around him and then things went dark all of a sudden. When he finally came to, he sat up and saw that the other men were gone…except for the wounded man lying next to him …and he was unconscious. *I must have been hit by another grenade*, he thought, since his head was swimming and he felt wobbly so he didn't try to get up. Then he heard wild screaming and weapons being fired out ahead of him somewhere in the jungle, but he still couldn't see anything through the thick underbrush. After a while the firing died down and it grew quiet. Okagi stayed still for thirty minutes…yet it seemed like hours…and then he heard strange voices yelling to each other as they were searching the jungle. *It must be the marines we were trying to kill*, he thought ominously. He rose up slowly and saw three of his men lying dead on the jungle floor nearby. Then he heard the voices again…this time closer…and he knew he couldn't stay there any longer. With no time to waste, Okagi reached down and grabbed the wounded private by his uniform shirt. With all his might, he hoisted him over his shoulder and trudged off in the direction of the river and friendly lines.

Keep going…just keep going. Okagi kept repeating this mantra to himself as he struggled towards the river, the pain of his flesh wounds increasing with every step he took. And even though the man on his shoulder felt like a boulder, he refused to drop him. He stopped only once…at the half way point…to briefly to catch his breath and rest his aching legs. When he finally reached the river, Okagi gently slid the emaciated man - the private had arrived on the island three months ago weighing one hundred and forty pounds and had lost nearly thirty pounds since then - off his shoulder and propped him up against a rotting log laying in the weeds along the shore. The wounded man moaned a little and Okagi saw that he had regained consciousness. The private smiled feebly and Okagi put his index finger to his lips...signaling him to be quiet...since the marines might still be in the area...hunting them. The petty officer knelt down and began dressing the man's wounds as best he could with a bandage he pulled from the pouch on his belt. The wounded man nodded thankfully and then whispered, "I am sorry, but I do not have any dressings. I used mine up long ago on some other wounded."

"That is quite alright, my friend. We will make do. Now just be quiet...your cheek is hurt and it must difficult to talk." Okagi then took his shirt off and cut off one of the tattered sleeves with his bayonet. He placed the dirty piece of cloth around a hole in his thigh and tied it off. "You know, Ono, I could've trained to be a medic back in Japan but I chose the naval infantry instead. The funny thing is that I somehow end up bandaging everyone I serve with on this evil island. I bet if I had become a medic, I wouldn't have had a chance to treat so many men. Strange how things turn out so differently than what we hope for," Okagi mused philosophically. The private smiled and Okagi gave the man a drink from his canteen, supporting his head with one hand while tilting the water container with the other. The thin soldier drank thirstily, but winced as the water hit his damaged teeth.

"What....what happened to... the....others?" Private Ono managed to eke out despite the pain.

Okagi told him that they must have walked into a marine ambush instead of the other way around and that several of the men had been killed. "I saw them laying there with my own eyes," he said emphatically, then added, "but I don't know where the rest of them went."

"Do you think they're okay," the private asked, concerned.

"I never saw anyone else. But I heard a lot of firing too...so something must have happened. For all I know, they could be evading the marines the same way we are. Or they could all be dead. The only way we'll find out is if we make it back to our own lines," the petty officer told him flatly.

The private nodded appreciatively, but Okagi could see, almost feel, the sadness in the man's eyes. "I know, my friend...I hope they are all alive too. But if they are dead...then there is nothing we can do for them anymore," Okagi responded, trying to console him. Then, to motivate him, he said, "Our mission now is to get across that river alive so we can fight again. And no one is going to stop us!"

They waited a quarter of an hour longer...gathering their strength and courage...before attempting the cross. Even though they hadn't heard or seen them in a while, the two men realized that crossing the river was still a big gamble since the marines could have snuck down to the bank of the river without their knowing it. "They could be hiding there now...on either side of us...waiting for us to cross over so they could wipe us out on the sandbar," Okagi theorized... and added cautiously, "It's now or never, Private Ono."

"I am ready when you are," the private stated confidently... and he pushed himself up with his good hand to a half-crouching, half-leaning position. Unable to put any weight on his injured leg, Private Ono grabbed Okagi for support and straightened up. They pushed through the last of the jungle entanglements and took a quick survey left and right...looking for anything out of place. When they saw nothing conspicuous, they left the jungle and trudged across the sandbar to the safety of the far bank.

• • •

Two days later a Japanese patrol on their way to the river found a man sitting against the base of a large tree. The man was in terrible shape and appeared to be dead, but he opened his eyes and smiled when the lead scout nudged his foot to see if he was alive. The scout jumped back, surprised, and asked, "What the hell are you doing out here all alone?" The patrol leader...a seasoned sergeant...walked up and eyed him suspiciously. The injured man opened his mouth to speak but the lead scout snarled, "He's a damned deserter is what he is." Then another man in the patrol came up, pointed his rifle at the man, and said venomously, "We should shoot him right now and leave him for the rats."

"You'll do no such thing," the sergeant said, and then he ordered the man to lower his rifle.

The soldier obeyed the command willingly but said, "But what about our orders? Aren't we disobeying our orders if we don't shoot this scum?"

"What makes you think he's a deserter?" the patrol leader asked back.

"Just look at him, sir. He's been living off the jungle for a while. What the hell else can he be?" the man argued forcefully.

The patrol leader looked at the man, considered the point, shook his head, and said, "He could be lost...got separated from his unit somehow...or maybe--"

"I'm not...not a deserter," Okagi blurted out, interrupting and surprising the patrol leader all at once.

"Get this man some water, quick!" he demanded, and when the water bottle was put to Okagi's lips, the patrol leader said, "Don't drink too fast or you'll just throw it back up."

"Thank you, sergeant," Okagi said, his voice barely above a whisper.

"Take your time...there's more if you need it," the patrol leader said softly...and after having his fill, Okagi began to tell them his story.

• • •

"Are you sure Ono was alive when you left him?" the patrol leader asked Okagi now that he had explained why he was alone by the tree.

"Yes…I'm sure he was," Okagi answered slowly, and to justify what he done, he added, "but he had lost so much blood…he may have died after I left him. At that point…I was so tired that I just couldn't carry him anymore. I hated leaving him like that, but I needed to keep going to see if I could find some help for both of us."

"Don't worry, Okagi," the patrol leader said, "you did the right thing," and then he jerked his head to the side and two other scouts took off down the trail to locate Ono.

The men returned later and said that they had found Ono right where Okagi said he'd be…and incredibly…he was still alive too. "Can I see him," Okagi asked, thrilled at the news.

"You certainly can…but not right now," the patrol leader said, and then he explained that they needed two stretchers…one to carry Ono out…and one for him…but they didn't have any with them. So he was sending two of his men back to get them…and that would take a little more time. "But," the patrol leader said, "Ono has managed to last this long on his own, so he should be able to survive for another hour or two until they get back with the stretchers." The alternatives were not as promising. One of the stronger men could carry Ono over his shoulder and walk out or they could design a stretcher out of tree limbs and uniform shirts and carry him out on that. Although both of these options might be faster, the brutal fact was that Ono was so badly injured that he would probably die from all the jostling he'd experience as he was carried fireman-style or in the makeshift stretcher. So Okagi concurred with the patrol leader's decision and he asked if he could help in any way.

"No, my friend," the patrol leader assured him, "you have done enough already. Just rest your eyes for a while and I'll wake you when they bring Ono in. How's that sound?"

"I don't know how to thank you," Okagi said, tears welling in his eyes.

"You don't have to," the patrol leader replied, and added, "now get some rest…and when you're strong again…you can go out and kill some Americans to avenge the loss of the men in your company."

"Yes…I think I will do that," Okagi said, and he closed his eyes and fell quickly asleep.

• • •

When Okagi finally woke up, he noticed that he and Ono were laying in a crude hospital area several miles from the river. Ono was still sleeping so he didn't disturb him. Intrigued, he sat up and he looked to see if the men from the patrol were anywhere nearby, but they were nowhere to be seen. Okagi then stopped a medical orderly who was walking by and asked him if he had seen the men who had brought him in. The orderly told him that he had spoken briefly to the patrol leader and that he had asked that he and his friend be given the best medical care possible. "We'll try to oblige him of course," he said reassuringly, "but we do not have much in the way of medical supplies here."

"That is alright. Please look to my friend, Ono, here first. He is in worse shape than I am," Okagi requested.

"Of course," the orderly replied, and smiling, added, "and we shall try our best to make your stay here a pleasant one."

Relieved, Okagi asked, "Where did the patrol go? Are they still here?"

"No," the orderly stately flatly, "they left right after I spoke to the one in charge." Then the orderly pointed his finger at the dense jungle and added, "They came in and went out…just like ghosts."

And in a strange way the man's depiction of Okagi's saviors captured their very essence…since these five men would disappear in the jungle… never to be seen again.

• • •

Okagi and Ono's wounds were bandaged and later that night they were treated to some rice and water. It wasn't much, but it was far better than laying in the jungle where the flies and mosquitoes had been their sole companions for the last three days.

Both of their conditions improved enough over the next few days that Okagi and Ono were moved to a rear echelon camp in a coconut grove near Tassafaronga Point. The two men were resting and enjoying the shade with the other wounded when a haughty Japanese officer in a fresh uniform appeared before them. Okagi looked the man over and thought, *there seems to be an endless supply of these types I'm afraid.* Fearing the worst, the men tensed as the major, rigid and formal in demeanor, pulled a set of orders from his breast pocket and began reading them perfunctorily. Okagi heard a man behind him moaning that they were doomed…that they were probably going back to the front. Instead, to their complete surprise, the officer gave them the best news they had heard since setting foot on Guadalcanal. The men were informed that their brave service on Guadalcanal had come to an end and that a destroyer was scheduled to arrive later that night to evacuate them off the island. The men would be transported back to Rabaul so they could rest and recover from their wounds in the hospital facilities there.

The major had expected the men to break out in wild cheering once he finished reading the order, but, to his consternation, the men just stared ahead solemnly, as if they had missed the portent of his message. "Did you not hear what I just said?" he asked incredulously, and then, waving the orders back and forth, added, "This is your ticket out of here." The officer gazed at the men quizzically, trying to gauge their reaction…but he had not been on the island long enough to understand their feelings and when the men remained quiet, he gave up the effort. *Ungrateful brood,* he thought dismally… and he turned on his heel and left…all the while shaking his head at the pathetic group.

Sometime after midnight, the wounded petty officer and his heavily-bandaged partner limped their way to the beach and struggled up the ramp of a landing barge that was grounded on the shore.

Ono was using a crutch that Okagi had fashioned out of a stout tree limb he had found...but nonetheless the trek was tedious and slow. Ono was out of breath by the time it was over...but nothing was going to keep him from leaving the island. The wooden deck of the barge was slippery and Ono nearly fell when the crutch skidded out from under him...but Okagi was there to catch him as he teetered over...and they were able to make it to the rear by the wheelhouse without incident. The rest of the walking wounded filed aboard and then the stretcher cases were loaded as well. When it was full, the coxswain backed the craft off the beach and headed towards a darkened form in the distance. As they got closer, the men were able to make out the shape of the Japanese destroyer that lay waiting to take them away. The boat's motor died down and it slid in against the side of the destroyer, bumping it gently as it swayed up and down with the waves. As soon as the sailors had secured the barge to the larger ship, rope nets were thrown down to the men in the barge below and the loading process began.

A sense of impending doom began to grip the men as the tiny barge continued to bang against the side of the warship. *How can those butchers back there on the island not hear all this racket out here*, they wondered nervously. The prospect of being taken under fire and sunk by the enemy shore batteries that were down the coast seemed to increase with each tick of the clock and time stood still as each man waited patiently for his turn to climb up the nets. The strain was too much for one wounded man to bear and he scampered up the net out of turn...ahead of some stretcher-bound cases that were still waiting to be hauled up. One of the other wounded cursed and went to grab him but Okagi blocked him and said, "Just let him go." The man glared menacingly at Okagi, but relented when the taller man - at five-foot-nine Okagi was usually a head taller than most of the men around him - showed no signs of backing down. "You're right. We'll all be up there soon enough," he said, returning peacefully to his place in line.

When it was their turn to go, Petty Officer Okagi and Private Ono hugged and clapped each other on the backs.

"We made it. Do you believe it, Sabo?" the young private beamed.

"I guess I don't really," the petty officer responded, "since it seems almost too good to be true."

"That it is…that it is," Ono said, savoring the moment, a look of joy etched on his bandaged face.

Okagi reached over and put his hand on Ono's shoulder and said, "You're the lucky one, Ono. They'll send you back home after we get to Rabaul. Your wounds are too serious to keep you out here."

"What do you think will happen to you?" the private asked, concerned about the fate of the man who had saved his life.

"I don't know, my young friend. It shouldn't take all that long for me to heal up. I certainly don't think my days of serving our Emperor and Japan are over quite yet. These Americans are tenacious fighters. They won't be satisfied with just taking Guadalcanal back from us. There are plenty more islands for them to attack if they are successful here. Something tells me that I will see them again…somewhere out there. And when I do meet them again…the outcome will be more to my liking," Okagi said confidently.

Just then a grizzled sailor leaned over the ship's railing and yelled, "Let's go you two love birds! You're the last two! Unless you want to end up as shark bait, get up those ropes so we can get underway. We linger around here too long and we'll get caught by the American bombers up the channel once the sun comes up. We've lost too many ships getting you in here and now we're going to lose just as many getting you back out. But I don't plan on being one of them. So move it!"

Ono went first and he made good time going up the net despite his bandaged hand and other wounds. Okagi watched him go, making sure he was okay, and then grabbed the ropes and pulled himself up. Almost to the top, he stopped and glanced over his shoulder for a last look at the formidable, black island in the distance and said,

"Farewell *Island of Death* ....may we never meet again." Looking back up, he saw Ono smiling down at him...bandaged face and all...waving him up with his one good hand.

• • •

Petty Officer Okagi spent the next two months recuperating at Rabaul and he was discharged from the hospital in February of 1943. Soon thereafter, he was transferred to the crack 7th Special Naval Landing Force...or SNLF...which was stationed there. In the meantime, the Americans had finally secured their victory on Guadalcanal and were conducting air raids against the other Japanese-held islands in the northern Solomons as they prepared to move up the island chain...just like he had predicted they would. And the petty officer figured the Americans would eventually come for Rabaul itself... since it was the headquarters for the Japanese Army and Navy in the Southwest Pacific and it possessed a wonderful harbor along with several formidable air bases...which is what the Americans seemed to cherish the most.

But this time the Japanese forces would be ready for them however...since New Britain...the island on which Rabaul was located...was at the northern end of the Soloman Islands chain and the marines were still several hundred miles away. The sheer distance between the islands guaranteed that there would be plenty of time to prepare a proper defense. They would not be caught unaware... like they had been when the Americans invaded Guadalcanal. *No, Okagi thought, when the Americans come for me this time...they will get a much different welcome than they did on the Island of Death.*

• • •

In the spring of 1943, the men of the 7th SNLF received a reprieve of sorts when the unit was ordered out of Rabaul however. For some strange reason, they were being transferred to a little island in the central Pacific that was well removed from the path of the fighting that was taking place in the Solomons far to the south. Some of the men were angry when they learned about the assignment...

since they had been looking forward to meeting the Americans on better terms so they could avenge the disgrace that had happened on Guadalcanal. Others…those who were sick of combat and its deprivations…had welcomed the move however. They were like drowning men who had just seen a life boat pull up beside them…and they were bragging to the young men that their combat days were finally over when they boarded the ship that would take them to their new home. Okagi, the sage veteran, warned them otherwise of course, but the joyful men would hear nothing of it…and his prescient advice was all but wasted on their deaf ears.

• • •

I tried to tell them…back in the spring…when we were headed here…but they didn't want to believe me. The young ones were so inexperienced that they just couldn't picture things turning out like this…and the old ones…well they just hoped it wouldn't, he thought ruefully. Now he was badly wounded and helpless…laying on the floor of a bunker that he had helped build to prevent just this sort of thing from happening. *I should have known the Americans were too powerful…I just should have known after what I had seen on the Island of Death.* And then he wondered if any of those young soldiers who had disagreed with him so adamantly so many months ago were still alive…and if they were…what they were thinking now.

Okagi focused his attention on some sand that was sifting downward from the roof. The image reminded him of an hourglass that he had seen somewhere when he was younger. It made him realize that he only had so much time left to try to make an escape…if he was going to make one at all. *I did it before…I can do it again,* he thought, steeling himself for the effort that lie ahead. Just like the last time he was wounded, he could hear American voices in the background… outside the bunker. *They'll be back soon…and this time they'll finish the job.* He thought about his options and decided that the best one was to sneak out of the bunker and head for the southern coast. It would be difficult to evade the marines lurking near the airfield…but if he did…then he'd turn east and head down the island's tail to rejoin the men that were holding out there. With a plan formulated in his mind, Okagi took a deep breath and rolled over. *So far...so good*, he thought. Then he tried to push himself up with his left hand, but a searing pain...like nothing he had ever felt before...tore through his body and he passed out. He never noticed the young marine standing at the bunker entrance...watching him intently...pointing his M-1 rifle at the Japanese soldier's head.

CHAPTER 13

Lieutenant Hackett saw the explosion in the first bunker and then watched Sergeant Endres and the two others begin their attack on the second. He saw Private First Class Cohen go down and thought, *keep going…just keep going*, silently commanding the sergeant and Private Scott to finish the job. He lost sight of them as they went behind the bunker…but when dust and smoke billowed out of the embrasure…he knew they had knocked out the second one too. Shortly thereafter, Sergeant Endres and Scott came around the side of the pillbox and Scott headed back to the trench line…using the wood line as cover…while Endres tended to the wounded Cohen.

• • •

"We got 'em, sir," Private Scott said proudly, taking a knee beside the lieutenant.

"Great job, Scott. How's Cohen? Is he hit bad?"

"He caught one in the shoulder, sir. I think he's gonna be okay though. Sergeant Endres was goin' to check on him as soon as I left," Scott explained. "He told me to tell you to bring everybody up."

"Okay. No problem. You wanna show us the way over?"

Scott looked at the lieutenant and a big grin spread across his face. "Sure, sir. I can do that. It's pretty clear as long as we stick to that wood line over on the left. There's a few small huts scattered about in there but they must be empty since no one took a shot at us goin' over and I made it back here safe enough," the private said, confident that he could handle the responsibility.

"Alright, lemme get the rest of the men over here. I want all of us to head over there together," the lieutenant told Private Scott. He turned to tell his runner, but PFC Petraglia had anticipated his instructions and was already heading towards the men on the right. Hackett heard him yell, "Already on it, sir," as he scampered down the trench.

Without waiting, Hackett and Scott headed to the left…where the last two men from Corporal Ingunza's squad were positioned. One man was bracing himself on one knee…watching intently across no-man's-land…his chin resting on the stock of his rifle…a coconut sliver protruding from his mouth. He turned his head slightly as they came up the trench, casually acknowledging their arrival. The lieutenant didn't know the man's name but he did recognize him. He figured the private was probably from one of the companies in Major Schoettel's 3rd Battalion and that he should have been over on Red 1 instead of here. *Wrong beach, wrong battalion, wrong company, wrong platoon, and wrong squad,* Hackett thought reflectively…*and yet he's doing his duty like a good marine. In the end, that's what's gonna be remembered most about this damn battle.*

Pointing to the man with the bad head wound, Hackett said, "Think you can get him down to the beach?"

"Aye aye, suh," the marine replied right back.

"See if you can find a corpsman. A few might have made it in with that unit that's trying to land right now. If you don't have any luck…try to get him over to the pier. Corporal Ingunza looks like he'll be okay in a few minutes…so we'll keep him here with us. He'll have one hell of a headache when he comes to...but he can still fight."

"Yes, suh," Private Drake Hall drawled in a lazy southern accent. The rifleman - he was from a small town north of Atlanta, Georgia - slung his M-1 over his shoulder and gently coaxed the injured marine up from his sitting position. "Come on, Johnny boy, we're gonna get y'all some help," he said, trying to encourage him. As they walked away slowly toward the beach, Hall added, "Don't worry, buddy. I'm gonna take good care of y'all."

The lieutenant watched the two men go and noticed several plumes of smoke rising in the distance. In stark contrast to the blue sky behind them, these spiraling, black clouds marked the spot where Higgins boats had been hit and were burning near the reef. Their demise meant that several large-caliber anti-boat guns were still in business...and they were still wreaking havoc on incoming landing teams. And though the lieutenant couldn't see it from where he was, artillery rounds were still exploding above the vulnerable marines who had left the protection of their boats and were now slogging their way in through waist deep water.

The lieutenant continued to stare at the two men until they were out of sight...and then he turned back around and sat down. Removing his helmet from his baking head, he wiped some sweat from his eyes and rubbed his forehead with the sleeve of his utility shirt. His helmet had a canvas camouflage cover stretched tightly over it...as most of the men's helmets did...and this tended to reduce the heat buildup somewhat...but not much. He left the helmet off for a while...hoping a cool breeze might come by...but none did...so he put the steel pot back on. Then he tended to his throbbing right hand. The metal sliver that had hit his palm was in too deep to pull out, so he took out his k-bar knife and dug it out. Then he wrapped a dressing around it, cut the extra length off with his knife, spliced the end, and tied it off. The wound still hurt, but it was not disabling, so he ignored the pain as best he could.

"Feel any better, lieutenant?" Private Scott asked, having watched the impromptu operation.

"Not really. How 'bout you?" Hackett could see the private staring at his canteen and knew where this conversation was headed.

"I feel okay...I guess. A little thirsty...but other than that...not bad. Ya think they brought any water in yet, sir?" Private Scott asked innocently.

"I don't know. It looks like we're having enough problems just gettin' men in here...let alone water," the lieutenant said. Then, reaching down, he pulled the canteen from his belt and offered it to Scott and the last man from Ingunza's squad and said, "Just don't drink all of it, you two. I gotta save some for the others."

"No thanks, sir. I...ah...I wouldn't do that anyway, sir. I mean... that's all you got...isn't it, sir?" Private Scott was shaking his head no, but the pleading look on his face said otherwise...just like the other marine's as well.

"What happened to yours? You drink all of it already?" the lieutenant asked.

"I used mine up yesterday afternoon with some of the other guys in the squad. They were running low too so I shared what little I had left with them," he explained honestly.

The lieutenant could see how desperate he was so he said, "Go ahead. Take it. You earned it," and he handed the canteen to him this time. "Try to leave some for the others," the lieutenant said again, knowing that severe thirst can make a person pretty greedy even though they don't want to be.

Putting the dull silver container to his lips, Scott took a sip, held the precious liquid in his mouth for a moment, savored it, and then swallowed. Then he quickly recapped it so he wouldn't take another sip and handed the canteen over to the other marine. "Thanks a lot, sir. I was damn near dried out," he said, and then, thinking he might be able to return the favor, added, "you know, sir, if you pull the back flap of your camo cover out, it makes a decent sun block for the back of your neck." He offered the suggestion up since a lot of guys were complaining about getting sunburned and he thought the lieutenant might be in the same fix.

"Yeah, I've seen some of our guys do that. I guess it works pretty well. I don't get sunburned for some reason. Never did. You think I would though…bein' Irish and all. When my folks took us to the beach…to Coney Island…I never had trouble with the sun. Maybe I'm black-Irish, even though I don't look it."

"What's black-Irish, sir?"

"Have you ever heard of the Spanish Armada?" the lieutenant asked.

"Spanish Arm…what, sir?"

"Armada," the lieutenant repeated.

"No, sir.…I don't think I ever heard about that," Scott replied hesitantly.

"Are you ready for a quick history lesson, Mr. Scott?" The lieutenant changed the tone of his voice, trying to mimic the voice of a helpful teacher he had back in high school.

The other marine…having finished his drink…recapped the canteen and handed it over to the lieutenant and he pointed to a jagged hole that was in his canteen pouch. The lieutenant acknowledged it with a nod and the private said, "Just lucky I guess…the round never touched me. I actually thought I had a one way ticket home when it hit me. But I quickly figured out that I wasn't hit…that the wetness I felt wasn't my blood…but the water leaking out of my canteen."

"See that's the problem, sir," Scott continued…bringing the conversation back on point. "I didn't pay much attention during my history lessons in school. The subject didn't interest me much. Then again, nothin' else did either…except shop class. I liked that class. I'm good at working with my hands. My father and I built a hockey rink in our backyard when it got cold out during the winter. I grew up in New Hampshire see…and it can get pretty cold up there. We flooded it with water and it froze just like a pond would. We could ice skate right in my own backyard." Then the private went silent as his mind drifted back to a safer, happier time.

"It could get pretty cold in Brooklyn too. During the winters, my two brothers and I would head over to Swan Boat Lake in Prospect Park and skate on it when it froze over. We did a lot of sleigh riding there too. They were good times….that's for sure."

The other marine…Private First Class Wykoff…was interested in the impromptu discussion and joined in too. "I've experienced cold like that at times…when I went duck hunting up in Arkansas. It can get real miserable sittin' in those blinds in December and January. There's no ice, mind you…but that damp cold has a way of eatin' its way through all your clothes."

"What was that Spanish thing about, sir?" Scott continued…not minding the interruption at all…but steering the conversation back to the history lesson since his curiosity was now piqued.

Lieutenant Hackett then gave the two privates a short synopsis of what happened to one of the most powerful fleets in the history of the world. He explained how Mary Stuart, the catholic Queen of *Scots* – he emphasized the last word in her title – had nominated the King of Spain…Philip II…to be her successor to the English throne. "Naturally," he went on, "this didn't sit too well with the actual Queen of England…Elizabeth the First…who was protestant and a member of the Church of England. She had Mary arrested for plotting against her and then had Mary beheaded in the Tower of London for good measure."

The lieutenant stopped to let that part of the story sink in. When Scott nodded his head, he continued. "Of course, the beheading infuriated Philip since England had been a thorn in Spain's side since Elizabeth had taken over the throne. Philip decided…like the rulers of some countries still do…that war was the best way to resolve the matter. So the King of Spain ordered his fleet of ships to attack and subjugate England in May of the year Fifteen Eighty-Eight."

"What does subjugate mean?" Scott asked, cutting in.

"It means to take over something…like a country…or a group of people and then make slaves of them. It's kind of what the Japanese planned to do to the Chinese when they invaded that country in the Nineteen Thirty-Seven," the officer explained, and then continuing the lesson, he added, "Elizabeth the First then sent Admiral Francis Drake out to defend England with an undersized fleet…just like Nimitz and Halsey did back at Guadalcanal. Well, like the good British Admiral he was, Drake fought the Spanish fleet to a draw in several sea battles in the English Channel."

Hackett stopped again, but this time he looked to see if Petraglia or anyone else was headed their way. Seeing no one…he looked back at Scott and Wykoff and said, "Still with me? I guess it's a longer story than I thought."

"Yes, sir. It's pretty easy to follow…at least the way you tell it. And you know what's weird?" Wykoff said.

"No…what?" the lieutenant replied.

"Drake…that's the name of the guy you just saw…the guy who's taking the guy with the head wound to the pier. He's from F Company. I met him a few times back in New Zealand when all of us were out on pass. The other guy is Donahue…but I never got his first name…or remembered it I guess. Now you don't run into too many guys named Drake…it's a Southern thing…the loftiness of it and all," Wykoff explained.

"Now that is a coincidence…cause that's the first time I've ever heard of someone being called that name too," Hackett agreed.

"He's pretty talented."

"Who?" the lieutenant asked.

"Drake…Hall…the guy I'm talkin' about. We were all together in some bar back in Wellington one Saturday night…and Hall jumps up and talks to one of the guys in the band that was playing. Well, the guy looks him over real close like as he's talking to him…and then gets up and hands him his guitar. Without missing a beat, Hall plays right along with them…and they were a real good band too. "

"There's a slew of talented guys in the Corps. I've met several since I got commissioned. And they're both officers and enlisted alike...talent isn't confined to rank...that's for sure," the lieutenant agreed again. "So how did you end up here, Wykoff?" he said, changing topics.

"I'm Private First Class Jeremy Wykoff, sir. I'm part of the Amphibious Tractor Battalion. I'm a driver...or should I say that I was a driver...of one of the amtracs in the first wave. We were taking the Second Battalion in. I almost made it all the way in when we got hit by something big...cause it blew the whole back end off my amtrac. The few guys that survived scattered and ended up who knows where. I headed over here and made it in without being hit...except for my canteen of course. Like I said...just plain luck I guess. They probably let me go since I was only one guy."

"Did you sign up to be a driver," the lieutenant asked.

"No...of course not," Wykoff scoffed. "I'm a trigger puller, sir. I qualified expert on the marksmanship course...and I wanted to be a Scout-Sniper...but then the Corps found out I was a good with engines and mechanical stuff and I got assigned to this new battalion. I had more experience than most of the guys to boot...and we didn't have enough much time to train everyone properly. I guess the idea of bringing the guys into the beach in these amtracs was sort of a new technique they wanted to try out. Doesn't look like it worked out like the generals envisioned, did it."

"Not exactly," Lieutenant Hackett answered dryly...knowing that Wykoff was indeed right. "So where are you from? Home wise?" the lieutenant continued.

"Me, sir. I'm from Louisiana...outside of Baton Rouge. I love it there. Did a lot of fishing and duck hunting growing up...which explains why I'm a deadly shot. Ducks hate me!" Wykoff smiled at the omission...and Hackett smiled right back...finding the young kid's enthusiasm and cockiness uplifting.

"What about the rest of that story, sir?" Scott asked impatiently...cutting in suddenly.

"Oh yeah. Where was I? Okay…I remember. Well that Spanish commander got frustrated and ordered the Armada to return to Spain, but this time he chose a route that took his ships north… around Scotland…and then back down the west coast of England to get home. Like most plans though, his turned into a disaster too… sort like what we got here," the lieutenant added, sweeping his arm wide to encompass the entire cove and reef area. "Believe it or not, the Armada ran into a violent storm as they rounded Scotland and the entire formation was broken up. Many of the Spanish ships were badly damaged and they ended up crashing along the coast of Ireland. And that," the lieutenant said, sounding satisfied, "is the story of the destruction of the Spanish Armada."

"Where'd you learn all that stuff, lieutenant?" Scott asked, still intrigued.

"I graduated the Naval Academy in Forty-One. I took all the history courses I could. I liked military history the best. For some reason it came easy to me and I always did well in it," Hackett answered.

"I never knew that any of that stuff ever happened. But what about the Irish bein' black part? You didn't mention what that was," Private Scott pressed.

"Oh yeah…the black-Irish. You were paying attention. That's good. Keep it up and you might actually live through all of this," the lieutenant said, complementing the young marine. "Well," Hackett said, continuing the story, "the Spanish that survived were able to- -" but he stopped when he saw Petraglia and ten others scrambling down the trench toward him. The lieutenant saw PFC Feeney among the familiar faces, still smiling and quite dirty. He nodded to him as he came up and Feeney returned the gesture…proud to be recognized. The lieutenant also acknowledged PFC Mornston and the private tapped the front lip of his helmet with his index and middle finger in a casual salute.

"Here's the deal," Hackett said, and the men crept up closer to listen. "Scott says that those two pillboxes have been knocked out.

Sergeant Endres is still up there so we're going to head over too. Scott here will lead us over. We're gonna use the wood line on the left for cover. Scott said that it was clear when he came over, but watch for snipers on the left flank. Some may have worked their way towards us in the meantime. Also, that big Nip bunker complex is still active…so stay low going over. They're the ones that probably dropped that mortar fire in on us before. No sense letting 'em know they didn't get all of us with that last barrage."

All the men nodded in agreement, having just seen the remains of the men who had been blown apart by the explosions. It was a sobering sight, and they felt both lucky and guilty at the same time. They knew alltoo well that a slight change in the deflection of one of those rounds could have left them lying dead back there…but… due to the luck of the draw…they were still alive and the others weren't.

"And spread out," Lieutenant Hackett ordered. "I don't want to see any of you bunched up. One round can take out a whole group of us if we're too close to one another. Scott will be in the lead goin' over. Then Feeney will follow with his men. Petraglia and I will go next. Mornston will follow with his boys to cover our backs."

Then, as if on cue, Corporal Ingunza came to and mumbled, "What the hell just happened? Where's…my squad?"

Everyone glanced at the bewildered corporal and their looks told him what he needed to know.

"But how can that…be?" Ingunza pleaded. "How come I didn't…get hit?"

After a painful silence, the lieutenant finally told him what he thought had happened. "I watched you when you left the trench and you made it several yards. Then it looked like you tripped and you hit the deck. That's when the mortar round hit. The fall saved your life. The others were caught right in the open and never had a chance."

The corporal sighed audibly, amazed that a dumb mistake like that had kept him alive.

The lieutenant waited a second or two and said, "You think you're ready to get back into the fight?"

"Affirmative, sir," Ingunza answered immediately, and then he added icily, "I got a damn score to settle with these Japs! I hope to hell they're ready is all I gotta say." With that, he picked up an M-1 rifle from the ground - it was Private Donahue's...the marine who had been wounded in the eye - and began dusting it off. As he did so, the other men checked their weapons too, making sure they were loaded and the safeties were off. Once that was done, the lieutenant shouted, "Okay...let's go!"

CHAPTER 14

Eyeing Lieutenant Hackett and the others coming up, Sergeant Endres said, "They're almost here," to Private First Class Cohen, who was laying against the left side of the bunker. He watched the marines make quick dashes and then squat or jump down...taking cover behind the trunks of splintered palm trees that were still standing or the sheared-off top sections that were lying on the ground everywhere. Sometimes they disappeared completely when they threw themselves into a shell hole or hid among some piece of battlefield debris that they found along their way. It could be an empty oil or gasoline drum or a bent section of corrugated tin roofing or siding that had come from a building that had been blown apart nearby... or a bunch of stacked wooden boxes that were marked with Japanese hieroglyphics that no one could understand. The men basically hid behind everything and anything that could shield their movements from the prying eyes of the Japanese artillery spotters, machine gunners, and snipers who were looking to kill them.

As point man, Private Scott led the group over...and thus he was the first one to get there. He slid in next to Sergeant Endres and the sergeant said, "Keep an eye on Cohen...he's actin' a little funny." As the others came up, the sergeant motioned them to find cover, and then he ran over to brief the lieutenant.

In the meantime, Scott...checking on Cohen as he had been told... suddenly tensed when he heard a strange noise coming from inside the pillbox. Getting up, he looked around the corner and didn't see anything so he approached the exit carefully. He raised his rifle and edged his head just inside the opening and saw that one of the Jap gunners was still alive. The man was in bad shape, laying in a pool of blood, with part of one leg nearly blown off below the knee. Scott saw that he was struggling to roll over and then he seemed to pass out and fall back. Scott raised his rifle and was about to finish the enemy soldier off, but something made him hold off. Instead, he rushed over to him and lifted the man's head off the dirty floor of the bunker...cradling him. The man was drenched in his own blood and Scott could tell that he didn't have very long to live. The enemy soldier opened his eyes and focused on the American who was holding him. Intuitively, the private could tell that the wounded man sensed what was happening to him. He murmured a word several times and Scott thought that he must be asking for water. Scott looked at the man apologetically and tried to show him that he was out of water himself. "I don't have any. I'd give you some if I had it, Mac," he said sadly. A slight smile crossed the Japanese soldier's face and Scott wondered if he was trying to tell the American that he appreciated the kindness Scott was showing him. Not knowing what to do next, Scott yelled, "Hey, sarge, one of these Japs is still alive in here. What should I do?"

But Sergeant Endres was too far away to hear him. He was over with the lieutenant explaining how they had taken out the two bunkers. Finishing up, Endres said, "Private Cohen was our only casualty. He got hit going after the second one. It's a shoulder wound... but he should make it."

Private First Class Petraglia, kneeling right behind the lieutenant, was listening to the sergeant's report and went over to check on Cohen himself. Petraglia knelt down next to him and saw that

Cohen was hit much worse than the sergeant realized. A thin trail of blood was now running out of the side of the private's mouth and his eyes were closed. *He's already slipping into shock!* Petraglia thought to himself. *The bullet must have nicked an artery and is causing some internal bleeding that we can't see.* "This man might not make it," he yelled to the lieutenant, "he's bleeding to death…and there's not a damn thing we can do about it out here."

"Whatta ya mean?" Endres yelled back, seemingly confused. "I was just talking to him. He's hurt…but not that bad." Both Endres and the lieutenant got up and ran over.

"See for yourself. That shoulder wound is bleeding inside… where we can't see it," Petraglia explained. "He might last another hour or two, but no more than that."

• • •

Back inside the bunker, Private Scott looked down at the wounded man and wondered who he was and what he was like. He also noticed how tall he was…in fact, he was the biggest Jap Scott had seen so far. *I didn't realize Japs could get so big,* he thought, and then he searched his pockets but didn't find anything that could identify him. Okagi moaned a little, and Scott said soothingly, "Don't worry. You'll be alright," and then he called out again for someone to help him. Okagi smiled weakly once again and he gripped the marine's arm and gave it a squeeze as he mumbled something Scott couldn't understand. Scott sensed that the man was really hurting…so he called out again that he needed help.

Kneeling beside Cohen, Sergeant Endres heard Private Scott's plea from inside the bunker. Without looking at the lieutenant, Sergeant Endres calmly walked away and entered the bunker. He saw Scott holding the wounded man and a rage overwhelmed him. "Put that Jap down and get away from him!" Endres spat out.

"What…you want me to just leave him like this?" Scott responded, not knowing what had just happened outside.

"You heard me. Now drop him and stand aside!"

"But look," Scott shouted, pointing to the man's shirt, "he's wearing chevrons...so he must be an NCO...just like you!"

"Get out of the way," Endres snarled, "that damn Nip could have a grenade hidden underneath him. The lousy Japs did that all the time on the *Canal*...and they killed more than one dumbass like yourself...so back away."

"I'd be dead already if he did," Scott pleaded.

Scott could see, almost feel, the hatred in Endres' eyes so he laid the man down gently, stood up, and slowly backed away from the injured Japanese soldier. "Whatta ya going do with him?" he asked, dreading the answer.

"Just get outside...and let me handle it," Endres said...his voice suddenly calmer.

The private slid past Sergeant Endres and stepped back into the sunshine of the day. Strangely, despite all the slaughter he had witnessed in the last day and a half, the thought of what was about to happen to this injured, helpless Japanese man bothered him for some reason. He hesitated for a moment, decided he couldn't let it happen, and turned back to put a stop to it. Too late, he saw the flash and heard the rip of a Thompson submachine gun inside the dark confines of the bunker.

• • •

Lieutenant Hackett knew right away what needed to be done for Private Cohen. When Endres came back out of the bunker, his Thompson was still smoking. The lieutenant looked at it...knew what had happened...thought about saying something...and then dismissed it. The lieutenant then told Endres that he wanted one man from his squad to serve as a stretcher bearer with Petraglia...who mumbled, "Oh, great," when he heard what his new assignment was.

"We don't have a stretcher, sir. Where are we gonna get one from out here?" Sergeant Endres said skeptically.

"Find one. Or make one. I don't care how you do it, but get one. We've gotta get Cohen back to the beach," Lieutenant Hackett responded firmly, no mistaking the authority in his voice.

"Right, sir…I'll get on it right now." Endres looked around, spotted the man he wanted, and waved him over. "Go with Petraglia there," he instructed, "and just do what he tells you to do."

"Aye aye, sergeant," the marine replied obligingly.

Petraglia looked the man over, seemed pleased with the pick, and said, "Follow me. We gotta go find a stretcher for Cohen there. And we gotta find one fast."

The two men headed for the first bunker and disappeared inside it. They rummaged around the dead bodies but the darkness made it hard to see. Finding nothing useful, the two left and ran over to the second one. Petraglia entered first and saw that it was much like the one they had just left…with dead Nips laying on the floor and empty ammo boxes and weapons scattered around along with a few other odds and ends that soldiers accumulate over time. It was essentially the same except for one thing…there was a canvas cot set up in one of the corners. It had been holed by some of the grenade fragments, but it was still serviceable. "Help me drag this thing outta here," Petraglia said…and then added, "it's just what the doctor ordered."

"Look at that," Lieutenant Hackett said, amazed. Sergeant Endres looked up and saw the two men lugging the cot across the sandy expanse between the two bunkers.

"I'll be damned," he exclaimed. "I'll never second guess the ingenuity of a marine ever again. I didn't look in that one after we blew it up. Who woulda known?"

The lieutenant helped Petraglia lift Cohen onto the makeshift stretcher and told him to do the best he could in getting him help. Once Cohen was taken care of, Petraglia and the other man…Private Joe Agresta…were to hunt up some engineers and bring them back with them. The lieutenant stressed that they would need some demolitions and flame thrower men if they were to have any chance at all of knocking out the big bunker complex to the right of them. "Explain our situation over here and hopefully someone will come back with you," Hackett offered as they left.

"Okay, sir, we'll try our best," Petraglia said, well aware of the predicament they were up against.

"I know you will...that's why I ask a lot of you," the lieutenant shot back, complementing him. "We'll be right here waiting on you. Without those engineers, we'd be wasting our time tryin' to take on that strongpoint. See ya when you get back."

CHAPTER 15

Back along the seawall near the middle of Red 2, First Lieutenant Hawkins stood up suddenly and looked down towards the pier. Refreshed after taking a ten minute break to catch his wind, he announced, "Everybody stay here. I'm goin' back to the CP to let them know what we've done here. Don't do anything crazy while I'm gone."

"Sir, can I take a look at that chest wound you got?" Pharmacist Mate Fumai asked, hoping that the leader of the Scout-Snipers would say yes.

"I'm fine. It looks a lot worse than it feels. Believe me," the lieutenant replied casually, and he headed down the beach in the direction of the pier. As he walked along, a burning rage consumed him once again. Up and down the beach were dead marines...and the closer he got to the pier, the more there were. Most of them lay in groups...probably killed by a mortar explosion or the sweeping blast from a machine gun. And Major Hays' battalion was still being slaughtered out in the lagoon...which added to the carnage. *I haven't done enough,* he thought angrily. *I'll kill these Japs one by one with my own bare hands if I have to!*

Anyone who served with the lieutenant recognized his deep love for the Marine Corps and the men around him. However…only a select few were privy to a physical condition that set him apart from the rest of the marines…and it certainly played a key role in driving his devotion to the Corps. At five-foot-ten and one hundred and fifty pounds, Lieutenant Hawkins was built like most of the officers and enlisted men that populated the ranks at the time. However… unlike the rest…his body was badly scared as a result of his being severely burned in a childhood accident. Being *different* from the other boys his age had presented its own set of challenges and frustrations when he was young, but nothing could prepare him for the disappointment and embarrassment he would experience as a young man when he tried to enlist to in the Army…and then the Navy…in an effort to serve his Country. In a stinging blow to his confidence and self-esteem, both services rejected him outright…and each cited his disfigurement as the main reason for their decision. Crushed, Hawkins went down to the Marine Corps recruiting office and pled his case to the men inside. Instead of turning him away…like the other branches had…the recruiters here welcomed him with open arms. *These guys must be pretty desperate…but they still want me just the same…and that's all that matters!* he thought happily at the time…and from that day forward he dedicated his life to the serving the Marine Corps since they had decided to accept him despite his physical deformities. He also swore that he would spend the rest of his days vindicating that decision…and his performance on Guadalcanal had done just that: he had been awarded a battlefield promotion for heroism under fire. And now he had the chance to show his appreciation yet again…on Betio…and nothing was going to stop him from doing it. Those who knew about his dark, little secret realized that he would keep fighting until every last Jap was dead…or until he had breathed his last breath…which ever came first. That was the debt this fearless marine felt he owed his beloved Corps…and he intended to pay it back…no matter what.

Striding along confidently, oblivious to the bullets flying by, Lieutenant Hawkins was almost at the pier when some movement in the distance caught his eye. He noticed two unarmed marines coming towards him. The men were checking the marine bodies lying on the beach to see if any of them were alive. If they were dead, one man would pause over the body for a moment...mouth something... and then moved on to the next one. Hawkins watched the men do this over and over again, apparently unfazed by the enemy fire all around them. Lieutenant Hawkins kept on walking...and then he realized who they were.

"Hey, preacher," Hawkins yelled out irreverently, "I thought you were a Navy corpsman at first. What the hell is a chaplain like yourself doin' out here? Tryin' to get your ass shot off? I'm sure Lee there has plans for the rest of his life...even if you don't."

"Oh... it's you, Hawk. Good to see you too! I hope your day is going well," Reverend Aaron Johnson replied, smiling. He slid over to another man...rolled him over gently...and seeing that he was still alive, he signaled to a marine crouching by the seawall. The young marine sprinted over and grabbed the injured marine under one of his arms. The chaplain's assistant...a young man named "RJ" Lee from Philadelphia...grabbed the injured man under the other arm and together they dragged him to the safety of the wall.

"If you're not careful there, reverend, you'll get picked off by a damn Nip sniper. Or your young protégé will be. These damn Japs mean business. It won't do your flock any good if you get yourself killed out here," Hawkins advised.

The chaplain looked up again, intrigued by the lieutenant's provocative comment. "Oh, that's alright, Hawk. Chaplains aren't supposed to live forever you know...just like Jesus wasn't. And if it happens...I'll be in good company...in more ways than one," the small-town preacher from Boaz, Alabama answered back.

"How about doin' some crawling then. I saw you from fifty yards away. If I can...then the Japs certainly can too. They don't give a rat's ass that you're a chaplain. You're just another lousy American to them," the lieutenant advised.

"I appreciate your concern, Hawk. But my job is to save souls out here...those that I can get too. I can't do that with my face in the sand...now can I?"

"I guess not, reverend...guess not. I'm on my way to the Regimental CP. You need me to tell 'em anything while I'm there?" Hawkins asked.

"Just tell them they're in my prayers," Johnson answered back passionately. "But I want you to do me a favor for me," the chaplain added.

"Sure, padre...what is it?"

"Clean up the lingo...you'll do that for me won't you? You know our Lord hates bad language...so humor me and Him and drop the expletives, okay," Chaplain Johnson asked sincerely.

"That I can do, reverend...since my mama didn't raise me to talk that way. Sorry about that," Hawkins replied, and he moved off...leaving the chaplain and his assistant behind with the dead and wounded. Then...despite the noise of the battle...Hawkins heard the chaplain yell to him, "And God Bless you too, Hawk!" The lieutenant waved his hand in appreciation and kept going...happy to have His Creator's protection from the dangers that lay ahead.

• • •

"It's been a while...you think he made it back okay?" one marine asked another.

Pharmacist Mate Fumai looked over at the scout-sniper who had summed up what everyone was wondering about. The one asking the question looked young...but the other one was a veteran...of that he was sure. This man...a sergeant...was leaning against the coconut log wall...using the sturdy structure to brace himself as he fired his bolt-action Springfield rifle. He had built an effective firing position for himself by piling up some debris along the seawall above him. He was scanning across no-man's-land through the sniper scope on his rifle…and he was squeezing off individual shots when a target presented itself. Hearing the question, he stopped what he was doing and glanced down at the marine.

"What are you…some kind of moron? Of course he made it back there. And he'll make it back. You seriously think there's a Jap on this island that's gonna be able to kill the skipper?" he asked skeptically. The marine he addressed didn't reply back…he just sat there with a grave look on his face.

The silence was eventually broken by the crack of the sniper's rifle. "That's one less Jap we'll have to deal with," the sergeant said dryly, his eye never leaving the scope.

Fumai got on a knee and raised his head up carefully along the log barrier, trying to see what the sergeant was shooting at. "I can't see a thing," he said, and sat back down. "You think they're dug in like this all over the island?" he asked Private First Class George.

"Probably so," George answered. "This outgoing fire is as heavy as it was yesterday…and yet I haven't seen but maybe three or four Nips since I landed. That's it. The rest must be holed up underground. We're gonna have to dig 'um out like you do with a chigger ya get walkin' in the woods back home. I hate chiggers."

"Can we do it, Bob? You don't think we can still lose this thing, do you?" Fumai asked, concerned.

"It'll be tough…make no mistake about that. But we're gonna win…and I'll tell you why," George said. "I saw a good omen early this morning…before I got here. You see we have a mascot for our company," and the private went on to tell Fumai about the saga of *Siwash*…the heroic duck from A-1-10.

Siwash was one of two ducklings that had been won by two men from his company at a carnival in Wellington when the 2nd Division was recuperating back on New Zealand. Early on, the marines fed the ducks beer…and as they got bigger…they gave them their leftovers from the mess hall. They must have liked the stuff because the two ducks continued to grow bigger and bigger…and they soon reached the size of a suitable meal. And then tragedy struck...or an axe actually...and one of them mysteriously disappeared one weekend. *Siwash* survived however and was soon adopted by everyone in the company. Besides drinking, the marines taught the big, black-and-white-feathered duck to fight and defend itself. And it learned to retaliate pretty well since the hung-over marines would antagonize him as he waddled and quacked his way through the barracks in the early hours of the morning looking for a meal. Anticipating that they would be leaving New Zealand, one of the men even built a cage for *Siwash* and they carried him aboard the ship when they finally pulled out.

"When I reached the main pier yesterday, I saw *Siwash's* cage sitting up there empty-like. Someone must have dragged it off the Higgins boat and let him out. I guess the guy figured that *Siwash's* odds of making it through this were as good as anyone else's," George said, pointing out to the end of the long pier.

All of a sudden, a mortar round exploded several yards inland, and everyone covered up as sand showered down on them.

"They must be tryin' to range in on us," the young marine...a private first class...exclaimed...sounding worried again. "Why don't you give that sniping a rest for a while, sarge? You're probably just pissing 'em off."

The sergeant grumbled, "Shut up, private. If you keep annoying me, I'm gonna make you get up and run back and forth behind me to draw fire. I'm sure I can get one or two of them that way."

"And what about me?" the private asked suspiciously.

"Oh, they might get ya...but you'd die happy...knowin' you performed an invaluable service for the Marine Corps. How's that sound?" The sergeant looked over at George and Fumai and winked at them...hoping they appreciated his sarcasm.

"I shoulda enlisted in the Navy...like my father said," the private first class moaned...and everyone started laughing.

"So what happened to the duck?" Fumai asked, intrigued by George's incredible story. "Was he killed on the pier?"

"No, he's still alive. I saw him before I got here...believe it or not. I was restin' against the seawall with a bunch of other guys and outta nowhere we heard all this racket. I got up and there was good old *Siwash* fighting this Jap rooster just over the seawall. *Siwash's* head was bleeding from the pecking of that damn rooster, but *Siwash* caught him in his beak and tossed him like a rag doll. That Jap bird took off real quick...heading for friendly lines as fast as it could go. I guess he knew his goose would've been cooked...so to speak... if he had stayed around there any longer. Well *Siwash* reared up and started flapping his wings...like he was declaring himself the winner of the battle! He was obviously very proud of his victory over that enemy bird and we all cheered right along with him. Then someone grabbed him and got him under the cover of the seawall. So it seems that *Siwash* will live to fight another day."

The pharmacist mate looked astonished. "Are you serious?" he said, not really sure if he could believe the tale he had just heard.

"As God is my judge," Bob George replied. "And I'll tell ya what. Right after that, several guys who had been laying around doing nothin' got up and started fighting back. Hell...they figured if a marine duck could do it...why couldn't they!"

"So a duck...a marine mascot...beat up a Jap rooster? Out here... in the midst of all this?" Fumai pressed.

"I'm telling ya I saw it with my own two eyes this morning. You wait an' see. When word gets out about it, the generals will probably award that damn duck a medal."

Another shot rang out, followed by, "Ahh damn...missed the son-of-a-bitch!"

The sergeant remained standing, reloading, but the marines below inched closer to the seawall, bracing themselves for a retaliatory mortar round or burst of machine gun fire. When none came...they all relaxed again.

Although the volume of fire directed at them had slackened somewhat, the noise of the battle had not diminished to their left and right. Fumai and George continued to sit with their backs to the wall and watched the activity in the water beyond them. They could easily see out to the reef and occasionally a wayward Higgins boat would pull in and drop its ramp. It was sickening to see the men emerge from the boat and be taken under fire immediately. The Japanese gunners were expert marksmen by now and they had the reef zeroed in perfectly. The marines that weren't hit coming out of the boat fanned out and started wading through the chest deep water. As if the Japanese fire wasn't bad enough, climbing over the coral was no picnic either…since its jagged, razor-sharp edges shred uniforms and cut deep into the skin along the legs, arms, and hands. In some places, the water covering the reef was much shallower… only one to two feet in some cases…and the marines tried to avoid these patches. When they couldn't though…they'd get down on their hands and knees and crawl or crouch down and duck walk over. The marines that survived this bloody gauntlet emerged from the water shocked and dazed and their first instinct was to head for the cover of the seawall.

One marine broke this mold however. George spotted the man first and tapped Fumai on the arm. Pointing to the man, George asked, "Look at this guy. Think he'll make it?"

The pharmacist mate scanned the water and saw the object of George's attention. It was a lone, determined marine…drudging in through chest-deep water. Both men's eyes locked on this one man now and they watched in awe as he came on despite the firestorm around him. The marine had his rifle slung across his back and he was holding a beach marker - a long pole with a pennant attached to its end - with his hands over his head. The man was responsible for planting the pole in a designated area on the beach so the Higgins boats approaching the reef could orient on it and drop their troops off at the correct section of the beach and then the marines ashore would head for it as well. This marine knew…but didn't care…that the boats couldn't make it past the reef however. He had been given an important mission to accomplish…and nothing was going to stop him from carrying it out. The Japanese gunners were also aware of the marine's mission…and how important it was…so they concentrated all their fire on him to take him out.

George and Fumai watched in fascination as the man plodded on…the water level getting lower with each step…until it was finally splashing around his knees…while machine gun bullets smacked into the water around him the entire time. Undaunted, the marine forged on…seeming to have some sort of protective halo around him…for other men were being shot down nearby. George and Fumai's excitement continued to grow with each step the marine took…especially as he got closer to them. They could see his face now…he was a young kid…probably no more than eighteen…and he had a determined, steely expression on his face. As he reached the beach, he hunkered down slightly…fully aware that the enemy gunners were directing all their fire his way. Both George and Fumai began to cheer for him, but the marine didn't pay any attention to them. Instead, the valiant marine trudged on undaunted and was almost to the seawall when he was finally hit. He was knocked backwards and fell flat on his back. Incredibly, the wounded boy got up…and started for the seawall again. George could see a dark splotch of red in the middle of his chest and he held out his hand…hoping the marine would take it and get down. The young marine ignored George's gesture and he continued to advance…the completion of his mission the foremost thing on his mind. He was almost at the seawall when he was hit again. This time he caught a machine gun burst and he was driven further back…almost to the water's edge. The man struggled to his feet yet again and staggered forward…never relinquishing his hold on the beach marker. He took a few more steps and then started to fall…the deadly wounds taking effect…and using the last bit of strength he had…he drove the pole into the soft sand in front of the seawall…and died.

PFC George and Corpsman Fumai stared at the marine...awe-struck. The young marine was laying there lifeless...only a few feet away...his eyes wide open...yet seeing at nothing. And despite it all... he had never let go off the very object that had marked him for death.

George looked at him...and then at Fumai...and said, "Look at that...his hands are still grasping that pennant. And he put it right where it was supposed to go."

Fumai looked up at the yellow flag that was flapping in the breeze...and said nothing...too overcome with emotion.

George...never at a loss for words...explained it best and said, "You were wondering if we'll win this battle. What you just saw tells you all you need to know."

Fumai ran the image of what he had just seen through his mind one more time...and said, "You know you're absolutely right...with guys like that...with that kind of courage...nothing will stop us from taking this island...nothing at all."

• • •

"I told you he'd make it back."

The young scout-sniper sat up and followed the sergeant's gaze down the beach. Sure enough...there was Lieutenant Hawkins... striding towards them...just like before. Only this time, there were several other men with him. "Hey, it looks like he's got Sergeant Hooper with him this time...and some of our other guys too." The private seemed quite happy that some reinforcements had finally arrived.

Lieutenant Hawkins had run into his platoon sergeant at the Regimental CP. Gunnery Sergeant Jared Hooper had just completed an attack against several Jap machine gun emplacements that were hidden in some of the airplane revetments that ran along the taxiway in the Red 2 area. Their accurate fire had stalled the marine advance in that area and prevented the expansion of the beachhead forward across the airfield. Hooper and the scout-snipers went forward and knocked the guns out, but they had also taken some casualties in the process. The gunnery sergeant had returned from that mission and was telling Colonel Shoup that it was okay for Lieutenant Colonel Jordan to move his men into the area when his platoon commander walked into the CP.

The two men grabbed each other by the shoulders and shook one another, happy to see each other still alive. Then the gunnery sergeant turned back to the colonel and said, "Sir, tell Lieutenant Colonel Jordan that it's imperative that he get his men into that area as quick as possible. We knocked several guns out over there...and it should be good for a little while. But it's seems like the Japs have an inexhaustible supply of men over there. If Jordan doesn't occupy those position quick like...the Japs are gonna filter right back into them."

Colonel Shoup admired Gunnery Sergeant Hooper immensely and he gave the platoon sergeant of the Scout-Snipers his full attention. "Thanks, gunny," he said, "I've been trying to light a fire under Jordan all morning...but he's really got his hands full. His men are all over the place...and he's doing the best he can with what I've dumped in his lap. I'll try to push some other units over that way as well." Then he turned and yelled, "Tom, come over here," to his operations officer...or Regimental-3...Major Culhane. The major came over and the colonel told him all that the gunnery sergeant had just related to him about the western taxiway area. "Get somebody over there now...or we'll have to fight the same battle all over again later on. Understood."

Culhane replied, "Yes, sir, I'm on it," and he left to go talk to another officer who had just called out his name.

The colonel turned away too...leaving Gunnery Sergeant Hooper and First Lieutenant Hawkins all alone. "Was it that rough over there?" Hawkins asked, having listened in to the conversation.

"It's like the Japs have a tunnel from one end of the island to the other and they can move their guys around wherever they're needed at the moment. We kept killin' them over there and it always seemed like they had more on the way. What about you…how'd it go on the beach down there?"

"Not too bad…we knocked out a few bunkers. There's one or two left…and then that sector should be all clear. At least it looks that way. I don't know if anyone has done anything west of there… so that's probably gonna be our next task."

"I guess we'll just have to keep killin' these bastards until there's none left to kill," the gunnery sergeant said dryly…and then he noticed all the blood stains on the lieutenant's uniform shirt. Since he knew his platoon commander as well as anyone else in the Marine Corps did…he didn't make a big deal about it. He only asked if the lieutenant felt okay and Hawkins replied that he felt as fit as a fiddle.

Colonel Shoup returned suddenly and called the lieutenant over to him. Colonel Shoup had a special affinity for Lieutenant Hawkins…like a father has for a son…and he always kept tabs on him and his condition. The colonel noticed the bloodstains on the lieutenant's uniform too…just like Hooper had…but he still asked Hawkins if he was up for another mission.

"Ready as ever, colonel," he replied confidently, "Me and my scouts can handle anything you got."

Colonel Shoup looked him over critically…decided he was okay… and gave the Scout-Snipers their next critical mission: an attack was needed against a troublesome complex of five bunkers along the west side of Red Beach 2…just what the lieutenant had anticipated. The colonel explained that these pillboxes were cutting Major Hays' battalion to ribbons and they were making any further landings in this area impossible unless they were eliminated. Hawkins looked at the colonel's map and saw that this complex was just west of the three bunkers he had just taken out. "No problem, sir. We'll get it done…or die tryin'," he told the colonel. Then the lieutenant turned to Hooper and said, "Make sure the men have plenty of grenades. Other than flame throwers…which we don't have…they're the best thing we can use against these Jap bunkers." Gunnery Sergeant Hooper heard the order and trotted off to the supply area with the rest of his men - they had been resting not far from the CP - to load up on grenades. The lieutenant watched him leave and then turned back to the colonel. "Any chance we can get some artillery support on this one, colonel?"

"I wish I could give you some, son, but everything we got is tied up already. Like everything else around here, we're short on seventy-fives too. Only a few of them made it in last night and they're working on the airfield and that large complex at the base of the cove. Those bunkers you're going after are the last nuts we've got to crack along Red 2. Once we're rid of them…we can go after the *Pocket* directly." The colonel jabbed his finger at the spot on the map and looked at the lieutenant…gauging him. "It's real important that you clean this place out for us, Hawk. We've got to open up these beaches so we can get some reinforcements in here in one piece. I figure the Japs could still have as many as three thousand men left…most of them to the east of us here. We still don't have enough people ashore to finish this thing up effectively. Hell, it looks like we'll be lucky if we get half of Major Hays' men in now. Half of a damn battalion…that's it. We can't win with those numbers," Colonel Shoup explained grimly.

"We'll get the job done for you, sir. Don't worry about that," the lieutenant replied, still confident.

"Well get going…but don't get yourself killed in the process okay. I've lost too many officers as it is. We've already got sergeants and corporals leading platoons in some sectors. The kids are doing a magnificent job…but we need some experience out there too," the colonel requested.

"I can't make ya any promises on that one, sir, but I'll do my best… how's that?" Hawkins then gave the colonel a thumbs-up sign for assurance. Then he turned away and headed towards the pier where his small band of warriors was patiently waiting…ready for their next fight.

• • •

Another reunion took place when Lieutenant Hawkins, Gunnery Sergeant Hooper, and the other scout-snipers met up with their buddies along the seawall. Some of them hadn't seen each another since the morning before and they were eager to find out what had happened to the rest of the platoon. Everyone was asking the same questions about the men who were missing: *Has anyone seen so-and-so?* Or *is so-and-so still alive?* Or *I think so-and-so might be wounded...did anyone else see him get hit?* They were followed by the typical answers...some disappointing...*No...he didn't make it...*or...*I saw him get hit...he's done for...*or...*Oh him...he's okay...he's just wounded.* And before long, the men had pieced together the status and whereabouts of just about everyone in the Scout-Sniper platoon.

Sitting off to the side, George and Fumai watched the happy gathering enviously, outsiders still. "I wonder how many guys in my platoon made it in last night...and where they are now," George said.

Scott looked at him and said, "Funny, I was asking myself the same thing. Seeing these guys so happy made me think about them. I hope they're doing okay." But they never got a chance to finish their conversation since Lieutenant Hawkins said, "Okay everybody... gather around," and he began explaining the situation on the island and what the colonel wanted them to do.

PFC George's spirits got a boost when he heard the lieutenant mention the part about the artillery unit engaging the cove complex and the airfield defenses. If the seventy-fives had made it in...then it was quite possible that some of his unit had as well...since his platoon's job was to set up a perimeter around the big guns and defend them against an enemy infantry attack. When the lieutenant was done with the briefing, George asked, "Sir, did you say that there are seventy-fives set up and firing?" to confirm his thought process.

"Yup, they're dug in along the beach...I saw them myself," the lieutenant responded.

George then explained his situation and asked the officer if he could head back to see if he could find his own unit.

"I hate to lose you…but sure…you can take off. Just be careful heading back to the pier. The fire is still pretty heavy in some areas. Thanks for your help this morning. I hope you make it back to that farm of yours in the Ozarks," Hawkins said, appreciating the young private's earlier efforts…and understanding his desire to link up with his buddies.

"Thanks, sir. It was a pleasure helpin' ya out. I won't forget you," George replied, surprised and humbled that the officer had remembered where he came from.

"I suppose you want to go too…right, doc?" the lieutenant asked, turning to Pharmacist Mate Fumai. "I won't order you to stay but I'd certainly like to have ya around for this next job we have," he added.

"I'll stay, sir, but only if you promise me that you'll let me look at those wounds you got," the corpsman answered, trying to strike a deal with the lieutenant.

The lieutenant glanced down at the blood stains on his dust-caked uniform, gently probing the area where the utility shirt had been slashed, and winced when he touched the punctures where the metal grenade fragments had penetrated his skin. "Okay, that's a deal, doc," he said, grimacing in pain, "but not until we've solved this little problem ahead of us. Good enough?"

"Deal, sir," Fumai beamed, happy with the compromise.

PFC George listened to the exchange and then grabbed Fumai by the arm when Hawkins turned away. "I'm gonna head back now," he said hesitantly, "…you know…to see if I can find my guys."

"Yeah…I heard you ask the lieutenant," Fumai responded stoically. "I hope they're back there. I'm sure you'll find them if they are."

"Thanks…and I hope I see ya again at the end of this. I promise I'll buy ya some pogey bait on the ship when we meet up," George said, hoping the corpsman would understand why he wanted to leave.

"Good deal," Fumai feigned. "That's the second good deal I've struck in two minutes… that must be some sort of record I imagine. I'll make sure I look you up aboard the transport and I'm gonna take you up on it. In the meantime, you take care of yourself. I'm sure glad I got to meet you. I probably woulda left already too if these scouts were the only guys I had for company," Fumai joked, nodding at the private and sergeant who were still jawing at one another...same as before.

George laughed and said, "Yeah, I hate to leave ya with those two."

Fumai laughed too and stuck his hand out. George grabbed it tightly and gave him a firm handshake. "Well...it's now or never I guess," George said, getting up.

"Bon voyage, buddy!" Fumai replied encouragingly, and George dashed off, hugging the seawall, crouching as he went. Fumai kept his eye on him until he was almost out of sight and then turned his attention to the lieutenant and his men...who were getting ready to move out. *Strange*, he thought, *I wonder if it was always like this in combat...where you spend three hours with a guy you've never met before...and then feel like you've known him all your life.* Little did the corpsman know that Bob George was thinking the exact same thing as he made his way to the pier.

• • •

Before long, Lieutenant Hawkins and the scout-snipers were working their way westward towards their intended target. They hadn't gone very far...forty yards or so...when they sensed they were near it...since the amount of outgoing fire increased significantly. It was so thick in fact that some of the men joked that they could actually reach up over the seawall and touch it as it went by. Yet they moved on...undeterred. After another twenty yards or so, the lieutenant put his hand up and the whole group halted. He and Gunnery Sergeant Hooper poked their heads up carefully and surveyed the layout of the bunkers. "This is it," the lieutenant said venomously, and Hooper gave him a glance, knowing full well what his tone implied.

"How do ya wanna handle it?" the gunnery sergeant asked, and then they both dropped down when a Jap machine gunner spotted them and fired a short burst their way. Sand kicked up in a neat, straight line a few yards in front of the seawall and sand showered down on them.

"You missed, you son-of-bitch!" Hawkins yelled, hoping to antagonize the gunner, and turning to Hooper said, "These Japs are pathetic...I woulda been dead a long time ago if they had any aim at all."

"Well just be careful...one of 'em is bound to get lucky sooner or later," Hooper advised, and added, "so what's the plan?"

Like the last time, Lieutenant Hawkins decided to go after the bunkers one-by-one. Starting with the left one first, they would work their way right and take the bunkers out in succession. With more manpower at his disposal, he decided to employ half the men with him in the attack while the others...under the control of Gunnery Sergeant Hooper...would stay along the seawall and provide covering fire.

"You sure you're okay," Hooper asked, glancing at the bloodstains on the lieutenant's shirt.

Hawkins caught the look and said, "Of course I'm okay...these scratches aren't nearly as bad as they look."

"Your call," Hooper answered affirmatively...knowing that he would not be able to deter the lieutenant once his mind was made up. Then he added, "Once you go over, we'll give you as much fire as we can to keep their heads down. But after this job, I got the next one. You don't want the boys thinkin' I'm slackening off...do ya?"

"Of course not, gunny," Hackett replied, smiling, and then he got serious again and said, "You got the next one."

The men took another five minutes checking their weapons and then the lieutenant signaled them to get ready. "We go on three," he said and then he held up his hand and counted the numbers off while raising one finger at a time. When he reached three, the lieutenant and the men he had picked to go with him rushed the first pillbox...a large position that housed two heavy machine guns. The Jap gunners saw the men and swung their guns to bring them under fire.

Hawkins and the men dove into a shell hole for protection and the enemy fire missed them. Once again...in total disregard for his own safety...the lieutenant told his men that he wanted to handle the first one himself. The men protested...but Hawkins scrambled out of the hole and charged the bunker...throwing grenades as he ran. The Jap gunners fired at him the whole way, but somehow they missed, and he reached the bunker safely and dove down beside the firing port. As he rolled over to unhook a grenade from his shirt, his luck finally ran out. A Jap rifleman in an adjacent bunker lined him up and shot him squarely in the chest. The round stunned him for a second...and his men thought he was dead for sure...since they had seen him get hit...but he wasn't through. Summoning all his strength, Hawkins tossed the grenade into the bunker and it exploded with a *whoosh*! The blast apparently killed everyone inside since no more fire came from it. Satisfied with the results, Hawkins pushed himself away from the aperture and waited as the other men came up. Tired and bleeding heavily, the lieutenant let his enlisted men lead the next charge. They took this bunker out quickly and continued on...charging the third and fourth bunkers in the same manner. They fell too...just like the first two...but one of the scouts was hit along the way; sadly, Private First Class Marcel Krzys had been shot in the head while running between the bunkers and was dead before he hit the sand.

Now there was only one bunker left...but it represented the biggest challenge yet...since it was the largest one of the five. This one was about thirty yards away and it was located at the top of a small knoll which gave the Jap gunners a three-hundred-and-sixty-degree field of fire. It was also protected by a double layer of coconut logs and completely covered in sand which made it impervious to everything but a direct attack. Lieutenant Hawkins waited for the men to return to his position and then he tried to psych them up to make one more charge. He pointed to the bunker and said defiantly, "Four down and one to go, men. It doesn't look like much...so I think I'll lead this one...just for the fun of it!" But they would have nothing of it. Instead, the men begged the lieutenant to stay down so they could get him help. One of the men put his hand on the lieutenant's shoulder and pleaded, "Sir, you're dying! Stay here and we'll get you that corpsman. Let us handle this one!"

Hawkins smiled weakly at the gesture and managed to eek out, "Don't worry about me, boys. I came here to kill Japs...not get evacuated!" Then, using his last ounce of strength, he stood up and started hurling grenades at the imposing bunker.

A Japanese gunner inside spotted the movement below and swung the barrel of his heavy machine over to engage the lone, exposed marine. He depressed the trigger and a bright, red flame lit up the dark interior of the pillbox as the machine gun spat out bullet after bullet.

Gunnery Sergeant Hooper...leaning against the seawall...saw the whole scene unfold and he screamed for the lieutenant to get down....but it was too late. Just like he had warned earlier, the lieutenant had run up against an enemy gunner who was a decent marksman...and Hooper and the others cringed as their fearless leader was struck down again. This time he was hit by a machine gun slug in the shoulder and the blood that was still in him poured out of the massive wound.

The sight of their heroic leader going down again galvanized the men around him and they charged into the open and ran up the hill like crazed men...just like their wounded platoon commander would've done if he'd been able to. Reaching the top, they surrounded it and plastered the gun ports with rifle fire...which kept the gunners inside at bay. Then the men stuffed grenades into the openings and they ducked out of the way. The explosions echoed one after another and most of the men inside were killed. A few seconds went by and then the metal back door banged open. Smoke poured out first...and then came the survivors...bloodied and disoriented. This desperate dash for safety was all they had left...but they didn't make it very far. The marines were expecting it and they simply shot them down as fast as they came out...leaving a grizzly pile of dead Japs at the bottom of the hill. One of the men continued to fire his machine gun into the pile for good measure…insuring that they were all dead. "That's for Lieutenant Hawkins…you lousy bastards!" he shouted at the bodies vehemently…and letting his emotions and anger get the best of him…he hacked up some phlegm and spat down on them. Lowering his smoking weapon, he drudged his way down through the deep sand and made for the first bunker, hoping he'd find the lieutenant still alive…and…thankfully…he was.

• • •

Fumai saw the marines waving frantically and heard them yelling, "Corpsman! We need the corpsman! The lieutenant's hit real bad!" He had seen Hawkins blown backward and knew instinctively that this wound would be far worse than the others he had already sustained. So he leaped over the seawall and ran as fast as he could to the injured officer. The scout-snipers were dragging the lieutenant back to the protection of the seawall, but they put him down when the corpsman reached them. They quickly moved aside and Fumai knelt down beside the injured officer. A quick look at the bloody wound told him all he needed to know: the large bullet had caused massive damage to the armpit and severed an artery inside the shoulder area. "We've got to get him back to the aid station at the pier. All I have is dressings…I'll stop as much of the bleeding as I can…but he needs more than that. He's losing too much blood. He'll die if we don't get him help right away," the corpsman said desperately as the men hovered over him.

Gunnery Sergeant Hooper ran past the group of marines and headed for the bunker. He quickly inspected the interior…making sure all the Japs were dead…and then raced back to the lieutenant. He barged his way through the bystanders and had Fumai give an assessment of the lieutenant's condition. Once he heard that Lieutenant Hawkins might not make it, he picked the two biggest men there and told them to carry the lieutenant to the rear immediately. "The lieutenant needs a blood transfusion. They got plasma back at the Regimental aid station by the pier. Fumai will go with you. He'll show ya where it is. Get there as fast as you can. Don't stop for anything," he told them. Then he pulled Fumai close and said, "We won't need you back here...and there's probably more for you to do back there anyway. Just do the best you can for Lieutenant Hawkins...he's as good as they come."

Fumai looked directly at Sergeant Hooper and said earnestly, "I will do everything I possibly can to keep him alive. I promise you... everything I can."

The two men reached down and lifted the lieutenant off the ground as gently as they could without hurting him. Then they carried him over to the seawall and lowered him down to the beach. Gunnery Sergeant Hooper hopped down as well and knelt beside the lieutenant. In a quiet voice he said that everything would be okay.

Lieutenant Hawkins looked up with glassy eyes and said in a forlorn voice, "I hate leavin' you like this, boys."

"Don't you worry about a thing, Hawk. We'll hold the fort down here until ya get back," Hooper replied softly, trying to reassure him one more time.

"We'll take care of the rest of these damn Nips while you're gone, sir," another scout-sniper chimed in.

"That's right, sir," the rest of the men echoed in unison.

"We gotta get going," Fumai broke in, and Hooper ordered them to move out. And as the three men left with the lieutenant...the entire section of scout snipers removed their helmets and stood at attention in a solemn tribute to their fallen leader.

"That's the bravest marine I've ever served with," Gunnery Sergeant Hooper said out loud and a corporal, tears streaking down his dust-smeared face, muttered softly, "Damn right...damn right." Then Hooper put his helmet back on and announced loudly, "Alright everybody...let's go knock out some more Jap bunkers and get this battle over with."

· · ·

As they got closer to the pier, Pharmacist Mate Fumai ran ahead to alert "Doc" Brukardt that they were bringing in Lieutenant Hawkins. When he described the extent of the lieutenant's injuries, the Navy doctor frowned and told him there was very little he could do. "We're practically out of plasma…and we're still short most of everything else," he said dejectedly. "I'm doing the best I can…but there are just some guys I can't save," he added in desperation, "but bring him in and I'll see what I can do."

The two marines carried Hawkins into the dark confines of the bunker-turned-hospital and laid him down on the ground next to the makeshift operating table. The doctor examined the wound and was amazed that the lieutenant was still alive. "These wounds would've already killed an ordinary man," he said to no one in particular. Try as he might though, Dr. Brukardt couldn't stop the bleeding and, exasperated, he stepped back from the lieutenant. "There's nothing I can do here," he said, holding his hands up in defeat. "I can't find the bleeder…everything's destroyed in there…and even if I could, I don't have anything in here to clamp it with…so just try to make him as comfortable as possible." He looked at the two burly scout-snipers and saw tears in their eyes. "I'm sorry, fellas" he said sadly, "I did all I could for him," and he stood back up to work on another marine who was moaning on the makeshift operating table.

First Lieutenant William Deane Hawkins lived on for several more minutes but his breathing eventually slowed and he slipped into shock. He died quietly…in the midst of other badly wounded warriors who…like himself…had put everything on the line for a cause they desperately believed in.

As his two men headed back to deliver the disheartening news to Gunnery Sergeant Hooper, one said to the other, "You know… had he been able…Lieutenant Hawkins would've refused to let the doc put any new blood in him…even if they had had some. He would've told him to save it for someone else that was worse off than he was."

"Old Hawk certainly would've," the other man said proudly... and they continued on...but in deference to their fallen leader...they strode a little taller.

• • •

Doctor Brukardt had seen the look on the corpsman's face when he pronounced the death of the brave lieutenant and he knew what he was feeling. "They'll be others you know," the Navy doctor said as the two scouts left, "just like him... brave boys that you won't be able to help. You learn to live with it...believe it or not. Don't ever get so full of yourself and think you have the power of God to save everyone...cause you don't. Just do what you can for those you can help and let the rest take care of itself."

Fumai thanked the doctor and asked him what he could do to help since his stint with the Scout-Snipers seemed to be over.

"Would you do me a favor?" the doctor asked. "Go up and let Colonel Shoup know what happened to Lieutenant Hawkins. He'll want to know."

The corpsman nodded that he would.

"Thanks. I'd do it myself, but there's just too much to do here," Brukardt said, obviously fatigued. "I keep wondering where the hell the rest of the docs are," he mumbled as he began examining the latest casualty that had been brought in.

Lieutenant Brukardt had no way of knowing that two entire battalion medical sections had been wiped out trying to land on D-Day...and that two others were still unaccounted for...a status that described many of the specialized units that were supposed to have made it in already. Another of the battalion surgeons did make it to the end of the pier...but he never got a chance to leave. With all the outgoing casualties piling up there, he set up a triage and clearing station and he coordinated the evacuation of the badly wounded to the transports beyond the reef. Sadly, another doctor, who was serving as an observer for the newly-formed 4th Division, had been killed too. His body and several others...possibly corpsmen...were found in an abandoned amtrac that was drifting aimlessly beyond the reef.

• • •

For the second time that day, Tom Fumai left the dark, musty medical bunker and emerged into bright sunshine. He shielded his eyes until they adjusted to the glare from the sun and made his way up to the CP. He could see Colonel Shoup speaking into a radio handset, gesticulating wildly as he spoke. "Keep pressing 'em!" he demanded, and then he listened for a few seconds to whatever the man on the other end of the line was saying. "Yes...yes...that's good," the colonel continued...his mind working ceaselessly....trying to calculate the impact his decisions were having on the course of the battle. "Right now the situation ashore is uncertain. I'm going to send Carlson out to the *Maryland*. He'll be able to explain to everybody what we're facing here. I need the Sixth Regiment freed up if Ryan can open up Green Beach for us! I'm trying to get word to him now. I'm also going to have Hays drive west towards the *Pocket* from the other side. That should take some pressure off of Ryan." The colonel listened for a second and finished up with, "Yes....yes...excellent. We're on top of the bastards. Great work on getting those supplies in. But what we need most is more men and more ammo. Keep it coming!"

Fumai had no idea who the colonel was talking to...but he could tell that it was an important radio call just by the colonel's body language. He was pacing back and forth as he held the radio headset to his ear...all the while yelling into the transmitter mike that he held with his other hand. It was obvious he was trying his best to be heard above the noise of the battle that was raging in the background all around him. And the colonel was excited...because he was finally able to communicate with the unit on his far right flank...although not directly. His call had to travel a circuitous route to reach Major Ryan...but something was better than nothing at this stage of the battle. His call went first to the Division Staff...who still seemed to be in the dark about a lot of what was happening ashore. Then they relayed the colonel's message to a destroyer that was steaming off of Green Beach. From there the message went to a lieutenant who been sent to Major Ryan that morning to act as a forward observer. News from Major Ryan had to travel the same route...only in reverse...but now the colonel had a better sense of what was happening on Green Beach at least. "It's about time we got some good news around here," he said happily, handing the radio set back to his communications officer, and then he slapped his fist into the open palm of his other hand. "Division is reporting that Major Ryan's kickin' some Jap ass over on the west end of Red One. He may be able to free up this logjam for us finally," he shouted to the rest of the men in the group. But strangely, the men of the colonel's staff didn't appear to share his enthusiasm over this good news. They just went about their business without paying much attention to the colonel...or so it seemed.

Fumai watched their odd reaction and thought, *this isn't over by a long stretch and they know it*. Then he noticed one man break away from the others and he recognized Lieutenant Colonel Carlson...the very same officer who had offered him a ride in the amtrac on D-Day.

Fumai watched Carlson walk over to the colonel and extend his hand...apparently over the good news from Major Ryan. Since no one else seemed to care...it looked like he was the only officer who shared the colonel's fervor over the recent turn of events. Either that or he felt he had a little more latitude than the others and could be less formal with the colonel since he wasn't part of the colonel's direct staff. "Congratulations, sir," he said, "that's definitely the best news we've had so far."

"Thank you, Evans," the colonel replied, shaking his hand heavily. "Now we need Major Hays to get his battalion organized and moving. Have we gotten any kind of status report from him yet?" Shoup asked, more confident now.

Carlson's expression changed all of a sudden. During the night, Colonel Shoup had sent him out to make contact with the Division

Staff to let them know what the conditions were like ashore and what the colonel's plans were for the following day. The trip out to the command ship took several harrowing hours and once his task was accomplished, he began the long journey back to the island. By coincidence, Carlson arrived at the end of the pier when Hays' men had begun landing so he had witnessed the horrific slaughter firsthand. "I don't know how many made it in, sir," he said, "but I saw a hell of a lot of them get hit. Like yesterday…it was basically another…well…I don't think that many made it in." His voice trailed off…disheartened by the memory of it…thus tempering his joy over Major Ryan's accomplishments.

Major Thomas Culhane, the fiery and upbeat operations officer, heard the colonel's question and came over. "Yes, sir, we do. Hays just reported in," and Culhane proceeded to tell Colonel Shoup the bad news…that Major Hays had reported that only half of his battalion could be accounted for on Red 2. Culhane stopped for a second…letting the bad news sink in…and then continued, "Major Hays estimates that he will have approximately four hundred and fifty effectives of the nearly nine hundred men that should have landed with him. He also decided to hold up the landing of his fifth wave." Hays had told Major Culhane that he thought it was senseless to feed the fifth wave into the meat grinder that his first four landing waves had run into…that getting them slaughtered made no sense at all… but the operations officer left that part of the message out. "Of the four hundred or so missing, Hays feels that some three hundred of them might have been killed or wounded. He's hoping the rest will eventually turn up on Red Two. And he thinks he saw some of them land to the west…where Ryan's men are…and they could be fighting there with them," Culhane said, finishing up the grim report. Then, shifting gears, he added, "Despite what happened out there, Hays is still ready to go with what he has left. He's just waiting for orders to get the attack started."

"Okay...it could be worse," Shoup said, trying to put a good spin on the bad news once again. "Tell him I want him to orient his attack westward...towards the *Pocket*. Explain that we've got some isolated units over there. We'll try to get them out of there so we're not killing our own people. He'll have to coordinate coverage for his left flank with Colonel Jordan. That should do it for now."

After issuing the order to Major Culhane, the colonel then turned back to Lieutenant Colonel Carlson...who was still standing there. He had listened to the whole conversation between the colonel and his operations officer and it validated what he had seen in the morning. "Look, Evans," the colonel said somberly, "I know you just got back...and I know how bad it is out there...but I need you to make your way out to the pier one more time. Catch a ride on whatever's available and let Division know firsthand what the hell is going on around here. Don't sugar coat it. Major General Smith has to be aware that this thing is nowhere near finished. Will you do that for me?"

"David...you and I have been around a long time....and we've been asked to do a lot over all those years. You're not asking me to do something out of the ordinary. I'll head out there and let them know what's going on...you can count on that," the former Raider officer said with aplomb.

"Thank you, Evans...I'll see you when you get back," the colonel said emotionally...knowing the tremendous task he had just laid in his friend's lap...yet again. And then he added, "And try to get those Navy boys to feed you some while you're there. You're looking a little thin. That Navy chow will fatten you up more than what we got around here."

Lieutenant Colonel Evans patted the colonel on the shoulder and then he turned and walked towards the pier...just like he had twelve hours ago.

• • •

Colonel Shoup watched his friend walk away and he silently thanked God for putting such wonderful...and courageous...men around him. Then...for the first time that day...he took a much-needed break. Sitting down, he removed his helmet and brushed his scalp with his dirty hands...trying to dislodge the sand and grit that had accumulated over the last twenty-four hours.

Standing off to the side...out of the way...Fumai could still see that the colonel looked extremely tired...his face drawn...his eyes bloodshot and sunken. Given that, he decided it was as good a time as any to do what he had to do...so he approached the marine commander.

"Sir...you got a moment," he said to Shoup, hoping he wouldn't get chased off by one of the staffers.

Colonel Shoup looked up and saw a Navy corpsman approaching...and he just assumed that he was there to treat his leg wound. He had bandaged it earlier but it had begun to aggravate him again. *Who the hell sent for him? I didn't tell anyone about it bothering me.*

"The leg's fine, son," he lied. "I'll get it looked at later...when there's more time, okay."

Fumai wasn't quite sure what the colonel was talking about and he wasn't sure what to do so he just stood there...staring at the officer. Colonel Shoup thought that the corpsman was being obstinate when he wouldn't go away, so he started to get angry and he reiterated the point about the wound being okay. Then he stuck his bandaged leg out and said in a demanding tone, "Look, son, it's not bleeding and there ain't a whole lot you can do about the shrapnel right now. I don't know who sent you over here but it's gonna have to wait."

Fumai suddenly understood *what* the colonel was talking about and he shook his head. "Sir, I'm not here to inspect your leg wound. I would if you'd let me...but you just answered that question for me," the corpsman said directly.

"Oh...then what the hell are you here for anyway?" Shoup shot back.

Fumai wasn't intimidated by the colonel's deprecating tone. He realized that the commanding officer was under intense pressure and that the current set of circumstances were weighing heavily on him...and he knew he was about to burden him yet again.

"Lieutenant Brukardt sent me up here, sir. I'm afraid I've got some bad news."

"Get in line, son. Now I already know the doc's short just about everything....but everybody else is too. I know he needs more plasma, more morphine, more dressings, and more amtracs to get the wounded outta here. Tell him we're doing what we can to get the word out to the Fleet. I got Lieutenant Colonel Carlson working on it too. He just left again...but the Division Staff assured him last night that we should be getting some of the stuff Brukardt needs anytime now. Hell...if it doesn't show up soon...tell him I'll swim out there myself to get it." Colonel Shoup placed both his hands on the corpsman's shoulders to convey his sincerity and said, "Now...anything else?"

"Yes, sir, there is. It's about Lieutenant Hawkins, sir. He was hit real bad, sir...taking out those pillboxes up the beach. He...ugh...he didn't make it, sir. Doctor Brukardt did everything he could for him, but the lieutenant was just bleeding too much and we couldn't stop it. We tried...but there was nothing we could do, sir."

The colonel looked at the corpsman for a while as the message sank in...and said nothing. Fumai could feel the pain the man was experiencing...just by looking into his eyes...and he said nothing as well. After a few moments, the colonel said stoically, "It's okay, son. I know you did everything you could. Lieutenant Hawkins was a brave marine. We'll need plenty more like him before this thing is over."

Despite his rough demeanor, the colonel couldn't disguise the overwhelming sadness he was feeling. It was common knowledge that the colonel had always saved the toughest jobs for the Scout-Sniper platoon and he was particularly fond of the man who led it. Of all the marines who had been killed so far, Hawkins' death seemed to affect the colonel the most.

"I was there, sir…and I don't think I'll ever see that kind of bravery again. Not in my lifetime anyway," Fumai said. "What he did out there was beyond the call of duty."

Colonel Shoup didn't respond …he just stood there…looking off in the distance…lost in his own thoughts. He pondered the corpsman's appraisal of Lieutenant Hawkins' actions and made a mental note of it. Then he reached into his shirt pocket and withdrew a cigar. He lit it, took a deep puff, and said, "You smoke?"

Fumai grinned and held his hand out and the colonel handed the cigar to the corpsman. Fumai took a deep puff…inhaled way too much smoke…coughed…and forced out, "No…but I had to… for the lieutenant and all," and then he handed it back to the colonel. He placed it in his mouth, bit down on it, and then rolled it around, still deep in thought. When the colonel finally spoke, he paid the lieutenant a fitting tribute: "It's not often you can credit a first lieutenant with winning a battle…but that Hawkins came as near to it as any man could."

"Are we really winning, sir?" Fumai asked hesitantly.

"I wouldn't have said so this morning, but I think we got 'em now. The Japs have a lot of fight left in 'em, but we've started to make good headway here and there, plus– "

Some commotion in the CP area suddenly caught the colonel's eye and he stopped abruptly. Fumai turned around and saw a young private coming into the center of the command post. All the staff officers and senior NCO's also stopped what they were doing and they were now riveted to the newcomer in awed silence. Even the deafening noise of the battle being waged around the CP seemed to taper off for a few, brief moments as this lone marine occupied center stage…adding to the drama of the scene playing out before them.

The marine had just crossed one hundred and fifty yards of open terrain to get to the CP. He had come from the area where the two smaller taxiways converged near the north shore to form the apex of the triangular-shaped airfield complex. That he had made it in alive astounded everyone…since Japanese machine gun crews were hidden in positions along these two taxiways and their fire swept the area clean…making back and forth movement all but impossible. His approach reminded Fumai of the way he had seen Lieutenant Hawkins walking down the beach earlier…ramrod straight and utterly defiant. The only difference between the two was that this man was limping. When he got to the CP, he smiled and asked in a raspy voice - he was parched and hadn't had any water to drink in quite a while - if anyone could spare a cigarette or two. He didn't seem to notice or care that his uniform was caked with dust and that it was shredded in different places…exposing his bare skin underneath. He pointed to a machine gun crew way off in the distance - they were firing at some unseen enemy from the cover of a shell hole - and he announced, "Not one of them's got a cigarette in the whole crowd." Someone threw him a pack of smokes and he took a cigarette out, lit it, and put the pack in his pocket. He took several drags and seemed to be enjoying himself when several bullets came whizzing through the CP. They smacked into the bunker with a dull thud and the men scrambled to get out of the way of the sniper fire. The dirty marine didn't budge an inch however; instead, in defiance, he screamed out, "Go ahead…try an' shoot me down ya son of a bitch!" Then he proclaimed proudly, "I just got my sixth sniper a little while ago….and me a cripple and all." He added casually that he had broken his ankle when he tripped and fell into a shell hole the day before.

After finishing his cigarette, the mystery marine just turned and limped away…with the pack of cigarettes still in his pocket. Before he had gotten very far, one of the men - he was a combat correspondent who was taking pictures of the battle - yelled, "Hey buddy, what's your name and where ya from?"

"Strange…Adrian Strange…from Knox City, Texas, partner," he shouted over his shoulder nonchalantly, not bothering to look back. The combat correspondent…Sergeant Norman Hatch…wrote the crazy marine's name down in his journal and shook his head in disbelief. Then he watched the young boy boldly walk back through the same dangerous ground yet again…seemingly invincible…as bullets flew past him the entire way.

The staff kept their eyes on him too and when he finally reached the machine gun crew, a muffled cheer went up among them. One man summed up the whole experience when he said simply, "I'll bet that guy Strange just met those guys in that machine gun crew…and yet he risks his life to go grab them some cigarettes."

A marine officer standing next to him shook his head in agreement and added, "With men like that, we're bound to win."

Pharmacist Mate Fumai had just witnessed another act of selfless courage - some would call it craziness - and thought, *maybe this kind of behavior is becoming commonplace all over this island.*

With his mission to the CP complete, he turned to go as well but his services were summoned yet again. This time it was Major Culhane who needed him.

"Hey you…the one leavin'," he said brusquely.

Fumai stopped in his tracks and turned to face the major. He recognized his voice because he had just heard him briefing the Colonel about Major Hays' situation. "You're a corpsman, aren't you?" he asked.

After Fumai said he was, the major asked, "Are you assigned to anybody right now or are you freelancing out here?" Fumai could tell by his demeanor that it was best to tread lightly in this man's presence…or suffer the consequences. He also noticed that he spoke quickly…and with a deep voice…which conveyed authority…and his eyes had a piercing quality to them…which could turn a man cold when he focused them on you.

"I'm with the First Platoon, E Company, Second of the Second, sir," he replied smartly. "But I've been separated from them since our amtrac got hit coming in yesterday morning. I was helping out Lieutenant Hawkins and the Scout-Sniper platoon before I got here, sir."

"Understood...and I can use you now. Private--" The major turned to a young marine standing a few steps away and gestured for him to come over.

"Lohuis, sir," the marine interjected quickly.

"Thank you," the major said, "Private Lohuis here just came in from the triangle out ahead of us and –"

"I was down the beach near the middle of Red Two, sir," Fumai interrupted, thinking this information might be pertinent.

Major Culhane glared at the pharmacist mate instead. His stare was frightening and Fumai felt his coal-black eyes burning a hole right through him.

"Sorry about that, sir," Fumai said, nearly gagging from fright.

"You gonna let me finish or you got something else I need to know about that's so damn important it can't wait?" the major said.

"Won't happen again, sir," was all Fumai could manage, badly shaken by the major's reproach.

The major's intense look softened just as suddenly and he replied, "Okay, no problem. Here's the deal." Major Culhane knew he had gotten his point across and dropped the matter. Although he was an ardent disciplinarian and noted screamer, the officer was also smart enough to know when a good admonition crossed the line and lost its effectiveness.

Fumai, his silent prayer seemingly answered, sensed he was off the hook and he breathed a sigh of relief.

"Lohuis," Major Culhane began, "is a runner from A Company of the First Battalion, Second Regiment." He then explained the situation so Fumai would understand why he was needed. The major told him that Private First Class Lohuis' company commander, Captain Bill Bray, had sent him back when his radio had failed.

"We began having problems receiving and sending early this morning...and by eleven hundred we had lost all contact with the rear. Our company and Captain Williams' company are out there together," Lohuis interjected, apparently unfazed by the admonition that the major had just given Fumai. "I think it was dead batteries, but out here, who knows?" he added for good measure.

Surprisingly, the major let the interruption slide and he picked up right where Lohuis had cut him off. "Captain Bray has requested that a land line be set up so he can communicate with our CP and receive further orders. According to Lohuis, Captain Bray has nearly fifty men or so with him and Captain Williams...the B Company Commander...has another fifty plus to their right. They are spread out between the center of the triangle and the northwest taxiway... basically right in the middle of *Indian Country*. And we don't have any reinforcements to send them right now...but we need them to hold that ground. And that's where you come in."

"Yes, sir," Fumai responded, knowing all too well what was coming next.

"It seems they have some badly wounded that could use your attention. You're to go with Lohuis here and do what you can for them. We're counting on the two of you making it through to them. I wish we could send more men with you, but we don't have any to spare. Stop by Doc Brukardt's and see if you can scrounge up any extra medical supplies before you go. That's all I got...now go get it done." And just like that Major Culhane turned on his heel and went over to talk to Colonel Shoup.

"Aye aye, sir," the two men shouted in unison, but the major never acknowledged it. He had given them their orders and that was that. Since they were marines - and even though Fumai was technically in the Navy...as a corpsman he was all but considered a marine by the men he served with - the major just expected them to get it done...one way or the other.

Fumai saw that Private First Class Lohuis had already picked up the spool of wire that he would need to complete his end of the mission and was thus ready to go. He had also pocketed some extra radio batteries…just in case his hunch proved to be right. "You gonna make it with all that extra equipment?" Fumai asked.

"Yeah, it won't be a problem. But can you shoot a rifle?" Lohuis asked. "Where we're going isn't exactly a walk in the park. The Japs got machine guns laid out all along that taxiway…and we gotta cross it. If I get hit…well…you just don't wanna be out there all by your lonesome…and certainly not unarmed. You heard the major…he called it '*Indian Country*' for good reason."

"Yeah, I can shoot a rifle if I gotta…don't worry about that," Fumai answered a little testily, remembering the Jap sniper he had killed under the pier.

"Hey, I didn't mean anything by it…I just don't wanna see you get jumped out there. The Japs ain't gonna show you any mercy just cause you're a corpsman," Lohuis replied defensively.

"I know…and thanks. But I think I'll pass on carrying a rifle for now," Fumai said.

Lohuis shrugged his shoulders and the two were about to leave when they noticed another ruckus breaking out in the CP. They could see that the colonel was livid and heard him yell, "God damn it, major!" An officer was standing in front of the colonel…and he appeared cowed to say the least. *I wonder what he did to deserve that*, thought Fumai, and he looked quizzically at Lohuis. Lohuis shrugged his shoulders as if to say, "Beat's me," and continued watching…fascinated…like Fumai was.

"One damn machine gun…that's it…that's all that's holding you up?" Shoup stammered.

"Yes, sir…and I can't get the men to attack it," the major replied hopelessly.

"Just one gun!" the colonel stammered.

The major looked totally dejected and pleaded, "The damn thing has the whole runway covered. Nothing can move without drawing fire."

"Major," the colonel replied tactfully, "sometimes you've just gotta stand up and say, 'Who's coming with me?' If you get five men out of twenty that'll follow you…then lead them. When the others see you go…they'll follow you too. Sometimes the men just want someone to show them it can be done. That's leadership."

The colonel's words seemed to do the trick because the major's demeanor changed immediately. Feeling his confidence returning, he straightened up, rolled his shoulders back, and said, "I'll try that, sir. If I can get just a few men to go with me…that'll be better than nothing." Then without another word, he strode off towards the airfield…a leader once again.

CHAPTER 16

Carrying a wounded man on a cot was exhausting...and PFC Petraglia knew they still had a long way to go. Even his partner...Private Joe Agresta...who was slightly bigger and a little stronger...looked spent. Petraglia knew Agresta well enough since he was in Sergeant Endres' squad...and as they struggled along...Petraglia realized that Agresta and Scott were the only ones still alive from the well-liked sergeant's original squad of eleven men. *Even Staggs would have missed that one*, the runner mused...while watching Agresta strain ahead of him. *Out of all those other guys with combat experience...only two green privates are left.*

Though he was just a newcomer, Joe Agresta had adjusted to platoon life on New Zealand very quickly after arriving with a large contingent of replacements from the United States several months ago. While he wasn't that tall...he was well-built...like a linebacker...and he never seemed to tire from the training. In fact, Agresta reminded a lot of the guys of a slightly smaller version of their squad leader...except he wasn't Irish or German at all. He was Italian... and Endres never missed a chance to remind him of this discrepancy in his background. But the easy-going Agresta never took the comments about his heritage personally...and he and Endres ended up being workout buddies whenever the opportunity presented itself. And now Private Agresta was thankful that the two of them had spent so much time working on their conditioning...because moving the wounded Cohen was taxing...and he and Petraglia were beat. They had tried switching positions...the one in front moving to the back and vice-a-versa...to reduce the strain...but after a while it didn't matter...since it was just backbreaking work all the way around. They had taken only one break so far...a brief respite to catch their breath...and then moved on...knowing that Cohen's fate was resting in their tired hands. Thankfully, the going was somewhat easier now that they were walking on the hard-packed sand along the beach instead of the soft, shifting sand that they had just trudged through inland. But now the heat was getting to them... sapping their strength and stamina all at once. After a while the two found that they could only go about thirty yards or so before they had to put Cohen down and take a rest...their fatigue and thirst overwhelming them. During one of these stops Petraglia simply collapsed after he lowered the cot to the ground as gently as he could. Sweat poured out of him, soaking his uniform, and he struggled to breathe. After taking several deep breaths he seemed to be okay and then, between gulps of air, he told Agresta that he had never felt more tired in all his life. Agresta, his lips cracked and parched, his face smeared with perspiration and dust, readily agreed and said, "I don't know about you, but I didn't get any sleep last night. I was too worried that a Nip would sneak up on us. I'd give anything to catch a few winks now though. I feel like I'm gonna keel over any second."

"We'll take a long break as soon as we get Cohen back to the pier. As beat as we are...we just gotta keep goin'," Petraglia replied, and then added, "If it was you laying on that stretcher and Cohen was lugging your wounded butt, you'd want him to keep goin'... wouldn't ya?"

The question Petraglia posed had a simple answer and Agresta answered it by standing up. "Let's go," he said, nodding in the direction of the pier with his head.

"Right," Petraglia answered, and the two hefted the makeshift stretcher back up and drudged off down the beach...grunting all the way.

They had gone another two hundred yards when they stumbled into Private Hall. He was sitting against the seawall, casually smoking a cigarette. The body of the other private was sprawled out on the beach in front of them...his one eye staring lifelessly at the sky. They lowered the cot and knelt in place at both ends, too weak to do anything else. Petraglia, huffing from exhaustion, finally spoke up.

"You...okay," he asked haltingly.

"Yeah, fine...what about y'all?" Hall replied, the cigarette tangling from his lips.

"Never better," he lied, and then asked, "What happened to him?"

"Crummy Jap sniper shot him in the neck. The bastard was hiding in that amtrac out there." Hall pointed to an abandoned, half-submerged LVT-1 thirty yards away. "The impact knocked us both down and I just laid there so he must have thought he got us both with just the one shot. I've heard things like that can happen, but I ain't never seen it myself. They say Cole Younger used to line up Yankee prisoners and shoot them three-at-a-time to save bullets." Hall took a deep, long drag on the cigarette and then sent the butt sailing into the water with a snap of his thumb and index finger.

"Who's Cole Younger?" Petraglia asked, mortified by the notion of a multiple execution with one bullet.

"Oh, he was a Missouri boy that rode with Jesse and Frank James after the Civil War. During the war he rode with Bloody Bill Anderson or with Quadrill's Raiders...I don't remember which. Supposedly he had a real nasty side and he took his hatred for the North out on the Bluebellies they captured."

"Is he still alive?" Agresta asked.

"Cole Younger? Hell no. He got killed or captured when the James Gang tried to rob some bank up in Minnesota. He's long since dead," Hall answered.

"I don't care about Cole Younger…or Cole Older for that matter. I mean that Jap sniper. Is he dead or is he still out there?" Agresta asked, and he crouched down, hoping to present a smaller target.

"Oh him. No…I took care of him. He had too many other guys to shoot at so he left me alone. He shifted his fire to the boys out in water. I saw him move over to the other side of the amtrac and that's when I made my move. I swam out and waited until he had to reload. When he did, I jumped in and knifed the little dumb ass with my good 'ol K-bar. I always wondered if I'd get to use it."

Petraglia and Agresta glanced at each other suspiciously and then looked over at the amtrac. Sure enough, the body of a Jap soldier was hanging over the gunwale…his arms tangling over his head…his fingers almost touching the water below him.

"Geez, I hope I never have to kill a guy up that close," Petraglia said, shuddering. He had already come to grips with taking another person's life on Guadalcanal…where he had killed several Japanese… or so he thought anyway. Before enlisting, the idea of killing someone had never even entered his mind. But that luxury didn't exist in a war zone and he had found that he could do it without remorse…if he had to…especially if the person you were trying to kill was trying to kill you at the same time. And the distances involved in a rifle shot made it easier to handle as well…since you rarely found the body of your victim…and thus seldom got to see the results of your work. That was quite different from being forced to use a knife or bayonet to end someone's life however…where the fighting was up close and personal…and Petraglia had always been repulsed by the prospect of having to do it that way. And thankfully…he'd never had to.

"Yeah…I don't know if I got the stomach to stick a man either. Why didn't you just shoot him and be done with it," Agresta asked, nodding towards Hall's rifle…which was propped up harmlessly against the seawall next to him.

"Hell…don't you think I would've done that if I could have. When I went to shoot him I realized I had no ammo left. I must have had an itchy trigger finger back at the trench and used it all up there. And I didn't wanna waste time rollin' Johnny over to get at his ammo pouches...so I just took off when I saw the Jap shifting his position to shoot at the guys in the water. You just do what you gotta do when the time comes I guess," Hall said defensively, since he certainly understood the feelings of the two men. "That's the first one I've ever killed," he added somberly. "Hell, he's the first one I've actually seen since we landed. I didn't really wanna kill him like that either, but what was I gonna do, let him sit there and pick off more of our own boys. We're trained to kill these bastards so that's what I did."

"You did the right thing," Petraglia said simply, and then added, "we could use some help." He then quickly explained Cohen's predicament...and Hall readily agreed to lend a hand.

"We need to get goin' if we're gonna have any chance of saving him," Petraglia said next.

Hall stood up, walked over to Petraglia, took his spot at the front of the cot, and said, "Come on, let's go y'all."

The three men took turns carrying Cohen and it made the difficult job much easier. The man that wasn't part of the carrying team was expected to scout ahead and flush out any Jap snipers that might try to take the group under fire. If one of the carriers got too tired, they would all stop and the fresh man on point would take over for the man that was worn out. They made good time using this arrangement and they had almost reached the pier when Hall replaced Agresta at the head of the cot for the last time. As they moved off, Petraglia, at the rear of the stretcher, suddenly asked, "Who was he?"

"Who?" Hall asked, glancing back at Petraglia.

"The marine back there on the beach...did you know him?"

"Yeah," Hall answered, "I knew him. He was my best friend. His name was Johnny Donahue. We got to know each other when we were boots back at Parris Island. I never had much use for New Englanders but we hit it off for some reason. Probably because he liked to drink Scotch just as much as I do."

"My best buddy's buried back on Guadalcanal," Petraglia said, "...or what's left of him." He remembered the incident sadly and felt the need to talk about it. His friend had taken cover in a foxhole when a Jap battleship had begun shelling the island one night nearly a year ago. "It was sheer luck where those rounds hit...you know," he said mystified. "It must have lasted maybe three hours or so and when it was all over, I called over to him and he never answered. A round hit near his hole--"

Hall cut him off suddenly. "At least he never knew what hit him. Johnny died with one eye blasted out and bleeding like a stuck pig from that neck shot. It didn't even kill him right away. The poor son of a bitch bled to death on the beach. He was beggin' me to shoot him. He wouldn't shut up. I thought that damn Jap would hear him for sure and that he was gonna drill the two of us again. I covered his mouth with my hand to shut him up. I guess it worked since the Jap never fired on us again. As far as dyin' goes...there's no better way to check out than the way your buddy did...believe me."

Petraglia considered Hall's point...saw the merits in it...but still came to the conclusion that dying was just a raw deal...no matter how it happened.

• • •

"Hey Fumai!" Private First Class Petraglia shouted happily when he saw the corpsman walking towards him. "Where the hell ya been?"

The runner, and now stretcher bearer, had just left PFC Cohen in the skilled hands of Lieutenant Brukardt. Hall and Petraglia had carried him inside the hospital bunker and the doctor had gone to work on the injured marine immediately. Hall left quickly but Petraglia had lingered inside, hoping to see if the doctor and his staff of pharmacist mates could perform one of their medical miracles on Cohen. In the midst of operating on Cohen, the surgeon had suddenly looked up at Petraglia and said kindly, "You don't have to hang around here. We have everything under control. You and your men got this man here just in time. I just might be able to save him. Good job."

Both Hall and Agresta were slumped against the side of the bunker sleeping so neither of them saw Petraglia come out or heard him greet his missing friend. The two men hugged each other tightly and then took turns explaining everything that had happened since they had last seen each another. At one point, Petraglia broke out in uncontrollable laughter. "You're kidding...you actually rode in with Colonel Shoup and his staff. What was it like to be surrounded by all that brass?" he asked hysterically.

"Oh, I'll tell ya what...those Japs must've known who was in that amtrac alright cause it seemed like bullets were comin' at us from every direction. Mortars too...I didn't think we were gonna make it. The officers were diving for cover and I stood up in that amtrac like I was a four-star admiral and I guided the driver in. Colonel Shoup said he was going to pin a medal on me himself!"

"Are you serious," Petraglia said, obviously impressed.

"Of course not! That boat got hit and we got sopping wet making the trek in...just like everybody else did," he replied sarcastically and the two of them fell into a fit of laughter yet again...the tension of the last twenty-four hours melting away like snow on a wet street.

The conversation turned serious when Fumai asked about the men in the First Platoon though. "How about the Old Man and Platoon Sergeant Roy? Are they still alive?" he wanted to know.

"The lieutenant is...at least he was when I left. Don't know about Sergeant Roy though. Nobody's heard from him or seen anyone else that was in his tractor." Petraglia then gave a rundown on everyone else who had come in on their amtrac...starting with those who had made it and finishing with those who had not.

"That's it. That's all that's left? Just you, Agresta there, Sergeant Endres, Feeney, and Scott?" Fumai said, sounding incredulous.

"Yeah...ya think I'm makin' this kinda stuff up? Besides everybody that got killed on the amtrac, we lost two more...Newell and Vandrisse...just tryin' to get to the beach. Then Friedman got machine gunned goin' over the wall after we made it in."

"Friedman…the handsome kid from Florida. He got killed? That's too bad…he was awfully nice. I liked him a lot…good baseball player. His sister's gonna take that real hard."

"He had a sister?" Petraglia asked…since everyone's interest always perked up when a female was mentioned in a conversation.

"Yeah…a real nice-looking girl too. You know the type…dark hair…dark eyes…the whole package. She took a train up to visit him while we were in boot camp…and we got that weekend pass. Everybody nearly lost their minds over her…smart too," Fumai said…and a smile creased his face as he pictured her jumping into her brother's arms when they met.

"So you and Friedman were close, huh?" This revelation had caught Petraglia by surprise since he thought he knew everything that went on in the platoon.

"We got to be as time went on…I'm definitely gonna miss him," Fumai said sadly…and then added, "So a machine gun got him?"

"Yup. He was the very first one that volunteered to head over the seawall. That took some guts…given the amount of fire we were up against. Nobody else wanted to do it…just him. I wish I had that kind of guts. Right after he got hit…Feeney…his buddy… jumped over the seawall and knocked out a bunch of pillboxes single-handedly. The LT promoted him on the spot to PFC for doing it," Petraglia continued.

"Feeney was Friedman's best friend. Both of them were in Second Squad," Fumai said, astonished…and added, "So there are just seven of us left out of the twenty men that started in on our amtrac?" He was hoping his math was wrong.

"That's about it…just eight outta twenty-one if you include the LT," Petraglia said matter-of-factly, letting the numbers speak for themselves.

• • •

Private First Class Lohuis listened patiently as Fumai and the other man told their stories and he just figured that the two had ridden in the same amtrac on the way in and then had gotten separated somehow. He understood their plight since his own company had been decimated and broken up when it landed too. His A Company had numbered one hundred and fifty men when it started in…and after the landing…Captain Bray…his company commander…had a little more than a platoon of men left to lead inland. The rest were dead, wounded, or missing…an astonishing seventy-five percent casualty rate.

Several minutes went by and then he interrupted the party and told Fumai that he had to get going. "I guess you're gonna stay here…with them," Lohuis added, figuring the corpsman would want to link up with his own platoon.

Fumai thought about the suggestion and came up with a better idea. "Are there any more wounded back with Lieutenant Hackett?" he asked Petraglia.

"No…Cohen was the only one," Petraglia answered, and then he looked at Lohuis strangely.

Fumai caught Petraglia's look and explained who Lohuis was and why they were there.

"Oh," Petraglia said, understanding the corpsman's dilemma…so he asked, "Well, what are you gonna do?"

Since Captain Bray had wounded with him, Fumai decided it would be best to follow Major Culhane's orders and go with Lohuis to see if he could help them out. But he also persuaded Petraglia to come with them down the beach. Then he said, "You can gauge how close Captain Bray's position is to where you guys are." Petraglia agreed with the corpsman's plan since he felt the lieutenant would probably want to link up with the captain's group since they seemed to be so close to one another and then they could operate as a united force. "The lieutenant sorta had us headed in that direction anyway," Petraglia added, but then he hesitated. "The only problem," he said, "is that the LT asked me to bring some engineers or flame thrower guys back with me. I haven't had a chance to look for any around here yet. I did get us some extra ammo though…since we're here."

Lohuis took over at this point. "I'll tell ya this much...you ain't gonna find any down here on the beach. The few that made it in are forward already. Not a single one got in with us that I could tell. If Colonel Shoup or Major Culhane found out that a flame thrower operator was crappin' out down here...he'd probably come over and shoot him himself."

Lohuis' explanation satisfied Petraglia because he went over and kicked the bottom of Private Agresta's boots. He ordered the sleepy private up and nudged Hall with his rifle.

Hall lifted his head slowly, groaned, and said, "Already...we just got here." He took his helmet off, scratched his head, put the helmet back on, and drawled, "Damn...and I was just fixin' to get some good shuteye too."

As tired as he was, Private Agresta jumped up immediately when he heard Petraglia's command. The young private was still responding to orders automatically... just like he had been taught in boot camp. *It's a good thing those lessons die hard*, Petraglia thought. Ironically, he had remembered hating all those mindless drills and repetitive tasks that the drill instructors had forced the boots to perform for weeks on end. *I guess I'm a slow learner*, he realized, finally appreciating the real meaning behind the Marine Corps' dictatorial approach to training. All the miseries and harsh demands that had been heaped on the recruits at San Diego and Parris Island...and on him in particular since he was always the *dumb dago*...suddenly made sense to him. *Out here, there's no time to think things over...you just react instinctively because you've been trained that way...which saves lives in the end.* Pleased with himself for finally figuring it out, he smiled...and then he told his two charges what they were about to do. Hall...his pouches now restocked with some of the ammo that Petraglia had secured from the supply deport...and Agresta listened to him intently. When the runner was finished they each checked their weapons...making sure they were ready to go should they need to use them. Before leaving,

Petraglia handed several bandoliers of rifle ammo over to each of them and they draped them over their shoulders for the trek back. Then…like the good marines they were…they all headed west…no questions asked.

CHAPTER 17

Petty Officer Tadashi Koshio raised the commander's hatch of the Type 95 Ha-Go light tank* and stood on the commander's seat to get a better view. The observation slit above the main 37mm gun provided limited visibility and he needed to see what was happening off to the right. The noise of the battle had grown louder in that direction over the last few hours as the marines intensified their attacks against the stubborn bunker complex southeast of the Burns-Philip wharf. He wiped the sweat off his brow and then diligently scanned the ground outside the blockhouse once again. He saw nothing and let the other two members of his crew...the driver...and the 7.7mm hull-mounted machine gun operator...know it.

Although it was very hot outside, it was still cooler than it was inside the tank. The burning, midday sun had already made the outside of the armored vehicle hot to the touch. When the tank was buttoned up, the interior became so hot that it felt like the men were baking in an oven. The open hatch gave some ventilation to the two men down below...but not enough to make it comfortable.

Koshio's tan uniform was soaked dark brown by now and he could feel a rivulet of sweat running down his spine. *And to think,* he thought, *I once considered this good duty.* The gunner leaned back and grabbed Koshio's leg, breaking his concentration on the terrain beyond. He glanced down and saw a grimacing face looking back up at him. "Any chance we can take a break?" he asked.

The petty officer considered the request and gave in. They had been cooped up in their tank for five hours already and he felt they could all use a turn outside to refresh themselves. "Okay, but don't stray too far away," he commanded. "I want you close by if I need you," he added.

Wasting no time, all three climbed out of the tank as fast as they could and jumped down to the ground. They sat in the shade along the wall of the bunker and relaxed. Several explosions erupted in the distance but they were so far away that Koshio and his crewmen were in no real danger.

"It's those damned American destroyers again," Koshio stated vehemently.

"Yup...they're still at it. I would've thought one of our shore batteries would've chased them off by now," the machine gunner said in agreement.

The tank commander had no way of knowing that the explosions had actually come from shells fired by the 75mm pack howitzers along the beach...their fire having been redirected at the Jap machine gun emplacements that were dug in along the auxiliary taxiway that lay just west of Admiral Shibasaki's command center. The Japanese defense scheme in this part of the island was living up to its commander's expectations...so much so that the marines under Major Crowe and Major Rudd had been hemmed in to the Red 1 beachhead area for nearly a day and a half now. The Japanese machine gunners had made it nearly impossible for anyone to leave the beach and cross into the eastern portion of infield triangle that was formed by the three runways directly in front of them. Thus confined, Crowe had directed the bulk of his forces to attack the beach defenses that controlled the Burns-Philip wharf area along the northeastern coastline...but they had been stymied there also. An impregnable complex of trenches, foxholes, pillboxes, and bunkers controlled this area and it was proving to be as tough a nut to crack as *the Pocket* was over on the western end of the island. Putting it plainly, Crowe's men had been stopped cold in every direction they tried to advance.

"What do you think will become of us, Tadashi," Private Jinzo Yoshizawa, the tank driver, asked. From the tone of his voice, it was evident that this man - he had been a simple rice farmer back home in Japan before the war and he was a little older than Petty Officer Koshio - still harbored hopes of surviving this battle somehow.

"Oh, I can't say for sure, Jinzo. I was never very good at predicating the future. If I could...do you think I would have chosen this line of duty? No...my friend...certainly not. If I had known then what was going to unfold here...I would have gone to cook school instead. That way I could have been inside this indestructible building...safe and sound...instead of sitting outside of it with the likes of you two. Just picture it...I am serving our fine admiral and his staff a wonderful dish of fish and rice. Then, after the meal, Admiral Shibasaki offers me a glass of sake...in appreciation of my efforts...and we would drink a toast to the Emperor in the cool confines of his Headquarters room. I have dreamed about it many times since being assigned here. But in reality, I'm not in there at all. Instead, I'm out here...swatting flies and listening to the rumbles of an empty stomach...and our brave admiral is now dead. Do not rely on me for advice regarding what the gods have in store for us on this little island of ours."

"Do you think we will die?"

"We may, Jinzo. The marines must know the importance of this building by now. Even though Admiral Shibasaki is dead...they don't know it. Even so, we are still in the fight. And we still have good leaders inside who are making decisions that will lead us to victory. Above all, we must believe in their leadership and not lose hope. And when the Americans come, we will fight them to the death. It is our duty. The Emperor and our countrymen expect nothing less of us. To do anything but that would dishonor our families back home...as you well know."

"So the Admiral is dead, Tadashi? You are certain of this?" the driver asked.

"Yes, my friend. I am sure the story is true. One of the admiral's guards heard the other officers talking about it. And he reported it to me. They do not want this news to get out. They feel the men will be demoralized by the admiral's death."

"How did he die? Weren't you talking with him just last night?" Jinzo pushed, still hoping the story could be false.

"Yes. He seemed fine to me when we spoke last night. I did notice that he was limping from a wound he had on his thigh...but that is not what killed him. The guard outside his door said that the admiral had gone into his room sometime around midnight to rest... and that he never woke up."

"Did he commit *hari kari*, Tadashi?" Jinzo asked innocently.

"No. He did not. When his staff tried to wake him, they found him stone dead. They searched his body and found a small wound... it had apparently gone unnoticed...behind the admiral's knee. He must have been hit by a small sliver of shrapnel when they got caught in that bombardment yesterday. It probably nicked the artery as it went in. We've seen other men die the same way. Shrapnel has no respect for rank. Admiral Shibasaki simply bled to death in his sleep."

Jinzo nodded in agreement and continued to listen with rapt attention...since it was rare that this kind of information would find its way to a lowly soldier like himself. "Didn't anyone try to help him, Tadashi?" he asked, wanting to pin the blame on someone for letting the admiral die unattended.

"Even though the admiral's boot was full of blood...he had not taken them off when he fell asleep so no attention was drawn to the seriousness of this wound. Whether the admiral knew about it is anyone's guess. I think he was aware of it...since it had to hurt on some level. Yet he knew there was nothing that could be done about it...so he left his fate to the gods...as all *samurai* do."

"That didn't turn out so well for our admiral...did it," the gunner chimed in irreverently...suddenly joining the conversation. He had never liked religion or its traditions...and did not think that the Emperor was a god...but he kept these dangerous thoughts mostly to himself...until now.

"Do not say such a thing...it is disrespectful," the driver said, trying to admonish him.

"I can say it...and I will say it, Jinzo," the man answered right back, refusing to back down.

Private Jinzo Yoshizawa looked pleadingly at his commander but the petty officer seemed nonplussed by the gunner's convictions.

Seeing this, the gunner added, "And what are you going to do about it, Jinzo? Tell one of the officers inside what I said? Do you think for one second that any of them would leave the protection of their royal cocoon and come out here and behead me?"

"That's enough, Kanji," the petty officer said, finally asserting his authority when the conversation took a bad turn. Then he added, "Don't take your anger out on Jinzo there...he means well...and that kind of talk serves no purpose anyway. I know you don't want to be here...none of us do. But I don't need an officer overhearing you and then chopping my head off too for allowing you to get away with it!"

The gunner respected Tadashi...since he had always been fair with him...so he honored his request and kept quiet. But an uneasy pall now hung over the group as a result of the confrontation. To offset it, the driver looked over at his commander and asked simply, "Are you afraid, Tadashi?"

The tank commander looked at his driver intently...and didn't answer at first...since he thought the question deserved a thoughtful response. After a few seconds went by, he said, "Yesterday...before the marines began landing...I thought I would be. But once the firing started...I became very focused and it seemed my fear disappeared. I imagine that it will be like that the next time they come. And from the sound of their guns...it shouldn't be too long before they do. I will tell you this though. I will do everything in my power to keep the two of you alive as long as I can."

"Thank you, Tadashi. I know you will. Can I ask just one favor though," Jinzo replied.

"Yes...what is it?"

"Please don't let me burn up inside this tank. Either shoot me first or drag me out...but please don't let the flames get me," Yoshizawa pleaded.

"Don't worry, Jinzo. I promise you that I will not let that happen to you," Tadashi answered consolingly.

Neither man said anything for a long while...their silence seeming to forge a bond between them. And Petty Officer Koshio knew right then and there that nothing would stop him from keeping his vow to Jinzo Yoshizawa...nothing.

In the distance, several more rounds landed...closer still this time...the crack of the exploding shells in sharp contrast to the gentle snoring of the tank crew's assistant gunner whose chin was now resting comfortably on his chest. He did not have the same interest in his fate as his two tank mates did...and he had given in to his fatigue and fallen into a deep sleep.

---

*This tank was misidentified as a Type 97 light tank on page 178 in early editions of *Annihilation Beach*.

CHAPTER 18

"Geeze…that sun is hot!"

"Oh shut up…will ya," the corporal responded, trying to stop the marine next to him from complaining yet again. The two men were sitting in a crater that a 5-inch shell had carved out of the sand not far from the stubby Burns-Philip wharf. The top of a palm tree that had been sheared off in the same bombardment was resting a few feet away from their hole and it offered excellent protection from the fire that sometimes came their way.

In the lagoon beside them, the destroyer that had fired these rounds continued to cruise back and forth just beyond the reef. The USS *Ringgold* - along with the USS *Dashiell* - had been performing yeoman's work for the marines on Red 3 for nearly twenty-four hours.

Detailed to provide close-in fire support, the *Ringgold* had entered the lagoon in the early morning hours of D-Day and it had already run aground once when its commander tried to bring the ship in as close as he could to provide better fire for the marines trapped on the beach. Running a parallel tack to Red 1, the ship was an irresistible target and it immediately drew the attention of the Japanese anti-boat gunners…who fired incessantly at her…but only two shells hit the ship…and both shells were duds. The first one hit just below the waterline and it plowed through several compartments and ruined some power lines before it finally came to rest. One brave sailor picked up the inert round and quickly tossed it overboard. At the same time, a quick-thinking lieutenant from the ship's company jammed his hindquarters into the puncture hole to stop the flow of seawater that was flooding into the ship. The enterprising officer remained in that exposed position until a mattress was brought forward and then he was able to remove his derrière from the hole.

The second round hit amidships a few minutes later while the ship was drifting under a loss of power as a result of the damage from the first round. This shell ricocheted around topsides and then slammed its way through the sick bay and the emergency radio room before finally exiting the ship…never to be seen again. As sailors scrambled above and below decks to assess the battle damage, several more rounds exploded over the fantail and up high among her radar equipment…but none of them caused any further harm to the ship. By the time her damaged side was patched and power was restored, she was listing slightly to starboard, but this didn't stop the *Ringgold* from getting back under way. As she moved back to her station off Red 3, the captain radioed his superiors that the feisty ship hadn't sustained a single casualty and was ready to resume firing.

A couple decks down in the wardroom of the *Ringgold*, Private "Whitey" Thompson sat with his back against a thick steel wall… but even now he didn't feel that safe. He would have preferred to have been on one of the big transports that were further away from the island…and out of range of those damn Japanese guns. As luck would have it, he had jumped aboard a Higgins boat that was already loaded with some horrifically wounded marines and it had made a straight dash to the destroyer so these men could receive immediate treatment from the medical staff aboard the *Ringgold*. Other coxswains had seen this and followed suit…so that the destroyer was now packed to the seams with injured marines.

Looking around at all the wounded men beside him, Thompson figured that the battle conditions couldn't be improving all that much…since more men were being brought aboard…even though there didn't seem to be enough room for them. *Maybe*, he thought sourly, *that hot reception we ran into yesterday morning wasn't a fluke after all.*

The dreadful condition of some of the wounded who had been carried below had certainly confirmed his opinion. And then Thompson watched one distraught sailor nearly break down in tears as he told one of his shipmates about a distressing scene he had just witnessed. The sailor explained that a marine lieutenant had been hoisted aboard who had both of his legs and his lower abdomen shot away. As his stretcher was lifted out of the Higgins boat, the man began thrashing around and his entrails had spilled over the side of the stretcher and tangled ten feet into the water below him. The sailor who was directing the loading…a senior petty officer…had looked away in revulsion and then thrown up…something he had never done while serving fifteen years at sea.

Steve Thompson was blond-headed and he had been given the moniker, "Whitey," when he worked in the mailroom of a broker-age house in St. Louis. That had been when he was sixteen years old…and in two years he had worked his way up to the trading desk as an assistant salesman. Now he was a few years older… but the things this twenty-year-old marine had seen during the last twenty-four hours had not made him any wiser. He cringed just thinking about it…replaying scenes in his mind that no young man should have to see. He had watched several men being carried on stretchers with horrible wounds to the head and face…and the sight of a man missing an arm or a leg was commonplace now. Others looked like chopped meat and the private guessed that these men had probably been in the amtracs or Higgins boats that had been hit by large-caliber, anti-boat shells or by the deadly 13-mm rounds fired by the heavy machine guns ashore. After a while, Thompson began to feel guilty that his wounds were so minor in comparison to some of the others he had seen...but he thanked God that he had been spared just the same. He had been hit while he was still inside his amtrac...fairly close to the beach. A Jap shell had punched right through the thin siding of the tractor and exploded against the engine housing...destroying the engine and killing several men who were in the rear of the amtrac beside him. Thompson had been hit by shrapnel in his arm and shoulder...and his platoon commander...First Lieutenant Hackett...had told him to stay with the corpsman...Pharmacist Mate Fumai...so he could get his wounds taken care of. The private wanted to complain...thinking he could still fight...but the searing pain in his arm told him otherwise...so he had obeyed the order. By the time he reached the end of the pier, his shoulder and arm were so numb that he needed help getting into the Higgins boat. A surgeon's aide aboard the *Ringgold* had examined him and removed several pieces of metal from his arm...and then he found a nasty piece of shrapnel - it came from the Amtrak's thin armor siding - in his shoulder and took it out too. After his wounds were stitched back up and bandaged, Thompson had wondered if he could get some morphine to dull the pain he was experiencing but the orderly had mentioned offhandedly to another sufferer beside him that there wasn't enough to go around. He then explained that most of the medical supplies aboard the ship had been destroyed when the Japanese shell tore through the lower decks earlier. With that in mind, Thompson had never asked for any...since he knew that there were many more aboard who were wounded far worse than he was and who needed the pain-numbing drug much more than he did.

Suddenly the loudspeaker in the room came to life and announced that the ship would be leaving the lagoon shortly to off-load the wounded and to replenish their own supplies. Incredibly, the *Ringgold's* 5-inch gun crews had exhausted their entire supply of shells in less than thirty hours while firing missions for the marines who had stormed the Red 3 beachhead. Not a single round…not one…was left in the magazines and now they were going back for more.

Private Whitey Thompson smiled at the news. *Maybe I'm gonna get outta here alive after all*, he thought happily. Then the faces of all the men he had served with floated in front of him and he wondered how they were doing and where they were. And he would have been shocked if he had known that one of the men he had played cards with on the *Zeilin*…Corporal Tim Staggs…was sitting only seven hundred yards away…and looking at the very ship he was on right now.

• • •

"I just hope it's not gonna be as hot as it was yesterday…that's all. My throat is already as try as leaf in winter," the private moaned, continuing to stare at the sun above.

"We both know that damn sun is gonna be sittin' up there for another six hours or so…and don't think for one dang minute that I'm gonna sit here and listen to y'all bitch about it all afternoon like y'all did yesterday. Try thinkin' about snow and cold weather…isn't that what you Swedes get a lot of up in there Minnesota…or wherever it was you said you were from. Is that too much to ask?" the other man asked.

"Wisconsin…I said I was from Wisconsin," the private stressed.

"I thought most of y'all Swedes lived in Minnesota?" Staggs smirked…jerking his chain.

"A lot do…but there are plenty of us in Wisconsin too."

"Who would know that…other than you blockheads. Just pretend I said Wisconsin instead of Minnesota, okay. There probably isn't much difference between the two anyway."

"My family owns a small farm there. I did a lotta hunting in the woods," Private Rolf Jorgenson said, thinking back on better times.

"Well that's good. Maybe your hunting experience will come in handy somewhere down the line."

"It might I guess…but hunting animals is a little different than hunting humans. I guess bounty hunters would be good at it though," the big Swede said thoughtfully…never having considered the idea before. "How about giving me a little swig from your canteen? If you let me have one, I promise you won't hear another peep outta me," he added hopefully.

Corporal Staggs pulled one of the canteens out of its pouch - he was carrying three of them on his belt – and threw it across the hole to his foxhole mate. The man removed the top, tilted it back, and took a drink. Jorgenson then screwed the cap back on slowly…almost treading it…and then he tossed the canteen back to Staggs who caught it easily. He shook it up and down to see how much of the precious liquid was left. It didn't sound or feel like much was. He frowned again and this time it was his turn to complain. "Whatta you doin' ya stupid ape…why do you keep taking such big gulps? You'll have us outta water in no time." Staggs unscrewed the cap and drained what was left. He put the empty canteen back into its pouch and checked the weight of the others still left on his web belt. "These will last us for a little while…so long as you keep your big mitts off 'em," Staggs said, admonishing the man who had saved his life the day before.

"Lay off will ya. I only took a little more this time. This heat's killin' me…can't ya see that." The big marine reached into his shirt pocket and took out a candy bar he had been saving. He tore the top of the wrapper, squeezed some of the melted chocolate onto his finger, and licked it off. The chocolate tasted delicious…and he would have liked to have some more…but he handed the precious commodity to Staggs nonetheless. "Here…take it," he said, hoping the corporal would grant him a pass on the water issue.

Staggs accepted the peace offering and ate what was left of the gooey mess…the melted chocolate now coating his lips and mouth. When he was done, the two men looked at each other and then started laughing immediately…their faces appearing clown-like with the dark chocolate smeared around their mouths.

As their laughter subsided, Jorgenson put his hand up to shield his eyes from the powerful rays of the sun. "If we don't finish this job quickly, we may end up dying of thirst. All the Japs gotta do is keep holding us up here...like they're doing...and we'll eventually run out of water."

"Do you have water on the brain or somethin'," Staggs asked the marine contemptuously. "Why don't ya just stop worrying about it? They'll get some water in to us...sooner or later," Staggs said confidently.

Deep down though, he wasn't so sure that the water supply problem would be resolved anytime soon. By his calculations, the odds of them getting anything they really needed at this stage...like water... or food...or flame throwers...or demolitions...or rifle ammo...were stacked against them...since it was still impossible to bring the supplies in via the most direct route...which was landing beaches.

There was no denying that the latest battalion effort to land had been a miserable failure...just like the other two landings that he had witnessed on D-Day had been. This morning's carnage was almost worst though...if that were possible...which proved his point. He had been excited at first as the landing got underway...and the marines around him cheered as a long line of Higgins boats pulled up to the line of departure...several hundred yards out in the lagoon. As the boats came on, water spouts began erupting around them as the Japanese shore batteries took them under fire...and then three of them were literally blown out of the water in quick succession as they pulled up to the reef. One second a boat was there...and the next it was simply gone...the force of the explosion obliterating everything...entire boatloads of men seemingly vaporized into nothingness. These boats were the victims of the excellent gunnery of the Japanese crews who still manned the 70-mm howitzers in *the Pocket* and the 127-mm and 75-mm dual-purpose guns situated throughout the island. The most menacing weapon of all though had been a 5-inch naval cannon that was located along the island's tail at

Takarongo Point...to the east of where the two men were currently sitting. This gun made a tremendous *crummmphhing* sound every
time it was fired and its shells had a devastating effect against the
thin-skinned Higgins boats approaching the reef. Thankfully, naval
gunfire spotters identified its position after it began firing at the
landing craft and counter battery fire put it out of action for good.
But that was about the only thing that seemed to go right for the
marines who were trying to land in the early hours of D+1...and now
they were experiencing the same brutal reception that both Staggs
and Jorgenson...and the men who had tried to land with them...had
the day before.

• • •

On D-Day, Private Jorgenson's platoon had ridden to the reef in
Higgins boats just like the men in the 1st of the 8th were doing now
on the morning of D+1. He remembered the crunching sound
his boat had made as it banged into the reef. "This is as far as
we go," the coxswain had announced loudly, shouting over the
engine noise...and then added, "Everybody out," as the ramp fell
forward and came to rest at an odd angle...making a smooth exit
a little tricky. As Jorgenson walked towards the ramp, he saw the
man in front of him slip on its slick surface. The man was so
laden down with gear that he found it hard to regain his balance
and he plunged head-first off the side of the ramp. Negotiating
the ramp successfully, Jorgenson jumped into about five feet of
water and watched as the man bobbed up beside him...apparently
okay. With seawater dripping from the space between his helmet
and the interior helmet liner, the water-logged marine said, "Now
don't that beat all! If this water were any deeper, I'd be in real
trouble!"

The water depth here wasn't so bad for Jorgenson since he was
slightly over six feet tall and he was only wet up to the middle of
his chest. It was a bigger problem for some of the shorter guys
around him though...since they were up to their chins in the stuff

and the waves began slapping them in the face. This made breathing somewhat of a challenge and more than a few men swallowed mouthfuls of seawater as they tried to advance through it while holding their weapons over their heads. Jorgenson saw two men ahead of him suddenly disappear when they tripped over an outcropping of coral in their path. The men struggled and thrashed about trying to regain their footing - each man was carrying nearly sixty pounds of equipment - and the water turned a soft pink as they began bleeding from the deep cuts that the sharp coral left on their shins and knees. Without thinking, Jorgenson slogged over to them and pulled each man up by the straps of their backpacks...which they were trying to discard...since that's what was weighing them down. Each of them said, "Thanks, Clutch!" in turn...using the nickname Jorgenson was known by in the platoon.

"Anytime," Jorgenson replied to each of them as they regained their footing...and then he watched as both men locked arms for balance and pressed onward towards the beachhead.

Joining them, Jorgenson looked up and down the reef and saw the same scene unfolding around him...marines scrambling over the coral barrier and then wading towards the island. He had gone about one hundred yards when the Jap defenders began shifting their machine guns and mortars from the boats to the men walking in the water. A few of them...the smarter ones...had begun to disperse once they got inside the reef but most of the men had made the mistake of confusing safety with numbers and they began bunching up...oblivious to the danger this put them in. Jorgenson watched as several Jap machine guns suddenly concentrated on one group of marines over to his right and the men fell as one as they were cut to pieces. Over to his left, a mortar explosion flung three men in the air...one of them clearly missing a leg as he tumbled end over end. None of them got up after they splashed back down into the water. Then he heard someone screaming *Spread out!* and *Get down!* as the carnage increased inside the reef. Some men dropped down on all fours and began crawling to present as small a target as possible while others squatted and duck-walked in to avoid the enemy fire. This technique worked for a little while, but eventually the water wasn't deep enough to hide them and then they were forced to make a mad dash for the seawall and safety.

If he hadn't seen this carnage with his own eyes, he would never have thought it possible...but he was part of it so it had to be true. In the span of a few minutes, whole units...entire platoons...his own included...had simply disintegrated. For Jorgenson and the rest of the men around him, the landing had become a ghastly nightmare... and he still had three hundred yards to go.

• • •

Corporal Staggs felt the mortar explosions and lifted his head groggily. *How the hell did I get out here?* As hard as he tried, he couldn't seem to remember anything other than the initial ride shoreward in the amtrac. Then he seemed to draw a blank...which was very frustrating...since his memory was usually pretty good. So good in fact that those who gambled against him claimed it was almost photographic. *Maybe if I just rest a little more it'll come to me,* he thought hopefully. The corporal laid his head back down across his arm and looked to his right. There, just yards away, was what he had been hoping to find...the catalyst that would spark his memory bank. Half-submerged, the empty hulk of the *Widowmaker* sat smoking...abandoned long ago by the men who had ridden in her earlier. Draped across the right .50 cal machine gun was the body of the one the amtrac crewmen...his corpse a grisly testimony to the horrific fire that had met the tractor once it was inside the reef. *Strange,* Staggs thought, pieces of the puzzle finally falling into place. *I remember the left gunner getting hit... not the right one...then an explosion...and tumbling...end over end...then darkness. They must have figured I was dead and left me out here like this.* The oversight wasn't particularly encouraging, but one he could certainly understand. *Probably couldn't get to me at the time anyway.* Staggs surveyed the beach and wondered where they might have gone. *Odds are that they're over there on the left somewhere.* From this vantage point…even as low as it was…he could see that very few amtracs had reached the cove area safely. As far as he could tell, most of the landing craft that had made it to the seawall were still sitting over on the left. *So that's where they would've headed too,* he reasoned.

He rose up on his elbows to get a better view and decided to do a quick check to see if he was hit anywhere. Much to his surprise, other than the ringing sound in his ears and a sore back, he seemed okay. He did have a small cut on his thigh but it was nothing serious. Examining his equipment, Staggs found that his poncho and backpack were shredded and his entrenching tool blade had a big dent in it so he discarded those. Then he removed the lifebelt from around his waist and tossed it too. The thing was useless anyway since he wasn't worried about drowning anymore and it had been punctured by the sharp edges of the coral outcropping he had landed on. Then he fished around to see if he could find his M-1 rifle…figuring the odds were nearly a hundred to one that he had held on to it. But all of a sudden his boot hit something solid and it moved. Thinking it might be the stock of his rifle, he reached down through the murky water and picked his trusty M-1 up. *What a shame,* he thought dejectedly as he watched a combination of water and sand drain out of it. *I'd just love to bet someone that this damned thing will still work…just like they said it would…*but there was no one around to take his wager.

Then…out of nowhere…he felt something settle on his shoulder. He turned his head and saw a big hand holding on to his utility shirt…and turning further…he saw the broad face of a huge marine smiling at him. "You okay?" the marine yelled.

"Yeah, I think so," Staggs said hesitantly, splashes now appearing beside them.

"I don't know if I did you any favors…the Japs seem to be using me for target practice right now! We'd better get outta here fast!" he screamed.

Staggs couldn't really hear what the marine was saying….since most of his warning was drowned out by the louder sounds of the battle swirling around them…but he got the gist of it…when more bullets splashed the water around them. Still a little groggy, he steadied himself by holding onto the boy's arm as they began walking towards the beach. That's when he realized why the big marine was so alarmed: a string of marines off to their right was being taken under fire by a Jap machine gun emplacement that was dug in behind the seawall in the middle of Red Beach 2. Staggs felt terrible as he watched the bullets kick up the surface of the water around the men. The Jap gunners adjusted their aim using the water splashes and honed in on their defenseless prey with deadly accuracy. Staggs could see…almost feel…the desperation of the men as they slogged their way through the waist-deep water. Some of them suddenly veered towards the *Widowmaker*, but the Japs spotted the move and shifted their fire to cut them off. Before long all these marines were hit…a fine spray of blood misting off their bodies…some tumbling forward…others falling backwards…the water turning a pinkish color as they bled into it. Then the Jap gunners redirected their fire back to the original group to continue their torment. Some of these men were hit as well…and some were not…and those that could struggled on…their indomitable will driving them forward. The enemy gunners found the survivors soon enough though…and they made every effort to stop them in their tracks. These marines eventually fell too…just like the rest…and then Jap gunners moved on to other prey…but only after all twelve men…an entire rifle squad…had been wiped out.

Corporal Staggs couldn't believe what he was seeing. He wondered if the saltwater was making his eyes play tricks on him. He rubbed them both just to make sure but the same chaotic scene was still there when he reopened them. He turned to the marine who was helping him along – he still didn't know his name – in hopes that he could clear up the confusion. "Is this still part of the first wave comin' in?" he asked, and, as an afterthought, added, "Who are you...anyway?"

"Private Rolf Jorgenson. I'm with the First of the Second. We're part of the first wave," he answered back, all the while pulling Staggs by his shirt sleeve to the left...towards the pier. "Come on...just follow me. Who are you with?" he asked offhandedly and then he felt Staggs pull up all of a sudden.

"Whatta ya mean...first wave. We were the first wave...I'm with the Second of the Second. You were scheduled to land behind us... and that was only if we needed y'all's help."

Staggs' southern twang caught Jorgenson by surprise. Up until that point, he hadn't been speaking with any sort of dialect at all. In fact, he thought Staggs had sounded like someone from the Northeast. "What can I tell ya," he responded impatiently, more concerned with reaching the pier than with debating Staggs over the landing assignments of the different battalions. Staggs, on the other hand, seemed determined to sort the details of the day out right then and there...not later on.

Jorgenson kept slogging towards the middle of the pier with Staggs in tow. He wasn't about to stop...not after what he had seen happen to so many others around him. But he did explain the circumstances of their landing to Staggs as he went. Look he said, "We got the call to land around ten this morning. It sure looked like your battalion needed our help." Then Jorgenson turned back towards Staggs to make sure he was getting it. When Staggs nodded, he continued, "You boys were gettin' the hell kicked out of you so they sent us in. We hit the reef a half hour ago and we were in the first wave for our battalion. We don't seem to be doin' any better I'm afraid."

Corporal Staggs felt his strength and wits slowly coming back and he finally told Jorgenson to let go of him. "I can make it...just like you can," he said, apparently peeved that the private was leading the corporal...instead of the other way around.

Jorgenson wasn't fazed by the corporal's concern for military protocol, but he did let go of his shirt. Then he said, "You sure sound mighty ungrateful for someone who was about to drown back there."

Staggs thought about it for a moment and decided an argument would make him feel better. "I wasn't drowning...I had just come to as a matter of fact. And when you saw me going under...I was just looking for my rifle...which I had dropped. The water wasn't very deep there anyway so don't feel like you went did me any favors."

The big marine stopped on a dime and swung around to confront the corporal. Staggs - like the good card player that he was - read the look on Jorgenson's face and knew instinctively that he had pushed his luck too far...so he quickly apologized.

"Apology accepted...and you can call me 'Clutch' or 'Hutch'... since I answer to both of them," Jorgenson said, a smile quickly replacing the aggravated look on his face.

"Let me get this straight...you have two nicknames?" Staggs asked skeptically.

"Yup," Jorgenson said straight up.

"So are you going to explain that or are you going to leave me hanging," Staggs answered...apparently more interested in Jorgenson's personal life than Jorgenson was himself.

"Well I grew up with sort of a speech impediment I guess...nothing big like...but I had trouble saying certain words. A lot of kids have this problem when they're little...or so I've been told. Maybe it had something to do with the fact that my dad spoke with a Swedish lilt...which he must have picked up from his dad...who must have picked it up from his dad...since he came right off the boat. Are you following me?" Jorgenson asked...since Staggs seemed to frown as Jorgenson went down his family tree.

"I'm not sure I'm following ya...and I'm pretty smart when it comes to stuff...so run that one by me again," Staggs replied mystified.

"Lemme put it to you this way," Jorgenson answered back, "my great granddaddy came right off the boat...and he couldn't speak anything but Swedish. He learned English after a while I guess...since he had to...but I figure everybody down the line was sort of influenced by his Swedish accent...but it must've just petered out with each generation that came along."

Staggs shook his head indicating that he was following along just fine so Jorgenson kept right on going with his explanation. "So I had trouble saying the word *much*...and a few other words too...but mostly it was *much*. Whenever I tried to say that word *much*...it came out as *hutch*...and so they started calling me *Hutch* as a kid...and it stuck with me all the way through high school."

"Okay...I get that part easily enough. But what about *Clutch*? Where's does that come from?" Staggs wanted know...still interested.

"Ready for this...I worked a lot of different jobs while I was in high school. Doing stuff around the farms in the area...you know...hay bailing...stuff like that. But I also cut lawns and did yard work for the people who lived closer to town...and I built myself a good little business doing it. By the time I left home I had two other kids working for me...and I ended up saving a good pile of dough while I was at it. So to reward my hard work...I bought myself a gorgeous Ford truck. It was dark green and I kept it in mint condition so to speak. But then the war came along...and I wanted to do my part...so I enlisted with the Marines. Well, I drove that truck down to Chicago with my brother so he could drop me off and then drive it back home...where it's waiting for me now," Jorgenson said proudly...picturing the truck sitting in his folk's driveway.

Staggs...who had been following the entire story word for word...cut in and asked, "Why Chicago? And get to the *Clutch* part... the suspense is killin' me."

"I was gonna get to that part...if you'd let me finish," Jorgenson replied while pretending to be annoyed at the interruption.

"Well, let's wrap this up, son, since I'm not getting any younger," Staggs countered quickly...now wanting the private to get to the point of the longwinded story.

Jorgenson then explained that he had to be in Chicago so he could catch a train to Atlanta...and from there he eventually made his way to boot camp in South Carolina.

"Okay," Staggs said, "I get that part of it...since most of us had to take that route to get to either Parris Island or San Diego," where the boot camps were located.

"Right," Jorgenson agreed, "but I pulled up in front of a bunch of guys who were standing outside the station...not knowing that they were all headed to Parris Island...just like I was. And when I got out, my brother yelled, 'Take care, Hutch,' and all the guys heard him. The problem was that my brother wasn't that good at driving a truck...so when he pulled out...he ground the clutch!" Jorgenson began laughing at this point...remembering how his truck was bucking as his brother was shifting and grinding the gears and he said, "Well...from that point on...I was no longer *Hutch*...but *Clutch!*"

Staggs broke out laughing at this point too...and said, "Well the wait was definitely worth it, Clutch, my boy! Nice to meet y'all!" Jorgenson then stuck out his hand and Staggs took it in his and they shook hands as mortar rounds began exploding close by. "Now can we just get on with it and get to that pier?" Jorgenson pleaded. "If we're gonna make it to that island alive...it seems to me that it's the way to go."

Staggs looked around and saw other men heading in that direction as well. A long line of marines was already snaking alongside the pier and they seemed to be making decent progress forward. About one hundred yards down, a group of officers and NCO's from the 1st of the 2nd who had survived the wade-in were waving to the lines of men in the middle of the lagoon to come their way. Others were yelling, "Head this way!" or "Use the pier!" and their exhortations seemed to be working since a lot of the men were now moving in that direction. Staggs figured they knew what was best, so he bowed to the private and said, "Lead on…mon general."

CHAPTER 19

"That was a nice thing to do."

"What," Corporal Staggs asked, "are y'all talkin' about?"

The two men were walking down the right side of the long pier...having miraculously survived the gauntlet of fire out in the lagoon....but they still had to be careful. Even though the guns in the *Pocket* were no longer a threat to them, they were still in the sights of the machine gunners and snipers in the pillboxes and foxholes behind the beach on Red 2.

Jorgenson nodded at two dead marines that were draped over the trestles that supported the decking of the pier above them. "Their friends must've left them there like that so they could find them later on...you know...so they can receive a proper burial when this is all over."

Staggs looked over at the two bodies and then caught sight of a dead Japanese sniper nearby. He had a neat hole in the middle of his head and he was slumped against the pilings as well. "What about him...ya think his buddies did the same thing for him?"

"I doubt it," the private said firmly. "It's more likely that he was a lone sniper...and he killed those two guys over there...before their buddies got him," the private theorized...thinking like a detective would at a crime scene. Then a frightening thought suddenly dawned on him: *What if there are more Jap snipers ensconced in these pilings...just waiting for the chance to shoot us as we pass by!* He expressed his concern to Staggs but the corporal didn't seem to be too fazed by this deadly scenario. Instead, Staggs was wondering something else...something just as troubling. Turning to Jorgenson, Staggs asked, "Do you think these Jap soldiers are just like us? Do they care about their buddies...the same way we do...and are they capable of humane acts too? Or are they just savages?"

"How would I know," the private answered quickly, and added, "I haven't been in combat before...and I don't know any Japs at all. There weren't any around where I grew up. The closest thing that comes to mind is an Eskimo family that lived near us. They sort look Japanese-like...I guess. And they were certainly nice people. Really hard-working and very close-knit...they did everything together. They even made ice fishing a family event. I guess I'm glad I don't know any Japs...especially any nice ones. Killing them would be much harder to do if I did."

"Oh, just forget it," Staggs said abruptly. "I shouldn't have brought that idea up. What's the sense of having any sympathy at all for these Japs...since they're the enemy...and we're probably gonna be forced to kill a few of 'em before the day's over. And the Japs aren't Eskimos either...so get that thought outta your head. If you end up cutting some Jap a break for sentimental reasons...you just might end up like one of those seals they hunt so effectively."

"No...I won't," Jorgenson said, resigned to the sad fact that combat and killing were inseparably intertwined...and that he would have to kill the enemy without remorse if he wanted to stay alive. And the likelihood of that macabre event happening was quickly approaching...since the island was now only two hundred yards away.

• • •

As the two got closer to the beach, they came across several more dead marines floating in the torpid water beside the pier and it made Jorgenson realize that Staggs had been right after all...that life and death out there was just a simple matter of odds. Staggs had made the comment when they were out in the open...vulnerable and defenseless. They had seen men getting hit in front of them...watched as others fell to their left and right...and even heard cries from marines being cut down behind them. Yet...for some strange reason...they were spared. Staggs had tried to explain it very methodically. "When we started in," he began, "there was a fixed number of Japanese alive on the island and they had a certain amount of bullets to fire at us. Obviously, it doesn't take a PhD to figure out that part of the equation." Staggs then paused, apparently pleased with the logic of his argument. "Hopefully though...in the interim while we've been trying to get ashore...the Japs have been whittled down by the guys that have already made it in and by the carrier planes that are bombing and strafing them. Concurrently—"

"Are you nuts?" Jorgenson muttered, cutting him off. The disturbing thought that Staggs may have gone crazy had crossed the private's mind...since combat veterans had told him stories about how men just snapped all of a sudden in the heat of battle. *Maybe this is what they were talking about*...but then it dawned on him that Staggs wasn't really rambling at all...that this was how the corporal dealt with stress. *But what the hell does concurrently mean anyway...he's acting like he's some stuck-up college kid tryin' to impress me with these big words.*

"Certainly not," Staggs proclaimed...and undeterred...the corporal continued his dissertation...as though he were a professor speaking to a student in a college classroom. But Jorgenson could only grasp so much of what Staggs was explaining...since it involved mathematical terms and calculations...something he had little interest in. He sort of remembered his teacher...Mr. Giglio...mentioning this type of stuff when he was a senior back in high school...but that had been a year and a half ago. To make matters worse, that class had also fallen during deer hunting season…so Jorgenson had not paid much attention during the lessons. Instead, the boy's mind had been occupied with thoughts of deer stand locations…corn feed applications…weather conditions…and anything else that would guarantee a successful hunt. And just as Mr. Giglio's math lessons had fallen on deaf ears…so too did the lesson on odds and outcomes that Corporal Staggs was trying to impart on the young marine ahead of him.

Jorgenson knew that Staggs was finally done when he proclaimed quite proudly, "So you see, Hutch old boy…the percentages are in our favor. Technically-speaking, we'll probably survive…as inconceivable as that might seem right now."

The private gave the statistics and probabilities lesson some thought and summed it up by saying, "So basically we're just gonna be lucky…like when the wind shifts all of a sudden and you end up bein' upwind of the deer instead of downwind. And yet it still comes towards ya…even though it smells ya."

Staggs…having hunted deer himself in Tennessee…considered his response, smiled, and said, "Exactly…you get an A."

• • •

Corporal Staggs and Private Jorgenson were greeted by yet another morbid sight as they continued to work their way cautiously down the pier. Now they had to push their way through hundreds of dead fish that were floating belly-up in the murky water around them. *Nothing is really safe out here,* Jorgenson thought grimly, *either above or below the water.* He used his rifle butt to plough a path through the shiny, white mass and realized, thankfully, that they weren't giving off that rancid odor that rotting fish do…since they hadn't been dead very long.

Their good luck continued as the Japanese fire seemed to slacken for a while and they were able to make good progress for the first time that morning. They attributed this respite to the fact that the third and fourth waves were now showing up along the reef and the Jap gunners were training their guns on them instead. They only had another hundred yards to go to reach the beach when an amtrac went churning by. It was heading for the small-boat cove that had been built at the base of the pier...not far ahead. An officer was clearly visible up near the front of the vehicle and he was waving to the men in the water...trying to get them to come towards the pier.

Staggs stopped in his tracks and turned back to Jorgenson and said, "Was that who I think it was?"

Jorgenson...who had finally relinquished the lead to Staggs... took the question in stride and replied, "Just another officer I guess... and one that'll probably catch a sniper's bullet sooner or later if he keeps standing up there like that."

Staggs stood there...working the possibilities over in his mind... and came to the conclusion that the man was definitely who he thought he was. *How ironic is that?* he mused...and then he caught up to the private who had just walked past him yet again. "Hey, Jorgenson," he said excitedly, "that was Colonel Shoup...our Regimental Commander...that just went by us. He's supposed to be a good card player."

Jorgenson didn't seem to be that impressed with the commander's sudden appearance on the battlefield. In fact, all he did was ask Staggs if it was normal procedure for the CO to be landing so early.

"I guess it can be," he answered, not really sure. "But if he's coming in, it must mean that things are looking up somehow. He must know something we don't...so maybe we're winning after all...right?"

"Well that's a good thing then," the private said, hoping the corporal's take on the situation was correct.

The two watched the amtrac continue to crawl forward through the surf until mortar rounds began landing all around it. One round exploded the pier itself and sand and crushed coral...which had been packed down on top to make a smooth surface way...went flying skyward in a big dust cloud. Then another round exploded in the water off the amtrac's right side...which had dire implications since it indicated that the mortar team that had targeted it for destruction had finally bracketed it. If they were as good as they seemed to be, the next round this deft mortar crew fired would be landing right between the two rounds that had just been fired…and smack into the rear compartment of the amtrac. This calculation wasn't lost on the driver of the amtrac either…and he was spooked beyond imagination. Without orders, he pulled back on the sticks with all his might and the vehicle slewed to a dead stop. Everyone in the rear fell forward from the shock of the stop…and then the driver jumped out of the LVT altogether. He splashed down into the water of the lagoon and fell on his backside. Without missing a beat, he got back up and looked around to see if anyone had seen this spectacle taking place. Satisfied that no one had, he then scrambled over to the trestles of the pier…just like Staggs and Jorgenson had done when the rounds started landing. Before long, an enemy machine gun crew in a bunker on Red 2 spotted the amtrac and they took it under fire as well…adding to the chaos.

Once Corporal Staggs saw that the colonel's ride had become a magnet for Jap fire, he grabbed Jorgenson and yelled, "Let's get outta here while we still can!" Jorgenson accepted the corporal's challenge and he followed along as Staggs climbed his way up to the top of the pier. They both waited a second…summoning their courage…but when bullets began smacking into the wood pilings around them, the two of them scrambled up and dashed across the pier to the other side. They lowered themselves down using the ends of the pilings…just like they had used on the other side in climbing up…and several marines ashore began clapping to celebrate that they had made it across unhurt. Both Staggs and Jorgenson had been so focused in their dash that neither of them had noticed that several marine bodies were laying sprawled out on the pier…having been shot down while trying to make the same move.

Staggs was hoping that the conditions on the left side of the pier would be better…but once he made it over, he realized that it was pretty much the same there as well. The only difference between the two was that the Second and Third Battalions of the 8th Regiment were catching hell on the left...while the First and Second Battalions of the 2nd Regiment were being shot to pieces on the right.

This had come about because Colonel Shoup had ordered Major Robert Rudd's battalion...the 3rd of the 8th...to land on Red 3 some thirty minutes after he had ordered the 1st of the 2nd to land against Red 2. And just like on Red 2, the Japanese defenders were ready and waiting when the marines tried to land on Red Beach 3. By then, the shock of the naval bombardment and air attacks that had helped cover the initial landing waves had worn off...and the *rikusentai* were now focused on their one main duty: to deny the beachhead to the invading marines. With their guns fully charged and their vengeance at a boiling point, the Jap defenders of Red 3 were making the marines pay in blood as they approached the island.

• • •

Since most of the enemy fire was being directed at the landing craft along the reef, Staggs and Jorgenson found the last fifty yards of the journey to the beach rather uneventful. When they hit dry ground, the two men knelt down and heaved a sigh of relief...their trek in finally over.

Catching his breath, Corporal Staggs glanced back to see how the 3rd Battalion was faring. Although it didn't seem possible given what they had just seen and been through over on Red 2...this battalion was having just as bad a time making it in as the other battalions were...if not worse! *Just how many damn Japs are on this island anyway?* The thought kept running through Corporal Staggs' mind as he watched Major Rudd's men being butchered as they came into the Jap kill zone. *It's a good bet there are probably a hell of a lot more of them than we thought there would be...that's for sure*, he thought cynically...since the carnage he was seeing did not square with the scuttlebutt that had been bandied about when he was on the transport. Many of the men had actually believed the rumor that they were going to have an easy time with the invasion and that they would be able to traipse

ashore and collect souvenirs…given the firepower the Navy intended to bring against the little island. *Most of the Jap garrison will probably
be dead after we get done shelling 'em* was a line that he had heard again
and again…and now he realized…too late…that it had been pushed
by the sailors who were still on the ships…and repeated by the guys
who were hoping it would be true! *It was a fool's bet…totally against the
odds…and yet I fell for it,* he thought dejectedly…and he swore that he
would never let himself be duped like that again.

The corporal was still considering the absurdity of it when a
young officer appeared and ordered them to head towards the left.
"That's where you'll find Major Crowe and Major Chamberlin.
They're the ones who are running the show over on Red Three.
They want all the men on this side of the pier headin' that way. And
you'll know Major Crowe when you see him…trust me," he said.

"But I'm with the First of the Second," Jorgenson protested, and
pointing at Staggs he added, "and he's with the Second of the Second."
Then…hoping he could still reason with the lieutenant…he said,
"We're supposed to be over on Red Two…not on Red Three, sir."

A tremendous explosion inland suddenly rocked the island…and
the three of them ducked down instinctively. Seconds later a shower
of sand, bits of wood, and other debris rained down on them…and
after it was over Staggs choked out, "Everyone okay?"

"What…the hell…was that?" the private stammered, shocked at
the violence of the explosion.

"You think that was bad? We had one go off earlier that made
that one look mild. They said that some engineer blew up a torpedo
storage building less than fifty yards from here. That one knocked
us all down. My ears are still ringin' from it," the lieutenant said,
grimacing as he put a finger into one of his ears and shook it up and
down a vain attempt to stop the annoying sound.

"I'm glad I wasn't around for that one then, sir," Jorgenson replied…and since the lieutenant seemed to be an easy sort, he added,
"I guess we'd better get over to Red Two where we belong then."

The comment had the opposite effect though and the young lieutenant suddenly became riled. "Look," he stated firmly, "we got guys from lots of different units scattered all over the place. Just do what I'm tellin' ya and we'll eventually get everything sorted out." The officer - he was a second lieutenant and he looked younger than most of them did - looked worn down and it was obvious that he had been carrying out this unenviable task since the first wave had landed. He shook his head up and down to assure them and his eyes conveyed a sincerity that was hard to disguise. Then he lowered his voice, as if trying to conceal something secret, and added, "It's fouled up…I know…but right now we need you two down there on the left."

"Aye aye, sir," Staggs replied and then he turned to Jorgenson and stated, "Let's go. You heard the lieutenant."

Jorgenson was torn…since deep down he wanted to head back to Red 2 to see if he could find his company and his buddies. But he also knew that he should obey this officer's order…even if it didn't make all that much sense to him. *They're probably right over there…on the other side of the pier…so close.* This tantalizing aspect had nearly won him over when the corporal intervened.

"Are y'all coming, private?" Staggs said abruptly. Jorgenson could tell by the tone of the corporal's voice that he was getting impatient too.

"Yeah…why not? We probably won't have to be over here too long…right, sir. I just don't want my squad thinking I bugged out on them or nothin'," he replied sincerely, his discipline and training winning out.

"We'll have you back in no time," the lieutenant promised. Then he said, "Now the two of you get going…you're needed over there!" The order had a sense of finality about it and Jorgenson knew immediately that the conversation…and the opportunity to find his buddies…at least for that day…had come to a close.

CHAPTER 20

Directly ahead of Staggs and Jorgenson was an abandoned amtrac that had gotten stuck as it tried to mount the seawall. Three marines were lying in the sand near the rear of the tractor and it was clear that they had been hit as they exited the vehicle. The rest of the marines that had come in on this LVT-1 were nowhere to be seen. They had already scrambled over the seawall and had advanced into the open area where the two taxiways of the airfield complex came together near the northern shore.

The corporal and the private crawled up to the amtrac and examined the bodies of the men lying in the sand to see if they could do anything for them. Staggs rolled the first two bodies over quickly and found them to be quite dead...both having been hit multiple times... probably from a machine gun. He looked over at the other man and realized that he would not have to roll him over though...since he was lying on his back...as though asleep. But Staggs knew the man wasn't sleeping...or taking a nap...since he had a neat hole right between the eyes. The accuracy of the shot was the telltale sign that a Jap sniper was in their midst...and they needed to exercise extreme caution when moving around...lest they end up like him. Staggs motioned to Jorgenson and pointed to the man's wound and mouthed *sniper* so Jorgenson was aware of the danger. The private...who was now knelling by the back fender of the amtrac...nodded that he understood and scanned the area carefully to see if he could spot the deadly assailant... but he was too well hidden to be seen. Staggs then searched through the men's web belts and backpacks - they had never gotten a chance to remove them - and he cursed after he had finished with the first two.

Thinking that Staggs was angry over their senseless deaths, Jorgenson said, "You're right. These poor guys never even got a chance to fire a shot. Why the hell didn't the Navy take out these crummy bunkers along the beach? It's not like they didn't know they were there. We knew they were dug in here...they had them identified on the mock-ups of the island that the officers showed us. What were they thinkin'... that the Nips were gonna just up and surrender to us when we landed?"

"A lot of guys seemed to think that way, didn't they," Staggs said wryly, and then added, "but I guess they know different now though...don't they."

Jorgenson nodded in agreement and watched as Staggs slid over to the third man and inspected his gear as well. Suddenly the corporal let out a yell as he patted the canteen on the dead marine's web belt. The private reacted like it was a warning however...and he hit the sand...thinking they were being fired on. Staggs gave him a puzzled look and asked him what he was doing. Jorgenson raised himself up on his elbows and said, "I thought you got hit by the sniper that got him." He pointed with the end of his rifle to the dead marine that was carrying the sniper's calling card. "He might still be out there ya know...even though I can't see him," he added defensively.

Staggs took the warning in stride and said, "Oh, he's probably moved on...since you would have been dead by now if he were still around."

Jorgenson...perplexed by the corporal's cavalier attitude towards the sniper...asked, "How do you know that? A few seconds ago you were telling me to keep a lookout for him."

"Because while you were kneeling by that amtrac, you made a perfect target for him. That's why so many of you new guys get knocked off so early in the fight...no combat common sense. Ya don't see me kneelin' around here do you? The less you give these Japs to shoot at...the longer you'll stick around. Trust me with that little piece of advice. Whoever spread that lie about the Japs being poor shots never had to face off against one of them. Some of them can shoot just as good as our best shots can...and I saw it with my own eyes on the *Canal*. The fact that your head is still on your shoulders tells me that our sniper friend is long gone."

"Why did you wait to tell me that now? It woulda been nice to know that beforehand...you know," the private pointed out.

"Ever heard of the canary in the coal mine, 'ol buddy?" Staggs answered back...smirking.

"No. What's that?" the private replied innocently.

"It's a pretty foolproof way of staying alive in a dangerous place. Miners used it to monitor the gas levels in the mines they were working in. They would bring a canary in a cage down into the mine with them...and keep the canary by them as they worked away. As long as the canary stayed alive and sang...they knew they were okay. But if that canary died...well then they knew they had to get out of there since the gas had built up to a dangerous level around them. The canary died...so they could live. Pretty ingenious really...don't ya think?" Staggs stated expertly.

"Are you pulling my leg...or was that some kind of sermon you heard in church," Jorgenson replied, not knowing whether to trust the corporal or not...even though it sort of made sense.

"No. I know this because my dad told me about it. My old man was a miner in West Virginia for a few years. He met my mom and she convinced him to move to Tennessee...so she could be closer to her kinfolk. Then they had me," Staggs explained.

"So let me get this straight then. In this scenario with the sniper...I was the canary?" Jorgenson said, already knowing the answer.

"Now you're catchin' on, Clutch! And if you stick close to me...
and keep following my sage advice...you just might make it off this
island alive and get back to that truck of yours after all!"

Jorgenson just shook his head in disbelief...but he knew deep
down that Staggs was being helpful...and doing everything in his
power to help keep him alive. So he would keep on listening to all
the corporal's lectures...even if it drove him crazy!

The corporal went back to what he had been doing beforehand...
and he removed the canteen and pouch from the dead man's belt.
"This is what I was lookin' for," he said proudly, holding the canteen
in his hand.

"Now you're gonna take the guy's water?" Jorgenson moaned,
appalled that Staggs was stealing the man's belongings.

"Why not...you think he needs it now?" Staggs shot back, de-
flecting the private's veiled reproach.

"Why don't ya just take all three then?" the private countered
sarcastically.

"Because the other two are shot full of holes...and this one isn't...
that's why. Consider it a gift from that sniper," Corporal Staggs said,
and satisfied with his find, he secured the new canteen and its carrying case to his web belt. That done, he said, "And here's something
else you can hang your hat on...if you want to stay alive out here."

"What's that," Jorgenson said, all ears now that the corporal was
willing to offer more tips on combat survival.

"Don't pass up any water you find. I don't care if it's in a marine
canteen...or a Jap canteen even. You see how hot it's getting out
here. In a few hours, most of the guys are gonna be dying of thirst...
but we're not. And you know why? Because I'm not stupid...and I
know how valuable the stuff's going to be. You watch...guys will get
killed just goin' to get water...especially as it gets hotter and hotter
and their thirst kicks in. But that's not gonna happen to us...cause
we're gonna husband what we got. So if you see any water...grab it...
understood," Staggs said authoritatively.

Private Jorgenson was humbled yet again…and said, "Sorry about that…I guess I have a lot to learn about combat…and what it takes to stay alive."

The corporal accepted his apology graciously with a nod and wink…and knew that he would do everything he possibly could to keep this young kid alive.

• • •

"You ready to go?" Corporal Staggs asked…but it was really a statement more than a question. Private Jorgenson nodded his assent and gripped his rifle a little tighter…eyeing the seawall ahead of them. Staggs glanced over at the seawall too and then looked down its length as far eastward as he could see.

"Are we headin' inland," Jorgenson asked…not sure of the corporal's intentions.

"Not inland," he answered. "We're gonna stay along the beach… behind the seawall for as long as it lasts…and try and find that major. That's what that lieutenant wanted us to do…so we have to try."

"What about these guys?" Jorgenson asked…pointing to several groups of men who were sheltering in place along the beach. It was obvious by their demeanor that they were going to stay where they were until the firing let up…or another officer came along and forced them to move. "They don't seem to be too concerned with following the lieutenant's order."

"I'm not concerned with them one bit," Staggs said harshly, and looking them over, he added, "some of them are just too scared to move and the rest don't know what to do…since their NCO's and officers were killed on the way in. They'll eventually get tired of sittin' around… and some of them will head inland. Trust me…it's always that way."

• • •

While nowhere was really safe on Betio that morning, the strip of beach that ran east of the main pier where Staggs was intending to go didn't appear as dangerous as some of the other beaches appeared to be. At least dead marines were not laying in droves in this area…like they were over on Red 2 and Red 3. But inland and farther east was a different story. Navy fighter planes were swooping down and strafing enemy positions all along the tail and Staggs could see geysers of sand exploding into the air and smoke plumes billowing off to the right... behind seawall...where the real fighting was taking place. "Okay, let's go," he finally said, and he scrambled up to the seawall and headed left...along the path they would use to link up with Major Crowe... the officer the lieutenant had mentioned in his order. They moved off in a crouch to keep their silhouettes below the log barricade and had not gone very far when Staggs pulled up. For some odd reason, he felt the need to explain his actions back at the amtrac to Jorgenson one more time...and turning around, he said, "Listen...water is gonna be just as important to us as ammo is in a little while. You just wait and see...you'll be beggin' me for some of this water later on. I'd bet y'all on it in fact...but y'all don't have anything I want right now." He then told the inexperienced private about how his squad had ambushed some Japs who had come down to fill their water bottles at a stream crossing on Guadalcanal. "They were desperate...and we weren't... and it cost them their miserable lives," Staggs said savagely...emphasizing his point. The private listened intently and when Staggs was finished Jorgenson reached around and felt for his own canteen. He grasped it and then jiggled it a little to make sure it still had some water in it...and he let out a sigh of relief when he felt the water sloshing around inside. Satisfied that he understood the lesson, Staggs moved out once again...only this time more cautiously.

The two men had not gone very far...only about seventy-five yards or so down the beach...when they noticed that the seawall stopped abruptly. For some reason, the Japanese had failed to complete this section of the barrier and the break in the wall ran for another seventy-five yards or so. Here the ground sloped gently upwards from the beach...and peaked about twenty yards inland...forming a berm. Fortunately, the Japanese pillboxes along the crest had already been knocked out by naval gunfire and by the machine gunners on the two amtracs that had been lucky enough to land in this over-looked weak spot. In fact, the two tractors had never bothered to stop at all. Instead, the drivers gunned their engines and they had rambled on in a move reminiscent of the *Charge of the Light Brigade*. Japanese machine gunners and anti-tank gun crews spotted them immediately and zeroed in on two amtracs...just like the Russian cannon cockers had done when the British dragoons under Lord Cardigan had ridden up the valley on October 25th, 1854 during the Crimean War. And like their English counterparts, the churning tractors somehow survived this gauntlet of fire and managed to cross over the narrow northeastern taxiway before coming to a halt almost three hundred yards inland. The forty-five men in the tractors piled out...formed a rough defensive line...and waited for the other two platoons from Easy Company, 2nd of the 8th to come up and join them. Incredibly, this would be the deepest penetration the marines made into Japanese territory on D-Day...and the achievement was credited to First Lieutenant Aubrey Edmonds - another decorated Guadalcanal veteran and prior enlisted man - who pushed the amtracs forward despite the risk. It was an honor his marines would've gladly passed up however...since they were all alone...and they quickly became the focal point for every Japanese soldier and gun in the area. To top it off, their armored escort then turned around and headed back for the beach...taking the firepower of their four .50 caliber machine guns and two .30 caliber light machine guns with them. Watching them go, one of the veterans in the group grumbled, "Those damn guns would sure come in handy...if things get real nasty-like around here." And even the privates...who were generally the last to know...sensed that they would be fighting for their very lives in the hours ahead.

To their credit, the amtrac crewmen didn't want to leave the marines out there all by themselves...completely isolated. Had it been up to them, they would have stayed put and fought side-by-side with the men they had brought in. But at this stage of the battle, the mission of bringing in the marines who were stranded along the reef was just as critical…if not more so…than helping the ones who were already in the fight. As the two vehicles drove away in a cloud of dust, one of the am-trac crewmen - a Sioux Indian from South Dakota - looked back at the forlorn group and gave them the thumbs-up sign. A marine he would never know and who would never know him caught the gesture and gallantly waved back. And watching the brave band of warriors fade out of sight, he remarked to the man sitting beside him, "I sure hope they have better luck than old *Yellow-Hair* did at the Little Big Horn."

• • •

Lieutenant Edmonds' advance wasn't the only significant accomplishment the marines made that morning on the left side of the pier. Another platoon from E Company had advanced across the island as well…and they weren't that far away from where Edmonds was holding out. These men were from the 1st Platoon and their mission was to storm the far right side of Red Beach 3…near the pier. Their two amtracs survived the run in to the beach and they hit the seawall with a jolt just to the left of the long pier. The coconut log barricade was intact here and it did its job just like it was supposed to. The marines inside were jarred by the violent crash and they braced themselves as the tractors tried to mount the obstacle. Neither could get over however and one of them backed off and then stopped. As if on cue, the marines inside poured out of it and sought cover. The other one…tractor # 45…got stuck when it was half way over and it was left straddling the top of the seawall. The men didn't hesitate for a second and began jumping out of the vehicle…but they were taken under fire and the platoon leader was killed almost immediately. A shrewd Japanese sniper had figured that the first man out would be the leader…so he waited patiently and drilled him in the head when he jumped over the gunwale. Two other men were struck down… one of them the platoon sergeant… in a fusillade of machine gun and rifle fire when they leapt out as well.

The loss of their two leaders did not stop the rest of the platoon however. Melvin McBride…a three-striper and Guadalcanal veteran…

took over behind the seawall and led the men forward. They vaulted over the seawall and charged the enemy positions behind it. The marines overwhelmed the Japanese in the nearest pillboxes and trenches with a shower of grenades and rifle fire and killed several more when they tried to run away. With the tide of momentum on their side, Sergeant McBride's marines kept going and they slashed their way across the small taxiway and took up positions in the aircraft revetments that ran parallel to the main runway. The revetments were designed to protect the Japanese planes on the island but they had failed in their mission since the carcasses of several Zero fighters were still sitting in them...completely riddled. They offered wonderful protection to McBride's men though...since they were constructed out of coconut logs about twenty feet long...just like the seawall was...only higher. In this case, the coconut logs were stacked lengthwise on top of each other until they were about seven feet high...and they were arranged in a U-type configuration...so they offered excellent cover and concealment from the Japanese units that were gathering around them.

Sergeant McBride looked around and knew immediately that he was in a tight spot...but at least he wasn't completely surrounded like Lieutenant Edmonds was. Instead, his men had created a bulge in the marine line...much like the German Army would do a year later during the Battle of the Bulge when they attacked the American Army in the Ardennes Forest in late December of 1944. The danger with this type of attack was that it left both flanks of the attacking unit *in the air*...which meant that it could be subsequently attacked from either side and cut off. A unit that found itself in this position was so vulnerable to a counterattack that Confederate Lieutenant General Stonewall Jackson had used the phrase himself to describe the condition of the Union Army's XI Corps which was under the command of Major General Oliver Howard during the Battle of Chancellorsville in May of 1863. Jackson had met with General Lee the night before the pivotal battle and told him that his cavalry scouts had reported that Howard's Corps was vulnerable to attack...

that his flanks…or wings…were uncovered and *in the air*. Lee understood the significance of the report…and in one of the most daring decisions of the war…he gave Jackson permission to attack his much larger opponent. Jackson then marched thirty thousand men for thirteen miles down an old dirt road through the wilderness the next morning and he destroyed Oliver's Corps in a surprise attack later that afternoon.

And now Sergeant McBride found himself in the same dire predicament that General Oliver had been in…but on a much smaller scale. The only bright spot was that he and his men weren't surrounded at that point…since they didn't have to fight off any enemy troops in their rear. There were no Japs behind them since they had destroyed them as they advanced ahead. But he did have enemy troops on either side of him…which meant that both his flanks were *in the air* as General Jackson would have put it…and out in front of him as well. McBride could only assume that the unit that was supposed to be covering his right flank…a platoon from the 2nd of the 2nd…had run into trouble and was still stuck on the beach. The same thing had happened to his own company too…since the platoon that should have been on his left flank was nowhere to be seen either. Sadly, he had no way of knowing that Lieutenant Edmonds' lonely outpost was ensconced only two hundred yards away from his own…off to his left…and they could have supported one another if they had known about each other's whereabouts. But the two intrepid leaders couldn't see each other…because of all the debris that lay between them…and they couldn't contact each other…since neither of them had a radio. So the sergeant took matters into his own hands…just like the lieutenant was doing…and he and his men dug in and waged a little war all on their own. And they would continue to do so…until they were ordered to do otherwise.

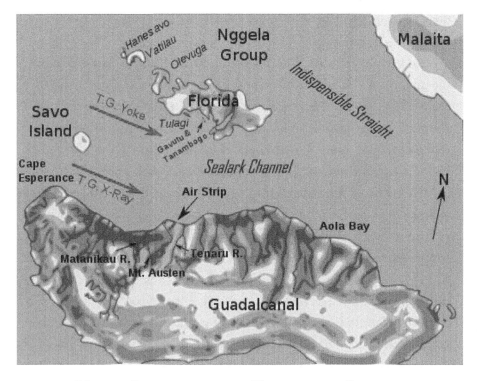

MAP OF GUADALCANAL AND TULAGI IN THE SOLOMON
ISLANDS. IRON BOTTOM
SOUND WAS LOCATED BETWEEN THE TWO RED ARROWS. THE 2ND
MARINE DIVISION FOUGHT THE JAPANESE FORCES ON THESE
TWO ISLANDS IN LATE 1942 PRIOR TO THEIR BATTLE ON TARAWA
IN NOVEMBER OF 1943.

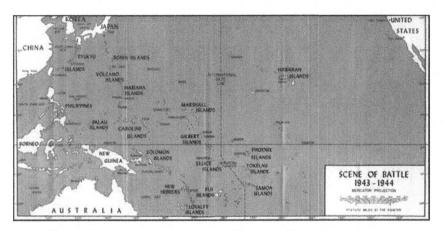

BETIO ISLAND IS PART OF THE GILBERT ISLANDS CHAIN...
WHICH SITS ALMOST IN THE CENTER OF THIS MAP.
GUADALACANAL AND TULAGI ARE IN THE SOLOMONS ISLANDS
CHAIN...WHICH LIES DIRECTLY EAST OF NEW GUINEA AND
SOUTHWEST OF THE GILBERT ISLANDS.

JAPANESE TROOPS BOARDING A DESTROYER FOR THEIR RUN TO
GUADALCANAL AS PART OF THE *TOKYO EXPRESS* IN OCTOBER
OF 1942. MANY OF THESE TROOPS NEVER LEFT THE *ISLAND OF
DEATH.*

A MARINE PATROL CROSSING THE MANTANIKAU RIVER ON
GUADALCANAL IN NOVEMBER OF 1942.

A HEAVILY-DAMAGED JAPANESE TRANSPORT LIES ABANDONED
ON THE BEACH OF GUADALCANAL AFTER BEING RUN AGROUND
TO PREVENT ITS SINKING IN IRON BOTTOM SOUND. MANY
SHIPS SAILING DOWN THE SLOT SUFFERED THE SAME FATE AS
THIS SHIP DID AT THE HANDS OF THE MARINE AND NAVY DIVE
BOMBERS FLYING OUT OF HENDERSON FIELD WHILE TRYING TO
LAND TROOPS AND SUPPLIES ON GUADALCANAL IN LATE 1942.

JAPANESE SOLDIERS LYING DEAD ALONG THE BEACH ON
GUADALCANAL IN LATE NOVEMBER OF 1942. THEY WERE
KILLED NEAR THE POINT WHERE THE MANTANIKAU RIVER
EMPTIES INTO IRON BOTTOM SOUND ON THE NORTHERN
COASTLINE OF THE ISLAND.

FRESH ARMY TROOPS LIKE THIS UNIT MARCHING IN COLUMN ARRIVED ON GUADALCANAL TO RELIEVE THE BELEAGUERED MARINES FROM THE 1ST AND 2ND MARINE DIVISIONS IN LATE 1942 AND EARLY 1943. AFTER LEAVING GUADALCANAL, THE 2ND DIVISION WAS SENT TO WELLINGTON, NEW ZEALAND FOR SOME WELL-DESERVED R&R UNTIL OCTOBER OF 1943.

JAPANESE OFFICERS SUPERVISING THE POSITIONING OF AN
8-INCH BATTERY ON BETIO ISLAND TO THE UPPER RIGHT IN
MID-1943. CONSTRUCTION MATERIALS FOR BUILDING BUNKERS
AND A COMPLETED BUNKER CAN BE SEEN IN THE MIDDLE OF
THE PICTURE.

ADMIRAL SHIBASAKI...THE COMMANDER OF THE JAPANESE
FORCES ON BETIO ISLAND. HE BRAGGED THAT A MILLION MEN
COULD NOT TAKE HIS ISLAND IN A HUNDRED YEARS!

JAPANESE TROOPS BEING INSPECTED BY THEIR OFFICERS PRIOR
TO NOVEMBER 1943.

WORK PROGRESSES IN MID-1943 ON THE SITE OF ONE OF THE
TWO 8-INCH GUNS THAT WERE PLACED ON TEMAKIN POINT
WHICH WAS AT THE SOUTHWEST CORNER OF THE ISLAND. BY
NOVEMBER OF 1943, BETIO ISLAND WAS A FORTRESS BRISTLING
WITH GUNS OF ALL TYPES AND SIZES.

MARINES INSPECTING THE TWO 8-INCH GUNS AT
TEMAKIN POINT AFTER THE BATTLE. THESE GUNS
WERE THE OBJECT OF MAJOR RYAN'S MORNING
ATTACK ON D+1 OF THE BATTLE.

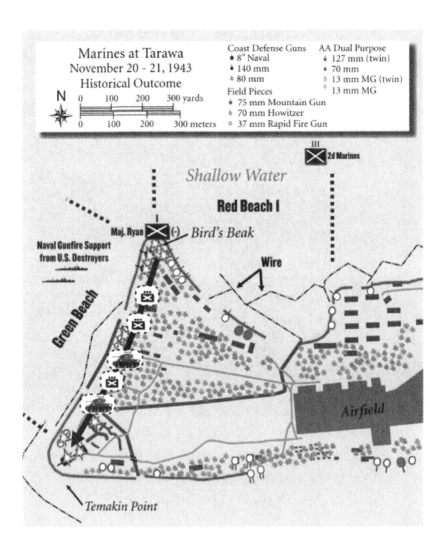

Marines at Tarawa
November 20 - 21, 1943
Historical Outcome

N
0   100   200   300 yards

0   100   200   300 meters

Coast Defense Guns
- 8" Naval
- 140 mm
- 80 mm

Field Pieces
- 75 mm Mountain Gun
- 70 mm Howitzer
- 37 mm Rapid Fire Gun

AA Dual Purpose
- 127 mm (twin)
- 70 mm
- 13 mm MG (twin)
- 13 mm MG

2d Marines

Shallow Water

Red Beach I

Maj. Ryan — Bird's Beak

Naval Gunfire Support
from U.S. Destroyers

Green Beach

Wire

Airfield

Temakin Point

MAP SHOWING THE ATTACK THE "ORPHAN" MARINES UNDER
MAJOR MICHAEL RYAN MADE WITH THE TWO SHERMAN TANKS
UNDER FIRST LIEUTENANT BALE ON GREEN BEACH BEFORE
NOON ON D+1 OF THE BATTLE. ON THE NORTHERN SHORE IS
THE *POCKET* WHICH CAUSED SO MUCH HAVOC TO THE MARINES
LANDING ON D-DAY AND D+1. THE *POCKET* WAS SO WELL-
DEFENDED THAT IT DID NOT FALL UNTIL WELL INTO THE THIRD
DAY OF BATTLE.

HEADING OVER THE TOP OF THE SEAWALL TOOK INCREDIBLE BRAVERY ON BOTH D-DAY AND D+1 OF THE BATTLE. SOME MARINES ARE STILL WEARING THEIR PACKS...WHILE OTHERS HAVE STRIPPED THEM OFF TO MOVE MORE EASILY.

A LEADER POINTS OUT A JAPANESE POSITION THAT HE AND HIS
MEN WILL HAVE TO TAKE OUT ON BETIO ISLAND. CASUALTY
RATES WERE EXTREMELY HIGH FOR UNITS LIKE THE ONE ABOVE
THAT MADE THEIR WAY INLAND ON THE FIRST AND SECOND DAY
OF BATTLE.

TWO HIGGINS BOATS AND A LANDING CRAFT MEDIUM...
WHICH CARRIED LARGER PIECES OF EQUIPMENT LIKE TANKS
AND CANNONS...WAIT FOR A BREAK IN THE ACTION BEFORE
HEADING BACK TO THE ISLAND. THE HIGGINS BOATS AND
LCMS COULD NOT GET ACROSS THE REEF THAT SURROUNDED
THE ISLAND AND THEY WERE FORCED TO UNLOAD THEIR CARGO
FAR FROM SHORE. EXPLOSIONS ARE OCCURRING ALONG THE
ISLAND IN THE DISTANCE...INDICATING THE FEROCITY OF THE
BATTLE IS IN FULL SWING.

MARINES ENJOY A PIN-UP BEFORE HITTING THE BEACH. THE SMOKE IN THE DISTANCE INDICATES THAT THE EASY LANDING MANY OF THEM HAD HOPED FOR WAS NOT IN THE CARDS.

MAJOR CROWE…COMMANDER OF THE 2ND BATTALION, 8TH REGIMENT…DIRECTING AN ATTACK FROM BEHIND LVT-1 # 23 ON RED BEACH 3 ON D-DAY.

THIS WAS MAJOR CROWE'S HEADQUARTERS FOR MOST OF THE BATTLE.
THE MARINE IN THE CENTER DOESN'T SEEM TO BE CONCERNED ABOUT
THE BATTLE BEING WAGED BEHIND HIM. HE IS PROBABLY SUFFERING
FROM A MILD FORM OF SHELL SHOCK AFTER SURVIVING THE WADE-IN
FROM THE REEF. THESE MARINES ARE WAITING FOR ASSIGNMENTS FROM
EITHER MAJOR CROWE OR MAJOR CHAMBERLIN...WHO WAS THE EXEC-
UTIVE OFFICER OF THE
2ND OF THE 8TH.

THIS MARINE PROBABLY HAD HIS LANDING CRAFT KNOCKED OUT...
SINCE HIS UNIFORM IS SOAKED FROM THE CHEST DOWN AND HE PROBA-
BLY JUST GOT DONE WADING IN UNDER FIRE. THIS IS RED BEACH 3 AND
THE STRAINED LOOKS ON THE FACES OF THE TWO MEN CAPTURE WHAT
MOST MEN WERE FEELING AS THEY WERE ABOUT TO MOUNT THE SEA-
WALL AND HEAD INLAND.

These marines are the extreme left flank of the Marine position on Betio Island. They are probably from F Company of the 8ᵀᴴ Regiment and they were tasked with stopping the Japanese from advancing past the Burns-Philip Wharf...which is in the background behind LVT-1 # 39 to the left.

THIS IS THE SHERMAN TANK *COLORADO*...WHICH WAS USED BY
MAJOR CROWE ON RED BEACH 3. *COLORADO* WAS HIT SO MANY
TIMES BY ANTI-TANK FIRE ON D-DAY THAT IT WAS BROUGHT BACK
TO THE BEACH SO THE RED-HOT EXTERIOR COULD BE DOUSED
WITH SEAWATER. FIRST LIEUTENANT LOU LARGEY TRANSFERRED
TO THIS TANK AFTER HIS COMMAND TANK...*CANNONBALL*...WAS
DESTROYED INLAND.

THIS IS THE TWO-STORY, CONCRETE BLOCKHOUSE THAT SERVED
AS ADMIRAL SHIBASAKI'S HEADQUARTERS ON BETIO ISLAND. IT
WAS LOCATED JUST EAST OF THE DEFENSIVE COMPLEX THAT WAS
HOLDING UP MAJOR CHAMBERLIN'S MEN IN THE RED 3 AREA.
THE BUILDING WAS GUARDED BY A TYPE 95 HA-GO TANK
THAT WAS POSITIONED UNDERNEATH THE OUTSIDE STAIRWAY
TO THE ROOF.

TARAWA U.S.M.C. PHOTO NO. 2-6

THESE MARINES ARE TAKING COVER ON RED BEACH 2...NOT
FAR FROM THE PIER...WHICH CAN BE SEEN IN THE BACKGROUND.
A SHERMAN TANK HAS ALSO MADE IT ASHORE AND IS LENDING
A HAND IN KNOCKING OUT JAPANESE BUNKERS.

TWO MARINES...ONE ALREADY WOUNDED...MAKING
THEIR WAY INLAND WHILE AVOIDING A BARRIER STRUNG
WITH BARB WIRE. DISCARDED MARINE PACKS AND
PONCHOS LAY NEXT TO THE OBSTACLE.

A WOUNDED MARINE IS DRAGGED BY HIS BUDDIES BACK TO THE
SEAWALL FOR TREATMENT AND EVENTUAL EVACUATION.

CARRYING WOUNDED MARINES BACK TO THE PIER FOR
EVACUATION WAS BACK-BREAKING WORK IN THE HEAT OF
THE DAY.

SOME OF THE WOUNDED WERE TAKEN TO THE END OF THE PIER
ON RUBBER BOATS AND THEN TRANSPORTED TO THE TRANSPORTS BY
HIGGINS BOATS AND AMTRACS THAT WERE STILL IN SERVICE.

A TREMENDOUS EFFORT WAS MADE DURING THE FIRST NIGHT ON
BETIO TO GET THE 75MM PACK HOWITZERS ASHORE...AND A NUMBER
OF GUNS WERE FIRING ON THE MORNING OF D+1 AS A RESULT.

FIRST LIEUTENANT HAWKINS MIGHT HAVE USED ONE OF THE BOW-MOUNTED .50 CALIBER MACHINE GUNS ON THE AMTRAC IN THE DISTANCE…AN LVT-1…TO FIRE ON THE BUNKER HE HAD JUST ATTACKED ON RED BEACH 2 ON D+1. A DESTROYED JAPANESE BUNKER OVERLOOKING THE BEACH CAN BE SEEN BETWEEN THE TWO AMTRACS IN THE PICTURE. THE TIDE FINALLY CAME IN AFTER THE BATTLE WAS OVER…AND THERE IS A DEAD MARINE FLOATING IN THE WATER BESIDE THE LVT-2 IN THE FOREGROUND.

TARAWA   U.S.M.C. PHOTO   NO.2-2

A MARINE CARRYING AN M1919 .30 CALIBER MACHINE GUN ON
HIS SHOULDER RUSHES FORWARD TO SUPPORT AN ATTACK. MACHINE
GUN TEAMS LIKE THIS ONE HELPED BREAK THE STALEMATE THAT
DEVELOPED ALONG THE WESTERN TAXIWAY ON D+1.

TWO MARINES CARRYING THE FIGHT TO THE ENEMY. THE MARINE
IN FRONT...WEARING HIS HELMET IN REVERSE...SO HE CAN SEE
BETTER...IS HOLDING AN M-1 CARBINE WHILE ALSO CARRYING AN
EXTRA BELT OF MACHINE GUN AMMO FOR A CREW THAT HAS RUN
OUT. THE MARINE BEHIND HIM IS GETTING READY TO CLEAR THE
WAY BY THROWING A HAND GRENADE.

ONE MARINE ENGAGES THE JAPANESE WITH A HAND GRENADE
WHILE HIS BUDDY...WHO IS HOLDING AN EMPTY CANTEEN...
TAKES A BREAK. LACK OF WATER BECAME A BIG ISSUE FOR THE
THIRSTY MEN AS THE BATTLE DRAGGED ON IN THE EQUATORIAL
HEAT.

THIS LUCKY MARINE TOOK A GLANCING ROUND OFF OF HIS
HELMET...AND LIVED TO FIGHT ANOTHER DAY. HE IS HOLDING
AN M-1 GARAND RIFLE.

WORKING RADIOS LIKE THIS ONE WERE IN SHORT SUPPLY ON
D-DAY OR D+1 SINCE SO MANY OF THEM WERE DAMAGED BY
SEAWATER WHEN THE MARINES CARRYING THEM WERE FORCED
TO WADE ASHORE UNDER FIRE.

THE REASON FOR THE ENTIRE OPERATION: THE MAIN RUNWAY.
MARINES FROM A AND B COMPANY OF THE 2ND REGIMENT RISKED
CERTAIN DEATH RUSHING ACROSS THE RUNWAY ON THE AFTERNOON
OF D+1 AND THEN OCCUPIED AN ANTI-TANK DITCH BEHIND BLACK
BEACH WHICH WAS IN THE WOOD LINE TO THE LEFT.

A DESTROYED JAPANESE ZERO FIGHTER THAT NEVER MADE
IT OFF THE ISLAND. IT WAS PROBABLY DAMAGED IN ONE OF
THE EARLIER BOMBING RAIDS THAT THE NAVY CONDUCTED IN
SEPTEMBER OF 1943.

CHAPTER 21

"Somebody made it off this beach alive at least." Staggs nodded towards the series of parallel tracks in the churned up sand that ran up to and over the berm to their right.

"Thank God somebody did," Jorgenson replied as the two men hurried through the open stretch of beach...trying to reach the safety of the next section of seawall that began again in the distance. It was about seventy-five yards in length along this part of the island as well...like the portion next to the pier they had just left...and Staggs and Jorgenson could see what looked like a battalion's worth of marines laying behind it for cover...just like the guys were doing by the pier and over on Red 2. Other marines...coming back to the seawall from the inland side...were dragging their wounded comrades over the log barricade and passing them off to corpsmen below. Taking the full scene in, Staggs glanced back at Jorgenson and warned, "Make sure you keep your head down once we get over there...cause that sniper you were worrying about back at the pier is probably over here by now...or someone just like him."

From this vantage point, Staggs could see that the marines were being stymied when they tried to advance inland beyond the seawall...

just like the guys over on Red 2 were. And they were being held up on Red 3 for the very same reason: many of the Japanese positions inland had been left untouched by the Navy's bombardment earlier that morning. Instead, the battleships and cruisers had concentrated most of their fire on the large, fortified gun positions that were located on the three main corners of the island and along some portions of the seawall. There was no mistaking these positions for what they were...since they could be seen and photographed from the air. And the Navy guns had done an excellent job in disabling or destroying most of them. But this plan...while successful on its face...had a major flaw in it: most of the bunkers and pillboxes that they couldn't see...which were hidden in the coconut groves behind the seawall... were left completely unscathed. And the Japanese made the marines pay dearly for this oversight...since they had excellent fields of fire from these positions and they were able to contest every attempt the marines made as they tried to expand their beachheads beyond it. To make matters worse, these positions...and there were hundreds of them...had been designed to blend into the ground around them... and the marines had just as much trouble identifying them as the Navy did. Then...when the marines did find them...in some cases by stumbling right into them...they realized that they were nearly impregnable to small arms fire. And since most of the weapons that would have worked against the bunkers had never made it ashore, the marine attacks against these positions were often turned back and a frustrating stalemate developed during the early stages of the battle.

• • •

As they got closer to the seawall, Staggs could see several empty amtracs backing away from the thin beach behind it. They had deposited their cargo...usually around twenty or so marine riflemen ...safely ashore...and now they were headed back to the reef to pick up more. But one amtrac would not be joining them...since it was hung up along the seawall...all by its lonesome. This amtrac – a big 23 was painted in white on its backend - had probably led the others in and it had tried to breach the seawall…but the obstacle had been too high and it came to rest with its bow exposed over the inland side of the wall. Seeing this, the other drivers had gone no further since they didn't want to get trapped like amtrac # 23 was. The situation reminded Staggs of what he and Jorgenson had just encountered back near the pier…where another amtrac had gotten hung up while trying to crawl its way over the seawall. Staggs just figured that the drivers who were getting them stuck like that were inexperienced - and a lot of them were - and had not trained on the vehicles long enough to know what they were capable of doing.

As Staggs looked the crowd over further, he noticed one man who stood out from all the rest. He was a very tall man…so tall in fact that he stood nearly a head taller than the other men around him… and he was peering over the gunwale of the LVT…even though it was canted at a high angle on the log wall. He was also talking into a radio handset that he held in his left hand and he was carrying a pump-action shotgun in his right. Staggs watched as the big marine propped the shotgun up against the side of the amtrac and then he turned to his left and pointed down the beach towards the tail of the island. Staggs could make out the remains of the small Burns-Philp wharf in the distance…and he could tell that the man was directing an attack against it. And as soon as he put his arm down, a group of marines began heading east…towards the wharf. *He's gotta be that officer the lieutenant was talking about*, Staggs thought confidently, *I'd bet my life on it!*

"There he is." Corporal Staggs motioned towards the group in the distance…figuring that Private Jorgenson would make the connection also.

"I sure hope you're right," he said right back. And then he added apprehensively, "If we keep heading away from the pier…like we're doin' now…I'm never gonna see my unit again."

Staggs could tell that the private was nervous so he sought to reassure him. "We're just doin' what that lieutenant back there told us to do. Somebody higher up the chain gave him those orders and he was just doin' what he was told to do too. If we all just struck out on our own…and everybody just did what they wanted to do…the whole system would collapse. If ya have any plans of staying in the Marines past your first cruise, then the first thing you gotta learn is to follow orders."

"I never thought about making a career outta this. I just joined up to get those Japs back for what they did at Pearl Harbor…and for everything else they've done since. I'll stay in right up to the very end…until we win this thing. But as soon as it's all over, I'm headin' back home to my dad's farm."

Jorgenson was about to tell Staggs that he agreed with him about the *following orders* part of his dissertation…but he yelled out a warning instead. Staggs swung to his right and saw that they had been ambushed by a wild-eyed Japanese officer and two *rikusentai*. The three had apparently been hiding behind the berm and were waiting for just this sort of opportunity all morning long.

These were the first living Japanese Staggs and Jorgenson had encountered so far and they were a fierce-looking lot from their appearance. The young officer – he was probably a lieutenant because he looked about as old as the American officer did back at the pier – was slightly bigger than the other two and he was brandishing a samurai sword above his head. The other two men were armed with *Arisaka* rifles that had long, deadly-looking bayonets attached to the ends of their muzzles. The officer and the two enlisted men had spent many hours polishing these weapons in anticipation of their use…and they were now gleaming in the sunlight…which made them look even more menacing than normal. And as they came over the berm, the three men began screaming in a hideous, primal manner to scare their adversaries…and to bolster their own courage as they made their charge. They were running as fast as they could… and were only about twenty yards away from their victims…when they hit a soft patch of sand. This inadvertently slowed down their advance…and allowed just enough time for their two surprised opponents to fend off their attack.

Since Jorgenson had seen them first...he was the first one to react. He swung his rifle up immediately and centered in on the Jap rifleman on the far left of the group. The private estimated that he was the closest...and therefore the most dangerous...of the three so he shot him first. *I'll pick some other time to be Sergeant York* was the crazy thought that ran through his mind as his first two rounds found their mark. The bullets blew two holes in his upper chest and the impact stopped the man dead in his tracks. Seeing that he was no longer a threat, Jorgenson pointed his rifle at the other *rikusentai* who was running next to him...which left the sword waver to Corporal Staggs. The private squeezed the M-1's trigger three more times in succession and his aim was just as good as it was with the first man. All three shots slammed home...two hitting the man in the upper chest while the third shot sailed a little high and exploded the man's throat. The soldier instantly dropped his rifle and reached up to stem the bleeding...but it was too late to do any good. The Jap soldier's momentum carried him forward even as he began collapsing like a knocked-out fighter. Plunging headfirst into the sand, his body skidded down the slope before finally coming to rest a few feet away from man who had killed him.

Thanks to Private Jorgenson's alertness, Corporal Staggs had plenty of time to pick his target...and just like the private had figured... the corporal picked the Japanese officer first. Staggs let the tall Jap fill his sights...but when he pulled the trigger all he heard was a dull click. His M-1 had misfired for some mysterious reason so he repeated the process and got the same result. *I can't believe it...I never thought this would happen*, he thought angrily. *They told us you could drag this damn thing through the mud and it would still fire...but I'll bet they didn't test it for sand and saltwater!*

He screamed, "My rifle's jammed!" and he lowered the rifle and pulled on the charging handle as quickly as he could to see if he could get the round to eject or recycle into the chamber. The rifle made a grating sound each time he pulled back on the metal handle though...indicating that it was still jammed for some reason.

Knowing it wouldn't fire, he gave up the effort and looked up in time to see the two other Japs going down from Jorgenson's shots. Staggs hoped that his warning had alerted Jorgenson to his predicament... and that the private would have enough time to finish off this third man too. But just in case he didn't, the corporal assumed a fighting stance with one foot ahead of the other and his rifle extended forward at an angle from his body to parry the Jap officer's sword blow. As the screaming Jap got closer and closer, Staggs noticed that he had several gold fillings and a single gold tooth in his mouth...which some marines on Guadalcanal had considered prized possessions. He was also wearing the normal tan-colored helmet that most of the Japanese were issued. But this man's helmet also had some webbing stretched tightly over it...for jungle camouflaging...and it had an anchor insignia attached to it just above the brim. *This guy's one of those rikusenatai they told us about*, Staggs thought, making the connection... *which makes him one of their very best.* And he also saw that this officer had not bothered to tie the straps of his helmet under his chin...so it was unsecured. This was not an oversight by any means...since the officer's uniform...while spotted with sweat stains...looked otherwise impeccable. Staggs knew that the Jap officer had done this on purpose...that he had left the helmet loose so that his head did not get blown off during the naval bombardment earlier that morning... and that he had probably left it undone afterwards. The veteran marines had told the inexperienced marines to do the same exact thing as they boarded their amtracs that morning too. They knew what the young guys didn't...that the shock wave from an explosion of a large-caliber shell could actually decapitate a man if it hit near enough while he was wearing his helmet and it was secured to his head with the chin strap. *Just my luck that I gotta tangle with one of their veteran officers too...and a squared-away one at that*, the corporal thought dejectedly... and he braced himself...anticipating the heavy strike from his sword. But as the officer raised his sword to deliver the vicious blow, his helmet suddenly flew backwards...and Staggs was pelted by pieces of scalp and brain from his attacker's head. Yet again, Jorgenson had delivered a perfect shot...and saved his companion in the process.

With this last threat eliminated, Corporal Staggs sank to one knee and exhaled a big breath of air. "That was...pretty close, huh?" he managed to stammer out...as he wiped the blood and gore off him.

"Let's get the hell outta here," Jorgenson replied right back and he grabbed the corporal by the shoulder for the second time that morning...and tossing caution aside...they made a beeline for the seawall up ahead.

When they finally got there, the two slumped down and sat quietly by themselves. Several marines glanced over at them casually... but no one approached them or said anything to them. Neither man minded the cold reception however...as it gave them a chance to catch their breath and let their nerves settle from the fight they had just survived. Eventually, Staggs reached over and picked up his M-1 rifle. He looked it over carefully to see if he could figure out why it had jammed...and let out a curse.

"What's...the...matter?" Jorgenson asked, still panting heavily.

"You okay?" Staggs asked...noticing his condition. He laid his rifle against the seawall and crabbed over to the private and said, "Let me take a look at you."

"It's okay...I'll be fine...I'm just washed out that's all. You must be in better shape than I am...even though I'm younger than you are," Jorgenson explained.

"It might be that," Staggs responded, "but I seriously doubt it. The fact that you've been lugging that backpack of yours all over the place might have something to do with it, ya know. The damn thing probably weighs over thirty pounds by now." The private considered the corporal's point and then glanced over his shoulder and eyed his pack suspiciously.

"You think it really weights that much? I packed mine just like they told me to. I was too scared to do otherwise. My squad leader would've killed me in the bay if he had inspected it and found something in there besides what he told me to bring," the private said defensively. "It didn't weigh that much when I put it on," Jorgenson added, "I mean how much can some shaving gear, an extra pair of pants, a shirt, some skivvies, some undershirts, three pairs of socks, and some extra chow weigh?"

"Not all that much...but that pack is water-logged. All your stuff is soaked...and that adds to its weight considerably," Staggs countered. "And you've been carrying it for several hours...so no wonder you're beat. I got rid of mine back in the lagoon. There was no way that I was gonna drag that thing all over the place. It would've slowed me down way too much," he said, finishing his point.

"I never even thought to get rid of mine," Jorgenson said, shaking his head. "I was too worried about what my squad leader would do if I lost it," he added sheepishly.

"Is your squad leader with ya now?" Staggs said.

"No...of course not," the private answered.

"So dump your pack. I won't yell at you...trust me."

"But what are ya gonna do when this thing is finally over? And we could be here several more days if the Japs keep fighting the way they are now," Jorgenson said sharply...confident that he was making a good point. "Can you imagine what we're gonna smell like," he said, wrinkling his nose, and added, "where are you gonna get a change of clothes from then?"

"From the same place that I got my extra water...from the dead guys that are strewn all over the place out here. That's where," Staggs stated unapologetically. "And there'll be plenty of packs to pick from too...trust me."

With all the dead marines he had seen, Jorgenson knew Staggs was right yet again...that there would be plenty of abandoned packs to pick from...since their original owners wouldn't be needing them anymore. So he slid the pack of his back and pushed it up against the seawall.

"Game…set…match," Staggs said victoriously…knowing that he had schooled his young protégé yet again.

Staggs then went back to what he had been doing before…checking the condition of his rifle. He pulled the charging handle backward…and this time it slid back and then released easily forward… so whatever had caused the snag in it before had been freed. Then he hoisted the M-1 up in the air so could peer into the chamber…but it was as clean as a whistle. "The damn thing wasn't even loaded! Sand probably caused the jam…that's what the problem was," Staggs said angrily. The corporal dug into one of his ammo pouches, pulled out a clip, and loaded it. "I must have forgotten to do it in all the excitement…or I never got a chance to load up when I was in the tractor. Either way, it's the kind of mistake that you rookies make all the time…and end up dying for it. I was lucky with that one. And it's never good to push your luck too many times…especially out here… where *Lady Luck* seems to be working against us."

"Well, it looks like you're set for bear now," the private replied, letting the veteran corporal gently off the hook.

"That was some pretty nice shootin' y'all did back there by the way. They do a good job on the rifle range with the boots…but not that good. Where'd ya learn to shoot like that?" Staggs asked, obviously impressed with the private's ability.

"From hunting up north…near home…and even in Canada sometimes."

"That makes sense…the huntin' part at least. I'm a good hunter too…as most Southerners are. I grew up in a town called Columbia. It's pretty small so you probably never heard of it though--"

"I know the place you're talkin' about," Jorgenson cut in.

Staggs kept on talking, oblivious to the interruption. "I've got kinfolk that go all the way back to the *War for the Lost Cause* and long before that and--"

Jorgenson broke in again. "What do you mean by the *Lost Cause?*" he asked skeptically.

"You know...the Civil War...the war for states' rights."

"States' rights...uh huh," Jorgenson replied caustically.

"Well, what the hell do you know about it then?" Staggs shot right back...figuring the private would know very little about history...and certainly not the Civil War.

"My great-grandfather fought with Colonel Opdycke's Tigers during the Civil War. I probably know just as much about it as you do...if not more," Jorgenson countered right back...and the look on the corporal's face changed dramatically.

"Are you referring to the Opdycke that fought at the Battle of Franklin in 1864?" Staggs asked, intrigued that Jorgenson seemed to know more than the average private...especially about a topic that interested him almost as much as gambling did.

"One and the same," the private answered confidently.

"Well don't that beat all! My great-granddad was a private in the First Tennessee Regiment. He enlisted in Eighteen Sixty-One and he managed to survive the war," Staggs proclaimed proudly...and seeing that Jorgenson was interested...he kept right on going. "He got captured at the Battle of Nashville in Sixty-Four and was sent to a prison camp up north in Illinois. That's where he was when the war ended. When he got older he ended up living with my pa and his dad since he had trouble walking. Maybe he had been wounded in the war and never told anyone about it. Who knows...but he was very proud of the time he spent in the Army...and he never missed an opportunity to enlighten others about it. He called it, 'his heroic service in the Army of the Confederate States of America.' My pa told us that he could spend hours talking about it. But Pa also said that the one and only battle that his grandpa never really liked talkin' about was the Battle of Franklin. And he said that he didn't like bragging on Bragg...that Bragg being Braxton Bragg...who was one of his generals...very much either. Said he was a tough disciplinarian...and would shoot guys at the drop of a hat for the slightest infractions."

Jorgenson...mesmerized at the story...cut in, "Good thing we don't shoot our guys like that anymore...since my squad leader's gonna have a fit when he finds out that my pack is missing. He'd probably try to shoot me himself if he could...like this guy Bragg was doing apparently."

"Will you forget about that stupid backpack of yours already?" Staggs said, exasperated, and added, "I'm givin' you an important history lesson here...and all you're thinking about is that damn pack."

"That's because you're not gonna get shot for losing yours!" Jorgenson pointed out. "I'm the one that's gonna have to explain it to my squad leader...not you!"

"If it makes you happy, I'll find him when this is all over and square it away for you. Happy now?" Staggs said diplomatically.

"Yes...as a matter of fact...it would make me very happy," the private said, encouraged.

"What's the guy's name? I might already know him," Staggs asked.

"Sergeant Trackman. I think his first name is Barry. I'm not positive about that so don't quote me on it. I heard one of the other guys say that's what it was...but I never heard anyone call him by his first name. This guy is a real stickler for the rules and he would never allow one of us underlings to call him by his first name."

"Trackman. Yeah...I know the guy. A real jerk...that one. I won a bunch of money off him after one payday when we were back in New Zealand and he couldn't handle it. He thought he was a much better card player than he actually was. He was good...don't get me wrong...but not in the same league as me. He was too cocky to know it too."

"Yup...that sure sounds like him," Jorgenson said in agreement.

"The idiot was such a sore loser and so arrogant that he tried to ban gambling in the barracks," Staggs said, laughing now.

"I heard about that! It happened before I got there...but they told me about it anyway," Jorgenson said enthusiastically.

"He almost pulled it off…since he found some arcane rule in the Regulations that he twisted around to suit his purposes…but your platoon sergeant liked to gamble too. I ended up taking a lot of money off him…but he could handle his losing…where Trackman couldn't. When he heard what Trackman was trying to do…he squashed it."

"I never heard about that part of it. I don't know if many of the guys know that's how it went down…but they were always wondering why Trackman just let the issue drop all of a sudden," Jorgenson said appreciatively, the riddle now solved.

"Well, your platoon sergeant still owes me a good chunk of money…so I'll go to him after this is all over and he'll keep that squad leader of yours off your back. So from this point on, I don't want to hear you mention that backpack one more time," Staggs said…and he stuck his hand out and the two men shook on it.

"Good deal," Staggs said, and then added, "now let me finish my story about my great-granddaddy's service in the Civil War."

"Fire away…I'm all ears," Jorgenson replied…happy to know that he was no longer going to be shot for losing his pack!

• • •

"Now where was I," Corporal Staggs said, trying to remember where he had left off.

"You mentioned Bragg…the mean general," Jorgenson offered.

"Right…Braxton Bragg. Well…like I was saying…my great-granddaddy didn't like him much. But he loved his replacement. He said that when General Joe Johnston took over for Bragg… the entire Army of Tennessee cheered. That was in late Eighteen Sixty-Three. Now there was a guy who loved his men and looked after them. And they loved him. He said anyone one of them would have taken a bullet for him…that's how much they cared about him. But just like always, politics got into it and screwed it all up. You see Johnston didn't get along with Jeff Davis…who was the President of the Confederacy…and Davis fired him the first chance he got. He said Johnston wasn't aggressive enough…that he was letting the

Yankees walk all over him...and that he needed to put up a fight to show those Northerners what the Southerners were made of." Staggs stopped...thought for a moment...and then said, "Kinda sounds like what we got going on here. These Japs definitely want to show us Americans what kind of moxie they're made of...no?"

"Definitely," Jorgenson answered.

"I'm not boring you by the way...am I?" Staggs asked defensively, and added, "I'm generally not this longwinded about much...but I guess I really do love to talk about my lineage...my people...and what they did."

"I'm okay with it," Jorgenson replied, adding, "Keep going."

"Well, Johnston eventually got sacked by Davis as the Yankees got closer and closer to Atlanta. He had put up a few good fights... like at Kennesaw Mountain...and at New Hope Church...but that bastard Sherman kept outflanking him so he was forced to pull back."

Jorgenson was startled for a second when Staggs called the Union General William Tecumseh Sherman a "bastard" and was about to defend him, but he let it go. The tone of his voice alone made Jorgenson realize that the corporal had a visceral hatred for the man who had supposedly burned down Atlanta...and then devastated an entire swath of Georgia...as he made his famous march to the sea to capture the city of Savannah.

Staggs noticed Jorgenson's reaction but dismissed it and kept going. "So Johnston gets canned...unfairly in my humble opinion... and Davis replaces him with a 'fighting' general named John Bell Hood. And Hood was a fighter...make no mistake about it. He had earned his fame leading a bunch of boys outta Texas. He was their Division Commander and when General Lee needed some ass kickin' done up in Virginia...well old Hood and his Texas maniacs got the assignment. And he pulled General Lee's butt outta the fire more than once...but his aggressiveness cost him dearly. When Davis finally put him in charge, he was missing a leg and one of his arms was useless. They even had to strap him to his saddle so he wouldn't fall off his horse. Well, Davis wanted him to fight…and fight he did…at Peachtree Creek…then at the battle for Atlanta…and finally at Ezra Church. The Army of Tennessee took it on the chin in all three of those battles…and they ended up losing Atlanta. Some say that's what got Lincoln reelected that fall in Eighteen Sixty-Four. Who knows…maybe it was…but I just hate the way politicians and politics work. Anyway, my dad said that his granddad said that after those battles the guys didn't like old Hood very much. He seemed to think that Hood should have stayed a division commander since he was better at leading men in a fight than strategizing and moving units around on the battlefield."

"Do you like our Division Commander," Jorgenson asked.

"Major General Smith seems to be a good one as far as I can tell," Staggs responded. "Julian's even-keeled and fair…and I've never heard any of the senior NCO's I know say a bad thing about him," he added. "It's the other Smith you gotta watch out for…he's the dangerous one."

"How so," the inexperienced private asked.

"Our Corps Commander is named Smith too…only he goes by Holland," Staggs explained, "and both of them are major generals and both wear glasses…but that's where the similarities end. Let's put it this way…Holland's nickname is 'Howlin Mad,' and it fits… trust me. You definitely wanna stay outta his way if you can. He's gotta a personality like Bragg's I guess…although he probably wouldn't advocate shooting his own guys…but who knows?"

"Geez…that's more good advice…but I doubt I'll ever run into him," Jorgenson said innocently, and added, "I mean what would be the odds of that happening…right."

"About a million to one, I guess," Staggs calculated, "but ya never know."

"You're right there…if I learned anything today…it's that anything can happen out here," the private replied.

"You got that right. Heck, if Jesus Himself showed up today, I wouldn't doubt it...like his friend Thomas did. Nope, I'd just salute Him and then I'd asked him to turn the water in my canteens to wine. Imagine that," the corporal intoned.

"This is certainly the place for miracles...that's for sure," Jorgenson...a Lutheran by denomination...said devoutly. "I've been praying to Him all morning in fact...stuff like *Please keep me alive, Jesus* and *Jesus, if you let me live through this, I will devote the rest of my life to your service.* You know...prayers like that," the private...a dedicated churchgoer...added.

"How's that workin' out for you?" Staggs replied condescendingly.

Jorgenson caught the sarcasm and wasn't fazed by it. "I'm still alive is all I can tell ya...and that's a miracle," he said mildly.

"I don't believe in miracles anymore," Staggs said, "since I never had any happen to me. And I certainly gave up on them after my dad was taken from us. He died a slow, painful death from black-lung disease. He and mom figured he got it from the mines...even though he didn't spend a lifetime down there. A few years of working under those conditions was all it took. I prayed for him day and night too...and God went and took him anyway. Since then I have kinda given up on Him and religion."

"That's tough. I'm sorry you had to experience that. And God works in strange ways sometimes. But when you're the one goin' through the rough times it's real hard to accept what He's trying to accomplish. I can't explain it any more than that...but I know that I experienced a miracle myself earlier today," Jorgenson said sincerely, fully comprehending the corporal's dilemma and the struggle he was having with his faith.

"What kind of miracle," Staggs asked...intrigued.

"You really wanna know?" Jorgenson asked skeptically.

"Yeah...maybe it'll restore my faith in God somehow," the corporal answered truthfully.

"Okay...well...when I was coming in this morning...it couldn't have gotten any worse. If there's hell on earth...I experienced it out there. All of the guys that were with me on our boat were killed…so when I got to you I was all alone. Just before I reached you, I said one of those little prayers I mentioned and out of nowhere I hear a voice say: *Move to your left.* I looked around and there was no one by me…I mean I was still all alone…no one had come up behind me. I'm thinking *did I really hear what I thought I heard…or am I just going crazy!* And then I heard it again…this strong yet gentle voice telling me to move to my left. I figured I had better listen to whoever or whatever it was that was telling me to do this…so I moved to my left. I go about twenty yards or so. No sooner did I do that than a mortar round explodes exactly where I just was…and if I had stayed there…well let's just say I wouldn't be here to tell ya about it. And that's not the end of it…cause no sooner did that happen then I felt a *presence* around me…and a feeling like someone…or something…was patting my shoulder…as if to say *You are going to be all right…I love you and will take care of you.* At least that's the feeling that came over me. I know it sounds crazy…or maybe it doesn't really…but I swear that is what happened to me. I think it was God… or my guardian angel maybe…if you believe in angels…looking out for me. So there you go…that was my miracle. And if I hadn't obeyed that voice…you and I would never have met this morning. Why God picked me…that I don't know. And probably never will."

"Which makes me question God even more now," Staggs said, "since He seems to play favorites. Why does He allow one guy to have his head blown off…and yet He spares the guy right next to him. Both guys are basically the same…yet one dies and the other one lives. There doesn't seem to be any rhyme or reason to it… nothing you can do to really affect the outcome of it all. And I like stacking the deck in my favor…but that doesn't seem to matter when it comes to God. It's frustrating…since the one real strength I have seems to be useless in God's eyes. Do you understand what I mean?"

Jorgenson had not taken his own eyes off the corporal as he was explaining his faith dilemma. It was if the war had suddenly disappeared while Staggs was speaking…and the private…knowing the importance of the topic they were discussing...had given the subject the attention it deserved. Even a mortar round exploding nearby was dismissed with a casual glance by the two men now...and then Jorgenson spoke. "I'm not a preacher...but some of the people back home used to tell me I had a gift. I have always been close to God...even as a kid. As I got older, my faith didn't seem to falter...the way it did with most of my friends. I guess it's because I didn't want it too. I love God...and I definitely know He loves me. And I know who He sent to save me. And how He saved me. That's the basis for my faith...and beliefs. It's pretty simple really. You just have to be willing to surrender your life to Him. There isn't much more to it than that. But some people have a problem with it...since it can't be proven completely. At least not in ways they are looking for. That's where the faith part kicks in. I wish I had a concrete answer for you...but that's all I can offer."

The corporal didn't respond at first. Instead, he considered what the young private had said...and weighed it against the argument he had made. As another mortar round showered them with water, he finally said, "You do have a gift. The way you explained it made sense to me. Deep down...I want to believe everything you just told me. And it's not just foxhole faith that I'm feeling...which I've seen guys experience when the chips were down. Maybe...just maybe... God'll speak to me out here too...if I just trust Him...the way you do. I certainly could use His help."

"Just start praying to Him...and He'll answer you. He always does...trust me," Jorgenson said confidently.

"I think those people are right. You do have a calling. Make sure you do something with it after all this is over with," Staggs said, impressed with the young marine.

"Thanks, corporal," Jorgenson said graciously, and added, "is there any more to that General Hood that you were telling me about?"

"Oh yeah...General Hood," Staggs answered...not missing beat...and he went on to tell how bad it got after Atlanta fell...and how Hood had then taken his army northward…with the goal of taking Nashville…and forcing Sherman's hand. "And that's what led to the battle…the only one…that my great-granddaddy wouldn't talk about. He claimed…so my father said…that he was in almost every major engagement in the West and that he had been in some rough fixes…but nothing like Franklin. And you say you have kin that fought there too…what are the odds of that happening?"

"Another one of those million to one chances," Jorgenson guessed. Then he began to tell Staggs about his family's experience with the Civil War. "You see my great-grandfather came over from Sweden…which you already know…and he was barely here when the war broke out…yet he signed up for the Army anyway. They told him it was a war to unite the country and to stop slavery and since he was going to be a citizen, he figured that he needed to be part of it. My father idolized his grandfather and he always told my brothers and me all about him. He told my dad that he enlisted at nineteen…just like me…and was badly wounded at Franklin. The Twenty-Fourth Wisconsin was his outfit. They were part of Colonel Opdycke's Brigade that fought there. His Regimental commanding officer was Major Arthur MacArthur…the father of General Doug MacArthur… who's fightin' the Japs down in New Guinea right now. I don't know if you know it, but old Dugout Doug's father won the Congressional Medal of Honor at Franklin for leading the Twenty-Fourth forward at the Carter House and capturing a Confederate regimental battle flag. I can't remember what unit they got it from…but who knows…it might've been the one that your kin fought with. Opdycke's men captured ten flags during that fight…imagine that? And the colonel had his horse shot out from underneath him…so he ended up fighting on foot…right beside his men in that inferno around the Carter House. Opdycke was promoted to brigadier general after Franklin…and he managed to survive the war even…but he died in New York City a few years after the war when he accidently shot himself in the abdomen while he was cleaning a pistol he owned. Talk about bad luck."

"Based on what his granddaddy said...my dad thought that Franklin was a battle that should never have been fought," Staggs seethed...and Jorgenson could see that the battle was obviously a sore spot with him as much as it was his great-grandfather. Then he added, "He felt that the Union Army under General Schofield got lucky and made it up to Franklin by the skin of their teeth. Hood almost bagged the whole lot of them just outside of Columbia...at Spring Hill... which is where I'm from...the day before the battle but our boys were just too tired to pull it off. By the time the Johnnies caught up to the Yanks, they were entrenched at Franklin...sorta the way the Japs are here. Hood was so mad that he just had them advance and attack without much preparation. We lost five generals storming the ramparts at Franklin. All of them good men and excellent field commanders...especially Major General Cleburne...who they called the *Stonewall Jackson of the West.* My dad would always say that the Confederacy lost its heart and soul that sad November day and he was right. It was worse than Gettysburg...but most people don't know that."

"I know what you mean," Jorgenson said, nodding his head. Then he spoke. "My father always remembered his grandfather tellin' him how horrible war was. He told my father that the hand-to-hand fighting that took place at the ramparts around Franklin was the worst he had ever seen in the war. When the Confederates broke through the Union line, his unit was preparing breakfast and the fact that the Rebs were disturbing their meal time made them as mad as hornets. They charged into the break and clubbed the rebels to death with their muskets and anything else they could swing. As bad as it was, my father said his grandfather always seemed very proud that he had fought with Opdycke's Tigers at Franklin. Maybe we'll be that way too someday...when we're older. I hope we'll be just as proud to say that we fought with Shoup at Tarawa."

The two men sat quietly for a while and though neither one of them said it, they were both thinking the very same thing: *Damn right I'll be proud to say it...if I can make it off this damn island alive.*

CHAPTER 22

"Hey, we'd better get up."

"Why, what's the problem now?" Staggs asked, sounding a bit perturbed. He was deep in thought calculating the odds on two men from different states meeting each other...especially under these conditions and circumstances...and having great-grandfathers who fought against each other in the same battle during the Civil War seventy-nine years earlier.

"An officer is waving us over...that's the problem," Jorgenson replied matter-of-factly.

"Astronomical...almost astronomical," the corporal murmured absentmindedly, and then he looked over to where he had last seen Major Crowe. Standing by the back of the amtrac was an officer... but it wasn't the tall one that he had seen earlier...and this one was signaling them to come over...just like Jorgenson said. "I believe you're right," Staggs muttered...and rocking himself off the seawall he added, "well, we're certainly not gonna to win this thing sittin' around on our backsides. Let's go see what this guy wants."

Staggs and Jorgenson...hunching over...threaded their way through the tightly-packed group of marines that were laying in the sand all around the stranded amtrac. Some of these men were seriously wounded and were being tended to by either a corpsman or by another marine if no corpsman was available. Others just seemed to be resting comfortably…doing nothing. Upon closer examination though it was evident that some of them were simply dead…shot down during the landing…their corpses mixed right in with the living who were lying behind the seawall. Sadly, the dead were being ignored for now…since there was nowhere else to put them and certainly no time to bury them.

The rest of the men…the ones that were alive…were sitting or lying around…apparently waiting for orders to head over the seawall. They watched expectantly as the corporal and private reported in to the major who had been waving them over.

"What unit are you two in…Two Eight or Three Eight?" the officer asked crisply.

Staggs spoke up since he was senior. "We're with neither, sir. I'm from the Second of the Second and he's from the First of the Second. We're supposed to be over on Red Two, sir, but we had a hell of a time on that side of the pier. We switched over to this side so we could get in and an officer sent us down here." Staggs then asked, "You're not Major Crowe are you, sir?" since this man didn't exactly look like the officer he had seen talking into the radio handset earlier.

"No, I'm not. I'm Major Chamberlin. I'm the XO of the Two Eight…Major Crowe's outfit. I'm gathering a headcount for him. Do you mind working with us for a while. I can certainly use you."

"We don't mind one bit, sir," Staggs said agreeably, but he felt Jorgenson nudging him with his foot. Then he added quickly, "I mean…we don't mind for now, sir…so long as we can get back to our own units sometime soon."

"I understand completely…and I promise I won't keep you all that long," Chamberlin replied, knowing he had several other men in the same predicament…and then he told them to wait by the seawall with the others who had recently come in.

As he turned to go, Corporal Staggs said, "Sir, mind if I ask you a question."

"Not at all," the major replied easily, "what is it."

"Sir, you look pretty familiar to me. I think I recognize you from the college I was attending before I signed up for the Marines. I was going to Northwest University on a math scholarship but I left after my second year. That was in spring of 1940...I just got bored I guess."

"Yes...that's where you would've seen me. I was a professor of Economics there before the war started," Major Chamberlin confirmed.

"What are the odds of that," was all Staggs could say.

Staggs left the officer and went over to Jorgenson who was sitting against the seawall. He sat down beside him and the private asked, "What was that all about?"

"Oh...just another strange coincidence...that's all. There seems to be a lot of 'em goin' on around here lately." The corporal didn't bother to explain the relationship he had with the major and Jorgenson didn't press him for one. The morning's trials had taken their toll both mentally and physically on the two men and they were more interested in getting some rest than shooting the breeze again. Exhausted, the two closed their eyes and drifted into a glorious state of semi-consciousness...completely ignoring the noise swelling around them.

They hadn't been out very long when a bellowing voice snapped them awake. Coming around the corner of the LVT was the big officer Corporal Staggs had seen directing the attack earlier. He was carrying his shotgun in one hand...like he had been before...but instead of the radio handset...he now held a swagger stick...or a riding crop... Staggs couldn't tell for sure...in the other. "Who's wants to go kill some Nips!!" he yelled at the marines taking cover below the seawall.

Staggs could see that the officer was well over six feet tall and that he wore a long red mustache... the trademark...of Major Jim Crowe. He strode in among the prostrate marines and cajoled and harangued them in a forceful, but good-natured way that bucked them up. He told the men that Major Chamberlin was going to lead their group over the seawall to launch another attack against the defenses that bordered the Burns-Philp wharf area. "Men," the forty-four-year-old officer said in a fatherly tone, "we need to reduce the bunkers and pillboxes over there so we can get some breathing room for the new boys that are gonna be comin' in real soon."

Staggs looked around and saw that everyone's eyes were riveted on the charismatic officer as he made his speech. What amazed Staggs was the fact that the officer did this while standing straight up...in full view of enemy snipers. Crowe...it seemed...was unfazed by them even though their fire was continually hitting and killing marines on the beach behind the seawall.

"So there you have it, men. That's what I need ya to do for me. Anybody not got the guts to act like a Marine and get that job done for me?"

Not a single hand went up. But the tension and excitement was broken when one young marine shouted out, "I'd charge into Hell if that's where ya wanted me to go, sir! Yes, sir, I'll get it done for you!"

"Well...as hot as it is out here...you might already be there," Major Crowe exclaimed and all the men started laughing. Then he looked from man to man, making eye contact with each and every one of them. "I can stand here and see it in your faces...you've had it with lying on your bellies. Now go kick some ass and show those lousy Jap bastards what the Second of the Eighth is made of!"

"Hey, sir," one marine yelled back, barely able to contain his enthusiasm, "I'm from the First of the Second...you mind if I tag along too!"

"What...there wasn't enough action for ya over on Red Two so you decided to see how hot it is over here on Red Three? Well, son, you must be a fightin' marine...you certainly look like one to me... and you came to the right place. We'd be right honored to have you kill a few Japs for us over here on our side of the pier. Welcome him aboard, boys, and I wish you all good hunting!"

When Major Crowe finished his speech, all the men immediately looked over to see who the big marine was that had asked for permission to fight with them. Corporal Staggs was just as surprised at the man's enthusiasm as the rest of them were...but he didn't need to see who it was. It was Clutch...his young protégé...who he'd been listening to for over two hours now...and he recognized his voice when he heard it!

• • •

While waiting for Major Chamberlin to return from his scouting mission of the left flank, Staggs saw a marine out of the corner of his eye scramble over the top of the seawall and trudge up to Major Crowe. Staggs could see that the man looked worn out and he felt Jorgenson elbow him and say, "Now what's all the commotion about?"

"Don't know yet," Staggs said hesitantly, alarm bells going off in his head. They watched as the tired marine pointed over the seawall and then bent over to catch his breath. Staggs got up on one knee and peered over the lip of the log wall but saw nothing but an empty expanse of sandy ground, shattered palm trees, and thick, black smoke billowing skyward in the distance.

In the meantime the major had confirmed via radio whatever the marine had told him and he strode purposefully over to their group. "Men," Major Crowe said earnestly, "I just got a report that there are two Jap tanks and a bunch of infantry headin' our way."

The word *tanks* sent a cold chill down the men's spines and they looked to one another for reassurance. Staggs heard one man moan, "Oh great, now we're gonna get shot at by tanks too."

"And make no damned mistake about it, gentlemen...they're comin' for us. If they can drive us outta here...they'll have us flanked and we could lose this entire beachhead."

"What can we do against tanks," another man said hopelessly.

Then the major pointed to the right down the beach and everyone's heads turned in unison. Resting hub-to-hub in the shallows were four 37mm cannons that had been dragged ashore by their gun crews. The cannon cockers had experienced the same frustrations as the infantry when they tried to land: one LCM carrying two guns had been partially sunk as it came up to the reef and the other had been forced to stop by the coral barrier. Knowing the guns were needed by the men on the island, the crews took matters into their own hands and they wheeled the gun carriages off the two LCM's and pulled the weapons in. Now the exhausted anti-tank gunners were waiting for orders when they saw Major Crowe pointing at them.

"Right now all we got to fend those tanks off is a platoon from K Company. That's thirty men with rifles and a few BAR's against two light tanks and some Jap infantry. You do the math. But if we can get these guns into the fight we have a damned good chance of drivin' them off us." Major Crowe let the impression sink in as the senior gun chief came running over.

"How are you fixed for crews?" the major asked.

"I lost two men to the shell that sank our boat, sir, and two more got separated from us on the wade in, but three guns are fully manned. I could use two men to help with the last gun...that's all I need," the staff sergeant replied in a low voice, still very winded from the journey in.

The major turned back to address the marines by the seawall. "Alright, I need two volunteers. Anybody out there got any experience firing a thirty-seven millimeter cannon?"

Staggs heard the question clearly, thought it over, and raised his hand in the air. "I do, sir. I helped out a gun crew on the *Canal*," Staggs said flatly.

"Excellent...anybody else?"

Staggs spoke up again and told the major he already had someone who could assist him. "He takes instruction real well...even for a boot," Staggs said, pointing at Private Jorgenson.

"Okay, it's settled then. Now...what I need the rest of you men to do is lift those cannons over the seawall...and right quick. The K Company boys told me they would do their best to delay the Japs but there's only so much they can do."

Crowe swung around and ordered the artilleryman to divide his four guns into two teams. "Send one team towards the airfield...to deal with the threat against the K Company position," he said, "and have the other team go with Major Chamberlin to lend support to F Company. They're slugging it out against that bunker complex to the east and they need help over there as well."

"I'll see it gets done, sir," the sergeant stated.

"Let's move," the Major bellowed, and the marines near the seawall sprang into action. Four groups ran over to each gun and they lugged them up to the log wall. With a heave-ho, they hefted each nine-hundred-pound gun and its attached carriage over the seawall one at a time and set it down in the sand on the other side. Then, in accordance with the major's wishes, the gun crews dragged the guns off in the appropriate direction...two going inland and two heading off to the left. About five marines stayed with each gun to help maneuver the heavy weapons through the soft sand and to also act as body guards for the crews once they began firing.

Corporal Staggs could hear Jorgenson grunting ahead of him. The private had grabbed a hold of the carriage trail and was pulling on it while Staggs was pushing against the steel gun shield behind him. "If you're keepin' notes, y'all can write that one down for posterity's sake," Staggs said to the strong Swede.

Without looking back, Jorgenson huffed out, "What are you talking about back there?"

"I guess you wouldn't know...would ya, Clutch," the corporal said laughing.

"Know...what?" the private asked, struggling under the weight of the gun.

"That as long as I've been a Marine...I never volunteered for a single thing before. Not one thing...until today. In fact...if I had been more of a volunteer, I'd probably be wearing sergeant's chevrons by now. But I like the cards too much...and volunteering has a way of interfering with my social life...so I'm still a two-stripe corporal.

It was your luck of the draw to be with me when I volunteered for the first time...of course. Sorry about that," Staggs replied, straining as he pushed with all his might against the gun shield.

"No problem," Jorgenson said, looking back over his shoulder and smiling at the corporal. "Heck, I don't know a single soul over here and I've never been one to do things on my own...I like being on teams...so I would've come with you anyway."

"Okay, just makin' sure that's all. Funny though...you'd have thought I'd be the volunteerin' type since I come from Tennessee and all."

"Why's...that," the private grunted back.

"You know...Tennessee...the Volunteer State," Staggs replied proudly.

From somewhere else along the carriage an exasperated voice drawled out, "Can't y'all just shut up and push."

"Semper Fi, Mac!" Staggs replied curtly...the standard refrain every marine seemed to use for everything...but he leaned harder into the gun shield just the same.

• • •

They hadn't gone too far when they saw the K Company marines waving up ahead. They were dug in along a jagged line and it was obvious that they had fought for every inch of it. Their position bordered the narrow northeastern taxiway and it stretched for almost thirty yards from end to end. A quick glance told Staggs there were only about fifteen to twenty marines defending this sector – about half a platoon – and they were using whatever cover they could find to conceal themselves. Some men were holed up in shell craters while others were lying behind small mounds of sand for protection. As he got closer, Staggs could see that these little hills were actually the tops of underground supply bunkers that the Japanese had abandoned as the marines had driven inland. He also realized that they were perfect spots to situate the two anti-tank guns behind...since the sand was piled just high enough to protect them.

As soon as the two gun crews began rotating the trails around, a lieutenant up front whistled back to get their attention. Looking up, the men saw him pointing to his left...towards the east. And then they saw them: coming down the far side of the taxiway were two tanks...and behind them a large group of enemy infantry. The chilling site froze them for a second...but then they realized that they had arrived just in the nick of time.

Staggs could see the sun reflecting off the bayonets on the Jap's rifles despite the thick dust that was being kicked up by the tanks as they rumbled brazenly toward the marine line. The gun crews loaded the cannons and the marines on the ground held their fire, letting the enemy force walk right into their ambush. The Jap tanks were only a hundred yards away when the cannon on the left opened fire. The first 37mm round scored a direct hit on one of the tanks and it began to smoke immediately. Another shell from the same gun penetrated the tank's thin armor again and it rolled to a stop...out of action. The command hatch came up and the tank commander tried to climb out but he was shot dead in a flurry of bullets fired by the K Company marines. Neither of the other two men inside made an effort to get out...so they must have been killed by the rounds themselves...or they suffocated from the smoke that was quickly enveloping the tank.

The Japanese troops suddenly stopped their advance when they realized...too late...that they had stumbled into an ambush when the first tank got hit. Being veteran troops, they scattered for cover immediately...and then a hailstorm of fire came their way. Undaunted, they began firing back at the hidden marines and a tremendous firefight ensued as they tried to save themselves. Bullets were flying everywhere and Staggs saw one of the cannon cockers operating the other gun suddenly rear up...his hands grasping at his chest...and keel over. Corporal Staggs shifted his gaze back to the Japanese line and noticed a man...obviously a Jap officer...trying to rally his men forward but he went down in a heap as he was hit across the chest by a blast from a BAR.

The gun crew that Staggs and Jorgenson were helping out didn't have as much success as the other one did though. Their first shot flew over the rear engine housing of the second tank as it slewed out of the cannon's line of fire. They got lucky however since the round exploded against the side of a plane revetment that was behind the tank and steel and wood splinters flew in all directions...inadvertently killing three Japanese soldiers who had sought cover next to it. The crew reloaded the cannon as fast as they could and managed to get off another shot but this one missed too as the tank cut a half circle and sped off towards the center of the airfield triangle. The Jap commander must have sensed the danger his tank was in and he turned tail and ran...a prudent decision. This left the Jap infantrymen in a terrible predicament: to stay and fight...and die in place...or to retreat like the tank had... and live to fight again. But their officer was now dead...and when no one else seemed willing to lead them forward in the attack...the survivors chose the latter option of saving themselves. Despite the disgrace of yielding the battlefield to the enemy, the men began making their way back to their own lines in small groups of two's and three's.

This was the first attempt at a counterattack in force by the Japanese against the Red 3 beachhead and it had been decisively repulsed by an under-strength platoon and two 37mm cannons...quite a feat given the odds were against them. Naturally, the marines were ecstatic when they sensed the fight turning in their favor. Staggs had a grin from ear to ear and he slapped Jorgenson on the back. The private shook hands with the man next to him and he saw the rest of the marines pumping their arms in the air and hugging each other. And the celebration was well-deserved...since this was the very first victory...small though it was...that they had experienced since climbing down the landing nets in the early morning darkness.

"One tank down and a platoon of infantry turned back...hot damn!" the lieutenant yelled as he scrambled over to the cannon crews to congratulate them on their tremendous accomplishment. "You sure

taught those Jap tanks a good lesson. It'll be a while before they'll
be back again," he said confidently. He then dug into his shirt pocket
and produced a cigar. He lit it up and beaming, said, "Gentlemen,
if you'd do me the honor." He took a big puff, drew it in, and then
slowly exhaled the smoke, savoring the moment despite the carnage
all around him. The lieutenant handed the cigar to the gun chief and
he took two long draws on it before passing it on to Staggs. The corporal held the cigar up to his lips, its sweet aroma wafting upward.
Staggs leaned his head back slowly, took a puff, and rolled the cigar
around in his mouth to get the full effect of the flavor. The smell of
the cigar seemed to trigger his memory somehow...and thoughts of
a happier time came flooding into his mind. He remembered sitting
around a card table in a Memphis saloon with a beautiful girl standing beside him...tenderly caressing his neck and shoulders...as he
was playing cards. He had been on a roll...and he had won several
hands already...when one of the best...and richest...gamblers in the
area had pulled up a chair at their table. Staggs played along innocently...winning some more games...but losing some too...all the
while watching his opponent closely...and spotting the man's tell.
Staggs noticed that the man would tap his cards with his index finger when he had a great hand...and that he wouldn't when he didn't.
Once he had that figured out...and that the man's large ego was
his weakness...he set his dapper victim up. Staggs used the man's
confidence and competitive nature against him and he baited him to
remain in the game by pretending that he had a fairly decent hand...
even though he didn't. Just like Staggs planned, the pot continued to
build...until it was well over ten thousand dollars. And when Staggs
noticed that the man wasn't tapping his cards anymore, he went in
for the kill. Staggs pushed all the money he had left in front of him
into the center of the table and challenged the man to meet it or fold.
Staggs did it so dramatically that he could have been a Broadway
actor...and the man threw his cards down and gave up...completely
cowed by Staggs' act. In triumph, Staggs flipped his cards over...

revealing a lowly pair of fives…which would have been beaten by the other man's hand of two Jacks if he had met Staggs' call.

Staggs smiled to himself now…thinking about the audacity of what he had pulled off in that Memphis bar. He had won his biggest pot ever by bluffing one of the best opponents he had ever faced into submission! And the memory of that great victory…on a different battlefield of sorts…made him forget…for a few moments at least…the butchery he had been witnessing over the course of the day on Betio Island.

Corporal Staggs handed the cigar back to the lieutenant reluctantly and said, "Thanks, sir. That really hit the spot! It made me think of some good times I had back when…memories I had almost forgotten about until now."

The young officer put the cigar back in his mouth and then announced that their little party was over. He said a runner had just come in with the news that Major Crowe wanted them to pull back so they could consolidate their lines. "He's got some air strikes comin' in to seal this area off. The major wants your two guns back with him on the beach. We're headin' over to the pier to strengthen our lines there." Before trotting back to his men, the young officer searched his pocket one more time. He withdrew another cigar and handed it to Staggs… even though he had never met the enlisted man before. "Take it," he said, and pointing at Jorgenson and the other men on the cannon crew, he added, "and share it with them. We'd all be dead out here if it wasn't for you guys. I got one more in my pocket that I'm saving for later. I'm gonna light it up when we finally get this damned island secured."

Staggs accepted the cigar and thanked the thoughtful lieutenant once again. Then the gun crew sergeant turned to Staggs and said, "You can keep it. I'm not a cigar smoker…and neither are my boys. I never really understood the fascination some guys have with cigars… and never will I guess. Anyway, let's lug these guns back before those flyboys come over and mistake us for a bunch of Japs. And the major's waitin' on us too…and he's the last guy I want mad at me."

● ● ●

The move back to the seawall went smoothly - there were no losses to snipers - and Major Crowe had the two cannons positioned
where they could stave off a frontal attack against his seawall re-
doubt. Before long the two missing members of the 37mm gun crew
showed up and a joyous reunion ensued. Knowing they were no
longer needed, Staggs bade farewell to the gun sergeant and then he
and Jorgenson went right back to the same spot where they had been
resting earlier and sat down again.

After a while, Lieutenant Edmonds' platoon came scrambling in
too. They had finally abandoned their lonely outpost after getting the
order to pull back from a runner sent by Major Crowe. It had taken
them a little longer to get back since they had to cross the dangerous,
fire-swept taxiway without the benefit of the armored protection that
the amtrac had provided on their way in during the morning.

Sergeant McBride and his men made it back as well…returning
in two and three-man teams. The plucky sergeant was limping badly
when he reported to Major Crowe and he told the major that some of
his men were badly shaken by an experience they had just had with a
single Jap *Ha-Go* tank…probably the same one that had just survived
the battle with the 37mm gun crew near the taxiway. This tank had
first approached Lieutenant Edmonds' position from the direction of
the taxiway…and they mistook it for a friendly Stewart light tank…
since they looked pretty much alike. At first the men were happy to
see some armored support rolling their way…but too late…they realized that their savior was an enemy tank instead. Unfortunately, they
had nothing in their arsenal that could stop it so they let it pass on
through…and in moments it was rolling up on Sergeant McBride's
position. Since none of his men were armed with anti-tank weapons either, the sergeant and a BAR-man took matters into their own
hands. Incredibly, the two brave men jumped up on the back deck
of the tank and tried to open the locked commander's hatch so they
could jam a hand grenade inside to kill the crew. Japanese riflemen
hidden in the woods nearby spotted them however and opened fire

to save the tank. Both men were caught in a shower of bullets and they tumbled off the tank...the BAR-man dead and McBride badly wounded. Free of its assailants, the tank drove up to the crater where the rest of the men had taken cover but the tank commander inside couldn't depress the tank's 37mm main gun low enough to fire at them. Fearing the marines would swarm over his tank like the other two had done, the commander ordered it forward and it skirted the foxhole and clanked off in the direction of the Red 2 beaches...leaving the surprised and thankful marines in its dust. Several marines crossed themselves as they watched it go, thanking God they were still alive. Then, risking their own lives, two marines jumped up and ran over to their wounded leader. Grabbing him under the arms, the men dragged him back to the cover of the crater and began dressing his wounds. Shortly thereafter, a runner arrived and told them that they were being ordered to the seawall...and Sergeant McBride began sending his men back in small groups in an orderly retreat.

When the squad leader finished his amazing account to Major Crowe, he passed out from loss of blood. The major was so impressed with the leadership skills of the young NCO that he had the sergeant immediately evacuated on an outgoing amtrac...and the timely medical attention he received on the ship saved his life.

In an amazing display of grit and determination, both Sergeant McBride and First Lieutenant Edmonds had occupied these forward positions for nearly five hours...and while doing so...they had proven to be an aggravating thorn in the side of the Japanese defenders. The marines in these two isolated outposts had surprised and shot down several groups of Japanese troops who were moving up from the south end of the island and they also tied up the enemy machine gunners and riflemen along the runways. Incredibly, it would take Major Crowe another two days to reoccupy the same ground that these two brave leaders and their men had held...and then been ordered to relinquish.

• • •

Sitting along the seawall, Corporal Staggs could see that a lot more men had made it ashore since he and Jorgenson had left to fight off the tanks. The thin strip of beach appeared to be far more crowded than it was before and Staggs noticed a strange phenomenon happening along the beach...something the men were calling suicide by sniper. Jorgenson sensed it too and he tapped Staggs on the arm and said, "Get a load of these guys."

"I was noticin' that myself," the sergeant replied incredulously.

Several of the new arrivals were acting a bit weird...as if they were courting or mocking death for some strange reason. Instead of running crouched over...or at the very least scampering from one place to the next...some of the men were strolling about as if they didn't have a care in the world. Staggs figured out the problem pretty quickly: these men had simply cracked under the pressure...and they were acting like they didn't have a care in the world. And sadly, they didn't. He had seen this odd behavior before...on Guadalcanal...and it occurred when men lost all hope of survival...when they became convinced they were doomed. These men had seen so much death and destruction so quickly that it had overwhelmed their internal defense mechanisms and their survival systems simply shorted out...just like all the radios had after being deluged with seawater. And once their instinctive gauge for sensing danger became damaged, they began taking inappropriate risks along one of the most dangerous stretches of beach on the island.

Jorgenson said dryly, "Do they actually think they can just walk around like that?"

"Get down, you idiot," Staggs yelled out in frustration at one young guy in particular. "This beach isn't secure yet, Mac," he added for good measure.

"You're gonna get himself shot if ya keep that up," Jorgenson joined in, hoping the marine would heed their warnings.

"Don't worry 'bout me, Mac!" he screamed back sarcastically and Jorgenson saw that the marine had that wild-eyed look and was muttering to himself as he went by.

A few other men joined in the chorus and began pleading with him to protect himself but their admonishments went unheeded as well.

The man they were yelling at had apparently seen one of his friends at the other end of the beachhead and he had boldly walked down to talk to him. He stopped when he reached his buddy and began chatting with him. His friend implored him to get down but the man laughed it off and looked around unconcerned. Their conversation over, he waved good-bye and walked casually down the beach like he was on a Sunday stroll back home. Everyone along the seawall became transfixed by his insolent disregard for his own safety and they wondered how long he could keep it up. Jorgenson and another marine decided the man needed saving and they began to get up. "This is gettin' outta hand," he grumbled to Staggs as he crouched over. "Every time I get comfortable somethin' else comes along. I'm gonna tackle him and talk some sense into him."

"I'll bet he doesn't make it another ten feet," Staggs said matter-of-factly.

"If I get wounded goin' for this guy, I'll shoot him myself and save the Japs the trouble," the other man said to no one in particular.

As Jorgenson crawled forward, a rifle spoke from a bunker beyond the seawall and the boy was hit in the side of the arm. He whirled around from the impact of the bullet and fell flat on his back. Everyone expected him to stay down and some men began screaming for a corpsman, but the marine bounced right back up and began examining his wound. Finding it a mere flesh wound, he looked in the direction that the shot had come from to see if he could locate the sniper. As the dumbfounded marines yelled for him to get down, another shot rang out and this one slammed right into the middle of the man's forehead. His head snapped back from the force of the bullet and a spray of blood, bone, and skin tissue flew off as his unbuckled helmet went sailing in the air above him. The marine stumbled backwards several feet, his arms flailing away, and then his lifeless body collapsed with a big splash as he fell into the water of the lagoon.

An unfortunate spectator to the sickening scene, Private Jorgenson now found that he couldn't take his eyes off the boy. The marine was laying there dead with his arms and legs outstretched - it looked like he had died in the midst of doing jumping jacks - and the macabre sight reminded him of the endless days he had spent exercising at the Marine Recruit Depot back in San Diego. While the body was floating in the shallows, it began to spin slowly in a tight circle while rocking rhythmically back and forth in the incoming waves. Disgusted at the uselessness of it all, Jorgenson turned around and crawled back to Staggs.

"The sorry son of a bitch must have had a death wish or something," he spat out, masking his true feelings.

"I shoulda bet y'all. I would've won that one easily. When guys get like that...there isn't all that much you can do for them. If they're lucky, a corpsman will get to them first and get them evacked out... but more often than not they end up like that kid there. It's a crappy deal...but ya get used to it...sooner or later."

The scene wasn't lost on Major Crowe however. "Damn it all," he screamed, "that sniper has shot his last marine! I need someone to go take care of that bastard right now!" Pointing the barrel of his pump-action shotgun at a bunker beyond the seawall, Crowe continued, "He's gotta be in that one right there...now who's gonna go get him for me?"

Two marines hugging the seawall must have thought the Major was talking directly to them since they quickly volunteered for the dangerous mission. One of the men - an engineer - was carrying two TNT charges and he began getting them ready by adjusting and checking the fuses attached to each load. He also had a cigarette in his mouth and he took a deep drag on it. The end of it burned bright red and he exhaled the smoke out easily. "I'm ready," he said, looking at the other man. His buddy - another survivor from the 18th Engineers - was armed with a formidable weapon that was making its debut on Betio: the flamethrower. The young marine nodded back to his friend and together they screamed, "Cover us," as they jumped over the seawall in unison. Bullets pinged and whined off the face of the bunker as the two men zigzagged their way across the deadly open ground in route to the bunker. As they drew close, they ducked into a shell hole for cover. As soon as the TNT charges were lit, the marine ran up to the bunker and jammed them into the aperture opening. The bunker must have been compartmentalized though because the sniper was not killed when the charges exploded inside. Instead, he immediately darted out the back of the bunker…racing for the safety of the Japanese lines behind it. The flame gunner zeroed in on his victim as he ran away and he squeezed the trigger of the flame thrower. A stream of liquid fire jetted out in a long, straight line and engulfed the man entirely. The sniper continued to run…a flaming torch now… and then he crumpled to the ground in a blackened, smoking heap. He continued to burn…and after a while it was hard to tell if what was left had ever been a human being. The flame gunner's friend patted him on the helmet and said, "You're gettin' pretty good with that thing!"

"Practice makes perfect, right!" the flame gunner responded proudly, patting the hot barrel of his weapon for effect. As they headed back to the seawall, he added, "And I'm definitely getting my share of practice today…that's for sure!"

• • •

Shortly after the sniper was eliminated, Major Chamberlin came up and gathered Staggs, Jorgenson, and about twenty other men around him. "We're going down to fortify the left flank of the perimeter," he said crisply, and then he leapt over the seawall. The marines followed in kind and they dodged some light grazing fire as they made their way down the inland side of the log barrier fairly quickly. They were heading east...towards the tail of the island...and the men noticed that the ground offered more cover here than it did over by the seawall. Far more coconut trees were standing in this area - the Japanese construction battalion hadn't gotten to them yet - and it was almost like they had entered a sparsely wooded forest. The pre-dawn naval bombardment had impacted in this area and some of the trees had been blown in half while others had been uprooted completely... but most...it seemed...had been missed. Fortunately, the naval gunfire had left large shell holes throughout the area and the marines scrambled into them for cover as they advanced.

They had almost made it to the stubby wharf when a long burst of Japanese machine gun fire forced them to take cover. The blast came from the top of a huge, twenty-five-foot-high, sand-covered, concrete bunker that was off to their right and forward of where they were. The monstrous position was the centerpiece of the defensive complex that controlled the northeast end of the island. It was supported by a steel-reinforced pillbox that was positioned by the lagoon and another hardened pillbox was located between the two. Trenches connected the pillboxes so troops could move under cover between them and the main bunker. In addition to these three structures, the massive concrete blockhouse that served as General Shibasaki's headquarters was within full view a little further southeast as well. To top it off, the whole site was so close to the marines' lines that the bomber and fighter pilots had avoided it altogether...since an errantly released bomb could easily end up detonating among their own men below. And the main bunker and the Headquarters building had even seemed to be impervious to the few direct hits they had received during the naval bombardment...so that option had been taken off the table as well. Thus, it was left to the men on the ground to take it out. And the only way to neutralize it was for the marine infantry to swarm over each structure and blast the occupants out with demolitions and flame throwers...no easy task given how strong the entire position was laid out and constructed.

Since the approach to the left flank had been effectively blocked, Major Chamberlin instructed Staggs and the others to stay where they were and dig in. He also warned them to keep a sharp lookout. "The Japs," he stressed, "are gonna try to push us outta here. They know, just like we do, that this place is the key to the whole sector. They're not about to let us get comfortable over here." The energetic XO then ran off to organize a two-pronged attack against the northern and southern entrances of the large, sand-covered bunker.

Following the major's orders, Corporal Staggs slid into a crater that afforded good frontal cover inland while also offering a perfect view of the Burns-Philp wharf up ahead on the left. About twenty-five yards out in the surf, Staggs noticed an ominous string of barbed wire that ran almost the entire length of the beach as far as he could see. It was attached to metal poles that had been driven into the sand and it some places it looked like it had been run over by some of the amtracs that had made it in. Shifting shoreward, he saw two empty amtracs that were laying perpendicular to one another about twenty yards from the wharf. Both had been shot up and then abandoned on the lip of a large shell crater…and dead marines were scattered around them. One of the LVT-1's had the number 39 painted in white above its left front fender…while the other… nicknamed 'Short Round'…had the number 27 on it. Staggs didn't know it…but a platoon from Fox Company in Major Crowe's 2nd Battalion had ridden these amtracs in…and they met a wall of lead as they left the water and crawled up the beach. In a bit of bad luck, the two amtracs had picked the worst spot to land in…since it was the most heavily defended section of Red 3 and the men had been slaughtered as they exited the vehicles. The lead alligator looked like it had taken the brunt of the punishment since it had slewed sideward and its left side was ripped open. Looking closer, Staggs saw that one the bodies sprawled beside it didn't fit in with the others… since it was wearing the tan-colored uniform of a Jap soldier. Staggs wondered if this soldier had made a suicidal charge and attached an explosive charge to the side of *Short Round* when it came to a stop. He was probably shot down as he was trying to get away…since it looked like he had succeeded in his courageous mission. *This Nip had obviously set his sights on much bigger game than the three that had come after us back down the beach*…and he was very impressed that the man had been so willing to sacrifice himself that way. *I sure as hell hope there aren't many more like him*, the corporal thought grimly, *cause if there are… we may never get outta here.*

The corporal continued his survey of the beach and saw another alligator that was less damaged parked just off their left flank. This LVT-1, # 33, was in fairly good condition but the driver and crew chief had left it there for some reason. The two amtrac crewmen who had manned the forward .50's had been killed as it came to a stop though. Heroically, the men had stayed at their posts until the very end despite the torrent of fire against them…and now their bodies were draped lifelessly across their guns. It was obvious to Staggs that these two men had sacrificed everything to complete their mission… and neither of them would ever go home. Looking along the seawall, Staggs spotted a group of fifteen or so marines who had made it out of this amtrac alive. These men had dug in and they appeared ready…eager almost…for a chance to even the score. Then he heard several rifles cracking and he saw another five or so men holed up in a crater by the other two amtracs. He hadn't seen them at first since they had been hunkered down…probably reloading…when he had looked that way. Still further up, beyond the wharf and almost out of sight, he spotted three other marines who were trying to expand the beachhead eastward all by themselves. After landing, these men had run to the left and survived a gauntlet of fire before taking cover in a shell hole. Completely isolated, they were soon exchanging fire with a small pillbox that was directly ahead of them and they became pinned down. Staggs tried to see if he could spot anyone else along the beach…but he couldn't so he stopped looking. The sad story was that out of the three tractor loads of marine infantry from F

Company that had assaulted the extreme left of Red Beach 3 in the morning...sixty men in all...just twenty or so men... maybe half a platoon at best...were left. These battered survivors...plus the twenty men under Major Chamberlin...were the only men Major Crowe had to defend his CP from an attack along the beach by the hundreds of Japanese who were still alive in the eastern end of the island.

The remnants of another F Company platoon were not too far away...and Staggs could see them. They were further inland and getting ready to storm the northeastern corner of the sand-covered bunker while another group was getting ready to hit the southeastern corner. Major Chamberlin had organized this group of marines around the combat engineers of the 2nd Battalion, 18th Regiment. These engineers had been assigned to support Major Crowe's 2nd Battalion...but just like everyone else...they too had suffered badly as they came in and most of their gear had been lost. Major Chamberlin organized what was left and then teamed them up with some of the orphans from the infantry companies that had landed in the area. Corporal Staggs could see the grim looks on the faces of the men from F Company as they were checking their weapons and making last minute adjustments to their gear before the jump off. Then a lieutenant shouted to get ready and the men yelled various lines of encouragement back and forth to one another to buck themselves up for the charge. Staggs heard one marine yell out to his buddy who was a few foxholes over, "These Nips sure picked the wrong platoon to mess with...didn't they, Al." Al, who was tall and lanky and looked all of eighteen years old, peered over his way and shouted back, full of bravado, "I'll tell ya what Lou...I'll bet they're so scared that they've already started committing *hairy-karey* by now!"

• • •

Major Chamberlin had worked very hard to coordinate the marines' first attack against the bunker complex and both groups took off right on schedule. To support the twin advances, the major had a 60mm mortar section lobbing rounds at the top of the bunker and two 37mm cannons firing at the bunkers beside it.

The Japs reacted immediately to the pincer movement and upwards of fifty soldiers streamed out of the bombproof and hurried to their designated positions. Some rushed into the trenches to reinforce the men that were already there while others made for the roof of the bunker where the heavy machine guns were located. The marines could even see the tops of the defender's helmets bobbing up and down behind the low parapet that ran around the top of the sand-covered fortress as they slid and crawled into place. And despite the number of shells that rained down on the roof of the bunker, the Jap gunners were still up there and ready to face whatever was coming their way.

Tragically, all hell broke loose when the marines from F Company made the initial move on the left. Forced to cross some open ground to get to the bunker, they became perfect targets for almost every Japanese gun in the area. The men were hit all at once by machine gun fire from the beach pillbox off their left flank and by rifle fire from the trenches and machine gun fire from the middle pillbox directly ahead of them. Added to this was the rifle and machine gun fire from atop the bunker on their right flank. Then grenades began exploding in their midst as well. Despite the overwhelming fire against them, at least twenty marines made it through this kill zone alive…and nearly half of them reached the far end of the bunker before they were stopped cold. Since they couldn't stay where they were…the only option left was to run back to their own lines through the shooting gallery they had just been through.

The same thing ended up happening to the group of marines that attacked the southern end of the bunker. They were led by a pioneer lieutenant from the 18th Marines named Alexander Bonnyman and his men were armed with a few flamethrowers and a cache of demolitions. Bonnyman also had several riflemen to protect them but it did no good. Looping his men around to the right, they encountered fire just as intense as the F Company men did…and he called off the attack after they had gone only fifty yards or so. Bonnyman saw that it was impossible to get within range of the bunker to use the

demolitions and flame throwers effectively so he decided…wisely…
to hold his engineers in check until a better opportunity presented
itself.

• • •

Corporal Staggs watched as the F Company men staggered back
from their failed attack. Exhausted and numb, each one would jump
into his foxhole as he made it in and then look back in the direction
he had come…hoping to see more men behind him. When it was
evident that no one else was coming back, the disheartened Staggs
turned to Jorgenson and said, "I counted ten men. That's all that
made it back. The Japs got the rest." Sadly, the officer who had led
the F Company attack…Second Lieutenant George Bussa…and the
two friends…Al Sheezer and Lou Morgineer…who had participated
in it…were not among the men in his headcount.

• • •

Major Chamberlin took the news of the failed attacks in stride…
which came as no surprise to the men who worked with him…since
very little seemed to rattle him one way or the other. "Okay…that's
all we can do for today," he said evenly, and added, "now let's get
ready to defend what we got…since the Japs are sure to hit us somewhere along the line tonight." The major knew…as did most of the
men around him…that there weren't enough marines available to
launch another attack…and secondly…he had no real means of supporting it even if he did have the men to carry it out. And if the
last two charges had revealed anything…it was that a single 60mm
mortar and two 37mm cannons did not have enough firepower to
pin the Japs down as the marines advanced. With no reinforcements
coming in and daylight slipping away, the major switched gears and
began concentrating on reorganizing and strengthening their tenu-
ous hold on the left flank instead…just like Major Crowe was doing
with his position along the seawall.

The Japanese weren't done however. Late in the afternoon, a
force of nearly two hundred men left the southeastern corner of

the island and cut across the island to reinforce the two hundred-yard-long defensive line that was anchored on the Burns-Philp wharf at one end and by Admiral Shibasaki's blockhouse on the other. Fortunately, a sharp-eyed marine sentry spotted the Japs advancing through the tangle of underbrush beyond the lines and Major Chamberlin was notified immediately. The one-time college professor understood the implications of the move and he ordered his two 37mm cannons over to the right flank to confront this new threat. The two six-man gun crews wasted no time in moving their guns over and before long they saw the enemy infantry approaching in the fading light. Holding fire, they let the unsuspecting soldiers walk right into their trap...and then they cut loose. The cannons were loaded with canister...the modern-day equivalent of grapeshot...and their shells had the same telling effect on the advancing *rikusentai* as the ones that were fired by the Union and Confederate artillery batteries did on the Johnny Rebs and the Billy Yanks during the Civil War. The short-fused, shotgun-like shells exploded almost as soon as they left the barrels and their scathing buckshot cut huge swaths through the Japanese ranks... killing or wounding over half the men...and cutting the rest of them off from their intended destination. The survivors hid behind anything they could find and sat tight, too frightened to move lest they end up like the men whose blood was now soaking the ground around them. Feeling trapped, several men lost their nerve and were cut down by the marine riflemen as they bolted to the rear. Later that night, using the darkness and the moaning of the wounded to conceal their movements, a quarter of the men wandered back to their starting point, dazed and broken.

This was the last significant action fought on D-Day...and Major William Chamberlin was extremely proud of his men and what they had accomplished. Though completely outnumbered, Chamberlin's marines had defended...and held...the far left flank of the entire marine line during a particularly hard day of fighting. And if he had taught history instead of economics, the major might have seen the similarities between his fight and one that had occurred eighty years earlier. In another famous stand reminiscent of his own, a small regiment of volunteers from Maine had been led by a man whose name was eerily similar to the major's. This man's name was Lieutenant Colonel Joshua Lawrence Chamberlain…and the coincidences didn't stop there. Both men had been college professors too…and both of them had put their teaching careers on hold so they could offer their services to their Country as well. And during the climactic battle that was fought for three days outside the small town of Gettysburg in Pennsylvania, Chamberlain's soldiers were positioned on the far left flank of the Yankee line…just like Major Chamberlin's men had been at Betio. And during the tumultuous day of fighting on July 2, 1863, Chamberlain's men…though outnumbered…had repulsed every Confederate attack they faced…just like Major Chamberlin's men had against the Japanese. Finally, the hallowed ground that Lieutenant Colonel Chamberlain's men had fought and bled for that day was called *Little Round Top*…which was a perfect moniker for the obstacle that Major Chamberlin's marines had waged attacks against all day long as well.

• • •

Sitting in their foxhole by the lagoon, Corporal Staggs and Private Jorgenson had heard the sharp crack of the 37's and the din of the rifle fire and they wondered what the commotion at the other end of the line was all about. As the cannon fire died out and it got quiet again, Staggs just shrugged his shoulders and indicated that he wasn't going to worry too much more about it.

They eventually got the scuttlebutt when a staff sergeant crawled up to their foxhole. He was draped with rifle bandoliers and dragging a wooden box full of grenades behind him in the sand. "Here's the dope," he said as he issued the two men some rifle ammunition for their M-1's and two hand grenades each. "There's dead Japs strewn all over the place over on the right …but there's plenty more where they came from so stay alert. The Japs gotta know that we're shorthanded over here…so they're definitely gonna hit us tonight. The major says we got a Sherman tank comin' over to help us out, but I heard Lieutenant Largey…the TC…tell him they're low on ammo. It's sitting over in the lagoon right now…and the damn thing looks like it got hit with nearly a hundred anti-tank rounds…but Largey says it's as fit as a fiddle and he'll do his best with the ammo on board to hold off the counterattack that's comin' tonight."

"Largey…he's on *Colorado*? What happened to *Cannonball*? That's his tank," Staggs asked.

"Yeah…how'd you know that?" the staff sergeant replied.

"I know the gunner on the *Cannonball*…Sergeant Glenn Kingrey…real well," Staggs answered.

"Well the lieutenant told us that he had transferred over to the *Colorado* after his tank got knocked out earlier in the day. He said it ran into a fuel dump and got stuck there after an anti-tank gun took it under fire. The fuel dump lit off and up went the tank. Largey said that everyone in his crew made it out alive though…in case you were worried about Kingrey."

"Thanks," Staggs said, sighing in relief over the staff sergeant's update on his friend's status. "He's a good man…he carried me out of a bar in Wellington one night when I got a little too hammered. That's another reason I'm still a corporal and not a sergeant," he said…and he nodded over at Jorgenson who said, "No kidding?"

"Too many beers…a good looking gal…you know the story," Staggs answered dryly…as if it were a common occurrence in his social life.

At this point the staff sergeant cut in and said, "So what happened? Did they take a stripe away from you as punishment?"

"Nah…I was still a corporal…so they just made sure I never got a chance to get promoted. It was my own fault so I don't hold any grudge or nothin' against the lieutenant or my platoon sergeant. Hell, they could've busted me down to PFC…but they didn't. Getting stupid drunk is no way to earn that extra stripe…if that's what you're after. I don't mind being a corporal though...trust me," Staggs explained without remorse.

"How pretty was the girl," Jorgenson wanted to know...picturing a stunning blond from back home in his mind.

"Hey, I would love to hear how this story plays out...but I gotta make the rounds to the other guys too...and get this ammo distributed," the staff sergeant chimed in sadly since he wanted to hear about this girl as well.

Staggs told him not to worry...that he would fill him in on the rest of the story...if he came back that way...and that it was a story worth hearing.

"Okay," the staff sergeant said, "I'll definitely try to head back this way...but if I can't make it...maybe I can catch you guys in the morning...if we're all still around...of course."

The staff sergeant's dire implication set off alarm bells in the corporal's mind and he asked, "What about those two destroyers out in the lagoon. Can't they do anything for us?"

"They've been firing to the south of us all day long to keep the Japs from coming up. Major Crowe's been on the horn with them since we landed so they should be available tonight too. That's what Major Chamberlin says anyway. The only problem is if the Japs get too close, the destroyers and the tank won't be able to help us one bit." Before crawling off, he made the same point that was being stressed all over the island. "You two know the deal for tonight. No one gets out of their hole for any reason whatsoever. If you gotta piss...do it in your hole. If you leave your hole...you get shot...no questions asked." The look on the man's face and the coldness in his voice told them the warning was no joke... and then he turned to Staggs one more time and said, "I'd bet anything she's got real dark hair, right?" before crawling off into the darkness.

• • •

"Was that supposed to cheer us up?" Jorgenson asked bleakly.

"You'd better hope the Nips don't break through the line, that's all," Staggs replied evenly, and then added, "but if they do...and we're cut off...then plan on doin' some swimmin' tonight."

The private looked at Staggs incredulously and said, "I can't swim that good. I only made it in here alive because the water wasn't over my head along the reef."

"Didn't you have to pass a swim test in training?" Staggs asked, mystified that his foxhole mate couldn't swim...or swim that well... as he contended. He thought that swimming was something everyone could do...and had to do...to get out of boot camp.

"I just faked it...and I somehow passed the test," Jorgenson explained.

"Well, whatever you do...don't let the Japs take you prisoner. I saw what the Japs did to a few of our guys they caught...and it wasn't pretty. If it comes to that...I plan on blazing away until I'm dead... cause I'm not gonna let any Jap take me prisoner!"

The private exhaled audibly and considered his options. His decision made...he swallowed hard...and then began inspecting his rifle to make sure it was clean and loaded before settling in for the night.

Staggs and Jorgenson spent the next several hours in relative comfort since the crater was big enough to accommodate both of them easily...and they had no reason to leave it. Heeding the staff sergeant's advice, they had even relieved themselves in it, shoveling the waste out of the hole with the private's entrenching tool. "I bet you're happy now that I went back and got my pack after we knocked out that tank," Jorgenson said cockily...twirling the entrenching too for added effect.

The corporal glanced his way but said nothing.

Not to be undone, the private added, "Cause if I hadn't, we would've had to use our hands to throw our crap out of the hole."

Staggs looked at him again, but his time he had a response. "First off," he said, "we didn't knock out any tank. That other crew did. If I remember correctly...we took two shots at it and they both missed. That's a *Maggie's Drawers* if there ever was one." Staggs was using the salty expression that was coined at the firing range in boot camp during the First World War to indicate that the person on the firing line had completely missed his target. If that ignominious event occurred, the person monitoring the target would wave a white flag to indicate the miss…and it had to be big enough so the riflemen and instructors all the way back on the firing line could see it. Someone must have been dating a very large woman at the time because the flag was said to be as big as Miss Maggie's drawers!

"Well at least we scared it off…that's better than nothing," Jorgenson said…once again on the defensive.

"We're not out here to scare things away, Clutch," Staggs said, stressing yet another point to the private. "Because sooner or later we'll probably run into that tank again…and then we won't have a thirty-seven-millimeter cannon with us…to scare it away. Wanna bet on it?"

"No…I get it," the downtrodden private mumbled…and then he said, "Am I ever gonna get the hang of combat…cause I don't think I've done a single thing right since I found you."

"You've done lots of things right, kid," Staggs said, trying to buck Jorgenson back up. "Look," he added, "you're a great shot…at least with a rifle…and to be honest…I'm gonna forgive ya for going back and getting that stupid backpack of yours. That shovel will come in handy in more ways than one. Trust me."

"Thanks," Jorgenson said, his confidence returning with the corporal's compliment.

"No problem. What else ya got in that pack of yours…since it's here. Anything useful?" the corporal asked.

The private reached in and pulled out some C ration boxes…so food wasn't going to be a problem either.

"Now we're talkin'," the corporal said hungrily, eying one of the boxes. "Throw one over here…I'm starving," and he motioned with his hands for the private to toss one over to him. Jorgenson looked one box over…read its contents…and said, "Meat…sliced…in gravy…sound good?"

"I'd take it if it was horse meat from World War One," Staggs said, licking his lips in anticipation.

"All yours," the private said, and he tossed the box to Staggs. The corporal caught it cleanly and tore into like the hungry man he was. The private picked a box out of his pack as well and began opening it when he suddenly stopped and said, "Hey, corporal...I only have one box left. Why don't we share yours...and then we can give this box to the guys next door. They might have nothing to eat."

Staggs stopped what he was doing and looked at the young private in silent admiration. "You just might make a good marine after all, Clutch my boy," the corporal said, and then added, "See if those guys are hungry."

Jorgenson turned and whispered to the two men occupying a hole several yards away. He told them that they had an extra box of rations...and that they were willing to share it with them if they were hungry.

"And how. We got nothing over here. We left our backpacks back by the seawall. We could use whatever extras you're willing to share," was the response that came back quickly.

Staggs gave Jorgenson a sly look and said, "I shoulda known that was coming." Jorgenson nodded knowingly and whispered, "Gottcha," and then said softly, "Incoming," as he tossed the box over to their foxhole.

A hand extended above the lip of the foxhole and Staggs and Jorgenson saw that the marine was giving them the thumbs-up sign...thanking them for their generosity and indicating the private had made a good throw. Staggs nodded appreciatively and said, "If the Japs hit us tonight...you can handle the grenades!"

"I've always had a good throwing arm," Jorgenson said, and then he told Staggs that he had once had a tryout with the Milwaukee Brewers. Staggs listened to the story while also opening the contents of the C rations box and he said, "You were going to be a pro baseball player?"

"Well the Brewers are a farm team for the Detroit Tigers. It was only a tryout...but I did okay. I was a pitcher and I struck a few guys out...walked one or two...and one guy hit a home run off me in five innings. I might have made it had I really pursued it...but I let it drop. I guess it wasn't in the cards for me," Jorgenson explained... and then he added, "how's that chow comin'...I'm pretty famished myself."

Staggs tore the lid off the box and placed it on the ground in front of him. Then he opened the can and quickly scooped out half the contents onto the lid. "Here ya go," he said, handing the can over to the private. Jorgenson looked at the contents and said, "Looks delicious." Without missing a beat, Staggs smiled and said, "Well it should be...I saved the tail just for you!"

• • •

As it grew darker and darker, Hutch began to get nervous. After a while his anxiety got the best of him and he began scooting around and piling sand along the edges of the crater to make the sides higher. Like the rest of the marines on the island, he was convinced that they'd be the recipient of a maniacal banzai charge sometime during the night. The young private became so terrified at the idea of being overrun and captured that he stayed awake the entire time. Corporal Staggs, on the other hand, had experienced this sort of thing on Guadalcanal and thus he wasn't fazed by the threat the way the young private was. Despite this, the wily veteran had been forced to catnap all night. Every time he had fallen asleep...Jorgenson...without fail...had shaken him awake to warn him of some surreptitious movement he had seen or noise he had heard in the shadows beyond their position. It was usually a palm frond swaying in the breeze or a smoldering fire crackling and popping in the distance that caught his attention, but the nervy private felt it was better to be safe than sorry. At one point Staggs got so annoyed that he hissed, "One more time...y'all wake me up just one more time...and I'll drag your ass over to the Japs myself," before rolling over and shutting his eyes yet again. The threat didn't work though since the instructors had warned the boys in boot camp over and over again that their throats would be cut if they fell asleep while on watch. And that prospect alone...of having his head tilted back and his throat slashed open by a stealthy, knife-wielding infiltrator...was more frightening to Jorgenson than any tongue lashing Staggs could ever dish out.

• • •

With the coming of dawn, Jorgenson finally began to relax...since he was still alive. And then his spirits really soared as D + 1 progressed and he spied the Higgins boats carrying the 1st of the 8th heading for the reef.

"Hey, it looks like we made it somehow...and we're gonna be getting some help here pretty soon too," the private said to Staggs excitedly, waking him up for the final time.

Staggs, who had been laying on his side, rolled over and sat up. He rubbed the cobwebs out of his eyes with his dirty hands and then looked sullenly at the private who had kept him awake all night long.

"Top of the mornin' to ya," the private said, smiling at the corporal. "Isn't that what the Irish people say when they get up?"

"Do...I...look Irish...to y'all?" Staggs mumbled, stifling a yawn. "I'm German...if you want to know."

"Oh..." Jorgenson replied, looking past him, more interested in what was happening out in the lagoon. The private then stretched up a little higher to get a better look at the advancing waves of infantry-laden landing craft. "Hot damn," he said, "the cavalry has finally arrived."

Staggs reached over and pulled him down by the back of his green-colored utility shirt. "Get down and stay down you big blockhead," he said sharply. "The last thing I want is to have your brains... what little there might be...splattered all over me."

"I'm just tryin' to see where they're going in. It looks like they're heading for Red Two...maybe Red One. It's hard to tell from this angle."

Now the corporal was interested too. He crawled up to the lip of the crater and he arched his back up in an attempt to see over the pier. "It doesn't look like they're headin' this way...that's for sure. Maybe they knocked out some more of the Jap defenses over that way yesterday afternoon. If so, it's better for them to go in there. Major Crowe and Major Chamberlin seem to have things under control over here at least. Even though we haven't made much headway against them on this flank, the Japs don't look like they're gonna be able to throw us outta here anytime soon. We're just gonna be tied down on this miserable island a little longer than we thought...that's all there is to it." Staggs reached down and picked up some sand in his hand and threw it back down in disgust. Then he added wryly, "I'll bet ya someone's butt is gonna be in a sling when the story about what happened here hits the papers back home."

"Why's that?" the private asked.

"Because when the press releases the casualty figures from this one, the public is gonna wanna know what the hell happened out here...that's why," Staggs explained sagely.

"I guess the Navy could've shelled this place a little more," the private countered, "but...other than that...there's really not much more that anybody could have done...is there. These Nips are so dug in here that the only thing that can get them out is guys like us... guys who can blast 'em out with rifles and grenades."

Staggs gave the private a deprecating look...and then said, "Did I miss something last night? During one of the few times I actually got some shuteye, did you change places with Clauswitz without telling me? How about having more amtracs...or tanks...or artillery? Hell, I've only seen one guy with a flamethrower over here. Don't you think havin' more of those things around might've made a difference?"

The private thought it over carefully and realized the corporal had a good point. He was about to tell him he was right when another thought crossed his mind. "Even if we did have all that extra stuff...could the Navy have carried it all here? Aren't they short ships? At least that's what I heard some of the swabbies saying on the ship I was on."

"How the hell am I supposed to know?" Staggs answered dryly.

"I don't think the Navy could really—"

"Ahhh just drop it," Staggs interrupted, knowing the private had defeated his argument soundly. But he wasn't about to tell him that. No good poker player would.

• • •

Before long the Jap anti-boat guns began zeroing in on the Higgins boats and Staggs felt a rage building in the pit of his stomach as he watched it happening all over again. The sight of another battalion being butchered was almost too much to bear. The fact that he didn't know what battalion it was didn't matter too much. Like all marines, he had good friends scattered throughout the Division...guys who he played cards with regularly...and in all likelihood, several of them were out there in those boats in the lagoon right now. The fact that he had survived what they were about to go through didn't really mollify him or dampen his anger. If anything, he felt worse...since he had already experienced...and survived...the horror they would soon be facing.

The most frustrating thing of all was that there was no way for Staggs to help them. He was stuck in place on the left flank of Red 3...unable to advance or pull back...feeling more like an observer than a participant of the battle that was being waged around him. As his anger built up inside, Staggs found there was nowhere to channel it. What he wanted to do was charge ahead and kill some Japanese to get even...like the other marines on Betio were doing. Unfortunately, bad luck had placed him at one of the few points along the marine line where Colonel Shoup's dawn attack order wasn't being implemented.

The defensive complex opposite the left flank of the Red 3 perimeter was just too strong and Major Chamberlin knew it. And that's exactly what he told Major Crowe. At this stage, the position didn't have any weak spots…as far as he could tell. Those Jap machine gunners and riflemen on top of the main bunker and in the smaller pillboxes on its flanks had all the approaches covered. Their mutually supporting fires crisscrossed the entire area so effectively that any attacking force was hit from several points on the compass as they rushed ahead. And the Japs had another advantage as well: the men on the roof of the bunker occupied the highest point on the island and they could see a marine attack developing well before it began. This gave them time to alert the rest of the Japanese soldiers inside the bunker…who could then rush outside to take their places in the connecting trench line and rifle pits. Chamberlin concluded…and rightly so…that throwing more marines at the complex at this stage would have accomplished very little…unless the goal was to get more marines killed and wounded. To launch an attack and expect success against such overwhelming odds would've been sheer folly…and more simply put…senseless murder…so he had them remain where they were. But the major didn't let the Japanese rest on their laurels. Instead of launching a ground attack, he had the two destroyers that were circling in the lagoon just off Red 3 concentrate their fire against the main bunker. He also ordered the two 37mm cannon crews and the *Colorado* to fire on targets of opportunity throughout the complex. And if this wasn't enough, he had also called for artillery support from the pack 75's that were now ensconced on Red 2 in an effort to soften the position up. If the complex could be weakened enough from all these efforts to warrant an attack…then Major Chamberlin would consider sending the infantry forward again later in the day.

Major Crowe had concurred with his executive officer's assessment of the situation and by mid-morning naval and artillery shells were raining down on the bunker complex. Corporal Staggs wiled away the time by listening to Private Jorgenson complain about the heat and his thirst…and before long the anger over his inability to help the men in the 1st of the 8th had simply faded away.

CHAPTER 23

On the other end of the island...eighteen hundred yards away from Major Crowe's Red 3 beachhead...the "orphaned" marines under Major Mike Ryan on Red 1 were tense...yet ready...as they prepared to forge ahead in compliance with Colonel Shoup's early-morning attack order. And though they didn't know it at the time, they would end up achieving the biggest gains of the day... and thus shifting the complexion of the battle in favor of the Marine Corps.

• • •

For one marine on Red Beach 1, the order to move out couldn't come soon enough. He was looking skyward for the carrier planes that were supposed to be overhead. At the last moment, Colonel Shoup had changed the plan and ordered an air strike against the long stretch of Green Beach that was still in Japanese hands. Shoup was hoping that the strike would soften up the Japanese defenses and make it easier for Ryan's men to retake the ground they had given up the day before. As a result, Major Ryan had ordered the marines leading the attack to hold up for the time being. The last thing he wanted at this stage was for some of his men up front to get bombed inadvertently…since some of the pilots who were flying close air support seemed to be having problems identifying friend from foe.

"No problem, sir," Platoon Sergeant Roy had replied, "but my boys and I wanna get goin'. We had that far shore in our sights yesterday afternoon and we don't want to give the Japs any more time to reoccupy the positions we fought over yesterday."

"I understand, sergeant. I tried to cancel this air strike but I don't know if the Colonel got the word." Major Ryan seemed to be as exasperated as the sergeant was. "And I hated giving up that ground too…but we bypassed an awful lot of active bunkers to get there. We would've ended up with too many Nips in our rear to stay where we were. That's why I pulled us back."

"It was the right thing to do, sir. No question about it. I just hate sitting around and waitin'…that's all," Platoon Sergeant Roy responded.

"Well, we're either gonna get this air strike shortly…or I'm gonna get some kind of message that it's been cancelled…and we can go ahead," the major said, summing up the situation as it now stood.

The other men at the hastily called meeting looked at the major and nodded in agreement. They were all officers…and everyone knew each other…to a degree…since they had trained together at some point in the past. There was Captain Jim Crain…the commanding officer of K Company…and his friend…First Lieutenant Sam Turner…the acting commander of I Company. Both of them had been part of the first wave with the 3rd Battalion, 2nd Regiment…and now they were leading the few men they had left after their landings had been shattered. The other line officer was First Lieutenant Kevin Kelly…the ad hoc commander of the men from the 1st Battalion, 2nd Regiment. Like Crain and Turner, Kelly had survived a brutal landing the day before and he was now trying to lead the mixed bag of men from his own battalion who had landed on the wrong beachhead.

The last two officers were going to play a pivotal role in supporting the ground attack on Green Beech. The first of these was First

Lieutenant Ed Bale...a tanker by trade...and the commanding officer of the two M-4 Sherman tanks that had made it ashore on Red Beach 1. The other one was Second Lieutenant Tom Greene...and he was a forward observer from C Battery of 1st Battalion, 10th Regiment...and he had just arrived on the Bird's Beak with a functional radio.

In strategizing the upcoming attack the night before, Captain Crain had suggested that Major Ryan try to get a destroyer to provide fire support to the marines as they attacked down the length of Green Beech. "Their five-inch guns would sure come in handy in knocking out those bunkers we're gonna have to butt heads with in the morning, sir," Captain Crain said.

"I agree," the major said, and added, "I'll see if Shoup can spare one for us. That kind of firepower might crack the Jap defenses wide open over here. If we can free Green Beach up pretty quickly...we just might be able to get some reinforcements in here early...and that could really change the look of things over here."

"If we do get a destroyer, sir, we'll also need a naval gunfire support officer to act as a liaison officer with the destroyer. We have no way of communicating with one even if it were out there," Crain advised hopefully.

And in one of the rare communication success stories of the day, Major Ryan's request actually got through to Colonel Shoup...and he approved the idea. But a naval liaison officer was nowhere to be found...so Lieutenant Green had been assigned the crucial job and he had been sent over instead.

Major Ryan looked the men over one more time...sensed their confidence...and said, "Okay then...we'll jump off as soon as I get the all clear from Higher. In the meantime, stay sharp and let your men know what's going on. They might enjoy knowing that the Japs up ahead are gonna be catchin' hell for once...instead of the other way around. All of them nodded in agreement again...and then Crain, Turner, and Kelly headed back to their respective commands to await the order to advance.

Watching them go, Sergeant Roy commented to Major Ryan that they were all good officers...certainly as good as any he had ever served with in his twelve years of service.

"That they are," the major said proudly, and then added, "And after what happened yesterday, it's lucky that any of them were left alive to lead this attack today."

And the L Company Commander knew what he was talking about...since the men of the 3rd Battalion, 2nd Regiment had drawn the roughest landing assignment for Operation Galvanic. Their task was to secure Red Beach 1...which ran from the tip of the parrot's beak in the west and ended where the bird's breast began on the left. In between these boundaries was the indented cove that gave the northwestern shoreline its shape...and resembled the parrot's neckline.

Major John Schoettel's assault plan split the landing beach into two sections and he assigned K Company the left half and I Company the right. The men of these two companies would comprise the first three landing waves so they got the amtracs. The marines in L and M Companies...along with the headquarters elements...would ride in Higgins boats behind them in the fourth, fifth, sixth, and seventh waves and their mission was to support and reinforce I and K Companies once they landed.

After negotiating the narrow passageway through the reef surrounding the Tarawa Atoll, the tractors carrying Major Schoettel's leading waves cut behind Lieutenant Colonel Amey's Second Battalion and churned to the right. This was when the Jap artillery fire started...light and probing at first...and several men pointed excitedly over the gunwales at the geysers of water sprouting up harmlessly in the distance. The battle noise increased though as the LVT's finally turned to the left and crossed the line of departure... and headed directly for the island.

The cakewalk the men of the Third Battalion had been really hoping for ended as soon as the amtracs hit the reef inside the lagoon. Machine gun fire began pinging off the vehicles and the marines hunkered down to avoid the bullets that were whizzing by overhead. The situation became dire when Captain William Tatom...the I Company commander...stood up to observe the beach and a round hit him in the middle of the forehead. Killed instantly, Captain Tatom's limp body fell back among the horrified men huddled in the troop compartment behind him. Moments later amtracs began exploding up ahead as they were taken under fire by the four 70mm dual-purpose guns and two 14cm guns that were dug in behind the beaches on the right side of Red 1. A palpable fear rippled through the ranks of the younger, green marines who had never experienced anything like this before...while the cooler heads...the veteran non-commissioned officers...sought to reassure them by speaking in measured tones...calmly rehearsing the plans they had practiced over and over again in their squad drills back in New Zealand. As they got closer to the island, the amtracs were engaged by the two 70mm howitzers and the 37mm rapid-fire heavy machine gun that were placed at the base of the *Pocket* and the fire from these weapons was so fierce that many of the amtracs were forced off course. By this point, the entire landing operation on Red 1 had fallen apart. Instead of approaching the beach in an orderly, line-abreast formation, most of the landing craft were driven to the right and the few tractors that did make it to their section of the beach drew the attention of every gun in the *Pocket*. The concave shape of the cove allowed the Japanese guns to fire down the flanks of the vehicles as they entered the cove and also into the rear of the tractors as they crawled up the beach. Once they got to the seawall, most of the LVT's stopped and the men inside scrambled over the sides and sought cover. Several tractors actually tried to grind their way over the barrier - in some places it was nearly five feet high - but none of them got very far...and a few...unable to go forward or back up...got hung up on the wall for their effort.

Exiting the amtracs became a deadly exercise as well...and marines were hit in droves as they jumped over the gunwales in a vain attempt to reach the seawall. Men were even killed as they huddled below the log barricade itself and as they darted back and forth along the beach trying to locate their squads and platoons. The sight of so many men being killed along the beach actually inspired a lot of men to scale the seawall quicker than they would have liked...in an attempt to seek better cover inland. Those that made it over alive quickly jumped into the craters that had been left in the sand by the exploding shells of the naval bombardment and they set up hasty defensive positions to fight off any attacks that might be coming their way. But this proved to be just as dangerous as the beach was...since several men were shot in the head as they peered over the lip of their craters trying to gauge what was happening out in front of them. The effect of seeing a friend's head being blown off beside you...after having made it through several hundred yards of hell already...was totally demoralizing...and for some...completely paralyzing...so the survivors hunkered down as best they could just to stay alive.

What probably saved the men on Red 1 from being completely wiped out was that the Japanese began shifting their fires onto the approaching Higgins Boats of the fourth, fifth, and sixth waves. Sitting stationary along the reef, the boats made perfect targets as they waited patiently for the amtracs to return from the beach. And sit they did...as many of the tractors that had survived the initial run in were subsequently hit as they sat defenseless on the beach disembarking troops or as they backed off and made their way out to the reef again. Anti-boat fire and mortar rounds took a tremendous toll on the surviving amtracs and so many of them were damaged that they became virtually useless thereafter. The conditions were the same on the other two beachheads as well...and it got so bad that by nightfall only sixteen of the original eighty-seven tractors that had been assigned to the first three waves of the operation were still in service for shuttle missions.

The ragged condition of the amtracs became a death sentence for many of the men in the later waves who were hoping to catch a ride in to the beach like the men had before them. Unfortunately, the marines from L and M Companies and the Headquarters and Support units for the Third Battalion were forced to wade in from the reef and they were shot down in droves by Jap machine gunners or killed by the artillery rounds that were exploding in their midst.

Many of the men from I and K Companies watched the debacle taking place behind them with morbid fascination…but after a few minutes the slaughter became so sickening that they just turned back to deal with the fight in front of them. Individually and in small groups, they began attacking enemy emplacements in their vicinity in an effort to expand their precarious toehold on Red Beach 1.

CHAPTER 24

O ne of the amtracs churning into this tornado of smoke and fire
had the number 57 painted on the side of its cab. Nicknamed
Rum Runner, this LVT-1 carried Platoon Sergeant Roy and the rest
of the men that made up the 1st Platoon of E Company: the platoon guide sergeant…the platoon demolitions corporal…two runners…the other half of the Second Squad…and the entire Third
Squad…for a total of twenty-three men. This was two more men
than Lieutenant Hackett had…but that was because the *Rum Runner*
was short a crewman to man one of its machine guns…so the lieutenant had assigned the demo corporal to Sergeant Roy's amtrac to
make up for the missing gunner.

The ride into Red Beach 2 had gone smoothly until their vehicle
slowed perceptively two hundred yards short of the reef. The other
amtracs in the first wave continued on, and then the second and
third waves passed them by as well. The problem became apparent
when the 146-horsepower engine cut out entirely. The crew chief
left the front cab and pushed his way through the men gathered
in the troop compartment to get at the engine housing in the rear.
Precious minutes were lost as he tinkered with the engine…all the

while speaking to it in a consoling tone…until it suddenly coughed back to life amidst a belch of smoke. The chief got up smiling and the men cheered and patted him on the back as he made his way to the front of the vehicle.

While its engine was out, the *Rum Runner* had been drifting to the right and it was now almost near the boundary line that separated Red 2 and Red 1. As the amtrac picked up speed again, the driver guided the vehicle back to the left to regain the heading it had been on in its approach to Red 2. In doing so, the lonely amtrac became a perfect target for the Japanese hiding in the *Niminoa* and they took it under fire immediately. One Jap gunner led the vehicle too much and missed with his first volley but he adjusted his aim and soon the machine gun fire was puncturing the amtrac's light side armor. Bullets riddled the cab, killing the driver instantly and injuring the crew chief's left arm and leg. In spite of his wounds, the crew chief managed to push the dead driver's body aside and he regained control of the tractor. To put some distance between the tractor and the incoming fire, the chief reversed course and began steering back to the right…away from the *Niminoa*…but…inadvertently…right into the kill zone of the *Pocket*.

Once the fire let up, some of the marines stood up and peeked over the sides to see what was going on, but Platoon Sergeant Roy ordered them to stay low so they wouldn't get their heads shot off. This seemed like a reasonable order and they all dropped down below the gunwale again, but the word was passed around that they were almost at the reef. After a few moments, the *Rum Runner* smacked into the reef…just like they had predicted…and the amtrac went up and over the obstacle with ease. Once on the other side, the men hunkered down, knowing they only had several hundred yards to go before they reached the beach on Red 2…and then they could link up with the rest of their platoon.

Onshore, five *rikusentai* in a hardened bunker on the right flank of Red 2 were licking their chops in anticipation…since they were

manning one of the most deadly weapons in the Japanese arsenal...
and they knew it. Their position contained a 13mm machine gun
that was mounted on a metal pedestal which was anchored to the
floor of the bunker - which helped improve its accuracy - and they
had spotted the *Rum Runner* coming in all alone. The tractor was
directly in their pre-registered field of fire and the gunner let loose
with a volley that rattled the pedestal mount as the bullets left the
barrel and headed towards the enemy landing craft.

One of Sergeant Roy's men...a new recruit...Private Doug
Schonkwiler...had been eyeing the men on the machine guns since
he had boarded the amtrac. He was jealous that someone else had
been assigned to man one of the two powerful, bow-mounted .50
cals...a job he had hoped to get since he loved working with heavy
machinery...while another man from the 2nd Squad had been put on
the rear-mounted .30 cal...a smaller but very effective weapon. The
coveted job of manning the fifty cal had been given to the demolitions corporal in the platoon...but the private didn't know him at all.
For whatever reason, the corporal had made it plain early on that he
was one of those irascible veterans who had no desire to meet...or
know...any of the new guys who had just come from boot camp and
had been assigned to the platoon back in New Zealand. Schonkwiler
and the rest of the new guys had given the man a wide berth ever
since...and none of them ever did learn the real reason for the corporal's ambivalence towards them. All sorts of explanations for his
behavior were conjured up in late night bull sessions of course...but
none of them were ever verified. And the veterans didn't seem to
know either...or if they did...then they must have made some kind
of pact with the corporal...since they never revealed it. What the
men in the platoon...both the veterans and rookies alike...would
never know was that the demo corporal's best friend had been killed
almost a year earlier...by a boot marine who had been sharing a foxhole with him on Guadalcanal. The boot had been assigned to the
friend's squad right before they shipped out and he quickly developed

a reputation for being a practical joker…yet very few guys seemed to appreciate the man's sense of humor and antics. This seemed to encourage him more though…and he continued to pull pranks on the guys around him…even on the *Canal*. One day…out of boredom…the boot had reached over and pulled the pin out of the grenade that was hanging from the shirt pocket of the corporal's friend. The spoon of grenade was inside the man's shirt…and practical joker figured…wrongly…that it would not pop off…since it would be pressing up against the man's chest…and it would hold in place. The veteran realized the boot's error immediately however…since he felt the spoon release inside his pocket…and then the two men watched in horror as the live grenade rolled down his chest and fell at his feet. Instead of diving out of the hole though, the corporal's friend jumped on the grenade and he smothered the explosion with his own body. In doing so, he saved the life of the very man who had caused his death. An investigation of the incident was conducted immediately…and the practical joker claimed that the man had caused his own death…which was technically correct…since he had jumped on the grenade of his own volition. He also said that he had warned the man not to wear his grenades in such a dangerous fashion…another lie…but his warning had gone unheeded. To cement his innocence…he claimed that the grenade's pin had been knocked out inadvertently by the man himself…and that he had tried to dive on it too…but the veteran had beaten him to it. What the joker never realized however was that two men in a foxhole nearby had witnessed the entire incident…and they had reported what they had seen to both their platoon commander and the man's best friend as well. With all the facts in, the platoon commander wasted no time in dealing with the situation…and the joker…despite his protestations… was removed from the platoon and never seen again.

Private Schonkwiler was still looking the trio of machine gunners over when they opened fire on the *Niminoa*…and the heavy *thump thump thump* sound the guns made reminded him of a tractor's throaty

roar…which was music to his ears. But his jealousy turned to consternation…and then anger…as the guns suddenly went silent when the
amtrac crossed the reef. In his estimation, the machine gunners were
the luckiest men on board since they were the only ones who had the
ability to fire back at the enemy…and therefore they should be doing
so. What he didn't know…or realize…since he was a rookie…was that
the gunners were holding their fire since they were just as liable to hit
friendly troops who were vaulting over the seawall as they were the
enemy targets inland. Because of this precaution, the men could have
easily stepped away from the guns and jumped down into the well
of the amtrac…where they would have been somewhat protected by
the thin armor siding of the amtrac. Then…as they got closer to the
island and were able to identify their targets visually…they could have
jumped back up and manned the guns again. But the two brave marines on the bow 50's chose not to; instead, they remained stoically at
their posts…behind the guns they would not fire…in an effort to in-
timidate the Japanese behind the seawall. They believed that the sight
of the two of them still manning their posts…gripping their guns…
might discourage some enemy gunner or disrupt his firing and…at
the very least…cause him to miss his target.

Schonkwiler…to solve the riddle…reached over and pulled on
the trouser leg of the left gunner…trying to get his attention. *I don't
care if it is him*, Schonkwiler thought warily…and he kept pulling until
the demo corporal glared down at him. The private let go of his pant
leg and he said sheepishly, "I was just wondering why you guys aren't
firing…that's all."

The corporal opened his mouth as if he was going to say something when Private Schonkwiler heard a loud whack and he instinctively ducked. The sound reminded him of someone hitting a heavy
punching bag in the gym, only much louder, and when he looked
back up…he was greeted with a gruesome sight. A burst of 13mm
bullets had hit the corporal square in the upper chest area and everything from that portion of the man's body on up had suddenly

disappeared in a spray of flesh, blood, and uniform fragments. For two horrifying seconds the man's hands and arms continued to grasp the rear handles of the .50 cal machine gun, and then they flew away in the slipstream as the tractor ploughed on. At the same time, everything from the man's waist on down was still standing on the gun platform despite the fact that his head and chest were gone... and then the lower portion of his torso tumbled into the troop compartment beside the other marines. The young marine had seen farm accidents before, but they paled in comparison to what he was staring at now. This grizzly baptism of fire caused Schonkwiler to throw up his breakfast of steak and eggs...a meal he had relished...but had seldom eaten while was growing up in the dusty fields of central Iowa during the depression-era 1930's.

• • •

"Go right! Damn it...go right! That gun'll chop us to pieces if we don't avoid it!" Platoon Sergeant Roy could see the heavy machine gun twinkling on the distant shoreline as its gun crew continued to blast away at the *Rum Runner*. The crew chief followed the big marine's instructions without hesitation...since his baritone voice was hard to ignore...even over the roar of the battle. Without thinking twice, he turned the vehicle back to the right. That seemed to do the trick since the gun stopped firing at them as they moved away and headed into the cove.

Next, Platoon Sergeant Roy turned his attention to the silent machine gun and the man who had been buggy him to man it. Roy's eyes settled in on Private Schonkwiler and he hollered, "After you're down puking...get on that gun. It's what you wanted all along, so get up there and do something with it!"

Schonkwiler lifted his head up and wiped the spittle from his lip with his sleeve. Then in one smooth motion he mounted the firing platform and began squeezing off accurate bursts from the machine gun.

• • •

In reality, *Lady Luck* had intervened on behalf of *Rum Runner* as it started its run to the beach…and that's why she wasn't hit and sunk like so many other amtracs were while approaching Red 2. In her case, the veteran *rikusentai* who was manning the machine gun that was firing at her decided to take a break…and this simple act had spared her…since the Jap sailor who had taken his place was not as experienced on the powerful gun as his mentor was. The young man was exhausted from the menial job of loading bullets into the empty magazines that were constantly being handed to him…and he had jumped at the opportunity when the tired petty officer asked for a much-needed break. Now he finally had the chance to dish out some punishment as payback for all he had been through so far…and he welcomed the chance to get even with the evil men out in the lagoon. Earlier, he and the four other men on the gun had cowered in the corners of the bunker while they endured the early morning naval bombardment from the ships far out at sea. He never envisioned that he could be so afraid…but as the shells exploded relentlessly around their position he thought he might go crazy from fright. It had been so bad that at one point he had heard one of the senior crewmembers crying helplessly above the din of the shelling.

He quickly sat down on the empty seat of the Model 93 heavy machine gun and got comfortable. This gun was accurate out to four thousand yards and it could fire four hundred and fifty rounds per minute. It was also magazine fed…and a single magazine contained thirty rounds apiece…so it required a crew of five men - a crew chief…a gunner…an assistant gunner…and two loaders - to operate it efficiently…and the assistant gunner had just placed a fresh magazine into the gun. This man…his buddy…looked at him and yelled, "Fully loaded…she's all yours!" He then bent over slightly and looked through the telescopic sight and immediately honed in on a single amtrac that was heading his way. He followed the gunnery procedures he had been taught months before and fired short, three-to-four round bursts as he tracked the vehicle's progress towards the beach. He assumed his aim was good when he saw a man who was manning one of the big machine guns on either side of the cab get hit and fall back out of view. Little did he know that the loss of this one man had probably saved the landing craft since it fooled him into thinking that his fire was effective…when…in actuality…he was firing way too high…a mistake made all too often by riflemen and machine gunners in battle for the first time. The vehicle made an evasive maneuver to the left to avoid his fire so he obediently swung his gun back to fire on the multitude of Higgins boats that were now coming into his assigned field of fire on the reef to the right of the amtrac. Like the dutiful, well-trained *rikusentai* that he was, he let the *Rum Runner* go…assuming that the gun positions to his left along the cove would dispatch the churning, green-colored landing craft as soon as it entered their designated lanes of fire. He had only fired a few more volleys when he felt a tap on his shoulder…and taking his eye off the reef and the targets… he turned and saw the petty officer patiently waiting behind him. Rejuvenated after a drink of beer - water was hard to come by on the island…but beer and saki were in plentiful supply - and a few moments rest, the veteran signaled with a jerk of his thumb that he was ready to resume his position behind the 13mm gun. The young sailor slid out from behind the gun and the senior gunner jumped back in and immediately acquired a new target on the reef. The petty officer began squeezing the trigger once again and his accurate fire raked a Higgins boat that was now approaching.

Five hundred yards away, Platoon Sergeant Roy and the corporal crew chief had no way of knowing how close the *Rum Runner* had actually come to being totally destroyed by this heavy machine gun position. They had been saved…for the moment…by the basic need of a veteran to relieve himself and quench his thirst.

• • •

Platoon Sergeant Roy took a quick survey of the cove and saw that the only place they could put in was on the right side of Red 1. There were about six amtracs sitting on the beach there and he could see marines huddled near the seawall and some men were actually vaulting over it. He pointed to the spot where he wanted to land and said, "Crank this piece of junk up and head over that way. I wanna go in near the tip on the right."

The corporal turned around and scowled at Roy. "Don't go callin' this amtrac any names. She's the only thing keepin' you and your boys alive right now!"

The platoon sergeant glowered back at the corporal in response.

"Her engine's a little long in the tooth...that's all. That's why she cut out before...but this old girl will get you boys to that beach...I promise," the crew chief said defensively, worried by the look on the sergeant's face. He then turned back around and pushed the throttle forward, accelerating *Rum Runner* through the fire-swept cove and onto the beach...just like Platoon Sergeant Roy wanted.

The crew chief had seen some other amtracs tottering on the seawall so he made no effort at heading inland. He stopped the vehicle on the beach and looked back and saw that the platoon sergeant was already ordering the men out of it. "Told ya she'd make it!" he yelled back into crew compartment over the noise of the .50 cal that was blasting away beside him.

Roy heard him while screaming, "Everybody out...everybody out," and he gave the crew chief the thumbs-up sign.

The corporal broke into a big grin and watched as the sergeant finally jumped over the gunwale, leaving the amtrac's once-crowded well entirely empty. With his first mission in the books, the crew chief put the vehicle in reverse and backed successfully off the beach. The other crew member...a private first class...continued to fire the bow machine gun at the targets along the seawall...and this marked it as a target worth destroying. Some fifty yards into the cove, he turned *Rum Runner* around and off she went...churning towards the reef to pick up another load marines...and right into the sights of one of the 75mm anti-boat guns in the *Pocket*. This gun had sunk several amtracs already and the gun crew methodically loaded a new round, closed the breach block, and registered in on the marine landing craft. The order to fire was given, the lanyard pulled, and a shell screeched across the lagoon in a flat trajectory on its way to *Rum Runner*. The armor-piercing round hit the back of the cab and exploded behind the corporal…killing both him and the machine gunner instantly. The explosion shredded the control panel as well and *Rum Runner*…with all three crewmen now dead and its steering mechanism damaged… chugged along in a lazy circle just inside the reef until it ran out of fuel. Dead in the water, seawater was soon seeping in through several bullet holes in the sides and then it was lapping over the gunwales as well. Twelve minutes later…without ceremony…amtrac # 57 sank ten feet down and came to rest on the lagoon bottom…along with her heroic crew…who also went down with her.

• • •

On Red 1, Platoon Sergeant Roy decided to spread all twenty-one of his men out along the seawall until he figured out what to do next. This seemed to be the safest place for the time being…but the dead marines lying nearby did give him cause for concern…so he called Corporal Phil Oliver, Sergeant Jeff Varner, and Sergeant Gene Flockerzi over to his side. As the right platoon guide, Flockerzi was second ranking sergeant in the platoon and he was a veteran with experience…so Sergeant Roy often relied on him to get things done. Varner was the squad leader of the 3rd Squad and he had his entire eleven-man squad with him…all alive…and no one wounded…a rare distinction on Betio. Oliver…a veteran…was a new man to the platoon…having been transferred to E Company after serving time as a ship-board marine on a cruiser. He was also the recipient of a recent promotion…since he had been given the Second Squad to manage. Oliver had just five men…or half the squad…with him. This was less than what he was normally in charge of…but no one thought anything of it…since he had earned the squad leader promotion by excelling in the training exercises on New Zealand.

The three leaders scrambled over to Roy and he explained that he was going to go find someone in charge to see where they were needed. As Roy got up to go, his group began taking fire from the left side of the cove...and he realized that they would be in trouble if they stayed where they were. Sadly, the seawall here couldn't protect them from the fire that was coming from the cove...since it was in their rear...so he changed his plans on the fly. "We'll get slaughtered if we don't move right away," he said, and added, "so we're going inland instead. I didn't come this far to die getting shot in the back!"

A hasty inspection of the area behind the seawall revealed one spot off to the right where the naval bombardment had destroyed a section of pillboxes and this is where Roy chose to go. He led the group in a crouching run to the right along the seawall, stopped for a second, peaked over log barricade to make sure the way was clear, and said, "Follow me."

The sergeant slithered over the log barricade and crawled to the ruins of a fortified machine gun position not far away. He found three dead Japs sprawled inside and two more were lying outside the exit in a connecting trench that led to an adjacent pillbox several yards to the right. Several unopened ammunition boxes and weapons were scattered outside this bunker but there were no more bodies to be seen. Roy figured that the second position must have been abandoned as marines fought their way off the beach earlier. Off in the distance, he could see three shell craters and several smaller foxholes and he decided that this is where they would make their first stand.

As the men began filing in behind him, a Jap machine gun team spied their movement and began firing at them as they darted over the seawall. Roy fired several shots at the gun emplacement with his shotgun but his fire had little effect. During the firefight that ensued, eighteen of the twenty-one men made it over successfully... with one man...the squad's grenadier...being killed outright as he mounted the seawall. This man...Corporal Bob Minkewicz from Hackensack, New Jersey...was tasked with carrying a Springfield rifle that could be fitted with a grenade launcher. This allowed him to fire grenades that were more powerful than the standard hand grenade...primarily for anti-tank defense. Horribly, he was hit by a large caliber shell as he mounted the seawall and he blew up when the grenades he was carrying in a pouch were ignited by the round that hit him. The force of the explosion was so strong that the rifleman waiting to go behind him was wounded too...and so badly so that he died shortly thereafter. One other man was also hit by a machine gun volley and he crumbled to the ground behind the seawall. Unwilling to leave the wounded man alone, Roy detailed one man to stay back with the injured man and this man...a private first class... quickly turned around and jumped right back down onto the beach. Wasting no time, he grabbed the wounded man - he had been shot in both legs - by the straps of his backpack and he dragged him roughly over to the cover of a disabled amtrac.

That done, Sergeant Roy pointed to Sergeant Varner and then pointed to the craters and foxholes up ahead. And though he didn't say a word, Varner knew from training what his platoon sergeant wanted done...and he and his eight remaining men advanced to the foxholes up ahead. Then they covered Oliver and his men with rifle fire as they scrambled into the holes beside them.

Once everyone was settled in, Platoon Sergeant Roy looked around and saw other groups of marines in the distance advancing to the left and right as well. Some of the groups were small... consisting of two and three-man teams...while others were larger... numbering as many as six or seven men in a bunch. They were led by lieutenants...or sergeants...or corporals...and...in some cases... by brave privates as well. Instead of waiting for orders, these men took matters into their own hands and despite the risks involved... they led their men forward...courageously taking the fight to the Japanese on their own. These initial forays inland were instrumental in clearing the tip of Red 1 of enemy machine gunners and snipers and this helped many more marines in the following waves get ashore alive...since there were fewer Japanese to shoot them down.

CHAPTER 25

Major Mike Ryan's men had begun making the treacherous, seven-hundred-yard trek from the reef at about the same time Sergeant Roy's men were landing on Red 1. Since the amtracs that were detailed to take them to the beach never showed up, the L Company marines left their Higgins boats behind and jumped into the turbid waters of the lagoon. Ryan's men were taken under fire as soon as they got inside the reef…and their landing had the earmarks of a total disaster until the major saw several marines scaling the seawall on the far right side of Red 1. Based on this key observation, the major made a fateful decision and saved his command…and inadvertently…his entire battalion. He immediately directed his men to swing to their right…away from the cove…and head towards the tip of the island… otherwise known as the Bird's Beak. In a stroke of luck, the men from M Company - the heavy weapons unit - and the other support units that were coming in behind L Company…primarily the demolitions engineers and flamethrower teams…saw what the major was doing and wisely followed his lead and made for the Beak as well.

From his vantage point, Sergeant Roy stared grimly at the lines of men being whittled down by the enemy machine gun fire and artillery fire. But Roy also noticed that some of the survivors had started to shift away from the blood bath in the cove and were now angling towards the section of the island that he and his men were occupying. *Good for them*, he thought, *someone out there seems to know what the hell they're doin'*...and though they had suffered terrible casualties...nearly two-thirds of the one hundred and fifty marines from L Company actually made it to the island alive by bypassing the Red 1 beachhead altogether. These men found their way to the northwestern corner of the island...which also overlapped the extreme northern tip of Green Beach...the long strip of beach that ran down the western side of the island. And like the rest of the men who had fought their way ashore that morning, the survivors from L Company flopped down behind the cover of the seawall... completely exhausted and in shock over what they had just been through.

As the marines lay there dumbstruck and hesitant, one officer decided to take charge of the situation and get them moving. Captain George Wentzel, the executive officer of M Company, climbed up on the log wall and began yelling at the men huddled below him...urging and cajoling them to head inland and start fighting. Oblivious to the bullets whizzing by him, the helmet-less, pipe-smoking former college professor strode back and forth along the seawall until some of the men began to stir. Whether they were inspired to do it or shamed into it was anyone's guess...but the major had struck a chord with them and they finally answered his call to action. Swallowing their fear, groups of marines began crawling forward into the maelstrom beyond the log barricade...which freed up space along the seawall as more and more men struggled in. Leading by example, the confident Captain Wentzel was the epitome of courage and boldness and he single-handedly broke up the logjam that had developed along the seawall on Green Beach. Sadly, Captain Wentzel would never make it off the very beach he helped clear. Later that morning he would die after being shot in the throat by a sniper as he continued to rally his men forward off the northern end of Green Beach.

• • •

By late morning, Major Ryan had a sizeable force of marines scattered around him and he began organizing them as best he could while he waited for his battalion commander to land. Before long it dawned on him that he might be on his own though...since it appeared that Major Schoettel, the battalion commander, was never going to make it in while the anti-boat fire coming from the *Pocket* was still so formidable. In his second crucial decision of the day, Major Ryan...a reserve officer...decided to hand L Company over to his executive officer and he took command of all the elements in the vicinity. It was a gutsy call for an officer with such limited experience to make...but a necessary one...and the major made it... the repercussions be damned. And just like that, Major Mike Ryan became the de facto commander of the entire Third Battalion on Red Beach 1.

With that fateful decision made, the major sent out runners to get a headcount from both I and K Companies and to find out exactly where their men were located. With that information at hand, he could get them organized and plan a coordinated, single-front attack against the Japanese that were dug in behind the northern end of Green Beach and along the western side of Red 1.

CHAPTER 26

"You see these defenses, Stonewall?"

Platoon Sergeant Roy kept scanning the terrain ahead to see if he could see any symmetry to the Jap defenses and then said casually, "Yeah, I see 'em...so what?"

"Whatta ya mean...so what? These bunkers beat anything the Japs had on the *Canal*. No wonder we had such a hard time getting in here. They must have been laughing the whole time we were comin' in. The beach side of this one has coconut logs a foot thick! And this is just a crummy, little pillbox! Can you imagine what they used to protect the bigger bunkers? No wonder so many of them survived the naval bombardment." Sergeant Gene Flockerzi, the platoon's right guide, was astounded by the meticulous construction and engineering of the Japanese defenses on Betio...at least the ones he had encountered so far. He continued his inspection of the bunker they were holding and whistled when he was done. "These bastards left nothing out...I'll tell ya that much. I wonder if they used concrete on any of them."

Competitive by nature, Flockerzi came from Franklin, a town near Pittsburgh in western Pennsylvania and was just twenty-three years old…but those that met him always thought he was much older than that. This mistaken notion was helped by the fact that he acted more mature than his age dictated…but he was also going bald so that fooled people too. He was also the senior three-stripe sergeant in the platoon and was considered E Company's resident expert on anything that dealt with woodworking and construction. The men in the platoon had long ago christened him with the nickname, "Flockerbee," since most of them felt he should have been a Navy Seabee instead of a Devil Dog…the nickname for a grunt marine. At the very least, the men thought he should have been an engineer or demo man but "Flockerbee" had always maintained that he had much more fun building things than blowing them up. His famous refrain was, "If you got the right tools, you can build or fix anything," and everyone who watched him work saw the merits in his simple philosophy. At six foot and one hundred and ninety pounds, he was bigger than most and as strong as an ox, but he rarely used his size to bully anyone…and when asked who their favorite non-commissioned officer was, nine of ten privates in the platoon would answer, "Flockerbee, who else?"

Platoon Sergeant Roy glanced back at Flockerzi - he was the only man that had ever been allowed to call the sergeant by his nickname - to see what he was doing…and was fascinated when the sergeant pulled a tape from one of pockets and measured off the length of one of the angle irons that was holding the coconut logs in place.

"Six feet…just incredible," Flockerzi stated emphatically.

Roy shook his head, said nothing, and turned back to the task at hand. He could never really understand why the sergeant found the length of a piece of steel or the thickness of a log in a Jap bunker more interesting than finding out where the Japs actually were.

CHAPTER 27

A cheer suddenly broke out from the marines on the Bird's Beak and it quickly spread to the men in the 1st Platoon. Platoon Sergeant Roy scrambled into the bunker and looked out into the lagoon to see what all the celebrating was about. Sure enough, climbing over the reef were six M-4 Sherman medium tanks and their pioneer guides. It was a magnificent sight and it certainly buoyed the hopes for all the men who felt isolated and trapped on the corner of the island. The men carrying the identifiable signal buoys jumped into the water ahead of the tanks and without hesitation began slogging through the chest deep water...all the time looking for dangerous shell craters and depressions that could trap the tanks. Roy watched them come on and realized all too well what they were doing. He turned to Sergeant Flockerzi and said proudly, "Remember what you see here, Flock. You'll never see any men braver than those guys out there in front of those tanks."

"What they're doing is suicide. The damn Nips know why they're there. They'll never make it in alive," Flockerzi said hopelessly and then he dashed out of the rear of the bunker to see if he could spot the Japs who were beginning to fire on the men in the lagoon. "Oh God," he moaned since he could see and hear hundreds of guns firing from the pillboxes, dugouts, and bunkers all along the base and far side of the cove. The cheering died down as the men on shore watched the pioneers being shot down one by one as they entered the fire-swept cove. By the time the tanks reached their landing spot at the base of the cove, not a single guide was left alive. Incredibly... one exceptionally brave marine...Sergeant James Atkins...actually made it in the entire way...and led the tanks right up to the beach. At the last moment, he was hit by a volley of machine gun bullets and he crumpled over and died right at the shoreline.

"What the hell are they doin' now?" Flockerzi said desperately.

"Beats me, Flock," Roy replied, not venturing a guess...since the tanks were almost three hundred yards away from where they were and it was too difficult to tell what was really going on.

Inexplicably, the tanks had rolled to a stop in the shallows and sat still for a few minutes. Then, instead of advancing up the beach and through the seawall as intended, the Shermans had backed up a few feet, slewed to starboard, and headed towards the Bird's Beak in a column formation.

Roy and Flockerzi watched the parade in silence and eventually two tanks came lumbered ashore near the tip of island off to their right. "Two are better than none, I guess," Sergeant Roy said finally...without emotion.

"I would've preferred to have all six going to work over here," Flockerzi countered, "since these defenses are gonna take a hell of a lotta work to destroy. More than just rifles and grenades in my opinion."

"Tanks or no tanks, it always ends up being the man with the rifle and bayonet who has to do the dirty work of getting in there and fighting it out with these jokers. That's the way it was on the *Canal*...and that's the way it'll be here too. Trust me," Roy replied right back, knowing that his guide sergeant would agree with him... since he was a veteran of Guadalcanal as well.

From their vantage point inland, both men could see why the tanks had driven over to the far side of the Beak. There was a small break in the seawall at that point...where a shell from one of the cruisers or battleships had hit...and the tanks were going to take advantage of it.

"I don't imagine that'll hold 'em up," Flockerzi said confidently.

Without hesitation, both *Cecilia* and *China Gal* crashed through the narrow opening...the sound of the coconut logs being crushed and pushed out of the way confirming that Flockerzi had been right. Then the tanks cut across their front and disappeared inland...heading for the *Pocket*.

The other four tanks never made it. They were strung out in a ragged line across the cove...completely helpless. Without pioneers to guide them over like they had on the way in, the tank drivers had inadvertently steered them into deep holes or shell craters that dotted their path...but they could not see. Seawater rushed into the engine compartments of the tanks and within minutes all four were stuck...their engines now useless. Two of them had nearly disappeared...the only thing still visible being the tops of their turrets.

The rest of the marines ashore found the sight especially depressing...since they knew...more than anyone else...that the firepower of those four tanks was desperately need ashore. The four 75mm cannons and four .30 caliber machine guns mounted in their turrets could have given the marines a tremendous edge in defeating the bunkers and pillboxes that were now holding them up. And the tide of the battle would have turned in their favor very quickly if all the tanks had made it in...but now the grunts would have to carry on the fight without their help...with just rifles and grenades.

• • •

Sergeant Flockerzi had returned and was back inspecting the inside of the bunker when he looked out the firing aperture and saw the commander's hatch of one of the Shermans stuck in the cove suddenly spring open. The TC...short for tank commander...popped his head out, took a quick look around, and then ducked back down inside. Rifle and machine gun fire ricocheted harmlessly off the tank's armor as Jap snipers tried to kill the man but it was obvious that he and the two other men with him were safe so long as they remained inside that part of the tank. The same could not be said for the other two members of the crew who were positioned in the driver's compartment...which was located below and forward of the main turret in the hull of the tank. Unfortunately, water was pouring steadily into the driver's compartment since the tank had fallen into a deep hole and the front end of the tank was completely underwater. Without waiting, the driver left his seat and squeezed his way into the turret...or he would have eventually drowned up front. The assistant driver...a man who had been recently assigned to the tank...decided that the risk of abandoning the tank altogether was a better option than remaining in it...so he chose to stay where he was until he was forced out of it. The *rikusentai* sensed that the tank crew was in a helpless position too...so they fired relentlessly at the tank...keeping it buttoned up...and hoping to entomb the five men inside the steel monster until they all drowned or a bigger gun could knock it out with a direct hit on its turret.

The driver's compartment was nearly overflowing with seawater when the assistant driver finally pushed his hatch cover fully open and he stood up. Flockerzi watched the man struggling with something near the hatch cover and in that brief moment he was stitched across the chest by a string of bullets. As he toppled over, the wide pocket on his tanker's uniform that had been caught on the hatch lever tore off...releasing the lever's hold on it. Now free of its snag, his lifeless body toppled off the front slope of the tank and fell into the water. Bullets continued ricocheting of the front of the tank and splashing around the man's body...even though he was already dead...but it didn't matter to the Jap gunners...since their blood was up. Now they were hungry for more kills...and they hoped the other four men inside would make the same error their buddy up front had.

Sergeant Flockerzi was anxious for the tankers too...and just like the Jap gunners...he was wondering what the other four men inside the tank would do next.

JAMES F. DWYER

Sergeant Roy had kept his eye on the tank as well and he could hear the men behind the seawall yelling instructions to the four men still inside. Some were telling them to stay where they were…while others…just as vigorously…were telling them to get out while they could. The crew must have weighed their options heavily…since their lives depended on it…and they obviously chose the latter option…to get out while the going was good…because the two hatches on the top of the turret suddenly sprang open. The TC's hatch… which was on the right side of the turret…was better shielded from the guns on shore because of the way the tank had tilted when it had slid into the crater…and it gave the four men a little more protection than the loader's hatch did so all four exited out of it…one at a time. Once they were out, the tank commander crept down the right side of the tank and grabbed the body of the assistant driver by the top of his tanker's overalls and dragged him back behind the vehicle. Then he opened the communications box that was attached near the rear fender and secured the dead private to the vehicle by tying him up with the long cord that was connected to the handset. The other tankers - the gunner…the loader-radio operator…and the driver - were huddled together behind the tank as well and they were watching the TC secure the dead assistant driver to the tank when the booming voice of Sergeant Roy caught their attention. Poking their heads carefully over the fender, they looked in the direction his voice had come from and they spotted a huge marine waving them over.

"You men need to get yourselves over here," he bellowed across the water.

The TC poked his head under the tank's main gun and pointed at himself…as if to say…*are you talkin' to us?*

"Yeah…you damn it! Who else do you think I'm talkin' to…the men on the reef? Get your asses over here. You ain't doing anyone any good sittin' behind that piece of junk."

The tank commander…a sergeant named Leon LaPorte… frowned and shouted back, "Screw you, Mac!" He then turned to the rest of the crew and said derisively, "Did ya hear that jerk! Who does he think he is…calling *Cougar* here a piece of junk?"

"Why don't you go over there and punch that guy in the nose," the loader said, egging him on.

"Because I'll get my ass shot off trying to get over there, that's why, you dummy. You really were at the end of the line when they were handing out brains weren't you, Cobb?"

The other two crewmen laughed at this exchange because their commander was a hair over five foot six inches tall while Private Tom Cobb was well over six foot tall when he stood straight up… something that rarely happened inside the tank. The gunner, a bright corporal named Toni Bruno, followed up with, "Yeah, why don't ya? That way we can trace your path if ya make it over there alive. I gotta tell ya, sarge, I'm gettin' real tired of standing in this water. Maybe it's about time we all headed over that way. Whatta ya say?"

Now the driver…Private First Class Sam Palmer…another Southerner like Cobb…chimed in and said, "Tony's got a point there, sarge. We can't stay here forever. And Cobber is right…that jerk does deserve a punch in the nose for talkin' that way about good old Cougar here." Then he added, "And y'all know I don't swim so good and they told us there were sharks in these waters in the briefings. I'd really hate to get eaten by a shark right now so why don't we just get it over with and go in?"

LaPorte looked at the men like he was stunned. It was the same type of look a guy gets when he's been punched in the nose but doesn't get knocked out from the blow…and the men had seen this look before. But this time their TC's resovle seemed to weaken just a bit. He looked the group over and said coyly, "Okay, I'm gonna give in…but just this once. We can't stay here forever…and I'd go crazy just listening to all your bitching and griping if we don't. So here's what we're gonna do."

The plan didn't have to be very complicated since they were only twenty-five yards or so from the beach…and about forty yards when you included the distance to the seawall in the calculation. "I'll go first and then each of you will follow me over one at a time. The Nips might not waste their ammo shooting at one man so we might get lucky and make it over okay if we go separately."

Sergeant LaPorte let a few minutes go by and then he said dryly, "Well, it's now or never." He made a quick sign of the cross and was off, pushing through the surf with all his might...and heading for the spot where he had last seen the big marine. The effort was exhausting but the TC reached the seawall safely and then collapsed against it.

As he sat huffing against the seawall, Sergeant Flockerzi ran over and jumped down onto the beach. "Hey, you made it," he said happily. He could tell the man was a tanker by the football-type helmet he was wearing. LaPorte looked him over and said angrily, "Are you the guy that made that comment about my tank?"

• • •

It took a while but the last of the tankers was finally ready to make his break for the seawall. The other two privates had followed LaPorte over and though they had been shot at...neither had been hit. But the Jap snipers had made all the adjustments they needed based on their previous misses...and they were ready and waiting when Corporal Bruno began his trek over. Bruno made it most of the way...but as he left the water and touched dry sand...he was shot in the belly. The tank gunner fell forward on his face and lay there for several seconds...and then he started crawling to the wall. When the marines and the tankers saw him moving, they scrambled over to help him. Two men grabbed him under each of his arms and dragged him to the seawall and set him down gently in Cobb's lap. PFC Palmer opened his shirt and looked at the ugly wound and knew instinctively that he was done for...and so did Bruno. One of the marines said sadly, "I wish we had a corpsman with us...but we don't."

"That's...okay," the corporal said in a labored voice, and then he added, "I got somethin' way better than morphine anyway." Bruno...smiling grimly...then reached into a pocket on his tanker's overalls and produced a silver flask.

"What's in that?" one of the young marines asked.

"Amaretto...no self-respecting Italian would be caught dead without it."

Palmer unscrewed the top and handed the flask to Bruno. He took a long swig and then looked at the flask with an appreciative glance. "Now that was worth it," he said. Then he handed it back to the driver and he told him to take a drink too. "So you'll have something...to remember me by," he said weakly. Palmer...no teetotaler...accepted Bruno's offer readily and took a good swig. "Here's to one of the best tankers the Marine Corps will ever have," he said, nodding to the gunner and Palmer passed the metal container to Cobb. He took his swig and passed it to the three marines who they didn't know...but who had helped drag Bruno over to the seawall. Each took a short nip and then the last man gave it back to Palmer. The driver could tell that there was a little left so he held the flask to Bruno's lips and the gunner drained it dry. Smiling at the men around him, he said weakly, "Sorry about that...didn't mean to take the last drop..."and he died in Private Cobb's arms.

CHAPTER 28

As far as Platoon Sergeant Roy could tell, the ground in front of the his position was lightly-wooded with coconut trees and pockmarked with shell holes from the earlier bombardment. He certainly couldn't see any bunkers that resembled the ones that had been built into and behind the seawall. *It's a sniper's paradise though,* he thought, looking through the pair of binoculars that Sergeant LaPorte had handed him and he asked the tanker if he could hang onto to them for the time being.

"Keep 'em…since it doesn't look like I'll be needing 'em any time soon. Even if I could get *Cougar* towed in, we'd have to pull the engine out and replace it. She went in above the fenders when we hit that sink hole. It'll be a while before she's back in action…which is too bad because she was a good tank."

Roy looped the binocular case over his neck and let it hang by his side, out of the way. "I never did have much use for tanks really," Roy said nonchalantly, and then added, "but that was before I got here." Since Roy didn't say anything else, LaPorte considered his remark a tacit thank you for the gift he had just given him.

The platoon sergeant then called his two squad leaders over and began outlining what he wanted done. "I don't intend to wait any longer for reinforcements or flank support. We're gonna start advancing with what we got right here." Roy then described the manner in which he wanted it done: they were going to attack across a broad front...with the men from the 2ⁿᵈ Squad under Oliver on the left...and Varner's 3ʳᵈ Squad on the right. Both squads would be advancing together...so it was up to the squad leaders to keep an eye on the platoon sergeant so they could coordinate their movements forward. Flockerzi would stay in the middle with Roy to take over if the platoon sergeant went down. When he was finished with the briefing, Sergeant LaPorte asked him if he and his two tankers could join him as infantrymen.

"Sure you can," he replied while looking the sergeant over. Then he asked, "Do you have any weapons other than that forty-five on your hip?"

"Cobb has a grease gun...but that's it. We never envisioned that we'd be fighting on foot," the tanker answered hesitantly.

"Well, have your guys go down to the beach and find something to fight with and hurry back. It shouldn't take them but a second since there are plenty of rifles laying around. You and your men can stay with Sergeant Flockerzi and me in the middle. Good enough?"

LaPorte didn't bother the sergeant with an answer. He simply turned to tell Palmer what needed to be done...but his driver was already scrambling down the trench and heading for the beach. *That man seems to know what I'm gonna say before I even say it,* the tank commander thought... impressed with his driver's innate sense of knowing what his TC wanted done. "And bring me a BAR if you can find one," he yelled at the driver's back as he jumped down off the seawall. Palmer just waved his arm to acknowledge his request...since he was going to do exactly that.

LaPorte then glared at Private Cobb who was crouching further back along the trench. Cobb looked confused at first and then he jumped up and said, "I think I'll go with him," and he ran off as well.

The tank commander turned back to the platoon sergeant and in an exasperated tone droned, "Privates..."

• • •

Sergeant Roy kicked his attack off at 1130 hours and it went better than he had anticipated. Fortunately for Roy's men, Captain Takeo Sugai - the leader of the 7th Sasebo Special Naval Landing Force and commander of the western section of the island - had concentrated the bulk of his forces along the Red 1 and Green beaches so they could all fire on the marine landing craft as they approached the island. But for some strange reason, the captain had left the ground behind the beaches lightly occupied. This created a soft spot that Roy's men were able to exploit...and they made good progress as they advanced through the open ground behind the beach. Many of the enemy soldiers that the platoon did encounter were the remnants of the forward beach defenses who had pulled back and a lot of them seemed to be demoralized by the constant pounding they had taken all morning long. Their recent retreat to these secondary positions had done nothing to spark their confidence or lift their tittering morale. Some of the *rikusentai* continued to put up a tenacious defense however...but their numbers were dwindling as their one, two, and three-man strong points were overrun. Before long, Roy and his men had driven nearly five hundred yards and were approaching the southern coast.

The cost in casualties to gain this territory was extremely light compared to the losses some of the other units had taken as they tried to advance inland. In all, Roy lost one man from each squad... both privates...one being the Iowa farm boy...Doug Schonkwiler... whose dream of manning the bow fifty on the amtrac had come true. The other was Private Cam Johnston...who at eighteen had left Penn State University to enlist in the Marines. Both men died attacking a particularly tough machine gun nest before it was wiped out by a perfect grenade strike thrown by another private in the Third Squad. Two other men had been wounded...but none seriously enough to be sent back to the beach …so they just patched themselves up and kept fighting beside their brothers-in-arms.

Roy's men had made such good progress in fact that they could almost see the southern shore of the island…or Black Beach…as it was called on the Regimental maps. At this point they had taken cover in the western end of a deep tank trap that started approximately a hundred and fifty yards inland from Green Beach and stretched another four hundred yards to their left…forming the northern border of a huge open area that extended eastward towards the main airfield. Up ahead, Roy's men could see another tank trap about half as long as the one they were currently hiding in. This one began all the way over by Black Beach on the southern shore and cut diagonally across the southwestern tip of the island…finally ending by a sandy trail that was some fifty yards inland from Green Beach off to their right. This trail…a rough roadway of sorts…ran parallel to Green Beach and basically connected Temakin Point…which lay up ahead and to the right…with the Bird's Beak…which now lay behind them on their right.

Roy could tell that the Jap defenses were stiffening again as his men got closer to the southern coast…and since he was satisfied with the progress they had made…he decided to halt right there. "Dig in," he ordered, and added, "If the Japs on the south coast get wise that we're over here…they'll probably mount an attack to drive us out. They can't let us sit here all by ourselves…we're too exposed and we'd be a thorn in their side." The platoon sergeant then placed himself in the center of the trench for control purposes and when he glanced up and down the line to check on the men's positions, an eerie feeling came over him. Although he hadn't thought about his real father in a very long time…years in fact…Roy was doing so now. His father…a teacher and lover of Civil War history…had often sat with him at night before bedtime when he was very young and read him stories about all the great engagements of that war. He loved those moments with his dad…had cherished them really…

and he had sworn right after his father's death that he would never get as close to anyone like that again. And up to this point in his life, he had followed through on that oath and kept everyone he met at an arm's length...to protect himself from losing someone close to him yet again. Then he smiled and thought sardonically, *you certainly didn't pick the easiest profession to accomplish that goal...that's for sure.* And as he thought more about his father and the different battles and gallant actions he had talked about...he remembered that there had always been one story that had seemingly struck a chord with the hardened platoon sergeant through the years...and he had never forgotten it. And it was coming to mind right now: the story of the desperate fight for the *Sunken Road* during the battle for Antietam on September 20th of 1862...where the outnumbered rebels under Colonel John Brown Gordon...who was wounded five times that day...fought off the Union soldiers in the center of the Confederate line and were almost wiped out for their effort. One of the aspects of the battle for the *Sunken Road*...which was also called *Bloody Lane*... that had intrigued Roy was what had happened to Colonel Gordon after he received his last and final wound...a bullet through one of his cheeks. Knocked unconscious, Gordon had fallen face-first into the trench...and was thought to be dead by those around him. As if by divine intervention, the colonel's kepi...a type of flat-brimmed hat that both he and General Stonewall Jackson wore famously...had been hit earlier as well...courtesy of a Yankee sharpshooter. So it now had two nice holes in it along its top...and while the bullet holes had ruined his hat...they also saved the colonel's life. When Gordon was hit, he had fallen forward and he landed with his face resting in his hat...and he should have drowned in his own blood as it filled up in his hat. But the two holes in the hat now allowed the blood to drain out harmlessly...into the ground...instead of building up and reaching a level that would have choked him to death.

Sergeant Roy pictured the scene in his own mind...since the tank trap resembled the sunken road...and the Japs up ahead certainly outnumbered his small band of warriors...just like the Yankee brigade made up of Irish immigrants had outnumbered Colonel Gordon's 6th Alabama Regiment at Antietam. Then he wondered if the *Man Upstairs* had the same intentions for him...or his lieutenant even...who gone through a similar experience back on Guadalcanal. Roy remembered how Colonel Gordon had been picked up by his men and taken to an aid station where he subsequently recovered and went on to fight until the very end of the war. *I sure hope the Man Upstairs will grace me with that kind of luck...and the lieutenant too...if he needs it yet again...wherever he is.*

The men picked up on Sergeant Roy's strange behavior as well... since he was staring off in the distance...not saying a word...something they had rarely seen him do. After a few seconds went by, they began nudging one another...as if saying, *what's up with him*...when they suddenly observed another band of marines leapfrogging their way ahead...off to their left...some seventy-five yards away. Other than the tankers, these were the first marines that they had seen up close since they had landed that morning...and it was exciting to know that there was a group of friendlies nearby.

Sergeant Flockerzi slapped Sergeant Roy on the shoulder and said excitedly, "Looks like the cavalry is showing up." Roy's mind quickly readjusted to the situation at hand in response to the Guide Sergeant's whack...and then he heard Flockerzi yelling and pointing to the other marines nearby. The sergeant spotted them easily and told everyone to stay put...and then he ran down the tank trap to see what these men were up to.

CHAPTER 29

"What unit are ya with, sergeant?" The officer asking the question was Second Lieutenant Jim Fawcett…a platoon leader in K Company, 2nd Marines…and other than a few of the men who were with him…he hadn't seen a single soul from his own company since he had landed on Red 1 at 0910 hours that morning.

"First Platoon…E Company…Second of the Second, sir," Roy responded automatically.

"Second of the Second?" the officer asked incredulously. "What the hell are you doing over here?"

"You want the short or long version, sir?"

"Don't bother, sergeant. You don't have to be a brain surgeon to figure that one out," the lieutenant said.

"No, sir, you sure don't," Platoon Sergeant Roy replied, agreeing with the easygoing officer.

"How many men do you have with you over there?" the former tanker and enlisted man from the state of Washington wanted to know.

"Well, sir, I landed with twenty-two and so far I've had five killed and three wounded…one badly. I detailed one of my men to stay with that one on the beach…so that leaves me with fifteen effectives. Plus the three tankers I picked up along the way. Eighteen total."

"Oh yeah…the tanks. Did any of them make it in? I watched them come in on my left and for some reason they stopped out there in the cove. I saw at least four of them sink on their way towards the Bird's Beak," the lieutenant said, still wondering why the tanks had made that move to the right.

"Two of them made it through the seawall, sir, but that was the last I saw of them. You know the strange thing about that move is that I was wondering why they did that maneuver too. And yet… with all that's been happening…I forgot to ask the tank commander that's with us why they did it. Hell…if anybody knows…he should."

"Well, if ya ever do find out and we end up crossin' paths again… do me a favor and let me know…will ya," Fawcett requested.

"Aye aye, sir. How are you fixed for men?" the platoon sergeant asked.

"Pretty good I guess. I've got about thirty-five men with me… maybe more…but we don't have any heavy weapons. I've picked up a lot of stragglers along the way. I lost my platoon sergeant though…to a damn machine gun…and my right guide…to shell fire. They were damn good men," the lieutenant said. Then he lowered his head, picked up some sand in his hand, threw it down hard, and added, "I'm gonna miss 'em."

The platoon sergeant knew what Fawcett was going through… since his own platoon leader was missing…and could be dead too… but he didn't say anything…having learned long ago to swallow the sadness and emptiness that went with the death of a person you cherished.

With no further ado, Lieutenant Fawcett pulled an aerial photograph out of his pocket and laid it out flat on the ground.

"Where'd ya get that from, lieutenant? Our CO collected all the aerials up before we left our ship," Roy said, quite impressed that the second lieutenant had managed to lay his hands on such a valuable piece of intelligence.

"I swiped it from a platoon leader buddy of mine by accident. I was gonna give it back to him once this operation was over…but his amtrac got blown up by an anti-boat gun back on the beach. He never made it out…he was firing the fifty cal to cover his men when the shell hit. I'm sure he's glad we're puttin' it to good use."

Like before…the platoon sergeant remained silent.

"Let me show you what were up against over here," the lieutenant then said, pointing to Temakin Point on the southwestern corner of the island. "Directly in front of us…about one hundred and fifty yards away…are two Vickers eight-inch naval rifles. The Japs got 'em mounted in tandem, one above the other, and they're surrounded by a concrete casemate for protection."

Roy liked this platoon leader right away and he was impressed with the officer's thoroughness as he listened to him describe the strengths of the Jap position up ahead. *He's got a good head on his shoulders, definitely cares about his men, and has the fighting spirit that's essential for leading men in battle*, the platoon sergeant thought appreciatively.

Second Lieutenant Fawcett…like the NCO he was talking to… had decided early on that waiting along the seawall was a no-win situation…so instead of digging in…he led his small force forward. He and his men had advanced along a parallel path to the left of Roy's platoon and they had just skirted the western end of the large, rectangular-shaped area that started near the western end of the main airstrip and stretched for four hundred yards towards Green Beach. Months before, the Japanese engineers had cut down the co-conut trees in this section of the island for use in their various building projects on that side of the island and their work had left the land barren of everything but tree stumps. Their route then swung roughly southwest and they soon found themselves up against the same tank trap that Platoon Sergeant Roy's men were now occupying. But Fawcett had lost his two leading NCO's along the way and

now his blood was up…and since he and his men had been successful so far…he was not about to stop and hold any ground. In fact,
he was doing exactly what they had trained him to do back in New
Zealand…he was advancing.

Fawcett and Roy were too far away to tell if the two 8-inch cannons in the distance had been destroyed in the pre-invasion bombardment…but they probably were if the terrain up ahead was any
indication…since it looked like one big junkyard to the two men
who were exchanging the binoculars back and forth. The southwest corner of the island had been designed as a labyrinth of fire
and communications trenches, machine gun nests, pillboxes, and
sand-covered bunkers with one purpose in mind: to protect and
guard the two big 8-inch guns on Temakin Point…and the five
smaller anti-boat guns …probably 75mm types…that were around
it. Now it was a wasteland. Rubble of every sort lay about: shattered palm trees…burned and splintered planks of wood from small
buildings that had been blown apart…chunks of concrete…broken
gun carriages…empty oil and gasoline drums…bent and twisted
sections of corrugated iron roofing…blackened steel beams…and a
few dead bodies…were scattered across the broken ground…and it
resembled a moonscape more than anything else. But "thinking" the
guns might be destroyed as well wasn't good enough…so Fawcett
and Roy just assumed the two guns were still operational and they
decided to go after them right then and there.

With that in mind, the lieutenant said, "I'm gonna try to get as
far as that Y-shaped trench system with my men. It's just beyond
the next trench up ahead of us. Have your men provide cover fire
for us as we go. If I can get my people in the next trench, I'll wave
you up and we'll play it by ear from there. If that Y-trench is open…
we'll take it too. But I don't think the Japs are gonna just let us waltz
in there and take this ground without a fight." The lieutenant then
pointed to the object he was talking about on the photo; like he
said, it resembled the letter Y…or a T depending on how the map

was oriented...that was located just beyond the tank trap up ahead. Lieutenant Fawcett knew it wasn't going to be easy to take the two trenches since he had seen a large force of Japanese shifting around amid the ruins beyond the trenches...but he was determined to attack them anyway.

"That sounds good to me, sir. Give me three minutes and when you hear my men firing...you go." Roy then gave the binoculars over to Lieutenant Fawcett and said, "Here...you'll need these when you get up there."

The lieutenant took the binoculars and looped the leather strap of its carrying case over his head. "Thanks," he said, "I appreciate it. I'll let you have them back when you join us up ahead."

"Don't worry about it...they're all yours. Binoculars are officer material...no self-respecting sergeant should really have them," Roy replied...knowing the young officer would appreciate the gift. Fawcett then slapped Roy on the arm in thanks and darted back down the trench to quickly brief his own squad leaders while the platoon sergeant ran off in the opposite direction to do the same thing.

At exactly the three-minute mark, Platoon Sergeant Roy's men began firing to their front just like they had been ordered. In most cases, the men couldn't see the enemy they were shooting at, but they hoped their fire would keep their heads down all the same. To their left, twenty men rose up and charged across the open ground between the two tank traps. Fawcett had wisely kept the other fifteen of his platoon back with him so he could exploit a breakthrough if the first group made it as far as the second tank trap.

Their first attempt carried the twenty men about half way across the open ground and they took shelter in several shell craters that were right along their path. Japanese riflemen and machine gunners hiding in the debris ahead began to fire intermittently at them now... but their resistance was not as strong as the lieutenant had expected...so he decided to give it another go. As his marines surged ahead this second time though, the Jap defenders really poured it into them and the twenty marines hit the ground without making any headway. A third attempt was tried and this time three of Fawcett's men made it to the second tank trap...but no more. The rest of the men were forced to hold up due to the fire directed at them and they laid low while the three up ahead heaved hand grenades at the spots where they thought the Japs were holed up.

Platoon Sergeant Roy was watching the advance and when Fawcett's men reached the first trench, he shouted for his men to get ready to go...thinking the lieutenant would send them all forward in one fell swoop. But the lieutenant held his hand up instead...signaling them to stay where they were for the time being. Roy figured that the platoon leader was being both smart and cautious at the same time...and he was more than happy to comply with the order. And the sergeant was right...since the lieutenant was gauging the situation to see what they were up against before he risked committing any more men to the attack. If the situation turned really bad...and the Japs attacked them in force instead...then Fawcett would need Roy's men right where they were to cover their withdrawal.

Lieutenant Fawcett waited a few minutes...but no attack came... so he got ready to send seven more men from his reserve forward when he turned and saw a welcome sight. Coming down the trench in his direction was Captain Jim Crain...his very own company commander...who he hadn't seen since they all left their transport, the USS *Middleton*, earlier that morning.

CHAPTER 30

"Who's in charge here?"

"Who wants to know?" The platoon sergeant kept his eyes fixed on the trench ahead...despite the fact that the man speaking to him carried a certain air of authority in the tone of his voice.

"Major Ryan. Is that good enough for you?"

Roy swung his head around and, sure enough, the lean major was standing right there behind him with his hands planted firmly on his hips. Several other marines were serving as his armed escort and they were crouching beside him and Roy thought to himself, *oh great...he's gonna come down on me like a ton of bricks.*

Despite the risk, the platoon sergeant started to get to his feet so he could address the officer in an appropriate manner but the major stopped him by placing a hand on his shoulder. "My apologies, sir," Roy said, feeling quite embarrassed. "I thought you might've been a runner when you came up. You usually don't see too many majors this far forward," he added defensively. The sergeant cringed inwardly yet again, realizing he had just stuck his foot in his mouth for the second time in less than thirty seconds.

Roy saw Major Ryan's eyebrows arch up in response to the un-intended slight, but he took it in stride. "Don't worry about it... sergeant...ugh..." The major recognized the NCO from somewhere in his past but couldn't place his name.

"Roy...sir. Platoon Sergeant S.T.J. Roy...at your service."

"That's right...I remember now. I met you and your platoon leader during one of the training exercises back at New Zealand. You probably don't remember."

"No, sir...I do remember it." But he really didn't...so he didn't say anything further about the supposed meeting.

"But I don't remember you being part of the Third Battalion. Weren't you two in the Second with Lieutenant Colonel Amey?" the major asked.

"Still am, sir. Just had a little problem during the landing this morning...that's all. It'll work itself out alright in the end. Me and my men decided to stay around and lend your boys a hand. Hope you don't mind us comin' over?" Roy joked.

"We can use every marine we can get our hands on. Welcome to the Third...we'll try to make your stay with us an enjoyable one," the major replied easily.

Major Ryan then explained that he had taken over the battalion on Red 1 and that he was ordering everyone to fall back so they could better defend themselves against a Jap counterattack that was sure to come later that night. He wanted to establish a stable defensive line...if that was possible given the fluid conditions they were un-der...in case the Japs came at them with the standard banzai charge that they had used in the past. He...along with First Lieutenant Turner and Captain Crain...were pulling all the marines they could find back to a line that affectively cut the Bird's Beak off from the rest of the island. The major felt that they had killed most of the Japanese in the Beak and therefore they could defend it without having to worry about getting sniped and attacked from their rear. The overall position was shaped like a ragged triangle that ran two hundred and fifty yards from the tip of the Bird's Beak east down the beach of Red 1and then turned to the right and ran inland...ending at Green Beach...nearly three hundred yards away. At this point it turned right again and it continued along the western shore for three hundred yards back to the tip of the island. For firepower they had a few 60mm mortar sections...several .50 caliber machine guns that had been salvaged from the damaged amtracs on the beach...a couple .30 caliber light machine guns...and the two Sherman tanks that had made it in safely.

"That's all we got to defend an entire battalion front, sir?" Roy asked, sounding a bit skeptical of the plan.

"That's it," the major replied evenly. And to drill the point home, he added, "The Japs did a job on our Weapons Company and the Engineer platoon lost nearly every man they had out in the cove. We'll just have to make do with what we got...that's all."

Ryan then told him that he wanted the sergeant and his men to guard a section of Green Beach in case the Japanese tried to make a night landing along the Battalion's right flank. "It's far-fetched...I know...but just when you think you have the Japs figured out, they pull something crazy out of their hat. They might have some boats on the eastern end of the island that they can use to make a surprise landing like that...who knows. The odds are they won't do anything like that...but my job is to make sure we're ready in case they do. You'll have I Company on your left flank further down the beach so make your arrangements accordingly. First Lieutenant Sam Turner is the acting CO over there and he's a good man. Elements of L Company will be on your right. They're under Captain O'Brian now. I'm gonna station one of the Shermans over there as well to prevent the Japs from coming up through the woods that are behind Green Beach. Talk to Lieutenant Bale and let him know where you're at. You need anything from me?"

"No, sir, I don't. But if you don't mind me saying so, it sure sounds like a damn good plan," the veteran marine said, changing his tune.

"Thanks...thanks a lot, Sergeant Roy," Major Ryan responded and then he turned to go since there were more units to find and brief. Looking back over his shoulder, the major saw that the platoon sergeant was already gathering his squad leaders so he could brief them on the change in plans and he wondered if the platoon sergeant had any idea just how much that one little remark had really meant to him. *Probably not*, Major Ryan thought...but that didn't diminish the feeling of pride he felt swelling up inside of him...and now he felt confident that they could actually hold on through the long night ahead.

CHAPTER 31

"Where we goin' now, sarge? First we were headin' forward...now backwards. We just gonna give this ground back to the Japs? What's the reason for that boneheaded move?"

Platoon Sergeant Roy didn't have to guess who it was this time. The man had been talking incessantly since they woke up in the dark aboard the *Zeilin* that morning. Roy had ignored the man all day... but as they retreated back north...he was quickly losing his patience. The kid just kept jabbering away...and the platoon sergeant knew that he wouldn't stop unless he told him to shut up. And then the kid would just turn to some other unfortunate soul and drive that person crazy for a while until he eventually came back to the platoon sergeant again. The only reason Roy let him get away with it for so long was because...deep down...the kid from New York City was so damn funny.

"Hey, sarge...are we gettin' back on the ships?" the skinny kid asked. "That's the scuttlebutt I've been hearin'. The word is that the Navy made a mistake and brought us to the wrong island...and now we gotta go attack the right one. Da ya think that's possible...and if so...are they really gonna make us do it all over again? Are they just writing this off as a particularly realistic live-fire exercise?" Even though the kid kept talking, his head never stopped moving from side to side…like it was on a swivel while he looked for Jap snipers. "How would they account for the ammo and stuff we've lost if it's true? Wouldn't somebody in the Government wanna know about it…you know…for accounting purposes and such. Would there be a reward if someone were to say…let them know about it? How much money–"

The platoon sergeant had finally had all he could take and cut him off. "One more word, Reisman…just one…and I will make sure your body never leaves this place. Am I understood," Roy said slowly, emphasizing each word, totally exasperated.

"Oh…yeah…sure, sarge. No problem. This is the last place I would want to end up being buried on. My family has a beautiful, little cemetery plot already picked out in Westchester…that's just north of the Bronx and–"

A smooth, metallic sound cut the private off. Roy had opened one of his ammo pouches and withdrawn a 12-gauge brass cartridge shell and loaded it into his Winchester Model 1912 pump-action shotgun. Reisman recognized the distinctive noise the shell made as it was racked into the magazine and immediately shut up.

CHAPTER 32

C aptain Jim Crain flopped down next to his platoon leader, smiled broadly, and said, "Good to see you made it. You're the only other officer from the company that I've seen alive today."

"What about the XO…and Schulte and Becker?" Fawcett asked hesitantly.

The CO's face said it all as he told him that the executive officer…First Lieutenant Clint Dunahoe…and Second Lieutenant Tom Becker…one of the platoon commanders…were both dead. "They got it during the landings," Captain Crain said, answering the lieutenant's next question before he asked it. Then the captain asked him if he had seen where Second Lieutenant Ott Schulte or Second Lieutenant Mike Hofmann's amtracs had landed or if he had run across either of them afterwards. "Maybe they're alive too…just like you…and I haven't found them yet," the captain said hopefully.

"Mike's dead, sir. I saw him get hit myself. I haven't seen Ott at all. His amtrac was off to my left just before we hit the beach. He could've made it in I guess."

"Well, let's pray that he did. Maybe he'll show up later," the experienced officer and Guadalcanal veteran replied. Then he raised himself up on his elbows, saw several marine helmets popping up and down, and added, "How many men you got up there?"

"Three in that far tank trap...and seventeen holed up between us and them."

"You need to get them back. Major Ryan's running the show now and he wants a perimeter set up before dark and he's ordered us to cover the left flank. I want you to withdraw your men to that long fire trench about three hundred yards from here. I've got some men in there already so look for them. I want you to put your platoon in on their right. We'll be tied in with I Company on our right and I'm gonna leave that job up to you. Where's your platoon sergeant by the way?" The captain had looked around but he hadn't spotted him so he assumed he was up ahead. The sergeant had been his own platoon sergeant when he was a platoon commander on the *Canal* and the sergeant...more than anyone else...had taught him how to be a Marine officer.

Fawcett knew that the two men were very close so it troubled him deeply when he told him that he had been killed only two hours ago. "He was leadin' a bunch of boys across some open ground when a Jap machine gun caught them. You should have seen him, sir. He was walking back and forth...just like he always did...not carin' a lick that the damn Japs were shooting at him. He was yelling at the men to fire back when he got hit. Seein' him go down must have rallied the men cause they all got up and charged that nest and knocked it out right after that."

Captain Crain listened intently to the story and when Fawcett was finished he said, "What a Marine! It sure was an honor to have served with that man."

"It sure was, sir. I was damn lucky to have him...that's all I can say," the lieutenant responded in kind.

The captain then reached down and picked some sand up in his hand and looked at it for a second. He tossed it up and down several times before he threw it back down to the ground. Fawcett realized that Crain was wondering the same thing he was too...*was taking this place worth the loss of so many good men?*

Neither of them said anything for a few seconds. They didn't have to...since both knew the answer to the lingering question: that despite the fact that many more men from K Company...and the rest of the Second Regiment too...would be killed trying to take Betio Island...the cost in lives was worth it...and the two of them would do everything they could to see their mission through to the end.

• • •

The word that they were heading back got around quickly...and it was confirmed when Lieutenant Fawcett alerted the men in front that they were pulling out. He then sent a runner forward to the three men that were isolated in the tank trap. The boy made it all the way over and as the four sprinted back a Jap machine gun team opened up on them. One man was shot down in stride...and the brave messenger...a private first class...stopped to check on him. Seeing that the man was dead...the boy left him where he was...and he sprinted to the rear. He had almost made it back to the tank ditch when he was hit in the rear for his effort.

Captain Crain watched him limp in holding his buttock and heard him yell out, "Shot in the damn ass of all places! Can you believe that?"

And with the field apparently clear, the captain asked the lieutenant, "Is that it? Is everybody back now?"

Lieutenant Fawcett took a quick headcount and replied that all his men were accounted for...so they could start for the rear.

"Okay...let's go then," the captain ordered.

Before leaving, the lieutenant took one last look at the complex with his binoculars...and then at the prostrate body of the man who had just been killed. He didn't know the man...since he wasn't in his platoon...or his company for that matter. He had just latched on to the lieutenant's group when they stumbled upon him as they had advanced off the beachhead...just like several other men had done.

Not knowing him didn't make his loss any more palatable however-er...and the lieutenant sighed...since a marine was a marine...no matter what unit he belonged to.

Despite the man's loss, the lieutenant could take solace in the fact that he had accomplished quite a bit since landing in the morning. He had rallied the survivors of his platoon and they had advanced inland...despite the odds against them. And they had come very close to taking their D-Day objective...which very few units could claim on the first day of battle. Now they were going to turn right around and head back the way they had come. Surrendering this ground back to the enemy would be hard to do...since his men had bled for it...but he was an officer who knew how to follow orders... so that's what he would do. But he wanted to remember this scene just the same...since he didn't know if he'd ever to see it again.

As he turned to go, Captain Crain asked him how he had managed to obtain the pair of binoculars he was using. The question jogged the lieutenant's memory and when he looked down the ditch to his right, he saw that Roy and his men had already left. "A platoon sergeant from the Second lent them to me. He's got half a platoon with him...all his boys...which is rare around here. They ended up on the wrong beach so they're fighting with us. I guess they pulled back already...since they were over on our right a little while ago. They covered us as we moved up," the lieutenant answered in a low, exhausted voice.

"Can I see them for a second?" the captain responded. The lieutenant handed the binos over to the captain and he placed them in his lap. He then rubbed his eyes to smear the dust away...and the lieutenant could see that he looked as physically and mentally drained as the lieutenant was feeling himself.

His eyes clear, Captain Crain picked up the binoculars and looked through them. He made a slight adjustment by turning the knob between the two lenses and the ground ahead suddenly came into distinct focus. "Ahhh...that's better," he said pleasantly and he scanned the southern shore out front. He then swung around and checked the open expanse to the east...and past that...the western end of the main runway to see if he could detect any friendly forces in the area. He saw hundreds of tree stumps, some coconut-log re-vetments, and a few aircraft that were littering the side of the large runway...but nothing else. *The Second Battalion couldn't have had any more success than we did*, he thought, *otherwise I would've seen somebody out there. They must be held up on Red 2 just like we are over here.*

When the captain tried to give the binoculars back, Lieutenant Fawcett pushed them away and he told the company commander that he could keep them if he wanted them.

"Damn straight I'll take 'em," Captain Crain said happily, thrilled with the generous offer, and he dropped the field glasses back into their brown carrying case. He then opened the buckle on the strap and lengthened it so the case would hang comfortably beside the .45 caliber pistol that was holstered on his hip. With that done, he put his arm through the loop, slung it over his neck, and said, "All set?"

"Ready when you are, sir," the lieutenant replied and the two officers led Fawcett's men back north towards their new position.

CHAPTER 33

Except for Private First Class Reisman's chattering, the men of the 1ˢᵗ Platoon were fairly reserved as they moved back over the same ground they had just taken. Platoon Sergeant Roy thought there might be a little bit more griping about the withdrawal, but he knew the men were too exhausted to bitch and moan about it. It was easy to see by just looking at them. The energized, fit marines that he had led down the cargo nets on the *Zeilin* were now physical wrecks: their heads hung down and their shoulders were sagging while their eyes already had that one-thousand-yard stare that guys get while enduring sustained combat for a substantial amount of time. As if that weren't enough evidence, their green, herringbone-twill uniforms were torn, soaked with sweat, and coated with a fine, white dust that seemed to blanket everything on the island. Roy also noticed that they were not moving with the same snap they had shown earlier. The heat and lack of water were finally taking their toll… and some of them…the ones that were dog-tired…were beginning to drag listlessly behind the rest. This made them vulnerable to Jap snipers so Roy called Sergeant Flockerzi over and pointed out their condition. "Tell Oliver and Varner to stay on top of their men,

Flock. Some of them look like they've really had it. The sooner we get to where we're going, the sooner they can rest. I don't wanna lose someone cause they can't keep up with the rest of us," the platoon sergeant advised.

"Aye aye," Flockerzi snapped and he dashed over to the two squad leaders to tell them to keep a sharp eye out for stragglers since they were going to pick up the pace.

The men had gone back another two hundred yards or so when Sergeant Roy and Sergeant Flockerzi saw the perfect spot to set up the platoon command post. They stopped beside an elevated observation post that stood on the beach not far from the stand of trees that they were creeping through. Roy figured that the height of the structure would make it easy to see…and locate…once nightfall hit. The structure was made of coconut logs and it had a square deck made out of wood planks that sat about fifteen feet above the ground. The Japanese had also constructed a bunker below it that was ringed by sandbags to protect the six *rikusentai* who were assigned to man it through the day and during the night. Around the tower was another semi-circular ring of sandbagged-reinforced foxholes and coconut-log-reinforced pillboxes that were connected to one another by a narrow trench. Roy jumped into the foxhole that was underneath the tower and saw that it afforded an excellent view of Green Beach. He turned to Flockerzi and stated, "We'll make this one our CP," and then added, "We'll keep the three tankers here with us. Have Corporal Oliver center his men on that pillbox to the left and have Sergeant Varner put his men in by that bunker on the right. Tell 'em to check those positions out carefully before they occupy them. There could be some Japs still hiding in them…or they could be booby-trapped."

The warning made the Guide Sergeant look up and he was able to see the outlines of two dead Japs lying on the floor of the OP. Without hesitation, Flockerzi fired two rounds into each of the bodies through the gaps in the wood flooring just to make sure.

"What the hell did y'all do that for?" PFC Palmer yelled out. His voice came from one of the foxholes that surrounded the tower and he was obviously annoyed at Flockerzi. He and the other two tankers had been sitting with their backs to the sergeant so they weren't prepared when he fired his M-1 Garand so suddenly. Naturally, they had all flinched at the sound of the Flockerzi's rifle going off and Palmer had actually dived to the ground... thinking they were under fire. Now that the firing had stopped, the tank driver stood up with a sheepish look on his face and dusted himself off. Sergeant LaPorte cracked up at the sight and Private Cobb...in a fit of laughter...managed to say, "You'd make a damn fine infantryman, Palmer!"

Flockerzi, pointing up at the OP, said simply, "Yeah...well out here I'd rather be safe than sorry."

• • •

Platoon Sergeant Roy gave the squads an hour to set up and then he went out to inspect their positions. Both squad leaders were veterans...trustworthy and good at their jobs...so Roy wasn't too worried about what he'd find. He headed to the left and found Varner's six men dug in around a pillbox that had housed a 13mm heavy machine gun. In a macabre scene, four Japs...the crew for the gun... were lying dead in the entranceway in the rear...almost blocking it. They were stacked on top of each other...like cordwood by a fire...but they didn't have a mark on them. With all the shell craters around, Varner guessed that they must've panicked during the naval bombardment and decided to abandon their post. A shell had probably hit nearby as they were trying to leave and it had killed them by its concussive effect rather than by shrapnel since they were protected from that by the solid walls of the pillbox. Varner told Sergeant Roy that he was going to keep one man with him and that they intended to stay in the exit trench during the night. The sergeant added that he had placed three men over on the left in a crater behind the seawall. "I know they have a lot of area to cover...but they're veterans...and I'll be able to see them from where

I'm at. They're also tied in with the men from I Company who are a little further down the seawall. The sergeant turned to the right and pointed to two men in another shell crater. "I put Reisman over there with one of the privates. He's got the only automatic weapon we got, but I didn't want to leave him with two rookies...so I took one and gave the other one to him. Any other time he could manage the two youngsters...but not tonight," he said, hoping the platoon sergeant would agree with his decision.

"What happened to Rampley's BAR?" Roy asked instead.

"Oh...he got real lucky. As he went over the seawall a Jap round hit it dead center and destroyed it. If it hadn't hit his BAR, we'd have one less man with us. Amazing luck, I guess."

"Yeah," Roy answered, "some guys have it and some don't. After all these years in the Marines, I still haven't quite figured out why some guys have it while others don't."

"So you're okay with my setup then?" the squad leader asked again.

"I don't see any flaws in it...good job," Roy said, shaking his head affirmatively, and then added, "but do me a favor. Send Reisman and one of those privates over to my CP in about twenty minutes. I should be done with Oliver by then. I'm gonna send him back to see if he can round us up any machine guns from the amtracs that are shot up on the beach. Reisman's always been good at scrounging things so maybe he can find us something useful to use besides these Garands."

"Will do, sarge," Sergeant Varner responded and headed off in a crouch towards Reisman's position.

Roy then made his way over to the right...where Corporal Oliver was set up. Like Varner, the lanky squad leader had chosen a bunker as the center of his position. This one was slightly bigger than the other positions around it...and it offered an expansive view of Green Beach from one end to the other. There were dead Japanese in this bunker too...like the one in Varner's sector...and they must have been killed by the shock wave of shell that had hit nearby as well... since they didn't have a mark on them either. With only four men to work with, Corporal Oliver put two men on the left and two on the right...the standard configuration. "I'll decide where I'm gonna spend the night once I get these guys settled in," Oliver said, hoping Sergeant Roy would agree with his decision. Roy looked them over and nodded his approval...and as he was about to leave, the corporal spoke up again. "Any chance we can get some more grenades, Sergeant Roy? My men are all out. And Lewis said he's running low on BAR ammo. Can Sergeant Varner spare any?"

"Sergeant Flockerzi will be making the rounds to inventory what we got. He'll be redistributing the ammo so let him know how you stand and what you need. I'm gonna head up to Battalion to see what I can squeeze out of them. We're short everything...I know it. Do the best with what you got until I get back...in the glorious Marine Corps tradition."

"Amen to that," Oliver answered, and then asked, "Any word on how Grasso is doin'?" The corporal was referring to the private in Sergeant Varner's squad...Private Vincent Grasso...who was his friend...and who had been wounded at the seawall earlier.

"I'll check in on him and let you know when I get back," the platoon sergeant responded with a smile...glad to see that Oliver was concerned about the welfare of the men in the platoon... a basic and necessary trait common to all good leaders...no matter what level of command they had.

The inspection finished, the Sergeant Roy walked back to the observation tower and told Flockerzi and Sergeant LaPorte that he was leaving for the Battalion CP. While he was gone, Flockerzi would be in charge...and he briefed Flockerzi on what he wanted done in the interim while he was away. "Get a status on the ammo and water situation and divvy it up evenly among the men. I'm gonna find out if Major Ryan can spare anything and see what they've got cooked up for tonight and tomorrow."

Just then Private First Class Reisman and the private from Varner's squad showed up and Roy motioned for them to follow him. "What'd you do with your BAR?" the platoon sergeant asked when he noticed that Reisman was carrying an M-1 instead of his normal weapon.

"Oh...Sergeant Varner told me to leave it with him. He gave me his rifle instead. Where we headed now?" Reisman, forever inquisitive, asked offhandedly.

The sergeant stopped immediately in his tracks, swung around, and glared at the private first class with cold, black eyes. Reisman held up...but the private did not; tired and looking down, the boy had just kept walking and accidentally bumped into Reisman who was in front of him. Reisman was pushed forward and he collided with the platoon sergeant in turn. This made Roy even angrier and the mortified private quickly backed up. Reisman thought the platoon sergeant was mad about being run into so he admonished the private behind him. "Watch what you're doing," he said caustically... and then he faced back around to accept his punishment.

Roy's stare indicated that he wasn't joking this time. "What did you just say to me?" the sergeant growled while staring at Reisman. The private first class was confused for a second, but then it dawned on him. By then the sergeant had moved his face much closer to Reisman's...so close that the tall NCO's nose was almost touching the end of the private's nose as he glowered down at him.

"Platoon Sergeant Roy...what I meant to say is, 'Where are we going...if you don't mind me asking?'" the frightened marine responded...hoping that the serious tone he was using would do the trick and get him off the hook. And it seemed to work.

"Now that's more like it," Roy said, satisfied.

The lesson in propriety over, Roy explained that he wanted the two men to check out the damaged LVT's on the beach. "Bring back whatever you can find...machine guns...grenades...water...anything you think we can use to hold off the Jap counterattack that's coming tonight. And don't forget ammo...we need that too. And one last thing...see if you can find Grasso and Hennessey. Grasso got hit earlier and we left him by the seawall near one of the amtracs with Hennessey to look after him. He's Corporal Oliver's buddy...and he wants to know how he's doing. Make as many trips as you need but keep Sergeant Flockerzi informed of your whereabouts. That way if you get into any trouble, we can send someone for you." Before they separated, Roy asked, "Do you have any questions?"

The two men shook their heads no and Roy said, "Okay then. Remember to be careful. Don't do anything stupid. And be back before dark!"

CHAPTER 34

Reisman and the private gave their platoon sergeant a final wave before he disappeared from sight in the wood line behind the beach. They continued north, staying close to the seawall, and passed other small groups of marines who were preparing positions for the night. They were digging in among the ruined pillboxes and bunkers that overlooked Green Beach...just like their platoon buddies were doing one hundred yards away. When they reached the Bird's Beak, they could see at least six amtracs that had been abandoned on the beach in front of the seawall along Red Beach 1and off to their left...one hundred yards offshore...the sandbar that sat off the northern tip of the island. Several marines had made the mistake of stopping there on the way in...and it had cost them dearly. Some had probably stopped to catch their breath...before going on...while others might have thought they could take cover behind the spit before making the final trek to the main island. Unfortunately, the Jap machine gunners had the spot registered perfectly and the men had been gunned down before they could take another step. Their dead bodies were now lying on the spit as a silent warning to anyone else who might think about doing the same thing.

As the two men approached the first LVT-1, Reisman and the private could see that the front of the vehicle had been chewed up by machine gun fire and the bodies of the driver and the assistant driver were still slumped over the controls inside the blood-splattered cab. The two men had obviously done their very best to get the amtrac in as far as they could and they had paid for the effort with their lives. Looking over the edge of the gunwale, Reisman could see that the crew compartment was empty and he noticed that the bottom was slick with blood so he didn't bother climbing into the vehicle. More importantly, the two bow-mounted .50 cals and the .30 caliber machine gun in the stern were missing...scavengers having already removed them...so the two men moved down the seawall to the next amtrac in line. This one had tried to get over the seawall and gotten stuck midway so its bow was sticking up high in the air...completely exposed. Reisman jumped down to the beach and stretched his body so he could see over the gunwale by the left rear of the tractor. This time he saw the bodies of seven marines piled in a heap in the back of the troop compartment. It looked like a mortar round had exploded in their midst and they had tumbled over when the amtrac had begun to climb over the log barricade. Like the first vehicle, the machine guns had been taken away by someone else but Reisman did see some hand grenades still attached to the web belts of the men who had been killed inside. Following Platoon Sergeant Roy's instructions, he climbed in and retrieved as many as he could find. He hooked some of them on his own web belt and passed the extras over the side to the private who did the same thing. None of the men had their canteens on them though...so someone must have taken them off the men before he got there. Reisman then vaulted over the left gunwale but he fell awkwardly when he landed in the sand below. His left foot had landed on a piece of coconut log that had been blown out of the seawall and it had rolled under his weight, twisting his ankle badly. Reisman hopped over to the log wall, sat down, and removed his boot to see how bad the swelling was. It didn't look as bad as it felt so he put his boot back on and stood up gingerly to see if he could still walk on it. He could...but it definitely hurt...so he said, "Let's hold up here for a second...I wanna see if this ankle is gonna keep giving me problems. I'm having a little trouble walking on it right now."

The private complied immediately...happy to take a break. He slid over next to Reisman and watched as he took his boot off again to inspect it one more time. The private looked at the ankle, grimaced, and said, "Sure looks like it should hurt. Want me to wrap it?"

"No...it's okay...but thanks," Reisman replied, appreciating the offer. Then he added, "If it doesn't get any better, we'll have to cut our mission short and head back to the CP with what we got."

"Whatever you say goes," the young private answered...deferring to the senior marine's authority despite his injury. Then he added, "While you're resting up, I'll go inspect that other amtrac to see if I can find anything useful."

"Go ahead...but be careful," Reisman advised, "there could be Japs anywhere around here."

The private looked around, saw nothing sinister, and headed over to the next amtrac...which was only twenty yards away. This one was sitting out in the open on the beach...just like the first tractor they had encountered. Reisman heard the private rummaging around inside the tractor and then he saw him peering over the gunwale. "There's nothin' in this one either," the private said dejectedly before climbing out and heading back to where Reisman was sitting. A large explosion inland caught his attention and the private ran up to the seawall and glanced over it...but he couldn't see anything so he plopped down next to the private first class. Both of them sat silently for several minutes with nothing more than the sound of the battle echoing in the distance. The young private finally broke the spell by pointing to the nickname that was painted in white lettering on the side of the third tractor and in an innocent voice asked, "Where's *Voyage* located?...I mean what state is it in? I figure the company workers that made these tractors must have been real proud-like of the town where their factory is...so they named a darn amtrac after it."

Reisman looked confused by the question and said, "What are you talking about?"

"There," the private said, jabbing his finger in the direction of the amtrac's moniker.

Reisman spotted it... *Maiden Voyage*...and said it phonetically... exactly the way the private was reading it. "Made...in...Voyage," he said slowly. Suddenly Reisman understood what the private meant and he asked him where he was raised.

At first the private looked quizzically at Reisman since he hadn't gotten an answer to his question. He thought that was somewhat strange since he had heard that the private first class was from New York City and the other men in the platoon had often said that he had real good "street smarts". The private just figured that a city-slicker like Reisman would know everything there was to know about everything. He certainly sounded like he came from that part of the country since he had the same sort of accent that the rest of the men in the platoon who had grown up in the Northeast had... in fact, his accent was worse than everyone else's. But the private suspected that maybe he had just been born there and then moved and lived somewhere else as a kid. That could've happened too and that would explain why Reisman didn't know what state that factory was in either. But the only way to find out for sure was to just ask... so he did.

"I'm from the Bronx..." Reisman answered, and then followed with, "why do ya wanna know?"

"Is that like bein' from New York City too?" the private pressed.

"Of course it is...you country hick. Haven't you ever heard of the New York Yankees?"

"Yeah, I heard of 'em. Who hasn't," the private shot back defensively.

"Well, where do you think they play all their games?"

"In Yankee Stadium!" the private said excitedly. "I know that cause Sam the barber listens to the ball games on his radio while he's cuttin' hair. He's roots for the Cardinals and the Chicago White Sox. He hates the Yankees...and the New York Giants too!"

"Yeah, I'm sure he does. And so ya know for further reference," Reisman said, sounding very intelligent, "Yankee Stadium...the home of the New York Yankees...is in the Bronx. I grew up three blocks from the place so I oughta know. And in answer to your question...you're definitely from New York City if you grow up there." Then he asked the private the same question he had asked him.

"I'm from Arkansas," the private said proudly.

Reisman just stared at the private and said, "Arkansas, huh?"

"Yup...Arkansas," the private repeated with a big grin.

"That figures...that figures," Reisman said dryly, shaking his head...and the conversation ended with the whereabouts of *Voyage* still a mystery.

• • •

With the sun setting quickly in the west, Reisman knew that their scavenging time was running out and they'd have to start back for the CP fairly soon. With only a few grenades to show for their efforts, he figured they could check out at least two more amtracs since they weren't too far away...only forty yards or so down the beach. Plus, the fire inland had seemed to be tapering off somewhat, so he thought it was worth a try. But the sixth amtrac was almost near the center of the cove...a long way from where they were...so he scratched that one off the scavenger list.

Reisman told the private what he had decided to do and then he stood up and put pressure on the bad foot. At first the ankle seemed to be okay...so he started to walk on it to give it a test. But as he hobbled towards the fourth LVT-1, Reisman quickly pulled up lame.

Even though he had given it a good rest, his ankle was still tender...
and it bothered him more than he thought it would. He began limping to take his weight off it, but with each step waves of pain shot up
his leg. When the private saw Reisman grimacing and falling back,
he put his arm up to stop the private first class from going further.
"Just stay there," the eager private pleaded, and running down the
beach, added, "I can do it...don't worry!"

"Get back here. They're too far away to go it alone," Reisman
yelled, but the private never heard him...or he acted like he didn't.
From experience, Reisman knew that you did nothing alone in
combat...that you always tried to have someone covering you...and
so he kept going...but at a much slower pace. He was somewhat
relieved when he saw the private reach the first amtrac safely but
then he got concerned again when he saw him disappear behind
the far side of the vehicle. This amtrac was stuck on the seawall like
the second one they had found, but it had hit the seawall at an odd
angle so that only one of its tracks was resting on the top of the
barricade. Instead of lying evenly, this one was canted over so the
right side was much higher up in the air than its left side was and
the private had run around to the lower side so he could climb in
easier. As the private boosted himself up on the gunwale, Reisman
knew that his silhouette would be outlined perfectly along the horizon behind them.

A Japanese sharpshooter in a bunker on the eastern side of the
cove happened to look up at the same time and saw a perfect opportunity: a lone figure climbing into one of the abandoned landing
vehicles across the way. He made sure his sniper rifle was loaded
and then he looked through the telescopic sight and centered it in
on the amtrac. The man who was now his target had already jumped
into back of the vehicle so he just waited patiently for him to climb
back out. It didn't take long before the man reappeared and he confirmed that he was a marine and not some friendly *rikusentai* out on
a hunting mission...like he was. With practiced precision he began

calculating the metrics of his shot. Since the marine was close to four hundred and fifty yards away and he was looking into the setting sun, it wouldn't be the easiest of shots to make, but he had hit static targets at greater distances than that so it was definitely worth a try. And since he was so far away...the target...or anyone else who might be hiding nearby...would never see or hear where the shot came from until it was too late so his position wouldn't be compromised either. With those factors in his favor, he figured the shot was worth the risk. Next he considered the wind effects, but since there was hardly any breeze blowing to shift the bullet left or right, he didn't have to make any adjustments and he aimed center mass. Last of all, to account for the slight drop the bullet would experience over this distance, he placed the crosshairs slightly above the marine's head. Next he took a deep breath...let some air out slowly...and then squeezed the trigger. He reloaded as quickly as he could...reacquired the target...aimed slightly lower...and fired a second time...and then a third time for good measure. The rifle bucked smoothly against his shoulder each time and that alone told him that he had gotten off three clean shots.

• • •

Private First Class Reisman had almost reached the amtrac when he saw the private coming back out of the troop compartment. He was exiting the vehicle the same way he had gone in...another mistake...and Reisman heard the private yell out that the amtrac was empty too...just like the other one had been. That was when his ears picked up the report of a bullet whizzing by him. He crouched down and looked around for the source of the shot but there was no smoke signature since the Jap sniper was using smokeless ammunition. And he didn't see any dust fly up either...since the amtrac was blocking his view across the cove...so there was nothing to indicate where the shot had come from. Then he heard three quick *cracks* in the distance and he knew they were under fire. Reisman quickly shifted his gaze to the private and he saw him clutching at his neck.

The private tried to say something...but all that came out of his mouth was a gurgled cry and then blood spilled down his shirt. He shouted instinctively to warn the private to get down but he knew it was too late...and the boy fell limply backwards into the well of the tractor.

The talented sniper watched the marine fall and he allowed a slight smile to crease his hardened face. He had killed many marines already...but this was his best...and most challenging...kill so far. His first shot had gone high...like he thought it might...since his rifle sometimes shot a little high. Knowing the vagaries of his rifle... like any good sniper would...he had adjusted perfectly...and his next two shots hit home. The second bullet he fired hit the private right in the neck...and while it alone had probably caused enough internal damage to kill the private...the next one really did the boy in. This bullet hit one of the ammo pouches on the private's web belt and the rounds inside began exploding one after another in a deadly chain reaction.

As Reisman hobbled up, he could hear the private moaning piti- fully as the number of detonations from inside the vehicle trickled off. The sound had reminded him of a bunch of fire crackers and cherry bombs going off in the street on the Fourth of July in the Bronx. The New Yorker knelt beside the alligator and waited several minutes before summoning the courage to check on the private's condition. With an active and skilled sniper still out there some- where, Reisman had to be careful about exposing himself lest he get shot too. But he also had a responsibility to determine if the private was still alive before he could head back. A quick peak over the gun- wale confirmed what he thought he'd find...but hoped he wouldn't have to see. Lying on his back, the young, eighteen-year-old marine was clearly dead. His eyes and mouth were wide open and his utili- ties had been shredded along his waistline...exposing his blackened and bloody torso...while grayish-colored smoke wafted up from his smoldering uniform. Reisman slumped back down on the sand and cursed out loud over the loss of his young companion. He also realized that save for a freak accident...his twisted ankle...it could easily have been him lying in that amtrac instead of the eager, inquisitive kid from Arkansas who died never knowing what state the city of *Voyage* was in.

CHAPTER 35

Sergeant Roy found the Battalion CP without much trouble. The major had set his command post up in an abandoned pillbox near the northern end of Green Beach and when Roy jumped down to take a seat, he caught sight of a tan colored uniform near the bunker's entrance. "Don't worry about him...he's as dead as he's ever going to get," Major Ryan said flatly when he saw the platoon sergeant nervously fingering the trigger on his shotgun. "I checked him myself," the major added emphatically, but the sergeant got up and looked him over...just to make sure. He had seen the Japs do some pretty strange things on the *Canal* in an effort to be overlooked and bypassed...and many a dead Jap - some men had even smeared blood all over themselves to make it look like they had been shot and killed - had miraculously gotten up and fired into the backs of the marines who had bypassed the corpse without a worry. As a result, Roy always made sure that a dead Jap was, in fact, dead. In this case, Roy saw that the enemy rifleman was lying in a large pool of stagnant, dark blood but his body didn't seem to have any wounds on it. The sergeant kicked the man's jaw and when his head rolled to the side, he saw that the entire back half of his head was missing.

JAMES F. DWYER

"If he's fakin' it, he's doing a damn fine job," Major Ryan said laughing.

"Sorry about that, sir," Roy apologized, "it's just that—"

"Don't worry about it," the major said, cutting the sergeant off. Although he hadn't seen it personally, he had heard about the Japs playing tricks like that too so he understood why the platoon sergeant was concerned.

Roy sat down and realized that he was the only non-commissioned officer at the meeting. The major introduced him to the other six officers in rank order and the platoon sergeant shook hands with each man in turn. The first one was Captain Jim Crain from K Company and Roy told him that he had recently met one of his platoon leaders… First Lieutenant Fawcett…up forward. The second officer was Captain Robert O'Brian…the L Company XO…or executive officer…and he had taken over the company when Major Ryan assumed command of the Third Battalion. Next was First Lieutenant Sam Turner…the I Company XO…who was now serving as the CO of I Company since Captain Tatom…the original commanding officer…had been killed during the landings. Roy mentioned that his platoon would be covering I Company's right flank and Turner added that the platoon leader on that side had already reported that they had tied in with Roy's platoon. Turner thanked Roy for getting set up so quickly and then he asked him to thank the squad leader who had affected the smooth coordination with his men on that flank as well.

The fourth and fifth officers were two lieutenants from units that didn't even belong to the Third Battalion. The first of the two orphaned officers was a platoon commander from G Company in Sergeant Roy's own 2nd Battalion. The next one was a fiery, red-headed first lieutenant named Kevin Kelly. He had limped up to the meeting since he was carrying mortar fragments in his left leg… the same leg that sustained a bad knee injury while he was playing in a college football game back in 1939. The lanky Irishman…he had the lean build of a marathon distance runner since his football

370

days were long over…was the executive officer of B Company in Major Wood Kyle's 1ˢᵗ Battalion, 2ⁿᵈ Regiment. He had started out as a platoon leader in the company and served admirably during the fighting for Tanambogo Island and later on at Guadalcanal as well. He had been promoted to first lieutenant on the *Island of Death* for his coolness under fire and given the XO's job as a reward for his performance. During this time, Kelly also acquired a reputation for being an officer who enforced Marine regulations to the letter of the law…without exception…and he was a severe disciplinarian when someone broke the rules. Even the slightest infractions met with heavy-handed discipline and he was so strict that the enlisted ranks had christened him with the unaffectionate nickname, "Old Iron Pants". In New Zealand, the XO had spent hours poring over the Marine Corps Field Manual and he even rewrote and improved parts of the Company's SOP - the standard operating procedures or guidelines which delineated the actions everyone was required to take in a myriad of situations and circumstances listed therein - on his free time. During the training day and on field exercises, he had pushed himself and his men tirelessly…so much so that they felt they could do their jobs and assignments in their sleep. *And that's just the way I want it,* he told himself, *because if the Japs fought hard on the Canal… wait until the men see what the Japs have got prepared for us the next time we meet them*…a prediction that would have made any fortune teller proud. But even Kelly had been humbled when he realized now that no amount of training could have prepared them adequately enough for the horrors of Betio. This was something totally different…and nothing in any damned SOP or manual…no matter how well-crafted or conceived…could have helped them survive what they faced out in the lagoon.

• • •

First Lieutenant Kelly had ridden up to the reef in a Higgins boat that was carrying half of the company's Headquarters Platoon. By then he had surmised that the naval bombardment had not been as effective as they first thought and they had a real fight on their hands. Like everyone else, he saw numerous amtracs burning on both the Red 2 and Red 1 beachheads and marines piling up along the seawall. Worse yet, he had witnessed several groups of men being shot down as they waded in from the tractors that had been hit out in the cove to his right. Off to his left, Captain Maxie Williams, his commanding officer, was already transferring the marines in his landing craft over to an amtrac for a shuttle run to the smoke-filled beach. Then, out of nowhere, water spouts began erupting around the captain's Higgins boat as the Japanese gunners found the range and artillery shells and mortar rounds began raining down on the reef. Kelly was fascinated by the drama playing itself out in front of him and wondered who would win: the Jap anti-boat gunners who were trying to sink the landing craft bunching up on the reef or the marines who were hurriedly completing their cross decking operations so their amtracs could get underway and out of the impact zone. The noise grew in intensity the closer they got to the reef and he was surprised to find that he wasn't afraid at all...but maybe some of the younger boys were. "It looks like it's gonna be a hot one boys!" he announced in a loud, firm voice and the men looked at him eagerly...desperate for reassurance. "But don't worry, men," he went on, bucking them up, "we've trained our butts off over the last few months and nothing is gonna stop B Company from accomplishing its mission...nothing!"

"Hold on tight," a voice suddenly yelled as the landing craft picked up speed and then plowed into the reef. The coxswain had revved the engine and sped up in a vain attempt to skim over the coral barrier but his assistant had seen that they weren't going to make it over and had screamed a warning to the men up front. Too late to brace themselves, Kelly and the rest of the men flew forward and then tumbled backwards as the Higgins boat slammed into the reef and ground to a halt.

"Are you nuts," the lieutenant said, struggling back to his feet. "Why would you do that?" he added angrily.

The coxswain got up from behind the metal shield protecting the wheel house and lifted his hands up in the air as if to say, *sorry sir, I thought I could make it over and get you men in safely.* Seeing this, Kelly understood that the man was doing his best so he let the matter drop and he turned his attention back to the beach…where the real problems were.

It wasn't long before a few empty LVT-1's rushed up to the reef and Lieutenant Kelly waved one over. The driver saw the lieutenant signaling him and immediately brought his battle-scared tractor up alongside the Higgins boat. He throttled the engine back to an idle and told the men to get in and stay down. "There's a ton of fire comin' from the beach and we don't want anybody losin' their heads on the way in…so stay down!" he warned as the men slid over the gunwale and jumped into the troop compartment. The first men in were stunned to see a series of jagged holes that ran along the sides of the vehicle and a mixture of blood and seawater was sloshing back and forth along the deck. As more men boarded, comments like, *sweet Jesus, I ain't standin' over there* and *oh great, we picked the one with a big bullseye on it,* were muttered by the veterans.

As soon as it was loaded, the crew chief waved good-bye to the coxswain of the Higgins boat and told him to let someone else know that they'd be back in a few minutes to pick up another load. Hearing this, one of Kelly's sergeants yelled out, "Hey, at least we got ourselves a ballsy sonofabitch at the helm!" The coxswain gave a thumbs-up sign in return and the driver of the alligator pulled away from the Higgins boat and circled back towards the reef. This time the men were prepared as the amtrac approached it and no one fell as the tractor clawed its way over the rocky obstacle and splashed into the water on the other side. As the LVT-1 began churning towards the shoreline, four other amtracs crawled over in unison and joined up behind Kelly's amtrac to form a little convoy. Without missing a beat, the crew chief of Kelly's amtrac, a thirty-year-old corporal and former train conductor from the mid-west, turned around and said in a jovial voice, "All tickets please...all tickets please...next stop Red Beach Two.....next stop Red Beach Two...my crew and I would like to thank you for riding with us today and have a pleasant day."

A Japanese gunner on Red 2 had a different destination in mind for the crowded amtrac and the other ones that were strung out behind it. As the amtracs approached, he drew a bead on the leading landing craft and opened fire. In seconds bullets were pinging off the armor plating on the front of Kelly's vehicle and along the left side as well. Several other guns on Red 2 began concentrating their fire on the group of amtracs and sensing the danger, the corporal started coaxing the driver to go to the right...to evade the fire coming at them from the beach directly ahead. It wasn't long before this slight course change brought Kelly's amtrac and the obedient ducklings behind it into the yawning mouth of the cove. Geysers of water began erupting around the small flotilla of landing craft, and the corporal, impatient now, yelled over the din of the battle at his bug-eyed driver. "Hurry up," he screamed, "they've got us bracketed...head for the tip," and just then the last amtrac in line was lifted out of the water in a violent explosion and split in two. The marines aboard were thrown up and out of the amtrac...some tumbling as high as fifteen feet in the air before falling back into the lagoon.

It took another ninety seconds - it felt like a whole lifetime to the men who were forced to endure it - to make the hellacious trip across the cove to the right side of Red 1. Miraculously, the four remaining amtracs reached the tip of the Bird's Beak and pulled up to the seawall unscathed...a gratifying accomplishment for all concerned. But as Kelly and the rest of the men scrambled out, a mortar explosion hit close by and the lieutenant felt a painful sting on his left side from his ankle to the knee. A quick inspection of the leg revealed that his pants and leggings were torn in several spots and there was some minor bleeding...but nothing too serious so he ignored it and set about organizing the men who had landed with him on Red 1. By noon, he had rounded up nearly one hundred of his compatriots from the

1st Battalion, 2nd Marines and he led them…stiffening leg and all… over the seawall and into the desperate battle for the Bird's Beak.

• • •

The last man that Sergeant Roy met at the officers meeting was First Lieutenant Ed Bale. He was a Texan and just twenty-three years old…but his serious demeanor made him look older. He was the commanding officer of the two medium tanks that had made it ashore earlier in the morning. The tanker studied the platoon sergeant very closely since he had a knack for identifying a good marine when he saw one and he was impressed with the sergeant immediately. *I won't have worry about this one*, he thought confidently and extended his hand to the tall sergeant.

Roy knew what the officer was doing and it didn't bother him at all. He had the ability to appraise someone very quickly too…a skill a leader on the battlefield had to learn and master very quickly if he planned on staying alive for any length of time. And Roy liked what he saw in Lieutenant Bale as well. The platoon sergeant sensed… correctly…that the tank officer was a fighter just by the way he carried himself…and he accepted the friendly gesture warmly. "I've got three of your tank buddies with me now," Roy said, pointing back to the beach.

"Three?" Lieutenant Bale answered right away.

"Yes, sir. Three of them. Their tank got stuck and two of the crew got killed. One was hit exiting the tank…and the other bought it trying to reach the seawall. The other three made it in safely and are attached to my platoon for the time being. They're back at my CP."

"You don't happen to remember the tank commander's name by any chance do you?" Bale asked since he was trying to keep track of the men in his company who had been forced to dismount when their tanks foundered in the cove.

"I have Sergeant LaPorte and two privates with me…actually a private first class and a private. One's real tall and the other guy…the private first class…is much shorter," Roy responded.

"The tall one's Cobb. The private first class sounds like Palmer. They were on *Cougar*...LaPorte's tank. He's as good a man as you'll find. Send them back to me. I need them right away."

"You got it, sir," the platoon sergeant answered immediately.

"I'm organizing a scavenger party to go out to the tanks in the cove and I could use LaPorte to lead it. My other tank is damaged and with some spare parts I might get it back up by morning. Otherwise, it'll just be a rolling pillbox with a machine gun. I'll send a man over to get them as soon as this meeting is over."

"That's fine by me, sir" Roy replied, "I'll send LaPorte and the other two over as soon as he arrives."

The pleasantries ended when Major Ryan laid a map of the island out on the sand and all the men gathered around it. He traced a rough line with his index finger across the base of the Bird's Beak to indicate the approximate location of their line for the night and told the men they must hold under all circumstances. "The likelihood of a massed *banzai* attack is fairly high," he said grimly, and the other officers and Roy mumbled their agreement. "It'll probably originate in the vicinity of the airfield to the east or along Black Beach to the south," he continued, "and they'll hit us sometime after dark...probably around one or two in the morning. It'll take 'em that long to get organized I imagine. When they do come, it's imperative that your men use good fire discipline. Tell your boys to hold their fire as long as they can... and remember, the Jap sappers will be looking for your automatic weapons...your thirty cals and the BARs. Use your grenades when necessary, but don't go too crazy with 'em either. One lousy Jap crawling up to your line doesn't warrant a grenade. You kill that bastard with a knife." Major Ryan paused and looked around the circle of men and all of them shook their heads. "Now," he went on, "about tomorrow. I plan on attacking on a broad front with I Company on the right and K Company on the left at oh eight hundred. We'll be going back over the same ground a lot of your men fought through today...that can't be helped. But hopefully the Japs won't have the foresight to reoccupy those same pillboxes and bunkers we overran earlier. In any event, we're gonna concentrate on freeing up Green Beach instead of Red 1. I don't think we have the manpower to tackle the *Pocket* over there, but I do think we can clean out Green Beach."

Once again the men nodded in unison...especially Captain Crain. His company had been shattered when it came into the *Pocket* earlier that morning and he had organized the survivors that were near the *Pocket* as best he could...much like Major Ryan had done with the men on the Bird's Beak. Crain had managed to round up only fifty men or so of his original company...and he had led several attacks against the Red 1 defenses along the base of the cove during the day...but he had nothing to show for it. The *Pocket* was proving to be one of the strongest defensive positions on the island and Crain's men were experiencing the same frustrations that Major Chamberlin's men were on the eastern end of Red 3. The complex was just too big and well-defended for an under-strength company of marines to overrun in one fell swoop so the captain finally resorted to the next best option... and he had his men wall the Japs off from the Bird's Beak.

Major Ryan went silent for a few seconds...letting his words sink in. He wanted his officers to digest what he had just said so there wouldn't be any mistakes or misunderstandings about what he wanted done. "Jim and Sam," he continued, "I want your two companies to advance as quickly as possible during the attack. To do it the way I want it done, I want you to jump off with your automatic weapons up front."

At this point, First Lieutenant Turner raised his hand and the major acknowledged him by saying, "Go ahead."

"Sir...you want our Bar-men and the guys carrying the Thompsons leading the attack? And then our riflemen behind them?"

"Yup," Ryan said with authority, "that's exactly how I want it done."

Lieutenant Turner made a gesture of acceptance...but the major sensed that he had some reservations with his tactics. To clarify his decision, he added, "Look, I know we don't ordinarily do it that

way…but I think the shock effect of your automatic weapons fire
will destroy whatever will power these Japs have left. I think the
gamble's worth it." He continued, "Destroy whatever obstacles you
can in your path. Use your flame gunners…if you have any…to fry
them in place…but if you run into a particularly tough one just bypass it. L and M Companies…plus the Second Battalion boys…will
be mopping up right behind you so don't worry about gettin' shot in
the ass by the Japs that get left behind."

"And if you do get shot in the ass…it'll mean you're not moving
fast enough…cause my boys will be doin' the shooting…so you'd
better step it up!" Lieutenant Kelly added and the group started
laughing in agreement.

Major Ryan sensed that the confidence he was portraying was
rubbing off on the harried officers who were gathered around him
and that in turn buoyed his own confidence even more. They had
arrived at the CP with looks of desperation on their tired faces and it
was heartening to see the men smiling and motivated once again…
like they had been back on the transports before the battle started.
Now they were convinced that they could repel a Jap attack that
night since the major had pulled them all back into a tight defensive
position…and they also liked his plan for the following morning.
They all realized…just like Major Ryan did…that the sooner they
took the fight to the Japs…the sooner they'd be off this hellhole and
headed for home. In that regard, they welcomed his plan and looked
forward to executing the attack aggressively in the morning. If nothing else, they could take pride in the knowing that they had done
their part to bring about the end of the battle as quickly as possible.

The major looked at his watch and realized he needed to wrap
the meeting up so the other officers could get back to their commands and make their own preparations for the night and day ahead.
The only thing he had left out so far was the fire support they'd
have for the attack and he addressed this in quick order…since there
wasn't much to report. "Besides Lieutenant Bale's tank…and some

mortars…we're pretty much on our own as far as the heavy stuff goes," the major said, "but we might luck out and get ourselves one of those destroyers to help us out. I sent a message over to Colonel Shoup a little while ago and I'm still waiting to hear back from him. Keep your fingers crossed…and maybe he'll be able to spare one for us." The major looked over at Captain Crain to let him know that he had followed up on the suggestion he had made at the meeting the two of them had had earlier…and Crain smiled back encouragingly.

"What about the other tank, sir," Kelly asked, "I was told that two of them made it in."

"Two did," First Lieutenant Bale cut in, answering the question. Then he added, "But my tank, *Cecilia*, had its seventy-five damaged by a lucky shot from a Jap tank that we knocked out behind the Red One beachhead earlier. The Jap gunner got a final shot off right before *China Gal* lit it up. I never thought I'd live to see anything like it, but that damned shot went right down *Cecilia's* main gun tube and exploded in the chamber. The gun's useless now so I gave our fifty cal to a lieutenant who said he needed it." He pointed in the direction of the *Pocket* and then added, "I don't remember his full name or what unit he was from…but his first name sounded a lot like Lieutenant Orr's there. That spitfire's got about fifteen men with him and a bunch of wounded. He said he's gonna stay there and fight to the death or until he's relieved."

The other officers looked at one another and wondered who the gutsy lieutenant was but no one could come up with an answer. Because of the confusion and misdirected landings, they all realized it could be any one of a number of officers from the companies that had tried to land along Red 2 or Red 1.

Captain Crain got excited however. "Was his name, 'Ott,' by any chance? 'Ott' Schulte is one of my platoon leaders. I haven't seen him at all. I just assumed he was dead too."

"Well, he's definitely alive, sir. Wounded…but alive," Lieutenant Bale replied back, "since Ott's the name of the guy I gave my fifty to. I remember that now…I mean how many guys are called, 'Ott.'"

"Hot damn," the captain said happily, and added, "and you say he's over by the *Pocket?*"

"Yes, sir. He told me he was going to hang on as long as he could. The fifty cal we gave him should help keep the Japs off his back for a while. He told me that he had some other machine guns with him too...that he had managed to salvage from some amtracs that were wrecked near him. Most of his men were wounded though. He's holed up way over to the east...near the boundary line between Red One and Red Two. Luckily, we were able to knock out a real tough bunker that was giving him problems. That took some of the pressure off of him. He's basically got a lone outpost set up near the beach."

"Can we get to him...to provide any help," Crain asked the tanker.

"I don't think so, captain. Not where they're at now anyway," Lieutenant Bale replied evenly. "There's just too many Japs between us and them. The only reason we made it over that way was because we were in our tanks. There are Jap pillboxes and bunkers scattered everywhere over there...and it's gonna take a lot more than a platoon of marines to take that ground."

Major Ryan had been listening to the conversation...as all the men were...and he understood Captain Crain's predicament...since he had men who were missing as well. He looked at the captain with empathy and said, "Jim...I know this is tough...but Schulte will have to hang on tonight with what he's got. Once we get some reinforcements over here, I will do everything I can to get him help. But for now, I need you and the men with you to help me here."

Captain Crain understood the bigger picture...and even though it pained him to do so...he looked the major in the eye and said, "Yes, sir. We'll do whatever you want us to. Schulte can handle it. I know he can."

"Thank you, Jim," the major replied...and then he explained that Lieutenant Bale was going to shift from *Cecilia*, his command tank, to *China Gal* since its 75mm main gun and top turret .50 cal and bow-mounted .30 cal machine guns were still working. The tank company commander had decided to employ *China Gal's* firepower against the bunkers that First Lieutenant Turner's marines would encounter as they advanced along Green Beach in the morning. At the same time, *Cecilia*, armed only with its forward-firing .30 caliber machine gun in the turret, would advance along the left flank where the terrain was flat and open. This tank...essentially a rolling pillbox now since its main gun was disabled...would be going up against *rikusentai* who were in foxholes, trenches, and rifle pits rather than the bunkers and pillboxes that honeycombed the ground behind the seawall on Green Beach. The heavy punch of a 75mm cannon would be far more useful along Green Beach than inland and Lieutenant Bale had picked *Cecilia* to support Captain Crain's men on the left flank for that reason alone.

"What about artillery support, sir? Weren't the pack howitzers slotted to land on Red One?" Lieutenant Kelly asked.

"They sure were...but once they saw what was going on over here...they probably chose to land somewhere else too. Right now... with the commo situation as screwed up as it is...I have no way of finding out where they are or if they can even help us out. To be honest with you, our radios have been so spotty that I don't know if Colonel Shoup knows what's really going on over here," the major replied.

"What about the password for tonight, sir? Are we sticking with the system of challenging with a state and answering with its capital?" the lieutenant pressed.

"Yes, it is. I would've gotten to that eventually, but you beat me to it. For tonight, the sign-countersign is just like the lieutenant said. But tell your men to pick a state with an easy capital so they don't end up shooting someone by accident. I don't want to have to write a letter to some kid's folks that he got killed because he didn't know the capital of Rhode Island okay."

The officers and Sergeant Roy laughed at the major's suggestion but they also realized he had made a good point. "What's New Mexico's capital...anybody know that one? Maybe we should stick to just a few states to play it safe?" Kelly wondered out loud.

"Albuquerque...isn't it?" the lieutenant from G Company guessed.

"It's Santa Fe y'all. I should know...I grew up next door in Texas...Dallas to be exact," Lieutenant Bale, the twenty-three-year-old tank commander, drawled.

"How about South Dakota...and North Dakota for that matter?" Kelly asked, continuing the discussion.

"Who the hell knows?" one of the other officers grumbled.

Sergeant Roy...who had remained silent until then...spotted the big, gold ring on Lieutenant Kelly's finger - Lieutenant Hackett...his platoon commander...wore a class ring just like it - and said, "Don't we have any other bookworms from the Naval Academy in this esteemed group that can answer that one?"

"Yeah, I should be so lucky," the G Company lieutenant named Conner Orr replied, the disappointment evident in his voice. He then explained that his application to the school had been rejected because his grade point average wasn't high enough to get him in. "I ended up going to *Ole Miss* though," he added quickly, "and I did alright I guess... good enough to graduate anyway...and get my bars."

Then Lieutenant Kelly spoke up. "Nope...I'm the only one," he said proudly, "Class of Thirty-Nine. But I majored in mechanical engineering...not geography...so that's my excuse. If I get off this island alive, I promise I'll go back there as an instructor and stress the importance of a liberal arts education to the faculty. Who knows... maybe they'll even listen to me." Everyone laughed at this and then Kelly asked the gunnery sergeant where he had gone to school.

"Sir, I went to the school of hard knocks," he responded just as proudly, and winking at the G Company lieutenant, he added, "and I guess I did alright too...cause it got me these chevrons."

The major jumped in at this point. "Alright...alright...let's knock it off everybody. Enough of the small talk. We'll have a big reunion party someday and then we can fill in all the details of everyone's life. But for now, let's stay focused on what we gotta do tonight and tomorrow. If anything changes between now and tomorrow's attack, I'll send a runner for you. That's all I got. Good luck tonight."

As the men stood up to leave, Major Ryan asked Lieutenant Kelly if he had any more questions before he let the men head back to their respective commands.

"No sir...I think that's about it...but...come to think of it...I think South Dakota's capital is--"

"That's all. You're dismissed!" the twenty-seven-year-old major from Osage, Kansas said, cutting the lieutenant off in mid-sentence... and the men left smiling...confident in their commander...and in his plans for the night and day ahead.

CHAPTER 36

O n his way back to his own CP, Sergeant Roy looked to his right and saw a solitary figure coming down the beach. The man was too far away to tell who it was but he could tell that Reisman's patrol must have run into some kind of trouble...since two men had gone out and only one man was coming back...and he was limping. As he got closer, Roy could tell that it was Reisman since the man was too tall to be the private that had been sent with him.

Reisman trudged up to the CP and look plaintively at his platoon sergeant and the right guide sergeant. Roy waited, letting the man rest a second, and then he asked him straightforwardly, "Well, what the hell happened?"

"Jefferson is dead...a sniper got him. He ran ahead on his on...a damn shame. I tried to warn him."

"What about you...are you okay?" Roy wanted to know, concerned about his leg.

Reisman was caught off guard for a second by the change in the platoon sergeant's tone and immediately felt better. "It's my ankle... twisted it when I jumped off an amtrac. It probably saved me and got that damn kid killed."

"Did you find anything that we could use…should we send any-one back?" The question came from Sergeant Flockerzi this time.

"No. I only found these grenades. Nothing else. Those tractors were stripped clean. Somebody got to 'em before we did," Reisman said, and he unhooked the grenades from his cartridge belt and gave them to Flockerzi.

"How about Grasso and Hennessey? Any sign of them?" It was Sergeant Roy again and he was asking about the marine from Corporal Varner's squad who had been wounded at the seawall and the man he had detailed to stay with him.

"Didn't see either one of them…alive or dead, sergeant. We checked all the amtracs near the Beak and a few further down…near where we came in…that's where Jefferson got it. I didn't see anybody down there on the beach…except dead marines."

"Okay, let Varner know you're back and then get some rest, pri-vate," Roy advised, and then added, "you did a good job."

Reisman looked confused. "Good job…sergeant?" he asked skeptically, "I took just one man out with me and he got killed." Without waiting for an answer, the dejected private limped off in the direction of the seawall to report in to his squad leader…just as he had been ordered.

• • •

"Looks like we got a visitor comin' our way, Stonewall," Sergeant Flockerzi announced a little while later. Before Sergeant Roy could re-ply, Sergeant LaPorte stood up and said, "Hey, guys, look! It's Platoon Sergeant Sooter…the best damn tanker in the Marine Corps!" The sergeant…Charley Sooter…was a veteran and the platoon sergeant of the four tanks that were assigned to the 1st Platoon of C Company. These four tanks…plus the two tanks from the Headquarters platoon under Lieutenant Bale…were the six tanks that had been assigned to attack Red 1. Cobb and Palmer rushed over and began bombarding him with their questions about the status and whereabouts of the rest of the men in the platoon. "First off, I'm sorry about Bruno and Day. They were both good tankers," Sooter…who was the TC of *Chicago*…said sadly, and added, "but I'm glad you three made it in okay. Everybody in my tank made it in safely. I am still looking for *Cobra's* crew and for *Cherokee's* crew. You haven't seen any of them by any chance…have you?"

"No," Sergeant LaPorte answered, "we have no idea what happened to those guys. We were too busy trying to make it in on our own after we got stuck."

"Well, hopefully they'll show up sooner or later. They could still be sitting out there in their tanks for all I know. But they're probably in the same boat as you guys…fighting as dismounted infantry around here somewhere," he added honestly. Then he told them that Lieutenant Bale had switched tanks and was now riding in *China Gal* because of the damage to *Cecilia's* main gun. "Unfortunately, the rest of us are gonna be ground pounders until we can get our rigs up and running again. With that in mind, the lieutenant wants me to put together a salvage operation to see if we can get any of the other tanks that we lost in the cove back in action. And if we can't, then we'll strip them of the parts we need to keep the *Cecilia* and *China Gal* running as long as possible. I am also organizing a team to bring up supplies for us too. I can use you guys for that too. We need water, food, ammo, and fuel…and the only way for us to get it over here right now is to lug it over ourselves from the pier. It's a suck job…I know…but what can I say. It's gotta get done. I just gotta figure out how to bypass the *Pocket* so we don't get any of you killed in the process."

"Where's *China Gal* and *Cecilia* now, sir?" Palmer asked, barely able to contain his excitement.

"They're hidden in a small stand of trees up the trail and to the right," Platoon Sergeant Sooter said, jerking his thumb over his shoulder.

"You and your men can head back with the sergeant as soon as you're ready then," Sergeant Roy said to LaPorte…and then to

Sooter he added, "I'm sorry we couldn't offer your tanker boys better accommodations during their brief stay with us."

"Are you kidding," Sooter answered, sounding mystified. "What more could a weary traveler have asked for? Your little spot here has a beautiful view...and there's a light tropical breeze blowing... to cool us off." Then he reached into his overalls and pulled out two cans of C-rations. Everyone's mouth dropped at the sight of the cans...and he threw them to the sergeant. "And some fine food, of course...to go along with the wonderful scenery."

"I hope somebody has a spoon so we can all share this," Sergeant Roy said, beaming.

Sergeant Flockerzi produced a spoon - he always seemed to have the right tool at the right time - and threw it over to his sergeant.

"What's on the menu, sarge?" It was the tall loader, Cobb, asking about the ingredients in the dark green cans. He was starving since he hadn't eaten a thing since breakfast had been served at one in the morning on his transport...over sixteen hours ago.

"Like you have a choice out here," Flockerzi wisecracked. Then he unsheathed his K-bar knife and said, "Toss them over here so I can open up our dinner."

Once the cans were opened, the men kept passing them around, each taking a spoonful of the contents - it was steak and potatoes, the standard fair for a C-ration meal - in turn until they were completely empty. The cans had made the rounds twice...so each man had two heaping mouthfuls to still his hunger...and they had eaten in silence...savoring not only the food...but the special camaraderie this moment engendered as well.

With dinner over, Roy took out his canteen and tossed it over to Flockerzi. The sergeant held it up in both his hands...like a waiter would in a fine restaurant...and in an effected voice said, "Gentleman, please honor Platoon Sergeant Roy by partaking in a glass of sherry for dessert."

Sergeant LaPorte, excited by the suggestion, said, "Hear, hear!"

This time the canteen made the rounds and the men had the added satisfaction of washing down their meal with a delicious swig of water. The canteen eventually made its way back to Sergeant Roy and he put it right back into its case on his hip…without taking a sip. As much as he wanted to quench his thirst, experience and discipline had taught him to conserve this precious commodity for when he really needed it.

Watching him, Sergeant Sooter said guiltily, "Now don't I feel like a jerk."

"Don't worry about it," Roy said lightly and he added a wink that no one else saw. Then he said, "But something has been bothering me for a while. Why did you guys back off that beach during the landing and then head across the cove to land over here. That move cost you four tanks. What was your lieutenant thinking? I met him and he seems pretty squared away to me."

"Well," replied Sergeant Sooter, clearing his throat, "when we pulled up to the beach…all we saw were dead and wounded marines laying right in our path. We coulda kept going but the lieutenant came over the radio and told us to stop. He said we weren't going to run over our own guys no matter what it cost us. Then he ordered us to back up and head over here. Since all our guides were dead…we didn't have anyone to spot any of the holes ahead of us and that's why we lost those four. I don't think a single one got hit by enemy fire… all four of them just foundered out. Even so, I still agree with what Lieutenant Bale did. We came here to kill Japs…not our own men."

"Damn straight," Sergeant Flockerzi said, listening to the explanation just as intently as Roy was.

Roy shook his head affirmatively and asked, "How are you guys fixed for water?"

"To be honest with you, sarge, we're not as disciplined with our water conservation as you are. It gets real hot inside those Shermans…especially in weather like this. As far as I know…we're completely dry," the tanker sergeant replied straight up.

Sergeant Roy reached back down to his hip and withdrew his canteen again. He shook it so everyone could hear the water sloshing around inside it. Then he threw it over to Sooter and said, "This is all I got…but you make sure and give it to your lieutenant…with my compliments. And you tell him I'd be honored to serve under him anywhere…anytime. Got it."

"I got it, sarge," Sooter replied…looking as proud as a peacock…as were the other three tankers who had been riveted to the exchange. Sooter then turned to Sergeant LaPorte and said, "Okay, let's head back to the tanks. I've been gone so long that the lieutenant must be thinkin' a sniper got me."

"Let's go, men!" Sergeant LaPorte ordered.

Palmer and Cobb…eager to return to their tank comrades and see Lieutenant Bale…sprang to their feet and dutifully followed the two tank sergeants back up the trail that led to the Battalion CP and their armored behemoths.

CHAPTER 37

For the marines lying in the foxholes, shell craters, and trenches scattered across the western tip of Betio, the most frightening part of the day…nighttime…and the darkness it brought with it… had finally arrived. Major Ryan's orphans would spend the next nine, nerve-wracking hours waiting for the Japanese to launch their wild charge to drive them into the sea. Knowing this, the men gripped their rifles a bit tighter as they peered into *No Man's Land* and listened for any sounds that might reveal the preparatory stages of an attack. To get ready, some men unclipped the few grenades they had left and laid them out in front of them…within easy reach…so they could find them quickly if they needed them in a hurry. Others pulled razor-sharp knives out of their sheaths and stuck them in the ground nearby…in similar fashion to what had been done with the grenades. This was the weapon the marines had been trained to use when their positions were being probed at night. The idea was to dispatch a sneaky, lone-wolf infiltrator as quietly as possible without giving your position away. With that aim in mind, a veteran marine who had shed his pack when he had landed removed the entrenching tool from the pack of a young marine who was lying next to him.

The man jammed the short, wooden-handled shovel into the sand beside him. When the younger man asked him what he was doing, the grizzled marine told him that the entrenching tool made a great battle axe and that it was just as silent as a trench knife or bayonet. "I'll also use it on the Nips if we're out of ammo and being over-run," he said matter-of-factly. The most conscientious of the men inspected their weapons and field stripped them to give them a good cleaning. Though they were not prone to jamming, the coral dust and sand had clung to everything and anything as the men had low crawled and run from one spot to another during the day and now their weapons were coated with the stuff. The marines who were too crapped out to do even that realized that a cursory cleaning of their weapons' components could prevent their rifle, machine gun, or BAR from seizing up...so many men...though exhausted...used the extra time to run a brush or rag over theirs. Those too tired and fatigued to care anymore left their weapons alone and simply lapsed into a series of restless catnaps while trying to stay awake. A few even fell completely asleep...a minor miracle in itself. Sometimes their foxhole buddies would wake them up when it was their turn for watch while others...those who were more concerned with their own self-preservation...let them sleep right through the night. They knew each other's tendencies all too well...since they had trained together side-by-side for months...and experience had shown them that nothing could keep certain men awake. So they covered for them and stayed up through their watch too...knowing these men's efforts to stay up would be in vain and that they'd fall right back asleep soon after they were awakened.

Just like everywhere else on Betio that first night, time seemed to drag endlessly by as the marines in the Beak waited for the Japanese to commence a *banzai* charge against their position. After a while though, the marines began to sense a strange calmness descending over their corner of the island. Now, in stark contrast to the pande-monium that had reigned throughout this section of the battlefield for the previous twelve hours, the only sound the marines heard came from the far left….over by the pier…almost a thousand yards away…where a faint echo of gunfire could be heard as the Japanese continued to fire at any movement they saw along the pier. On the Beak however, everything had gone eerily quiet.

• • •

"Did you just hear something?" the big private asked yet again. If there had been any light to see by, the private may have been less jittery…but it was so dark he could barely see anything more than a few yards away.

"Yeah, I'm pretty sure it was a Jap. He ran down the beach waving a big, white flag. I think he was trying to surrender…now let me get some sleep," Private First Class Reisman said derisively. He was lying next to Private Chris Nelson and the burly private had just elbowed him awake…again.

"Shut the hell up. I'm only doin' what you told me to do," Nelson whispered back. "I thought I might've heard something that sounded like a motor launch out there. The Japs probably got boats hidden at the other end of the island. Maybe they're gonna land somewhere over here." The eighteen-year-old private from South Florida squinted into the distance to see if he could detect anything else but all he heard was the sound of the waves washing softly up on the beach in front of them.

If it had been anything at all, it's long gone by now, Reisman thought as he laid his head back down on his arm, convinced that this latest invasion attempt had fizzled out…just like the other two that the private had already sighted. "Nelson…" he said monotonously, "the next time you spot the Japs, let them come all the way in. In fact, let them get so close that you can count the buttons on their uniforms. That's when I want you to get me up. Those are your new instructions. Forget about what I told you earlier…okay. Now let me get some rest or else I'll be very grumpy when it's my turn for guard duty. And I know you don't want that."

And he certainly didn't. The big marine had spent the entire day running alongside the skinny New Yorker as the assistant BAR-man and he was worn out. He had started the day as a normal rifleman… but when the original assistant BAR-man had been killed at the seawall, the job had fallen into his lap…since he was one of the bigger guys in the squad. His new assignment required him to carry several bandoliers of extra .30 caliber ammunition for Reisman to use if he ran low. This job obviously required the private to stay close to Reisman…which…in this case…also meant that he was forced to listen to him rant and rave all day long too. The only break he had gotten from his partner's incessant jabbering was when the platoon sergeant had sent him back to look for more ammo that afternoon. Reisman had handed him the Browning automatic rifle as he was getting ready to leave and told him…in that nasally, sarcastic tone of his…that he didn't want his rifle any dirtier than it already was when he got back… or he'd have to clean it. So Nelson had just cleaned it while he was gone…knowing that Reisman would make him clean it later anyway.

To pass the time, Nelson removed his helmet and scratched his scalp. It felt gritty with sand and sweat, but that was the least of his worries. Being dirty was something he was used to…since he dug golf courses for a living. He wasn't used to being hungry and thirsty at the same time however. And he was hungry…with a capital H. He could even hear his stomach grumbling at times and he knew that if he could hear it…then some Jap sneaking up on them could probably hear it just as well too . *How would you explain that at a court martial hearing with the CO*, he wondered: *Yes, sir. That's right, sir. I jeopardized my entire platoon… well what was left of it…because the enemy heard my empty stomach making those crazy sounding noises and I was forced to fire on them when they charged my position.*

The temptation to get up and go find some discarded backpack - the marines had carried enough rations to last three days in them - was overwhelming. *Hell…there must have been hundreds of them strewn along the beach where we had landed*, he thought. *On the other hand, the odds of finding one and making it back here without being shot dead by some nervous sentry is extremely slim… so what's the use,* he realized sadly. To take his mind off his hunger he told himself to think about something else so he picked up his helmet and looked inside. Even though it was dark, there was just enough light for him to see the picture of his high school sweetheart. He had placed it inside the webbing of the liner of his helmet and he considered it a good luck charm as long as it stayed there. Right then and there he decided that he would marry Micky as soon as he got some leave and a chance to go home…*so long as I don't get killed in this damn battle first,* he thought realistically. Unlike Reisman…who made the same decision after dating the love of his life for only a few months while they were all stationed in New Zealand…Nelson had met his future bride - until a few minutes ago the term had been girlfriend - when they were both in the high school almost four years ago. They had gone out a few times, found out that they liked each other's company, and continued dating. In the process, they had also become best friends and had been inseparable ever since. But strangely, the subject of marriage had never been discussed…or even brought up between them…not once. *Funny,* Nelson thought, *how a war can change your view of things in a hurry.*

• • •

"Is it my time yet?" It was Reisman all of a sudden. He had an uncanny ability to wake up at the right time - it was almost like he had an internal alarm clock - and the question had caught Nelson off guard and startled him. The assistant gunner checked his watch and…sure enough…it was midnight and time for Reisman to take over the watch. They had arranged it so that each man would spend two hours on guard duty while the other slept…or at least tried to.

"Yeah…it is," Nelson answered, and then added, "nothing happenin' here. Maybe the Japs are gonna leave us alone tonight," and he rolled over and went right to sleep.

"Don't count on it," Reisman replied, "the Japs can hit at any time." His warning fell on deaf ears though since Nelson was already fast asleep.

• • •

"Nelley...get up...we've got movement to our right."

Nelson, still groggy, blinked his eyes and saw his partner staring at him. Reisman's face was very close to his own and he was whispering the words as softly as he could. Nelson also sensed that there was something very different in the tone of his voice and the way he was acting so he roused himself quickly.

"Where?" he said, rubbing his eyes so he could see better. He then looked at his watch and saw that it was almost 0200 hours...and time for him to relieve Reisman.

"Down by the seawall...about twenty yards to the right. There's four of them...five...maybe more. They lift their heads up every once in a while to see where they are. I don't think they know we're here though. They must be looking for gaps in the line so they can get in behind us...the sneaky bastards," Reisman hissed.

"We need some damn flares," Nelson complained.

"Yeah...and more ammo and more men too, but we don't have any...so shut up and get ready to hand me those extra clips of ammo. Don't take 'em out until I tell ya. I don't want any sand getting into them and foulin' 'em up, okay."

"You got it. Let me know when you want them...I'll have them ready for you...trust me," Nelson said confidently.

"I always have," Reisman replied matter-of-factly, still squinting into the darkness ahead.

The private smiled at the remark and pulled the bandoliers for the BAR closer to him...within easy reach. "With all the crap you give me," Nelson whispered, "I never thought you did."

Reisman, still staring at the seawall intently, laughed lightly and said, "Nelley...you might not be the smartest kid in the class...but I never said I didn't trust ya."

Smirking, Private Nelson took the jab in stride. It was common knowledge among the men in the platoon that Nelson...with a year of college already under his belt...was one of the smarter guys in the unit. To enlist in the Marine Corps, Nelson had even promised his mother that he would finish up his studies at Florida State in Tallahassee and graduate before doing anything else once he got back. Now he realized that he should have hedged his bet and told her, "When I get back," of course. *Well...things might have changed slightly*, he mused, but he didn't think the vow he had made to himself a little while ago...to marry his hometown sweetheart...would upset his mother one bit...since she loved Mickey as much as he did. It might delay his educational plans...and his football career too... since he was the fullback on the football team...but some things were worth it.

"There they are again," Reisman suddenly whispered, pointing with his finger. "Do ya see 'em?" he asked.

Nelson looked in the direction he indicated and saw some shadowy figures running bent over at the waist near the seawall. "I see 'em," he replied quietly while tracking the enemy soldiers over the barrel of his rifle.

Their movement attracted the attention of the two marines outside the bunker to their right and a shaky voice called out, "Halt... who go dare?" Hearing this, the Jap squad...all nine of them... dropped out of sight behind the seawall.

"Oh no," Reisman moaned, "he's gonna get us all killed."

"He probably doesn't know half of the states...let alone their capitals," Nelson whispered.

Both he and Reisman recognized the accent immediately. It belonged to Private Ragnar Svansson...one of the new recruits who had joined the platoon in New Zealand. Based on his appearance, most of the men had thought that the young private was from somewhere in the Mediterranean like Italy, Greece, or even Turkey...since he had jet black hair and dark eyes along with an olive complexion. But the handsome private had shocked them though when he informed them that he came from Iceland of all places...which accounted for his Nordic accent. He explained that he had only been an American citizen for about a year or so and that he would have enlisted sooner but his father had told him that the marines wouldn't let him join until he was eighteen. Only later did he realize that his father had lied to him when he met other kids who were seventeen during boot camp.

To make more money, Ragnar's father had moved the family to the United States in early 1942 and they had settled in eastern North Carolina...so he could be within easy driving distance of the new Marine base that was under construction. It was later named Camp Lejeune...and while the base did have fourteen miles of beach to remind the family of home...it was still quite a bit different from the cold environs that Ragnar was used to. Before that his father had worked as a contractor on the military base in Iceland where the 6th Marine Regiment was billeted. Ragnar had accompanied his father to the base on many occasions and the jaunty marines had treated him fairly and squarely...especially the guys that seemed to be around his age. Svansson had never forgotten their kindness or the thrill of seeing the marines training and he swore that someday...somehow... he'd be a marine too. The fact that he was from Iceland...which made him a Norwegian citizen...didn't concern him one bit...and now the family move and the war had given him the chance to fulfill his dream...two years later.

The easygoing Svansson was accepted into the platoon rather quickly...in part because the suave private acquired a reputation for being a hit with the young ladies of New Zealand. It wasn't long before he was nicknamed, "the Latin Lover," and on one weekend pass Svansson had met a pretty girl named Tammy at a dance that the locals had arranged for the homesick marines. Private Reisman had been there too and when he expressed an interest her...the private had been kind enough to introduce the young lady to his friend. For Private Reisman, the rest was history...and thankfully...it didn't seem to bother Private Svansson one bit...because...as far as he was concerned...there were plenty more good-looking fish in the sea... plenty more.

• • •

The Japanese petty officer leading the engineer squad knew he had to act quickly. With a deft hand signal, he motioned the fourth man in line forward and he slid up as quietly as possible. "Ready?" he asked.

The private indicated he was by shaking his head affirmatively.

"Do it then," the petty officer ordered immediately.

"Corpsman...I need a corpsman," the private moaned quietly in perfect English. He had lived in the United States for ten years before his father, an ex-Army officer and businessman, had taken the family back to their homeland when the Japanese Army had invaded Manchuria in 1937. Now he was getting a chance to put all those years of hardship - neither he nor his family had ever been fully accepted into the community in Los Angeles - to good use and he couldn't be happier. "I'm hit pretty bad...I need help...somebody... anybody out there...please get me a corpsman," he pleaded over and over again softly...hoping the dramatic flourish would draw some of the marines out of their positions...or...at the very least...get them to respond...so they could identify where they were hidden.

His plaintive calls were loud enough that the two men from Corporal Oliver's squad...Private Svansson and PFC Doug Tuchmann...who had been positioned nearest to Sergeant Varner's men heard them too...but Reisman and Nelson had no way of alerting them to the danger that was lurking only twenty yards away. "Whatta we gonna do?" Nelson whispered, hoping the more experienced Reisman would have some sort of solution to the problem already figured out.

Without uttering a word, Reisman reached into his utility pocket and retrieved two hand grenades. He had given the others that he had found in the amtracs to Platoon Sergeant Roy, but he had held onto these two for himself. *I ain't no dummy*, the streetwise marine thought...and he handed one to Nelson. "Throw yours to the right...I'll go for the ones on the left. On three," Reisman ordered.

Nelson nodded and Reisman counted off, "One...two...three." At three, both men pulled the pins on the grenades...held them for two seconds...and then heaved them in the vicinity of the log barricade where they had last seen the helmets bobbing up and down. Then they ducked down and closed their eyes.

The bright flash of the explosions blinded both Tuchmann and Svansson for several seconds. They had not been aware that the grenades had been thrown and they were both staring at the seawall to see if they could spot where the wounded marine was...if it was a wounded marine. To be safe, Tuchmann had even yelled out a clever challenge...or so he thought. Since they were using states and capitals as the sign and countersign...he picked Louisiana...since he figured its capital...which had an R in it...would be hard for a Jap to pronounce properly. But he never got an answer. What he got instead was a silent stampede by five enemy soldiers...but neither he nor Svansson could see them since they were still dealing with the night blindness caused by the grenade explosions.

Once the initial shock of the grenades had worn off, the petty officer pointed at the four men nearest to him and said, "You are coming with me." Then he saw that one of the grenades had done its job...since the last man in line had been mangled in the explosion. This left three effectives...and he detailed them to head to the right...to outflank the position they were going to charge. Wasting no time, he and the four others climbed over the seawall and he led them in the direction where the American's voice had come from...since he couldn't see either Tuchmann or Svansson. While they were doing that, the last three men in the squad crawled past their dead buddy and moved back down the seawall in the opposite direction in order to outflank Tuchmann's position...and right towards Sergeant Varner's two men.

Reisman and Nelson had shielded their eyes from the brilliance of the grenade explosions so they weren't affected by it. And when they lifted their heads back up, they immediately saw the enemy movement to their right. *Why aren't Tuchmann and Svansson firing,* they both wondered, and then Reisman swung his BAR around to engage the Japanese troops. His BAR barked loudly as he fired short, sustained bursts and he quickly dropped one of the men on their way to Tuchmann's position. Nelson...taking the cue from Reisman...started blasting away with his M-1 rifle as well. He nailed one of the Nips too, but out of the corner of his eye he spied three other figures crawling over the seawall just to the left of their position. "I got three more comin' at us to the left of the other ones...almost straight on!" he screamed and Reisman turned towards this new threat and began firing at them.

Back on the right, PFC Tuchmann had regained his sight just in time to see two crazed Japs darting to the left of the foxhole he and Svansson were manning. Only moments before the Japs had dropped down to avoid the automatic weapon's fire that was coming at them from their flank, but they had gotten back up when that gunfire had suddenly shifted off them...and that's when Tuchmann saw them.

"Are you alright," Tuchmann asked Svansson calmly.

"I think so," Svansson answered, rubbing his eyes frantically.

Seeing that his foxhole mate appeared to be okay, Tuchmann left the foxhole and moved into the small trench that led off to the left... and just in the nick of time. In seconds, the Jap petty officer and another man came barreling around the left corner of the bunker... their dark silhouettes plainly visible so close up. PFC Tuchmann... always cool under fire...was ready for them and he put two rounds into each man's chest before they ever knew what happened. The two men collapsed in a heap and their blood drained out of them... soaking the sand beneath their bodies.

• • •

The last soldier in this party had watched helplessly as his petty officer leader and the other man in front of him rose up and dashed off to the right of the bunker...bravely carrying out the wishes of their Emperor and nation. But he just laid there...petrified of losing his life. He had never been a good soldier...at least in his own mind... and he had only stayed in the service to protect his family from the repercussions and shame that would have been leveled against them if he had dropped out of the Army...especially in wartime Japan.

From the very beginning, this free spirit had found the suffocating discipline and order of military life an unbearable burden...and he never felt comfortable in a world where the other men around him loved carrying guns and wearing uniforms. He knew...or felt somehow...that he would never fit in. In a stroke of luck, he had been assigned to the 111th Pioneers Construction Battalion...an elite engineer unit...after basic training...since he possessed skills in that area...but even that gift seemed to fall flat after a while. He came to accept the sad fact that he would never be happy...that he would never measure up or flourish the way the other dedicated men in his unit did. And he felt like a failure now...yet again...as he watched his fellow engineers run off without him. Then...out of nowhere... something clicked in him. Whether it was from the training he had hated...but endured...or from sheer guilt he didn't know...but he just knew he had to act...whether he wanted to or not. Summoning his courage, he forced himself up and charged to the left of the bunker...and ran directly into a marine who seemed to be oblivious to his presence.

Private Svansson was kneeling on one knee in the foxhole...still trying to blink his night blindness away...so he never saw the frightened soldier coming his way. But he did hear a man grunting from exhaustion as he ran through the soft sand...and then he heard what sounded like equipment jingling as the enemy soldier got closer still. In a desperate attempt to save himself, he squeezed off two shots in that direction...hoping to hit whatever was coming his way. Then, all of a sudden, he felt a sharp blow to his chest and he was knocked backwards into a sitting position against the back of the foxhole.

PFC Tuchmann heard Svansson issue a shriek of pain off to his left and he turned just in time to see a tan-colored figure standing over Svansson's body. The man was grunting loudly as he was tugging and pulling at his rifle…and the private first class knew immediately what had happened. The enemy soldier had bayoneted the private and the long blade at the end of his rifle had gone almost entirely through Svansson's body and become stuck in the process. Tuchmann saw the amazed look on the young boy's face as he struggled to dislodge his weapon from his victim's chest but it was no use. If he had paid better attention during training, the young private would have known that the simple technique for dislodging a bayonet that is stuck in a victim's body is to fire off a round into body that the bayonet is stuck in. This will often dislodge the bayonet so it can be pulled back out without much effort. But the bored private had never really been interested in hearing what the veteran instructors or older engineers had to say…whether it was about stuck bayonets or anything else for that matter…and this stubbornness and aloofness would cost him his life.

PFC Tuchmann didn't give the Jap soldier any more time to solve his problem. Without compunction, he fired one round right into the side of his head and the boy…who had never wanted to be a soldier… simply crumpled on top of Svansson…who was by then just as dead.

• • •

Over on the left side, Reisman and Nelson had just killed one of the three soldiers who were still trying to outflank Tuchmann's position…but in doing so, one of the two remaining Japs had spotted them. The Jap soldier took aim where he had seen their rifle flashes and he fired…hoping to keep their heads down. The tactic worked since both the marines ducked to avoid the incoming fire. With only fifteen yards or so separating the two parties, the other enemy engineer seized the opportunity and charged the crater containing the two marines. The five-foot-nine, two-hundred-and-twenty pound, muscular engineer - he was one of the biggest Japanese on an island full of heavily built Japanese men - covered the distance quickly and leapt into the hole with a dull thud. He lunged at the bigger marine first with his bayonet - he had discarded his rifle since he had never been a good shot and he felt far more comfortable using a weapon worthy of a *samurai* - but the marine parried the jab deftly and struck him with the butt of his M-1 as he went by.

Nelson heard the man grunt in pain as the stock of his rifle connected against the side of the Jap's head but his adversary recovered quickly and he turned to face Nelson once again. Before he could charge, Reisman laced the man down the side with a string of .30 caliber bullets. A look of shock registered on the Jap's large, meaty face as the rounds slammed into him and he sank to his knees very slowly, seemingly in deep thought over what had just happened. The man remained kneeling like that for a few seconds...willing himself to stay alive...and in that time he uttered a simple prayer that he had been taught as a young boy back in Nagoya. Finishing the prayer, a feeling of contentment spread through him...for in the end he knew he had championed over death...by leading a life of honor...and that was as much of an accomplishment...if not more...than anything he would have ever achieved back home. With that peaceful thought to ease his mind, the man keeled over and died.

Reisman and Nelson had both watched the eerie scene in the crater while also keeping a wary eye out for the other Jap rifleman. No sooner had the big Jap fallen over then the last commando jumped up and sprinted for the seawall. Reisman figured that he had seen his buddy go down and had just run out of nerve. *He's probably gonna try to swim back to his own lines*, he thought wryly, and for a brief instant he was going to let him go...but then decided not to. His well-aimed shot caught the runner right in the middle of the back and the man threw his arms up as the bullet struck home. The man went down in a heap as his legs suddenly went limp and Reisman and Nelson watched as he began dragging himself through the sand in a valiant attempt to reach the seawall and the water beyond.

"I definitely got him," Reisman said coldly.

"I think so…but he's still movin' from what I can tell," Nelson replied, rising up so he could see the Jap better.

"Finish him off then before he gets away. I might've just winged him and if he makes it back alive to his lines, he can show his buddies where we are."

Nelson stood up and set himself firmly for the coup de grace. He brought his rifle up until the enemy's body filled his sights and then pulled the trigger…just like on the firing range. This round found its mark as well and the man died with his arms hanging in vain over the ledge of the log barricade.

"Nice shot," Reisman said, surveying the private's work.

Although he knew he had gotten him, Nelson didn't exactly know where he had hit him so he shrugged his shoulders. In fact, his bullet had hit the man just under his shoulder blade and had gone straight on through…shattering his heart along the way…before it exited the front of his body. Nelson sat back down without acknowledging Reisman's compliment and he suddenly felt very tired…in fact more tired than he had ever felt in his whole life. But he wasn't about to go to sleep now…not with all those crazy Japs still out there somewhere. All he wanted…besides something to eat and drink… was just a little peace and quiet so he could make it through the rest of the long night ahead.

CHAPTER 38

When dawn finally broke over the western end of Betio, every marine in Major Ryan's command breathed a sigh of relief. They...like the rest of the marines scattered across the island... were wondering just why the Japanese hadn't attacked them during the night. They had been forced to fight off a few small, spoiling attacks across their entire three hundred yard front...but nothing more than that. These tactics had certainly deviated from everything the Japanese had used prior to that which left the marines theorizing why it had played out that way. One explanation seemed more plausible than all the rest: *Maybe the Japs are so well dug in...that they want us to attack them!* With that grim thought in mind, the elation the men felt at having survived their first night on the island quickly gave way to a new worry...because they all knew that they were going to have to wage another attack against an enemy who was sitting back waiting for them. A dicey proposition at best...but that's exactly what Major Ryan intended to do.

• • •

"So do you have anything else for me," Major Ryan asked the platoon sergeant. All the other officers had just left the early morning meeting on D + 1 to head back to their respective units...but Sergeant Roy had lingered around longer...since the confidence the officer was exuding was infectious.

"No, sir. That should do it for now," Roy answered, and added, "I guess we'll just wait for your word on when we shove off."

"I'll send a runner over your way as soon as I get the all clear from Colonel Shoup. I still don't trust those flyboys enough to let them drop their ordinance around us. I just can't risk having one of them drop their bombs short and killing some of our own guys. Plus we got Lieutenant Greene here...and he assures me that he's got excellent commo with those two destroyers out there."

Roy acknowledged the lieutenant and then glanced out to sea and saw the two majestic ships steaming back and forth off of Green Beach and smiled broadly. "They sure are a sight to see, that's for sure," he said, appreciating the firepower the two heavily armed ships would bring to the gunfight that lay ahead of them.

"They sure are," Major Ryan agreed. "The funny thing is that I can talk to the captains of those two ships right there...over a thousand yards away...yet I still can't talk to my own Regimental CO... and he's only a few hundred yards away. Makes one wonder, no?" he continued, the frustration obvious in his tone.

"Well, somebody's ass is gonna be in a sling after this is all over, sir...at least I hope so. Whoever put this commo package together should probably lose some rank...do you agree, sir?"

Major Ryan looked at the platoon sergeant and smiled at the idea and then said, "Those decisions are way above my pay grade, sergeant. I'm just a lowly reserve officer with no say so whatsoever. Trust me...the higher ups are not going to come asking me for advice on what should be done for that mishap. And to be honest with you, I don't know exactly what should be done anyway. I'm sure the officer in charge of communications took every precaution possible to make sure the radios would work here. Hey, he'll be in good company since there'll be plenty of blame to go around when this one's all said and done…that's for sure."

"I guess you're right, sir. No point in crying over spilled milk, right. We're here…so let's just get on with it and get it over with. The sooner the better in fact. I'll be waiting on your runner," Roy replied forcefully, still confident of the outcome…despite all the mishaps that had already occurred on this small island. That said, Platoon Sergeant Roy gave the major a quick salute…the snipers be damned. *This man earned that one*, Roy thought, *that's for sure*…and he turned on his heel and left the CP.

• • •

Sergeant Flockerzi turned to the two men who were with him in the sand-bagged bunker at the base of the tower and said, "Look lively…he's comin' back." The two marines were assigned as the platoon sergeant's runners and they had been snoozing like many of the others while waiting for Sergeant Roy to return. They perked up immediately and both men pulled out toothbrushes and began cleaning their weapons. Both men were privates first class and they knew their platoon sergeant would go ballistic if he caught them crapping out while there were still things to be done. PFC Lerman Mudd…the bigger of the two men - and they were both big guys - glanced out of the foxhole and said, "Sure enough…that's him alright. There's no mistaking that man y'all," in a lazy southern drawl.

"Hey, Kentucky," the other runner said with a slightly different accent…since he was from southeastern Pennsylvania, "who do you think would win a fight between you two? Ever thought about it?"

"Are you serious," Mudd answered back, "that man would kill me before I got a punch off. His eyes alone could scare a man to death!" The awe the big marine had for his platoon sergeant was unmistakable…and it was a feeling generally shared by every man in the platoon.

"I was hoping you would have thought otherwise," PFC Larry Rickard said dejected, and added, "I would have placed a bet on that fight with Corporal Staggs for sure. And just so you know…it would

have been against you…since no one can beat up our platoon sergeant…no matter how big they are!"

"Thanks for the support there, Lar," the big Kentuckian replied
and then went on cleaning his M-1 carbine…which looked small in
his hands.

"I wonder how Staggs and the others are doing?" Rickard asked,
now talkative. "I wonder if he asked about them at the meeting?
Don't you think it would be nice to know what's going on with the
other half of our platoon?"

"I've been thinking about them myself since we got here. We have
a lot of buddies in the first squad…and Endres and Staggs are both
topnotch leaders too. I hope they made it in safely…put that's a pipe
dream…I know. I imagine they're over on Red Two somewhere fightin'
for their lives…just like we're going be doin' again at some point today."
PFC Mudd was about to say something else when Sergeant Roy jumped
into their bunker and crouched down…ending the conversation for the
time being.

The platoon sergeant…wasting no time with pleasantries…told
Sergeant Flockerzi to gather up the two squad leaders so he could
share the dope about the upcoming attack. Flockerzi jumped out and
ran off towards their positons…ducking all the while…since it was
now daylight…and while not likely…there just might be some sniper
still lurking about unseen within the marine lines.

In moments, Flockerzi and the two others came running back
and all three of them jumped into the spacious bunker. Sergeant Roy
was already aware of what had happened during the night…since
he had made his rounds of the platoon's positions when dawn first
broke. Taking that into consideration, he addressed Corporal Oliver
in a conciliatory tone and said, "You okay?"

The corporal looked at him and answered, "Yeah…I'll get over
it. I just hate that we had to lose that kid…that's all." Oliver…just
like everyone else…had been fond of Private Svansson and he was
carrying the weight of his death pretty heavily.

Sergeant Roy knew the feeling...since every man that the squad leaders lost was one of his own too...and he told Oliver to put it behind him. "Look," he added, "Varner lost Jefferson yesterday afternoon... and you lost Svansson last night. We didn't see either one of those losses coming...since things seemed to be pretty low key once we got here. It happens...and the longer you're a leader, the more men you're gonna lose. It's something you just gotta come to grips with if you're gonna lead men in combat. Your men did a good job last night...given the circumstances...and we're lucky that we only lost one man. It could have been much worse. They could've gotten all of you if your men hadn't been alert...so let it go and drive on."

The corporal nodded that he understood so Roy let it go and then he began to brief the men on the attack that was scheduled for later in the morning. He explained the details of Major Ryan's plan and where all the units would be located in the attack. Then he told them how they were waiting for the air attack to be cancelled...and that they would be jumping off once that was done. And then he laid out the best news of the day so far...that they'd have two destroyers supporting their attack. All five of men perked up when they heard that good news...since they understood the destructive power of a 5-inch shell just as well as their platoon sergeant did.

Sergeant Roy was starting to tell them about how Major Ryan wanted their Bar-men...Reisman from the 3rd Squad and PFC Kevin Lewis from the 2nd Squad...upfront during the attack when two more men came running over to their bunker.

Lieutenant Greene poked his head over the top of the sandbags and asked, "You guys got any room in there for us?"

"Hop over," Roy said, and all the men inside slid closer to make more room. The two men jumped in and everyone introduced themselves to each other. Then the lieutenant explained why he was there. "I was looking for a good spot to observe the ship fire from...and when I spotted this observation tower I figured it would work perfectly." With that, the lieutenant climbed up the wooden ladder that led to the platform up above them...and within seconds he yelled back down to the runner who was with him, "Tell the major this will work...I can see all the way down to Temakin Point...and over to the east as far as the airfield. This couldn't be better!" The excitement in the officer's voice was unmistakable...and the runner dashed off in the direction of the major's CP with the good news.

The lieutenant then yelled down that the air attack had been cancelled...that a runner from Colonel Shoup had made it over...and he had called it off per Major Ryan's request. Then he added, "The major said to tell you that our attack is going to kick off at eleven hundred hours...and that's after thirty minutes of prep fire from the destroyers. We might even get some of the heavies to lend a hand too!"

"That's great news," Roy shouted back up to the lieutenant...knowing that by heavies he meant battleships and cruisers.

"It sure is," Lieutenant Greene shouted right back, and then he warned, "Look out below!"

Roy looked up quizzically and he watched as the lieutenant pushed the two dead Jap observers out of the sand-bagged OP and over the wooden railing that was built around the edge of the platform. The bodies fell about eighteen feet and hit with a dull thud below and Roy looked at Flockerzi and shook his head. Flockerzi understood the gesture and replied dryly, "Officers...can't live with them...can't live without 'em."

Sergeant Roy smiled at the remark...since he liked the enthusiasm of this young officer...and he appreciated how important his job was. Next, he looked at the watch on his wrist and saw that it was nearing ten o'clock...or 1000 hours...which gave them thirty minutes to get ready. As he turned to alert the men, Sergeant Varner and Corporal Oliver both leapt out of the bunker and headed towards their squad positions. And looking over his shoulder as he ran, Varner yelled out, "Already on it, sarge!"

• • •

At precisely 1030 hours, the western end of Betio began to reverberate as a slew of shells began landing on Temakin Point. The two destroyers hove in close and used their big 5-inch guns to blast the positions on the southwestern corner of the island...but they didn't stop there. They pushed the envelope and moved in closer... knowing that the marines ashore were depending on their fire...and within moments their 40mm pompom guns and 20mm cannons were blasting away as well. The shells left a swath of destruction in their path...killing and wounding many of the Japanese defenders who had managed to survive the first day of battle unscathed. And true to their word, the cruisers and battleships got into the act as well...and their fire completely destroyed whatever hope the intrepid Japanese troops had left.

Like a master at work, Lieutenant Greene then shifted the ships' fire northward...and he walked the rounds right up the beach in a methodical pattern that obliterated most of the bunkers along and behind Green Beach...the very same bunkers that had proved to be so troublesome to the marines as they moved southward the day before.

Even the marines knew something special was happening...and many of them began to cheer as loud as they could in appreciation of the Navy's efforts. They were literally shaking in their holes from the force of the explosions as the rounds hit south of them...and then the explosions began to slowly walk their way towards their lines. At one point, the shells were hitting so close to the marine positions that Lieutenant Greene had to get special approval from the Division Staff to continue the bombardment. The men who would benefit the most from the shelling...the grunt marines...kept yelling, "Keep it coming," and, "that's it, boys, let 'em have it!" over and over again as they got ready to make their attack.

At precisely 1100 hours the shelling ceased...and the silence was incredible. One minute it seemed like the world was falling apart... and the very next minute everything went eerily quiet. But the silence didn't last very long...since the orphans of Major Ryan's command commenced their attack...and they moved down the length of Green Beach with incredible speed. The few Japanese who were still capable put up a tenacious fight...as they always did...put their numbers were nowhere near as plentiful as they had been when the day started. Marine lives were lost of course...since no one was immune from all the fire that came their way...but the casualties were unexpectedly light given the number of men who had been killed on D-Day taking the same exact ground.

Word of their success filtered back to Major Ryan and he reacted just like his men thought he would. "Good...good...good," he kept telling the small staff he had assembled to help him to control the myriads of different units under his command. Then he added, "Tell them to keep pushing...to keep it up! We need this entire beach clear of Japs so we can get some help in here...and then we'll get some rest!"

The men followed his orders to the letter...and by noon...nearly one hour after the attack had started...a young marine put his boot in the water off Temakin Point! Shortly thereafter, a navy spotter aboard one of the destroyers spied one of Captain Jim Crain's men using two flags to communicate via semaphore. His message read, "Marines have secured Japanese from point. Need water badly."

• • •

The incredible success of Major Ryan's attack on the morning of November 21st could not be overstated...since it cut the western end of the island off from the Japanese...and it also freed up an entire beachhead that could be used to land an additional battalion of fresh marines. In addition to that, the thorn known as the *Pocket*...which had been so deadly to so many marines...could be now be attacked from its western flank with renewed vigor.

When the news of Major Ryan's victory finally reached Colonel Shoup's headquarters, a shout of joy went up from both the colonel and his staff...since this was the first real success they had experienced during the battle. Major Culhane walked over to the colonel and extended his hand. Colonel Shoup took it gladly and said, "I've been waiting to hear something good for a while now... and even though it's only a small amount of ground, it's still significant, Tom."

The veteran major...a screamer by nature...smiled a broad, grizzled grin and replied softly, "Now the bastards know we're here to stay. I'll bet Shibasaki will need a new pair of trousers when he catches wind of this!"

The colonel smiled too...even as tired as he was...and replied, "That he will, Tom...that he will!"

Little did either of them know...since they couldn't...that General Shibaski would never learn of the defeat of Commander Takeo Sugai's forces on the Beak and along Green Beach...and given his condition...that a new pair of pants was the very least of his troubles!

CHAPTER 39

While the conditions on the western end of Betio had certainly improved, the situations surrounding the marine forces on Red Beach 2 and 3 had remained stagnant at best. On Red 3, Major Crowe's men were still locked in a life and death struggle with the large bunker complex to the southeast of his command…and with the airfield taxiway directly ahead of them…and no headway had been made whatsoever. The Jap defenses were just too strong and too in depth for the men in his two depleted battalions to overcome…no matter how hard they tried. So Major Crowe had concluded that the best course of action was to play a waiting game and to hold on to what he had. The red-mustachioed major was too much of a fighter to just sit there though…and he had his men continually probing the Japanese lines to spot any weaknesses…but they never found any. Forced between a rock and a hard place, the major realized that his forces would be hemmed in to their beachhead until something broke elsewhere on the island and then he could get more help.

The conditions inland of the Red 2 beachhead had not changed dramatically either. If anything, the situation was actually worse than it was on Red 3 since the men that were there were from three different units…and their ad hoc commander…Lieutenant Jordon… wasn't even a member of the 2nd Division. Jordon was acting as an observer for the newly formed 4th Division…but he had been quickly recruited to take over the 2nd Battalion of the 2nd Regiment when their commander…Lieutenant Amey…had been machine gunned out in the water as he was trying to land. The transition had not been an easy one for Jordan since he didn't know anyone in the 2nd…but he was doing the best he could with a bad hand. During the landings, most of the units in the 2nd Battalion had been decimated…with some companies suffering almost fifty percent casualties as they tried to land on the beach and then move inland. And their officer and senior enlisted men's ranks…from the captain level on down…had been so shattered that many of the platoons and squads that had somehow survived were being led by junior sergeants and corporals. On top of that dilemma, these very same units had landed in a haphazard fashion so there was no symmetry in their positioning. Large gaps existed between them and the coordination that was so necessary to shore up the gaps was non-existent given the heavy fire everyone was under.

The same thing had basically happened to the 1st Battalion of the 2nd when it tried to land behind the 2nd Battalion on D Day. It had met the same fierce fire that the 2nd Battalion had…and it had been cut to pieces as well. But the survivors from the 1st had managed to push through the beachhead and they were now ensconced…trapped was more like it…in the V-shaped area that was bordered by the western end of the main airstrip and the northwestern taxiway. The Japanese had let these men from A and B Companies move into this kill zone and then they sealed it off with machine gun teams that covered both the taxiways and the main runway so there was no means of escape.

The last unit to land on Red 2 was the 1st Battalion of the 8th Regiment and they had come in under intense fire on the second morning of the battle. They were chopped up in identical fashion… just like the first two battalions were…which seemed almost criminal in nature. And to the marines who were forced to endure the spectacle, it seemed like no one in the upper echelons had learned anything from the landings that had already taken place. But the survivors from the 1st of the 8th Regiment were quickly organized by their battalion commander, Major Larry Hays, and he led them over to the right flank of Red 2 where he launched the first coordinated attack against the right flank of the *Pocket* late that afternoon. Even the assistance of another healthy Sherman tank that had finally made it ashore during the night couldn't shift the outcome though…and the attack stalled…just like the ones against the bunker complex on Red 3 did. With no further help coming his way, Major Hays was forced to postpone any additional attacks and he had to wait it out too…just like Major Crowe was doing on Red 1.

• • •

Despite the fact that this was Colonel Shoup's first combat command, he seemed to be a natural at it…which allowed him to see opportunities that other officers in his shoes…or boots…might have missed. He went over to a map that was secured to one of the coconut logs of the bunker his CP was adjacent to and looked it over…yet again. And there it was…the chance he had been waiting for all day. With Green Beach now open to a landing…the next thing he had to do was make sure it stayed that way. And to do that he needed to cut the island in half…which would bottle the Japanese up in the east end of the island. In addition to that…and probably more important now…it would prevent the Japs from using the corridor along the southern shore to move west so they could contest the new marine build up that was about to begin along Green Beach.

The colonel looked around and spotted the man he wanted and called him over again. "Whatta you got, sir?" Major Culhane, his operations officer, asked with aplomb. Even though he had hardly slept a wink, the major was still full of energy…an ability that amazed the colonel given the circumstances they were operating under.

"I need someone to cut this island in half…who can do it?" Colonel Shoup asked in a tired voice.

The major looked at the map and then used his finger to point to the western side of the triangle that was formed by the three runways of the airfield. "Right now we have elements from two companies in there. By all accounts...and I'm not gonna dispute it... they're trapped there. They've been there since yesterday afternoon. So far I haven't been able to get anyone into them...and they can't get anyone out. It's those damn Jap machine guns that seem to be everywhere and anywhere. They've got the two taxiways...the small one in Crowe's area plus the bigger one to the west that Jordan's up against...and the main runway to the south sealed up as tight as a drum. I've lost several runners to those guns already...and it's likely that anyone else I send over won't come back as well."

"What units are in there," the colonel asked, sounding concerned...since he already knew what he was going to ask them to do.

"We've got two companies in there for the most part...all from the First Battalion...and some smaller elements from the Second Battalion as well. Let's see...we got about seventy men from A Company under Captain Bill Bray...and another sixty men or so from B Company under Captain Maxie Williams. We did have wire communications with Bray until about an hour ago...and then the line went dead. But I have a wireman and a corpsman heading that way now. Hopefully, communications with Bray and Williams will be back up in no time. Behind them...on this side of the western taxiway...is Captain Jim Clanahan. He has about seventy-five men with him. Clanahan said that he also managed to corral some machine guns...both light and heavy...from the Regimental Weapons Company and he's gonna use them to help him get across the taxiway so he can join up with Williams and Bray. But so far he and his company are still stuck on this side of the triangle. Now mixed in with Bray and Williams are about twenty-five men from E and F Companies of the 2nd Battalion. As you know...and can see by these figures...the Second Battalion really took it on the chin yesterday when they came in. I'm not telling you anything you didn't already know in that regard."

"Twenty-five guys total? That's it? Those two companies probably started out with nearly one hundred and fifty men each...and
you're telling me that only twenty some odd men made it to their
objective?" Shoup could hardly believe these numbers...but deep
down he knew they were accurate.

"Well...these figures are somewhat old...so we could have lost
more than what I just reported. There are more Second Battalion
men scattered about...here and there...some under Jordan of course.
In fact, they could be right out in front of us for that matter...since
he says he's got about a hundred men with him too...but it's still
hard to account for everybody's whereabouts," the major answered
defensively.

"Yeah...you're probably right," Shoup answered back quickly...
not meaning to challenge the accuracy of Major Culhane's numbers.
Then he told the major that he wanted the men in the triangle to
attack directly across the island. "I want those Japs that are dug in
along the center of Black Beach driven out and I want this island
split in half. I need this island to be cut in two by nightfall. Now get
it done...one way or the other."

There was no mistaking the tone in the colonel's voice...and
Major Culhane...a tough customer in his own right...responded just
like the colonel knew he would.

"I'll get right on it, sir," Major Culhane said unequivocally...and
then...despite what he had already told the colonel about the fate of
the men he had already tried to send over to the triangle...the major
yelled out, "I need another runner over here!"

CHAPTER 40

PFC Lohuis stopped along the seawall and pointed inland. "This is the spot. I remember it perfectly. This is where we make our turn. Captain Bray and Captain Williams are about three hundred yards that way," he said to Pharmacist Mate Fumai.

"Okay," the corpsman answered, "I'll head that way with you...since I told the major I would...but these guys are gonna head back to my platoon. That way they can let them know where we're at. Like I said...Lieutenant Hackett might want to join up with us once he knows there's a bunch more guys over this way." Fumai looked over at PFC Petraglia for confirmation and the lieutenant's runner nodded to the corpsman like he had earlier. "I'll let the lieutenant know as soon as we get back to our perimeter," Petraglia said, agreeing with Fumai's appraisal of the situation.

"Okay...well hopefully I'll see all you guys again real soon. Oh... and don't forget to tell the lieutenant that Thompson made it off the island alright...but Rosenau and DeGeralomo were killed. He'd wanna know that," Fumai added...and then he jumped over the

seawall as PFC Petraglia, Private Hall, and Private Agresta continued their trek westward down the beach.

• • •

PFC Lohuis already had a head start on Fumai since he had kept
walking while the others had stopped to talk. When Fumai caught
up to him, he had paused and was sharpening a stick with his K-bar
knife. Once he had one end sharpened, he flipped it over and cut a
V-shaped notch in the other end. His project done, he slid his knife
back into its scabbard and then he jammed the sharpened end in the
ground. Next, he laid the thin black commo wire across the top of it
so that it was no longer laying across a jagged piece of roofing that
had been blown off a destroyed shack nearby. Then he picked the
spool of commo wire back up by its handle and continued on his
way…the commo wire unraveling softly as he went. Every so often
he would stop again and repeat the process when he came across
something that might cut, snag, or damage the wire he was laying.
At one of these stops, he glanced up at Fumai and said, "It's a little
trick my sergeant taught me. This wire looks tougher than it actually
is…and most anything can cut right through it…so I take these pre-
cautions to protect it. Whatever works, right."

"What if a Jap sees it…won't he cut it?" Fumai wondered, thinking the question sounded reasonable enough to ask.

"There's wire all over the place out here…some stupid Jap will
probably think it's their own stuff and leave it alone. That's what I'm
counting on…at least."

The explanation sounded plausible enough so Fumai never bothered to mention that most of the Jap wire had been buried…and
that it was only exposed…and already cut…where a shell had landed
nearby and blown it up.

As they continued on, Fumai could not help but admire the dil-
igence of Private Lohuis' work…and he complemented him on it.
"Yeah," the private replied, appreciating the gesture, "I try to do my
best. I always have I guess. Plus, the guys up ahead are counting on

me to do it right...since there's nothing worse than when you are stuck and need help and you can't talk to anybody."

Shifting topics, Pharmacist Mate Fumai asked offhandedly, "Do you smell what I smell?"

"Yup," the private answered, crinkling his nose, "what is that?"

"That's all the dead bodies around here beginning to decompose," Fumai answered with authority...even though he had never smelt anything like it before in his life. "It doesn't take too long for a body to swell in this heat. Eventually the bodies split open from the pressure and the insides will burst out. And there must be hundreds of dead men laying around. Heck, we passed nearly a hundred on the beach alone. You add in all the dead Japs out here...the ones we can see...and the ones we can't...and you've got a recipe for disaster. Who knows how long these bodies are gonna lay around before we get some burial parties in here? It could take days at this point...and already the smell is gagging me."

"Geeze," Lohuis replied, "and I thought it was just me. I've never smelled anything so bad in all my life. And I'm from Chicago...so you'd think I'd have developed an immunity to it...with the cattle stockyards and all. It must have been worse for my dad...and his dad before him...with all those slaughter pens going full bore...I guess they just got used to it."

"You like livin' in Chicago?" Fumai asked, steering the conversation away from the topic of dead bodies. And he had never met anyone from there...so he was interested in hearing what Lohuis thought about it.

"Oh yeah...I love it there. Big city...all the stores...nice lake there... it's top-notch in my opinion," Lohuis answered proudly. "Where are you from?" he asked back, happy to be talking about something else besides decomposing human bodies and the smells they created.

"I grew up right outside of New York City...on Long Island. It's a great place...lots to do...but it is getting a little crowded...even for my tastes."

"Sounds nice. I never met anyone from New York City before... so I'm glad we met. Maybe someday I'll get to visit there. I mean who doesn't grow up wanting to see the Statue of Liberty...and the Empire State building...and Wall Street!"

"Yeah...I'm glad we met too. You're good company, Lohuis," Fumai agreed...but the rest of their journey was spent in silence... since the western taxiway...and the enemy machine gunners who were guarding it...were right up ahead.

• • •

The two men sat in a foxhole on the fringe of the taxiway and considered their options. "It doesn't look like much...but when those machine guns open up, you'll wish you were somewhere else...that's for sure," PFC Lohuis said in a whisper. He then went on to describe how harrowing it had been when he crossed it the last time. "Getting there wasn't so bad," he explained, "it was almost like the Japs wanted us in there. But when I crossed over a few hours ago it was a nightmare. There must have been at least five machine guns firing at me...bullets were flying by so thick I could almost touch them...yet all I got was this nick in my pants. How's that for luck, huh."

"You think they're still out there," Fumai asked...wishing he had not come now.

"Oh, they're out there alright. Where would they go? They obviously know this area is important...just like we do...so they're gonna do everything they can to keep us out of it."

"Wonderful," was all Fumai could muster in return.

"So here's my plan," Lohuis said.

"I'm listening," Fumai replied...still unnerved.

"I say we go over together...instead of separately. We make one mad dash and just get it over with. The Japs will be ready for the next guy if one guy goes over and makes it...and I don't plan on going second so I think you'll agree with me."

Fumai couldn't agree more and before they knew it, both men were sprinting across the small runway with reckless abandon. This one was only one hundred yards wide…but it felt like a thousand to the two men when the Jap gunners opened up on them. Just like Lohuis had said, bullets began ricocheting off the packed surface of the taxiway all around them and Fumai could hear the zipping sound as other bullets flew by his head. They had made it almost half way when Lohuis suddenly lost his balance and fell down…and the spool of wire and the batteries went flying ahead of him. He had been slightly ahead of Fumai when it happened…and Fumai had not seen him get hit…so he just assumed the private had merely fallen. Despite the fire, Fumai came to a stop and grabbed Lohuis by the arm and helped him to his feet.

"Thanks," the PFC said, "I can't believe I just tripped out here like that…with the Japs trying to kill us and all."

"No problem," Fumai shouted back…and then he watched in horror as a stream of machine gun bullets laced Lohuis right through the mid-section…and nearly cutting him in half. Fumai knew he was dead…there was no mistaking it…since he had seen plenty of men get hit and killed already in two days of fighting. Reacting instinctively, he let go of Lohuis' arm and left him where he had fallen… since there was nothing he could do for him. Then he spotted the spool of commo wire ahead of him. He ran over to it…retrieved it… and then he dashed the rest of the way across without being hit…a miracle if there ever was one. No sooner had he made it across then he spotted an empty shell hole and dove in…exhausted and out of breath from his latest brush with death. He crossed himself and said, "Jesus…I will go to church every Sunday…even if the Giants are playing…for the rest of my life if you let me live through this in one piece…I promise!"

All of a sudden a man appeared out of nowhere and he jumped into the shell hole with Fumai. At first Fumai thought it was a Jap… and he wished that he had taken a weapon with him…like Lohuis had advised back at the CP. But the pharmacist mate had passed on the recommendation…and he now he was going to pay the price

---

for doing so. He reached to his web belt and tried to pull his knife out...but then he realized that his adversary was wearing a marine uniform that was covered in dust...and carrying an M-1 rifle. "You nearly scared me to death," Fumai yelled out excitedly as the adrenaline still pumped through his body. "Who the hell are you anyway!" he added as an afterthought.

"I'm with Alpha Company. Captain Bray saw what you did and sent me over to get the commo wire." The marine held out his hand...and Fumai...still reeling from the whole experience...simply handed the spool over to him. "Thanks. Our company's right over there," he said, pointing to the left, and looking at Fumai's kit, he added, "You're a sight for sore eyes...we got several guys that are wounded...and they can use your skills."

Fumai thanked the man for the compliment and asked him how many men were wounded. In reply, the private told him that there were three guys with wounds that required his attention... and another guy who was probably going to die no matter what Fumai did...since he had been shot through the head. "The guy's still hanging on somehow. He's breathing, doc, but it doesn't sound very good."

Since he was a pharmacist mate, the young private had immediately christened Fumai with the esteemed title of "doc" and it always made Fumai feel good about the decision he had made to be one. The private then went on to say that they had lost a man during the night... that he had bled out after being shot in the neck by a sniper. "You wouldn't have been able to do anything for him either," the marine emphasized...seemingly granting Fumai forgiveness for not being there to help.

"Well, I'll do the best I can with the others...count on that," Fumai assured him...and then he told him he was ready to head over that way...since he had a chance to catch his wind.

"Let's go then," the marine said...and they dashed over to Captain Bray's makeshift CP.

Pharmacist Mate Fumai immediately introduced himself to the captain and he noticed that he had a dressing wrapped around his left leg. "Are you okay, sir?" Fumai inquired…and added, "Nobody told me you were wounded."

"Don't worry about it," the captain replied…and he told the corpsman that he had been grazed by a bullet yesterday. "It's not bleeding as far as I can tell…and it doesn't really hurt so I'm dealing with it. We got guys hit far worse than me…just look after them, okay." Fumai replied that he was there to help out as best he could and the captain nodded agreeably. He pointed over to three men who were laying on their backs…and he said, "Those are your customers…treat them right…they're good boys." Then Captain Bray thanked him for getting the wire over to them…since they had been able to reestablish contact with Major Culhane already as a result of his efforts. "The major told me that he wants us to launch an attack against the southern shoreline," he added, "and we're gonna have a devil of a time crossin' that big runway out there. The Japs gotta have that damn thing covered from one end to the other with machine guns. Who knows how many men we're going to lose trying to get across that one?" The captain looked at Fumai plaintively… and understanding his predicament…Fumai nodded back. The captain then looked at his watch and said that the attack would kick off shortly…since it was just after thirteen hundred hours…and the major wanted their men over there as soon as possible. "Since we're going to be moving out of here, do what you can to make those men as comfortable as you can…and then follow us over. You're probably going have more patients to take care of after we're done fighting our way over there."

Fumai acknowledged the captain's request and headed right over to the three men who were lying on their backs inside a twenty-foot wide circle of debris that the other men had piled up in the hopes of giving themselves some cover from the snipers in the area. The little fort had seemed to work since no one inside it had been wounded or killed after they built it. Fumai then noticed that a body was lying off by itself...and it had a poncho draped over it so he knew this was the man who had died during the night. Nearby was another man who looked like he might be alive...but on further inspection Fumai could see that he was dead too...and that he was a first lieutenant. He had been shot through one eye and there was a fairly large exit hole on the backside of his head. This was the other man that Fumai had been told about...the one that had been struggling for breath... and given the severity of his wound...it was no wonder why. That the marine officer had lasted as long as he did was a testament to his will to live...but he had eventually lost that battle and now he was stone dead. Fumai noticed a backpack laying nearby and he found just what he was looking for secured to it. The pharmacist mate untied the poncho and unrolled it so he could cover him up...just like the other man was. In doing so, Fumai noticed that no one had removed the officer's map case and a nice pair of binoculars were still tangling from his neck. *Strange*, Fumai thought...but he left the two items where they were...since he didn't need either one to perform his job. Then...as he placed the poncho over the man...he ran into a problem. He quickly noted that this man was several inches taller than the other guy was...so his body couldn't be completely covered by the poncho. Fumai realized this when he slid the poncho up over the man's face and his boots...or boondockers as the marines like to call them...popped out. Fumai knew that leaving his feet exposed was a far better option than leaving his mangled face uncovered...so he just left it like it was.

Then the corpsman went over to the three wounded men and looked each of them over. They were all conscious and each of them had a large wound...which seemed consistent with the fact that the area was ringed by Japanese machine guns...but none of the wounds appeared to be life threatening. The wounds had also been bandaged already...and whoever had done it had done a fairly good job of it... since none of the wounds were bleeding...so there was very little for

Fumai to actually do. Thankfully, the men were alert...since they hadn't been given any morphine...and they were still holding on to their rifles...so they could defend themselves if they were forced to. One man with a nasty thigh wound was struggling to get up and Fumai went over and helped him into a sitting position so he could be see what was coming his way. That...and the fact that two other riflemen had volunteered to stay back with them...made Fumai feel a lot better about the prospect of leaving them behind. And when the attack against southern shoreline finally got underway...he bade his charges farewell...and he took off running in the direction of Black Beach.

• • •

While the number of men involved in the attack against the southern shoreline was not that significant...what they achieved was certainly so. In a stroke of luck, the one hundred and fifty or so men under Captain Bray and Captain Williams suffered minimal casualties as they cut across the main obstacle that had been blocking their path to the south for over twenty-four hours...the large, flat, and fully-exposed main runway that dominated the middle of the island. Maybe it was the sight of so many men getting up at once that intimidated the Jap machine gunners who were supposed to be guarding it...and rather than poking this hornet's nest and stirring it up... they just let them go across unimpeded. Or maybe they thought that the defensive network that had been set up along Black Beach was so formidable that the troops over there could take on and defeat this large marine force all on its own. For whatever reason, most of men under Williams and Bray were able to cross this wide, daunting gauntlet in one piece...an outcome they would never have predicted or anticipated while they were surrounded and cut off in the airfield triangle.

And *Lady Luck* wasn't done with the men of the 1st of the 2nd quite yet...since their attack led them right into the one and only soft spot in the Japanese defensive scheme along the southern coast. Instead of butting their heads against an intricate complex of bunkers and foxholes, the men found a shallow, two-hundred-yard-long anti-tank ditch that had been dug parallel to Black Beach and they jumped in and occupied it from one end to the other. And from their new home they could easily see the ocean sparkling in the distance beyond...and thus they had achieved the incredibly crucial goal of cutting the island in two...just like the colonel wanted!

It didn't take the Japanese long to discover that their lines running along the southern coast had been punctured since the marines from A and B Company began disrupting the movement of their troops from the eastern end of the island to the western end...where reinforcements were needed. To repair this breech and drive the marines out, the Japanese began attacking both ends of the tank ditch simultaneously and the fierce battle that the marines had been anticipating all along now ensued. It lasted the rest of the afternoon and well into the night and the marines were slowly whittled down as the number of killed and wounded began piling up. And Pharmacist Mate Fumai...who had made it over to the ditch safely...found himself in the thick of the fighting yet again!

• • •

When Tom Fumai had first jumped into the trench, things had been relatively quiet...but they didn't stay that way for long. As the afternoon dragged along, Fumai quickly figured out that the two most dangerous places to be in the trench were at both ends of it... since that's where most of the casualties were occurring. It was no picnic to be stationed near the middle either though...since the Japanese were firing down the length of the trench from both directions when they waged their attacks against the ends. He heard, "Corpsman!" being yelled continually...and he would scurry down to the end of the trench that the call had come from...locate the wounded man...and then drag or walk him back to the center of the trench where he had established a casualty collection point. There he'd tend to the marine's wounds as best he could...using whatever bandages or dressings the man had on him first...since his medical supplies were dwindling away as the casualties mounted up. And before long he was completely out...so he resorted to taking the first aid packets off the dead men that were laying around him. When that option was exhausted, he would turn to the men who were not wounded and ask them to donate theirs... and no one refused his request. In that simple way he was able to do the best he could for all the men who came under his care...and everyone...from the two captains on down to the junior privates... appreciated his efforts and the dedication he displayed in keeping them alive.

• • •

Captain Maxie Williams, the CO of B Company, watched in admiration as Pharmacist Mate Fumai struggled with a wounded marine. Williams glanced over at another marine who was laying against the inland side of the trench and yelled, "Hey, you!" The young marine...who was guarding against an attack from the direction of the main airstrip...looked over his shoulder and saw the captain.

"Me?" he mouthed, pointing at himself.

"Yeah, you!" he shouted back, "Come over here."

The marine obeyed the captain's order immediately and left his position alongside the trench and knelt beside the captain...who was standing up. The grizzled-looking officer looked down at the private and said, "I want you to assist doc there with the wounded. We got too many wounded for just one man to handle so from now on you are his assistant. Do whatever he tells you to do... understood."

"Yes, sir!" the boy marine responded enthusiastically...and he ran over to the corpsman who was dragging another marine down the center of the trench. The kid tapped Fumai on the shoulder and the corpsman stopped to see what he wanted.

"Captain Williams thinks you need help...and he sent me over," the marine proclaimed proudly, honored to be given such an important assignment by his commanding officer.

"Well, that was nice of him," Fumai responded, "I can definitely use a hand...dragging all these guys around has about worn me out. So what do I call you?"

"You mean what's my name?" the young private asked back happily.

"Yeah, what's your name? I gotta call ya something...so I might as well call you by your name, right," Fumai answered, and added, "I mean if I just yell out *Private* every time I need you...well, half this place will come running over."

"Oh," the private said laughing, "I guess that makes sense. My name is Private Marcy...Reed Marcy...I'm from Georgia. And I'm eighteen...but everyone thinks I look younger." Just then several bullets went whizzing through the trench and the private and the corpsman both ducked down to avoid getting hit. Neither of them were hit and both men stood back up and Fumai noticed that Marcy still had a big grin on his face. *This kid's got more guts than brains,* Fumai thought to himself...*since he doesn't appear to be fazed by what's going on around here.*

"Okay, Private Marcy," Fumai replied, "nice to meet you. And my name is Pharmacist Mate Fumai...Tom Fumai. And I am twenty...but I think I've aged about a hundred years while I've been on this island," and the corpsman stuck out his hand and the private shook it with his own. And for the rest of the afternoon, the two of them kept hauling one wounded man after another down to the collection point...with the young Marcy smiling the entire time.

• • •

Around 1600 hours, Captain Bray met with Captain Williams to talk over the dire situation confronting them. After two hours of hard fighting, the two companies could only put up about a hundred effectives between them...since ten men had been killed and another thirty were wounded. Plus, they now running short of everything a marine unit needed to survive for any amount of time as well... especially in combat.

"How are you fixed for ammunition?" Captain Bray asked his counterpart from B Company, and then he added, "cause we hurting. I'm short rifle ammo...and we're down to almost nothing for our automatic weapons. And we just used up the last of our grenades."

"We're in the same boat," Captain Williams said gravely...and looking around at the men baking in the hot sun...he added, "and we need water desperately...and food too for that matter."

"So do we," Bray confirmed sadly.

"Well, the bottom line is that we'll just have to gut it out as long as we can," Williams said firmly, "I've already witnessed some of our boys fighting hand-to-hand with the Japs. Brutal stuff...rifle butts and bayonets. I thought those days were over...but I guessed wrong."

"Well, we don't intend on leaving--"

"Wait a minute...what the hell is that?" Major Williams said, interrupting Captain Bray in midsentence...and the two of them looked up to see an amtrac approaching their position.

The amtrac was moving as fast as it could travel...around twelve miles per hour...since the driver was pushing it to the limit. All of a sudden the driver spotted the marines waving from the anti-tank ditch and he pulled back on the steering gear and it slewed to a stop...just short of the lip of the trench. "How'd I do," the driver yelled as he peered at the marines through the glass window in the cab.

"Nice work...real nice work there," one of the marines yelled back, appreciating the driver's skill in handling the big, fourteen-ton vehicle.

With that, several marines jumped over the gunwale and quickly took up firing positions along the side of the trench...mimicking the men that we're already there. Then two more men jumped out...both officers...and the two captains looked at each other and smiled.

One of the arriving officers...a first lieutenant...shouted at the men who had just laid down against the trench. "Boys, that amtrac ain't gonna unload itself..." and the men jumped back up as the driver and the crew chief began throwing crates of ammunition over the side. Next came five-gallon metal cans filled with water...and then boxes of C rations were tossed over the gunwale as well. The men picked them up and began stacking them in separate piles in the ditch so the contents could be distributed as needed.

"Now that's more like it," First Lieutenant Ken Konstanzer said, "I knew ya had it in ya." The man's New York accent came through clearly...and several men smiled at the sound of it.

"Well, it's about time...LT," Captain Williams drawled. Williams was good friends with the lieutenant...who was the executive officer of F Company...and he addressed him by his nickname...which stood for *Long Time*. Konstanzer had been an enlisted man before he became an officer so he was slightly older than his lieutenant counterparts...and he had also spent more time in the Marine Corps...thus earning the pithy sobriquet.

"Yeah, I thought I'd better get over here and give you First Battalion boys a hand. It seems I've spent my entire career looking after you guys...when are you gonna cut me a break," the lieutenant joked right back...and he went right over to the captain and the two embraced in a hug. "It's good to see ya, Maxie," Konstanzer said...and then he turned to Captain Bray and said, "You too, Bill."

Captain Bray went over and shook his hand...and then said, "Let's be careful out here...there are Jap snipers all over the place," and he pointed to a line of marines laying on the ground dead.

"So it's been that rough over here? Can ya hold?"

"We can with those extra men you just brought in...and those supplies are a big help," the officer answered back.

"That's the spirit," Konstanzer said, offering encouragement to the two men who had done so much already. And then the lieutenant turned to the other officer who had been standing quietly by...just listening to their conversation...and said, "I'm sorry about that, sir. It was just time for a little *Auld Lang Syne* since I served with this yard bird Williams for a long time and we know each other well."

"No problem, lieutenant," the lieutenant colonel said, then added, "it was nice to see given what we've all been through so far." Then Lieutenant Colonel Walt Jordan...the observer from the 4th Division...turned to the two other officers and introduced himself. "We didn't get a chance to meet yesterday...for obvious reasons," he said directly.

"How are things going with the Second, sir?" Captain Williams asked.

"Well, I brought over all of them that I could find. Twenty in all. I'm sure there are others scattered about throughout the beachhead. We'll find out when this donnybrook is over, I guess," he said...and he nodded at the men who were taking up positions along the walls of the trench.

"Just twenty, sir. That's all?" Captain Bray questioned.

"Just twenty...like I said," the acting commander of the 2nd Battalion replied dourly.

"My God," Captain Williams said, joining in. "We have a little over twenty of them here with us. So with your twenty that makes--"

"Just shy of fifty," Lieutenant Konstanzer jumped in, adding, "You were always horrible with numbers, Maxie. And you do know that I went to Prep School...so my intellectual capacity is nothing short of marvelous!"

Captain Bray didn't know Konstanzer quite as well as Captain Williams did so he wasn't sure if the lieutenant was being serious... or just joking like he normally did. And given their current predicament, he focused in on the losses of his sister battalion and said, "Less than fifty men out of an entire battalion?" Bray sounded like he couldn't believe what he was hearing. "That's about a platoon's worth of men left out of nearly eight hundred and fifty? That just can't be right. There have to be more somewhere. They couldn't have lost that many men...it's impossible."

"All I can tell you is that the ones I had with me are here now," Lieutenant Colonel Jordan emphasized...and then he added, "And the good news I have for you is that your battalion commander is on the way over too. At least he should be...if he can fight his way through the triangle. With so few men of the Second here, Colonel Shoup thought that it would be better to have your own commanding officer take over. I will leave the men of the Second under his control...and then you can sort it out later when the shooting stops."

"Major Kyle is coming over here?" Captain Williams asked incredulously.

"He is," Jordan replied. Then he explained that Major Kyle would be arriving in about an hour...that he would be coming in an amtrac loaded with supplies...and that the battalion's C Company was on its way too...if they could break through.

"Do you know who's in command of C Company, sir," Captain Bray asked...hoping that his friend, Captain Jim Clanahan, was still alive.

"I believe Clanahan's still in charge of C Company...but his officers have taken a beating. I believe he's had two of his platoon leaders killed already and another wounded. Clanahan was alive though," Lieutenant Colonel Jordan answered, "at least he was when I headed this way. He got hung up on the western side of the airfield triangle too. The Japs must have shifted some machine gun teams from the *Pocket* over to that area along the western taxiway during the night...cause he was having a devil of a time trying to get across it earlier today. But Colonel Shoup told him to just keep trying...and then to link up with your position here...once he's broken through."

Captain Bray smiled at the announcement and he turned to Captain Williams and said, "Good old Clanahan's on his way. How about that, Maxie! When he gets here we'll have all three companies...A...B...and C...together in one spot. I bet there aren't too many battalions that can say that!" The excitement in Bray's voice was evident and it made the other men feel confident that the battle was finally turning a corner.

And just like Jordan had predicted...at 1800 hours an amtrac carrying Major Wood Kyle came roaring into the area. Marines jumped out...just like before...but this time Major Kyle was the first one out. He immediately went over and shook hands with his two company commanders and congratulated them on doing a spectacular job. Then he got with Lieutenant Jordan and told him that he would assume command...since Colonel Shoup wanted it that way.

"Okay then," Jordan said, "I guess I'll head back. Anything you want me to tell the colonel?"

"No...I've got everything locked down. Just try to take as many wounded outta here as you can...that would be a big help."

"No problem there," Jordan replied...and then the major turned and yelled over to Captain Bray and Captain Williams to start getting the wounded loaded aboard the two tractors. Then he turned back to Lieutenant Colonel Jordan and said, "By the way...everyone...and I mean everyone...appreciates what you did yesterday. And I'm not telling you that to blow smoke up your ass, sir. I spoke to the colonel himself and he knows that you're one of the reasons we're finally licking the Japs. You were tasked with an impossible situation...and it was handed to you at the worst possible time...and you still kicked butt...and I...for one...know that the Fourth Division is getting themselves one fine officer."

"Thank you, major, that means a lot to me," Jordan replied, shaking his head affirmatively...and when the loading of the wounded was finished...he climbed back into the amtrac and the driver pushed the starter button. The engine roared back to life...white smoke belching out of its exhaust...and Jordan noticed that the am-trac was just as crowed as when he had come over...only this time the cargo was different. The driver manipulated the steering levers and the amtrac...following his deft guidance...made a tight U-turn. With its bow pointing northward, the driver gunned the engine again and he made a beeline for the opposite coast and safety...just as the sun began to set in the western sky. Jordan glanced in that direction and saw some movement in the distance. Shielding his eyes against the last rays of the setting sun, he was able to make out a large group of marines heading towards the southern shore...and he knew that Jim Clanahan had finally broken through.

CHAPTER 41

"**D**o you think Cohen made it?" The lieutenant asked off-handedly. He had taken a black book out of his utility shirt pocket and was scribbling something in it as he asked the question.

Sergeant Tom Endres, a squad leader of the lieutenant's platoon, looked over and replied, "Cohen?"

"You know...the man that Petraglia and Agresta carried outta here. Do you think they were able to get him back in time to save him?" the platoon commander clarified.

"Oh, him..." Sergeant Endres replied, suddenly realizing who the lieutenant was referring to. "Yeah, I think he did...now that you mention it. He's big...and certainly looked strong. I'll bet he could do a lot of pull ups and push ups. Did you see the size of his arms?" The sergeant...a workout freak and a legend in the gym...was obviously impressed with Cohen's appearance. Then he noticed the book the lieutenant had in his hands and asked, "What's that you have there?"

The lieutenant finished drawing a line through one of the names that he had written down during the night when he had popped suddenly awake to check on the men in the foxhole with him. The entry read: McGovern, Charles SGT. Then he had added to it: KIA 21 Nov 1943 Red 2. He had a few more updates to make when the sergeant asked him about it. "Oh…this," he replied, holding up a small, tattered, black book. "I have kept this on me since I made second lieutenant. I keep track of all the guys that have served under me. It even made it through Guadalcanal intact somehow."

"That thing made it through the *Canal*? With as wet as it was there?" Endres was astonished. "That's one tough little book you got there, sir!"

The lieutenant held the book up…admiring it…and then said, "You're in here too."

"Lemme see," the tough sergeant said…eager to see his name for some reason.

Lieutenant Hackett held the book open to where his name was written down…and Endres noted all the other names with lines drawn through them. *I sure hope mine doesn't get one of those lines*, he thought to himself. Then he said, "That's great that you do that, sir. Keepin' track of all of us like that. Heck, I had already forgotten Cohen's name…and you got a lot more guys to keep tabs on than I do. I admire that, sir."

"Thanks, sergeant," Hackett said…and added, "I just hate having to draw those the damn lines through them. I guess that's what war really is…a line through a name…not much more than that. I can't wait until it's all over with…I'm tired of losing men."

The sergeant understood exactly what the lieutenant was feeling…since he had lost a lot of his men here too…and on Guadalcanal as well. And like the lieutenant, he had wondered many times when it would all be over with…but he had never expressed it in front of the men the way the lieutenant was able to. He had worked very hard to maintain a tough exterior to all the guys he led…and he didn't want to jeopardize the *persona* he had created by letting his men know how he felt. In an odd way, he was sort of jealous that the lieutenant could bare his soul and still keep the respect of the men in place. *I'm gonna have to lighten up at some point*, he thought silently again...*if the lieutenant can do it...and not lose respect...then so can I.* Suddenly the sergeant felt like a weight had been lifted off his shoulders...and a big smile creased his big red face.

The lieutenant noticed it and said, "What's got you feelin' so good. We've seen nothing but death out here...and you're smiling about it? Come on...lemme in on your secret to staying happy through all of this."

"If I gave away my secret...everybody'd be happy and we'd never get down to the business of killing these Japs, sir...so I can't let on what it is that just made me feel that way...okay, sir," Endres answered back...wanting to tell him...but not wanting to as well.

The lieutenant accepted his response and let it go...knowing that Sergeant Endres would cave in somewhere down the road and tell him. Then he said, "Is it me...or is this place starting to stink. We've been around dead bodies before...on the *Canal*...but it never got this bad. Do you remember it being like this?"

"No, sir. I don't. I've never experienced anything like this either. It seems like the smell is sticking to everything. I can even taste it when I take a drink outta my canteen. The men have begun to complain about it too...I mean who can exist under these conditions. I wonder if it bothers the Japs the same way it does us?"

Now that he had mentioned water, Hackett noticed that one of the sergeant's canteen pouches was empty...but the other one was there. "You got any water left?" he asked.

"Yes, sir. That I do," he answered.

"What happened to your other canteen?" The lieutenant was curious since Sergeant Endres had always been hard on his men about keeping tabs on their own gear.

"Oh, I must've lost it somehow. Not like me...I know. Can't really tell my men to do something if I don't," the sergeant said back... knowing that he had never lost any of his gear...ever...and certainly not one of his canteens!

The lieutenant was going to pay him a complement...but all of a sudden a voice yelled out, "We got runners comin' in!"

Everybody turned in the direction of the beach to look...and before long they could tell that the three men coming in were Petraglia, Agresta, and Hall...the same ones who had left earlier to bring the wounded men to the pier.

PFC Petraglia...the platoon commander's runner...came over and sat down beside the lieutenant while the two others made their way over to the squads they had been assigned to. "Well, that job's finished...and don't ask me to do that again, sir...since it's backbreaking work...and a runner isn't supposed to be doing stuff like that," Petraglia said without waiting. He and the lieutenant had a very good relationship...one that went all the way back to Guadalcanal...so he could get away with a lot of stuff that no one else in the platoon would ever think of saying or doing around the lieutenant.

"Quit your griping and give me a proper report or I'll put you on stretcher duty from here on out," Hackett said seriously...making his point but doing so without really coming down on Petraglia for acting so casual towards him.

"Okay, sir. We got Cohen back to the pier and the doc there said he was going to make it. On the way, we ran into PFC Hall and Private Donahay...or Dona something...I can't remember the guy's name exactly...but he was the guy that got hit in the eye. Well he's dead. He got hit again by a sniper...but Hall made the Jap pay for it. He killed him with his knife...Jim Bowie style. Oh...and while we were at the pier, we ran into our corpsman...Fumai!" Petraglia then gave Lieutenant Hackett the breakdown on the casualties that Fumai had told him about.

While Petraglia was still talking, the lieutenant pulled his black book out of his pocket again and he started drawing lines through a few names and then he made the appropriate notations based on what Petraglia and Fumai had reported. His runner had seen him do this before…especially on Guadalcanal…but he had not seen him do it on Betio so far so he let him finish. When Hackett put his book away, the runner continued his report. "Things are really starting to shape up back at the pier, sir. A ton of supplies are making it in and they're stacking the stuff all over the place."

"Did you see any water down there? It would have been in five-gallon cans. That's what we were told in the briefings anyway."

"No, sir, I didn't," Petraglia answered, "and I went looking for it while Agresta and Hall there took a snooze. I did get us some ammo at least. I'll have them distribute it evenly…like we normally do."

"Okay…do that," Lieutenant Hackett replied back.

"Oh…and one more thing. It seems our corpsman got detailed by none other than Major Culhane himself to help out with some guys from the First Battalion that are surrounded somewhere over that way." Petraglia stood up and pointed to the left…towards the southeast…where the western taxiway and the main runway met. He quickly sat back down and said, "Are there still snipers over this way?"

"Of course," the lieutenant replied, "they're all over the place." No sooner had the words left his mouth then a bullet went zinging through the area and he added, "See what I mean."

"Thanks for the heads up, sir," his runner quipped back.

"Ahuh," the lieutenant shot back…and then asked, "Is that it?"

"I went over everything with a fine-toothed comb, sir…that's all I got."

"Outstanding work…as usual. You just might get yourself a battlefield promotion if you keep this up, PFC Petraglia. Now go do whatever you got to do…cause we're going to be moving out shortly. Time to get back in the war!" the lieutenant said seriously…and then added, "and let the other guys know as well. It's time to get our game faces back on."

"Yes, sir!" Petraglia responded…knowing that the lieutenant liked to use football analogies a lot…especially since he had been a star defensive back at the Naval Academy. And Petraglia had been around the lieutenant long enough to know that when he started using football references, he usually meant business.

"Everybody up and adam," Petraglia yelled getting up, "it's game time again," and the lieutenant smiled as he called for his three squad leaders...Endres...Ingunza...and Mornston...to come over so he could give them the dope on the upcoming move.

• • •

Within minutes, Lieutenant Hackett and the rest of his charges were heading to the southwest...towards the area Petraglia had pointed to earlier. The lieutenant had consulted his map one more time...so he knew exactly where he was...and where he wanted to go. Based on the information Petraglia had given him, he figured that the men who were trapped in the airfield triangle could probably use their help the most...so his plan was to head that way and hit the flank of the Japanese that were positioned along the smaller western taxiway. With them out of the way, he could move his men into the triangle area bordered by the taxiway and main runway and link up with the men from the 1st Battalion who were holding out there. The three squad leaders agreed with the plan as well...and the men under them liked it too...since it made them feel like they were *the cavalry riding to the rescue!*

To orient their move, Lieutenant Hackett had picked out a large, three-sided airplane revetment that sat on the northwest side of the western taxiway all by itself. He figured that it would be as good as any spot to fight from...since it looked like a small fort...minus one side...on his map. *If we end up running into something we can't handle,* he thought, *we can always hole up there until someone comes for us I guess.*

The platoon hadn't traveled too far when they noticed the large, rectangular-shaped apron of the main runway off to their right. Even at this distance it looked intimidating...since it was flat and open and it seemed to stretch on forever in all directions. A long line of eleven aircraft revetments ran down the northwestern corner of it and a few of them had been damaged in the naval bombardment… but most were still standing in perfect condition. The revetments were there to protect the Japanese fighters, bombers, and reconnaissance aircraft that had flown off the island in better times…but they were completely empty of aircraft now. The revetment they were looking for was built just like these were…out of stacked coconut logs secured by braces…but it was still another one hundred or so yards away from where they were.

At this point, the lieutenant and his sixteen men began angling their way to their left and the terrain seemed to open up more since there were fewer trees in the area. Debris still littered the ground as far as they could see…so it wasn't hard to find cover to hide behind…and like before…Hackett's men advanced by leapfrogging from one place to another. PFC Feeney was out front…as usual… and all of a sudden he raised his arm as a signal to hit the deck. Everyone jumped down and stayed right where they were…except for the lieutenant…who quickly made his way up to Feeney…who was hiding behind a metal 55-gallon drum that had been tipped over. The lieutenant took a whiff of the air, looked at the drum, and said, "You ever smell aviation fuel before?"

"Yes, sir…why do you ask?" the private first class answered evenly.

"Because we're lying behind a barrel that's about full of the stuff…that's why…and all it takes is one bullet to touch it off…and then you and me end up like burnt matchsticks…that's why," the lieutenant pointed out.

Feeney…no dummy…took the reprimand in stride and said, "Sorry, lieutenant," and then he pulled out two pieces of cotton that he had stuffed up his nose. "It's the smell of the dead bodies, sir…I couldn't take it anymore. I've already puked twice from it."

"I hear you," Hackett replied good-naturedly…and then he grabbed one of the cotton balls and jammed it up one of his own nostrils and added, "Good idea…I appreciate that."

Feeney shrugged, put the other ball back into his nose, and said, "Look over there...to the right...along both sides of the runway." As the lieutenant scanned the ground, Feeney said, "You see what I see?"

"Am I missing something...what am I looking for?" Hackett answered back, squinting to see what his point man...who had incredible eyesight...was seeing.

"They're hard to make out...crafty little bastards that they are... but if you look closely...you can make out a bunch of foxholes. I spotted their tan helmets popping up and down as they were firing on that group over there."

"What group?" the lieutenant responded, still trying to see the Japs.

"Them." Feeney pointed to his left and before long the lieutenant was able to make out a large group of marines who...like his men... were hiding behind whatever cover they could find. "I wonder who that is," Hackett replied. "Maybe they're our guys who made it in on Red Two. I wonder if Platoon Sergeant Roy is over there...wondering where we're at too."

"Could be...no telling this far away though," the private first class replied evenly.

As they were watching, half a squad of six men from the group of marines they had spotted jumped up and tried to advance their way across the taxiway. Just as suddenly, a torrent of machine gun fire was unleashed their way by the Japs that Feeney had pointed out. Only the first three men made it across successfully. The trailing three marines never had a chance...and they were gunned down near the middle of the strip. The lieutenant looked more closely now and he could make out more marines laying lifeless in the distance... men who had been shot down trying to cross the taxiway earlier. And then ...to his horror...the Jap gunners began machine gunning the dead men laying on the taxiway...chopping their bodies to pieces...and sending a message to the marines who would try to cross in the future. "They can't get across," he said angrily, "not with that Jap machine gun fire as heavy as it is." To confirm this, a man in a crater across the way held up a hand and kept moving it back in forth in an attempt to warn the other marines not to cross.

Sensing their desperation, the lieutenant said, "I'm going to bring everybody up...and we're gonna take those Jap guns on. Maybe that'll take some of the heat off those guys up there and a few more of them can get over."

Feeney nodded his head...knowing the lieutenant never passed up a fight...and he made sure his Thompson submachine gun was ready to go. He blew some sand dust off the receiver and pulled the charging handle all the way to the rear. When it hit the stop, he released it and it snapped forward...locked and loaded.

Lieutenant Hackett slithered his way back to where Sergeant Endres was waiting and indicated that he wanted the two other squad leaders and his runner to meet him there. They immediately made their way over to him and he explained the situation confronting them. Then he told them that they were going to crawl up to Feeney and form a lazy L with the short side of the L angling back towards the revetments they had just passed. "I want our line set up that way so we can put the bulk of our fire on the Japs that are across from us. But I also want to refuse our line to the right... just in case there are some Japs holed up around those revetments behind us. Everybody got it," he said.

"Refuse, sir?" Ingunza asked.

"Yeah...refuse our line...you know," the lieutenant replied back.

"Uhhh...what exactly does that mean," Ingunza said shyly.

PFC Edward "Harry" Mornston...a veteran who had fought with the 1st Marine Parachute Battalion on Gavutu Island and at the battle for Edson's Ridge on Guadalcanal...smirked at Ingunza's lack of military terminology and said, "Corporal...you *refuse* your line to counter a flank attack. It simply means to bend it back...in Jersey-speak."

Ingunza shot a glance at Mornston that looked like he wanted to kill the private with his bare hands…something he may have been able to do even though Mornston was a little bigger than him. But the veteran…taciturn by nature…didn't back down a bit and threw fuel on the fire by adding, "You'd think you'd spent your entire career in the Army being that dumb."

Ingunza reached over to grab Mornston but Lieutenant Hackett blocked his arm from reaching him and he admonished the two of them. "Knock it off, you two…or I'll shoot the both of you and be done with it. We got bigger fish to fry…and I need the two of you focused on the Japs and not on killing one another."

Ingunza kept glaring…but when Mornston finally cracked a smile and thrust his hand across to the corporal…Ingunza relented and stuck out his own meaty hand. The two men shook hands… ending the confrontation. Then Ingunza smiled too…since he respected the fact that Mornston had not really backed down…when many others would have…since he had quite a reputation for winning fights.

"Good," the relieved Hackett said, "I wasn't really interested in shooting either one of you…but if you ever pull that crap again… make no mistake what I'll do. We got marines lying dead out there and you two are my leaders. Act like it…or I'll get someone that can. I'm gonna head back to Feeney…and if nothing has changed… I'll signal for you guys to bring your men up." Then he pointed to Sergeant Endres…who had been quiet for some reason…and told him that he wanted him and his six men on the left of the long stem of the L. Then he looked at Corporal Ingunza and the two men he had left…PFC Hall and PFC Wykoff…and said, "I want you three on their right…you'll complete the stem. Your job is to rain death down on those Japs who are across the taxiway. They're the same ones who are machine gunning the bodies of our friends who are laying dead out on that runway." He let that sink in for a second… and then he continued. "Now those Japs have several machine gun teams over there...so we're gonna be outgunned...but we gotta risk it. These Japs are holding up a much larger group of guys down to the left from crossing that taxiway...and those guys could be some of our own Second Battalion boys for all I know. As far as I can tell the Japs have no idea that we're over here...or how many guys we have...so it surprise them when we open up on them. And make your men shout at the tops of their lungs when we engage them. Maybe we can trick them into thinking there's a lot more of us over here than there really are."

"You sound like the old Swamp Fox," PFC Mornston...who had grown up in Beaufort, South Carolina...said to the lieutenant.

"How'd you know about him," Hackett asked, suddenly intrigued...since the private had spoken very little over the last day and a half.

"Who hasn't heard of him?" Mornston replied back evenly.

"I haven't for one," Petraglia quipped...and Mornston shot the runner a frown...since he had heard about Francis Marion's exploits since he was a little boy. Then he said, "Well, you should've...since he's pretty famous down around the parts I come from."

"And how were we supposed to know that...since you've said all of two words since we found you on the beach yesterday morning," Petraglia shot right back...never at a loss for words.

"I like to keep to myself. I'm not a big talker," Mornston said truthfully...hoping it would satisfy Petraglia...and keep him from asking any more questions about his past or his upbringing. It wasn't that he was secretive...since he wasn't. Instead, he had found it easier to remain somewhat aloof since someone always thought he was bragging when he brought up his family life. So the private first class had never told anyone in his unit that he had made a vow to himself that he would follow in his father's footsteps and attend the Citadel...a military college in Charleston...and become an officer... just like his father...if he managed to survive the war. And no one knew...since it made some guys jealous...that his dad was a colonel commanding a bomber group in England...and that he had flown twenty combat missions over France and Germany so far.

Petraglia seemed to accept his explanation however...since he didn't push him any further on it...and Mornston added, "We'd be speaking with an English cocknee if it weren't for him. When General Washington was stymied up north, it was Major Marion who turned the tide of the war against the Brits in the South. He did it mostly alone...but later on he got some help from General Hale. General Horatio Gates...as most everyone knows I guess...never did any good once he got down there. He can be damned for all I care."

"You definitely know your history...that's for sure," the lieutenant said, praising him. And then he added, "Yeah, I guess I am using one of his old tricks. Hey, it worked on the British...so it might work on those Japs over there. And it seems they got an officer who thinks he's a Banastre Tarleton-type. I just didn't think those Jap marines would treat us marines that way...even if we are the enemy...unless they were ordered to...or encouraged to...which is the same thing as far as I'm concerned. I guess it was just wishful thinking on my part. I was still hoping that marines were marines...no matter what country they fight for...but I guess a Jap is just a Jap unfortunately."

Mornston knew that the lieutenant was referring to Colonel Banastre Tarleton...a young, tarnished cavalry officer who had fought for the British under General Cornwallis in the Southern Campaign in the Revolutionary War. Tarleton had gained fame...or infamy...depending on which side you were on...by being extremely cruel to both the Americans he was fighting against and the local citizenry in South Carolina...and he was hated by the men under Major Marion's command as a result.

"If that officer doesn't get killed outright...then leave him to me," the private seethed...since he had seen more than enough atrocities committed by the Japanese troops on Guadalcanal. And to hammer the point home he added, "And I won't be takin' any prisoners...just so y'all know."

Sergeant Endres had been listening to the discussion quietly... apparently unfazed by it...but after hearing Mornston's assertion... he suddenly joined in. "We do what we gotta do to win this war. And sometimes the Japs throw the rule book out the window. But that doesn't mean we got to. I've seen us do some pretty rough stuff too...some of it warranted...some of it not. Just do what you think is right...at least I will."

"I understand," the lieutenant said thoughtfully...genuinely surprised...but heartened just the same...by the fact that Sergeant Endres had been willing to challenge Mornston over the morality of killing a man who has surrendered or is wounded. Hackett thought it over and said, "What I just witnessed out on that taxiway makes me sick. Sometimes I can lose my bearings too...and I just wanna get even with the bastards. But you're right...so I won't condone or support anyone who kills a man who surrenders. We're not savages...no matter what happens. Understood?"

All squad leaders nodded their assent...even the chastened Mornston. The veteran held no grudge against the lieutenant for warning him...and the others...the way he did however. He had seen some horrible things done to captured or wounded marines on Guadalcanal...and one of them had been a close friend...who had been butchered with a bayonet. Nothing he had seen in several months of combat had come close to the savagery of it...and the image of his buddy...who had been tied to a tree...kept him awake at night. The Japs who had tortured him had obviously enjoyed their work...since they had curved him up and then pulled his intestines out of him while he was still alive. But they had not killed him. Instead, they left him alive...to prolong his agony...and he was still breathing when Mornston and the others found him. But he died shortly thereafter...which was a gift...and from that moment on Mornston and the men with him had sworn that they'd get even with the Japanese for their barbarity and cruelty. The retribution they had delivered to the Japs on Guadalcanal had been merciless as a result. Yet...strangely...he felt empty just the same...and the pain of it all never left. So deep-down he knew that the lieutenant... and Endres for that matter...were right...and he swore he'd abide by their rules for a change.

Then PFC Petraglia chimed in...as he always did...and said, "We got it, sir. But if we gotta listen to one more history lesson out here...some of us might start committing *hari kari* ourselves! So can we please just get on with it!"

• • •

Lieutenant Hackett crawled back to Feeney and the private first class told him that nothing had dramatically changed in his absence... that he hadn't seen any more movement from the marines since he left. But an additional squad of Japs...two of whom were carrying a Type 92 7.7mm heavy machine gun...had moved into the area across from them. With that, the lieutenant raised up his bandaged right hand and waved the men over. They all began low-crawling in teams of two and three and after a while all the men had made it forward without being spotted. The squad leaders directed their men to where they wanted them...and before long a lazy-looking L had taken shape. Just like the lieutenant wanted, Sergeant Endres was on the left...with his shadow...Private Scott...laying right next to him. Then came Private Agresta...and next to him were the three other marines who were not part of Hackett's original platoon. PFC Feeney anchored the right end of his line...and then came PFC Petraglia... the platoon runner. Next to him was the lieutenant...at the center of the line...and then came PFC Wykoff...Corporal Ingunza...and then PFC Hall. There was a small gap in the line at this point...since this was where the base of the L began to curve back to the right so PFC Mornston and the four men with him could keep tabs on the area around the aircraft revetments in their rear. PFC Mornston took the first spot...so he could still moniter what was happening along the taxiway…and then next to him were the three privates that were under his command. First in the order was Private Kevin McCaffrey…who was a Third Battalion orphan…and then came Private Dave Beach…and next to him…Private Marty Poffineger. These last two men were from G Company of the 2nd Battalion… and they had veered way off course trying to get ashore…since their company had been scheduled to land near the pier on Red Beach 2. But the two raw recruits were feeling lucky all the same…despite their circumstances…since the lieutenant and the NCO's had treated them fairly the entire time they were there. As a result, they were willing to do anything that the lieutenant or PFC Mornston asked of them.

Further down the line was PFC Martin Mychale…the assistant driver of *Widow Maker*…the amtrac that had been carrying the lieutenant and his men to Red Beach 2. Mornston figured that he could trust Mychale with the tail-end-charlie position since he had not panicked while he was sitting in the cab of a lightly-armored amtrac that was under direct fire from hundreds of guns that were situated on the very beach he was trying to land on. *I'll fight beside any man with that much guts*, the veteran marine thought to himself as he watched the amtrac driver diligently scanning the ground beyond for any sign of movement that might reveal an enemy attack against their position.

• • •

Lieutenant Hackett glanced over at all his men…and seeing that they were ready…he screamed, "Fire!" as loud as he could. On his order, the men began firing and yelling at the tops of their lungs as well…just like he had asked them to. And his plan worked…since the Japanese did think they were under attack by a much larger force than the seventeen men who were firing into their flank. The most devastating fire came from the two BARs in the platoon…since this weapon fired a large thirty-caliber bullet out of a twenty round magazine. Private Scott…the big marine from New Hampshire…was handling one of them. He had found the weapon the day before…lying on the beach...next to a dead marine who had been shot through the head. Scott had picked it up and he had been carrying it ever since...which meant that he had surpassed the thirty minutes of life expectancy that was normally associated with a marine or soldier who carried this weapon in combat. The other one was being fired by PFC Wykoff... who had swapped his M-1 rifle with the BAR that belonged to Private Poffineger. Wykoff had asked the private to make the trade...since he was going to be firing on the Japs in the triangle while Poffineger would be on lookout duty on the right. Poffineger had handed the weapon over graciously...so Wykoff didn't have to order him to do it...which he would have...if the young private had refused.

The fire from the BARs was intense...and it forced the Japanese machine gunners to keep their heads down while they tried to re-orient the direction of their own guns to cover their vulnerable left flank. Hackett's men also had two Thompson Submachine guns firing as well...but this gun...while effective...was better suited for close-in work. This was the weapon that had been made famous in the Chicago gang war between Al Capone and Bugs Moran in the 1930's...and it could fire about seven hundred rounds per minute at a velocity of nine hundred and twenty feet per second. Sergeant Endres was armed with one of them...while PFC Feeney had the other...and both were experts with it. Endres had already used his Thompson to great effect during a firefight he had been part of on Guadalcanal...while Feeney had put his to good use in clearing several bunkers right after they had landed on the beach.

Everybody else in the platoon was carrying the M-1 Garand rifle...except for the lieutenant...who was armed with an M-1 carbine. The eight-shot Garand was a revolutionary rifle since it could be fired as fast as the trigger was pulled...while the Japanese were still using the bolt-action *Arisaka* rifle...which was not as accurate... and much slower to operate. This enabled the marines to put a lot of fire on the Japanese in the initial foray...and several of them were killed outright before they could reorient their weapons to meet this new threat. But once the nine Japanese machine gun teams and fifty or so riflemen did shift their fires, Hackett's men were forced to take cover...just like the men who had been trying to cross the taxiway were.

• • •

Although Lieutenant Hackett was too far away to tell who the men along the taxiway were...he was still willing to help them. And Captain Jim Clanahan of C Company was in same boat...since he had no idea who the unit off to his right was either. But he appreciated their help nonetheless.

He and his company of over a hundred men had been held up for almost twenty-four hours at the taxiway...and the stalemate looked like it was going to go on forever. He had been able to push a few men across...and they had jumped into shell holes on the other side for cover...but he had lost just as many in the effort...so it was a deadly tradeoff.

In the early afternoon, the complexion of the battle had suddenly changed in his favor however. He had been requesting heavy weapons support for some time now...and several machine gun crews from the Regimental Weapons Company had finally showed up to lend a hand. These men were armed with several types of machine guns...including the standard M1919 air-cooled, thirty-caliber light machine gun and the M1917 water-cooled, thirty-caliber heavy machine gun. But they had also salvaged two Browning fifty caliber heavy machine guns that they had found on the Red 2 beachhead... and they put them all into action against the Japanese along the western taxiway.

Without planning it that way, the machine gun crews began engaging the Japanese at the same time that Lieutenant Hackett's men had begun firing at them as well...and their combined fires shocked the Japanese...since it all happened so fast...and now they were the ones who were pinned down. Suddenly caught between a rock and a hard place, the Japanese were forced to divide their assets to fight off the two attacking parties...and this gave Captain Clanahan just the break he needed. Sensing the lull in enemy fire coming his way, he immediately ordered his men to race across the taxiway...and they made the trek virtually unopposed this time. And they didn't stop there. Exploiting the breakout, they pushed through the triangle and then kept right on going across the main runway...their momentum carrying them all the way to the far side of the island! It was yet another miracle...in an afternoon that seemed to be full of them... since Clanahan's C Company men were able to link up with the men from A and B Companies who had been fighting for their very lives in the anti-tank ditch behind Black Beach.

Having just patched up yet another wounded marine...Pharmacist Mate Second Class Fumai looked up and saw the reinforcements coming their way and he breathed...like so many others did...a sigh of relief...and said, "Finally...thank God!"

• • •

First Lieutenant Hackett watched as the marines darted across the taxiway in the distance...and he broke into a big smile. "Hot damn... they made it," he said to no one in particular...and the men around him clapped each other on the backs...feeling the same sense of satisfaction that their leader did. Then he yelled out, "Everybody ok?"

Sergeant Endres looked down the line of his men and everyone seemed okay...so he gave the lieutenant a thumbs up to indicate that no one had been hit on that end.

Then Lieutenant Hackett looked over at Corporal Ingunza...and he mouthed, "Well?"

"I dunno, sir," he shouted back...his voice almost lost amidst the sound of gunfire still coming their way. Ingunza then started crawling towards PFC Hall...since Hall had not responded when he called over to him. PFC Wykoff pushed back on his elbows to get a better look at him but he couldn't tell if he was hurt or not...so he just shrugged his shoulders when the corporal looked over his way.

Ingunza had almost reached Hall when he heard PFC Mornston yell over that everybody he had was okay as well...which made him feel somewhat better...but he was still concerned about the private who was just a few feet away. He was almost on top of him when he noticed that Hall's head was slumped forward and resting on his rifle... so he reached over and shook him. Hall didn't respond at all...so Ingunza rolled him over...and he saw what he had hoped he wasn't going to see...a neat, red-rimmed hole in the middle of Hall's forehead. The bullet had hit him just below the brim of his helmet...but if it had come in slightly higher it still would have killed him...since his helmet would never have stopped a bullet traveling with that much speed and force behind it. Ingunza sighed and then yelled out, "Hall's had it, sir. Shot straight through the head," and he crawled back to his own position...all the while wondering if he was going to bring anybody in his squad home alive.

• • •

Any hopes that Lieutenant Hackett had about crossing the taxiway like Captain Clanahan had done were dashed by the amount of machine gun fire that kept coming at them from the Japanese who were stationed further back along the inland side of the triangle. Hackett's fire had killed a few of these Japs...but not enough to make a dent in the fire that was enveloping their small outpost. Now they were just as trapped as Captain Clanahan's men had been earlier...so the lieutenant made another wise decision...one of several he had made over the last two days of fighting. "We're gonna sit tight for now," he told the squad leaders who had crawled over to him. Then looking at his watch, he said, "And we'll probably spend the rest of the night here too...since there's really nowhere else for us to go at this point. We'll lose too many of us trying to cross that runway...so that's out... and there's no sense turning around since we got the cove complex behind us now. We're sort of surrounded I guess...so let's make the best of it. Tell the boys to get comfortable...and we'll go with the same rules that got us through last night. One guy up while another sleeps. And if they probe us tonight…which they probably will… no rifle fire…use your knives first…then your fists or whatever you have to…but no one fires his rifle…unless we're being overrun. Let the Japs crawl all over the place trying to find us in the dark. Don't lend them a hand and make it easier by giving our position away with rifle fire. Everybody good with that," he said finishing up…and the three men nodded their approval before crawling off to brief their men…just like they had been told.

And as the sun began to set in the western sky over the island of Betio, Lieutenant Hackett once again looked into the billowing clouds above him…and he wondered if the God who made His home up there was still looking down on him and offering him protection. As if on cue, he heard a silent voice that said, "You're still breathing…aren't you." The lieutenant looked at his wounded right hand and he realized that he had been pretty lucky so far…that despite all the dangers he had faced over the last thirty-six hours… he had come through it pretty much okay. That's when it dawned on him that he was more than just lucky…that he was truly blessed. Blessed beyond all measure in fact…and still looking up at Heaven, the young lieutenant bowed his head in thanks and said, "Yeah… Father…I guess I am at that…I guess I am at that."

It is well that war is so terrible…or we would grow too fond of it.
Lieutenant General Robert E. Lee…December 13th, 1862…
commenting on the
slaughter of the Union Army units that made fourteen
unsuccessful attacks
against the Confederate position along Marye's Heights
during the Battle of Fredericksburg

Made in the USA
Coppell, TX
11 December 2020